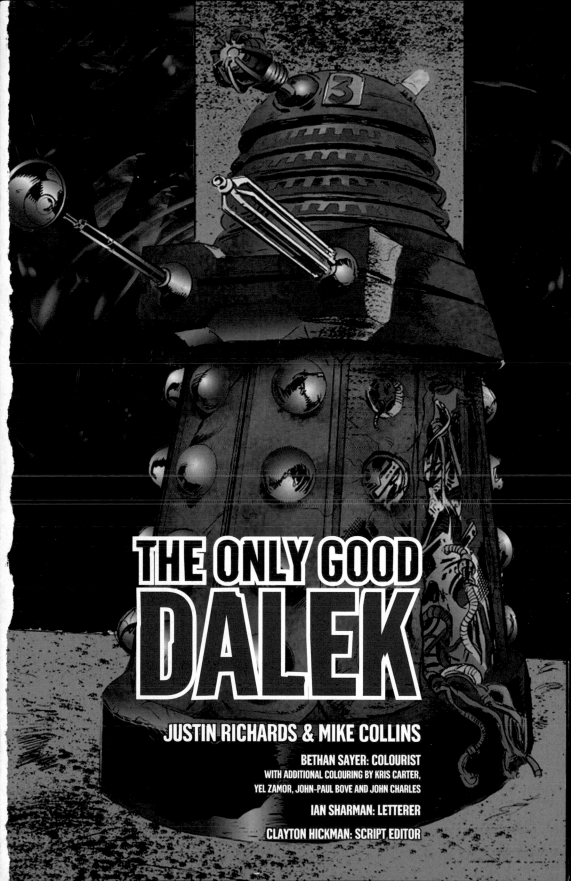

THE ONLY GOOD
DALEK

JUSTIN RICHARDS & MIKE COLLINS

BETHAN SAYER: COLOURIST
WITH ADDITIONAL COLOURING BY KRIS CARTER,
YEL ZAMOR, JOHN-PAUL BOVE AND JOHN CHARLES

IAN SHARMAN: LETTERER

CLAYTON HICKMAN: SCRIPT EDITOR

THE ONLY GOOD
DALEK

THE WAR HAS RAGED FOR A HUNDRED YEARS — HUMANITY STANDING AGAINST THE MIGHT AND TERROR OF THE DALEKS. ALL THAT IS GOOD AGAINST ALL THAT IS TERRIBLE. BRAVERY, COURAGE AND DETERMINATION AGAINST UNFEELING, PITILESS MONSTERS...

1 3 5 7 9 10 8 6 4 2

Published in 2010 by BBC Books, an imprint of Ebury Publishing.
A Random House Group Company

Copyright © Justin Richards 2010
Artwork © Mike Collins 2010
Justin Richards has asserted his right to be identified as the author of this Work in accordance with the Copyright, Designs and Patents Act 1988

Doctor Who is a BBC Wales production for BBC One.
Executive producers: Steven Moffat, Piers Wenger and Beth Willis

BBC, DOCTOR WHO and TARDIS (word marks, logos and devices) are trademarks of the British Broadcasting Corporation and are used under licence. Daleks created by Terry Nation.

The Random House Group Limited Reg. No. 954009

Addresses for companies within the Random House Group can be found at www.randomhouse.co.uk

A CIP catalogue record for this book is available from the British Library.

ISBN 978 1846079849

The Random House Group Limited supports the Forest Stewardship Council (FSC), the leading international forest certification organisation.
All our titles that are printed on Greenpeace approved FSC certified paper carry the FSC logo. Our paper procurement policy can be found at www.rbooks.co.uk/environment

Commissioning editor: Albert DePetrillo
Editorial manager: Nicholas Payne
Series consultant: Justin Richards
Project editor: Steve Tribe
Cover design: Mike Collins & Lee Binding © Woodlands Books Ltd, 2010
Design: Lee Binding @ tea-lady.co.uk
Production: Phil Spencer

Printed and bound by Firmengruppe APPL, aprinta druck, Wemding, Germany.

To buy books by your favourite authors and register for offers, visit www.rbooks.co.uk

For Terry Nation and David Whitaker - who first translated The Dalek Chronicles

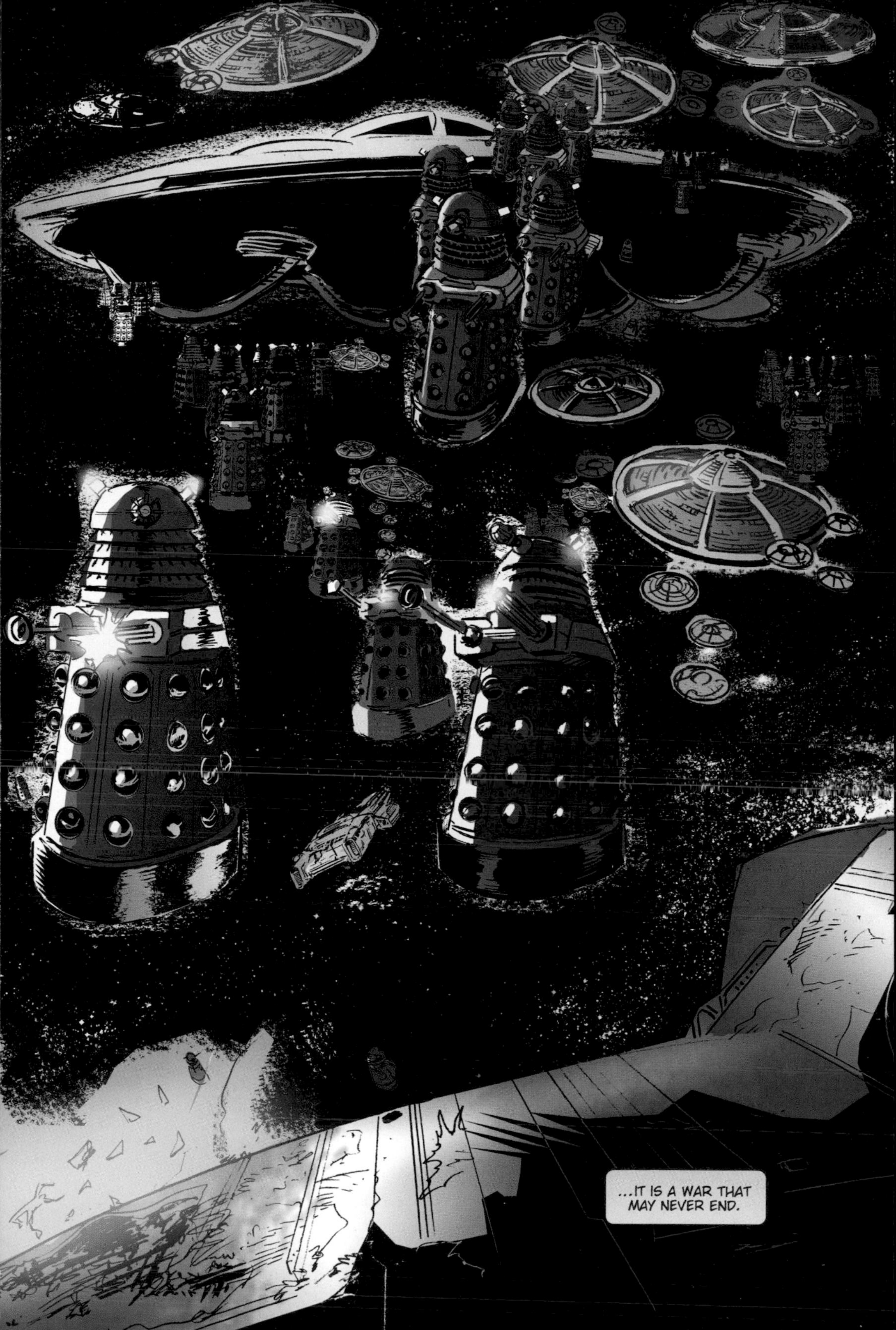
...IT IS A WAR THAT MAY NEVER END.

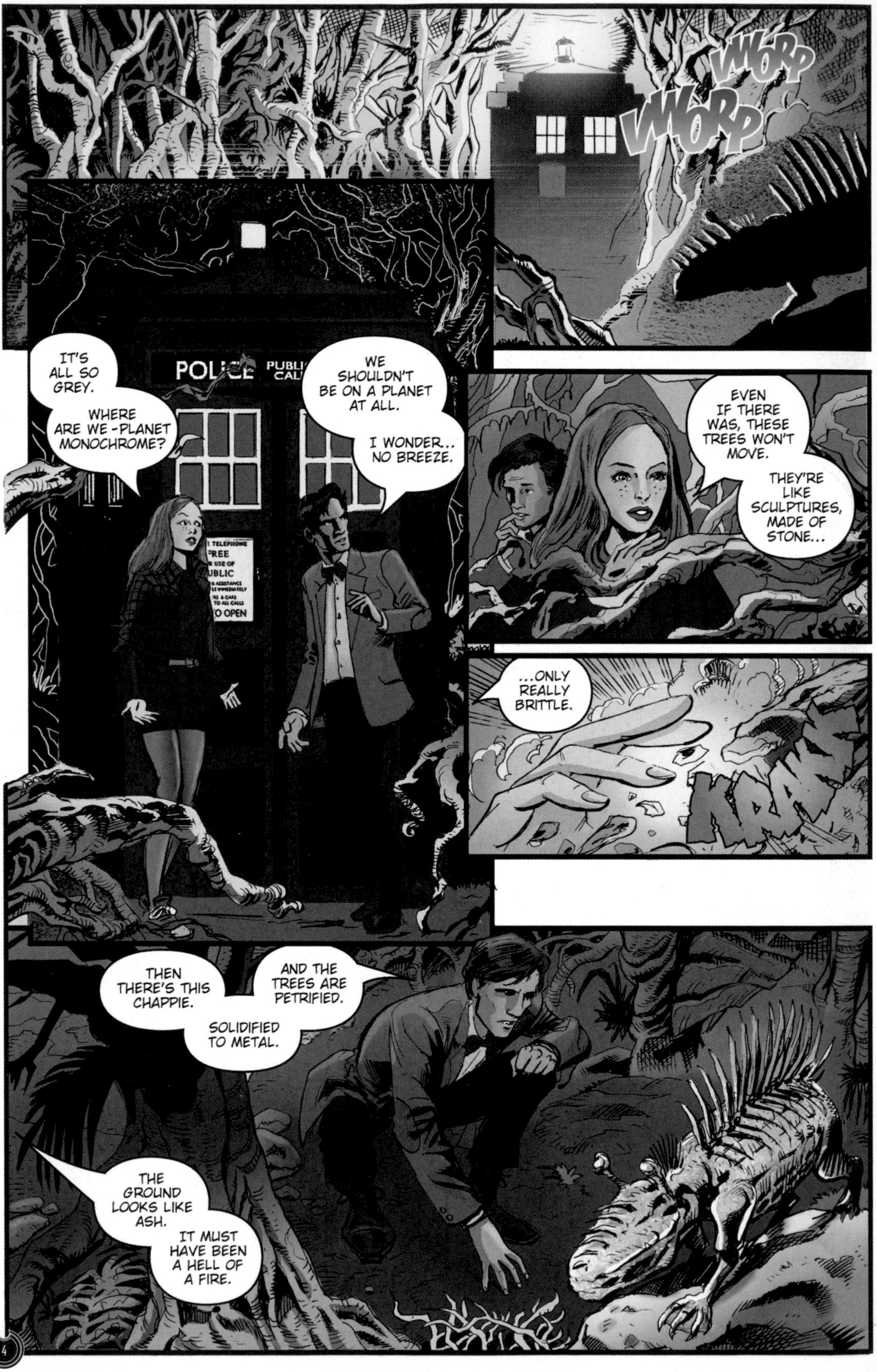

VWORP
VWORP
IT'S ALL SO GREY.
WHERE ARE WE - PLANET MONOCHROME?
POLICE PUBLIC CALL
WE SHOULDN'T BE ON A PLANET AT ALL.
I WONDER... NO BREEZE.
EVEN IF THERE WAS, THESE TREES WON'T MOVE.
THEY'RE LIKE SCULPTURES, MADE OF STONE...
...ONLY REALLY BRITTLE.
THEN THERE'S THIS CHAPPIE.
AND THE TREES ARE PETRIFIED.
SOLIDIFIED TO METAL.
THE GROUND LOOKS LIKE ASH.
IT MUST HAVE BEEN A HELL OF A FIRE.

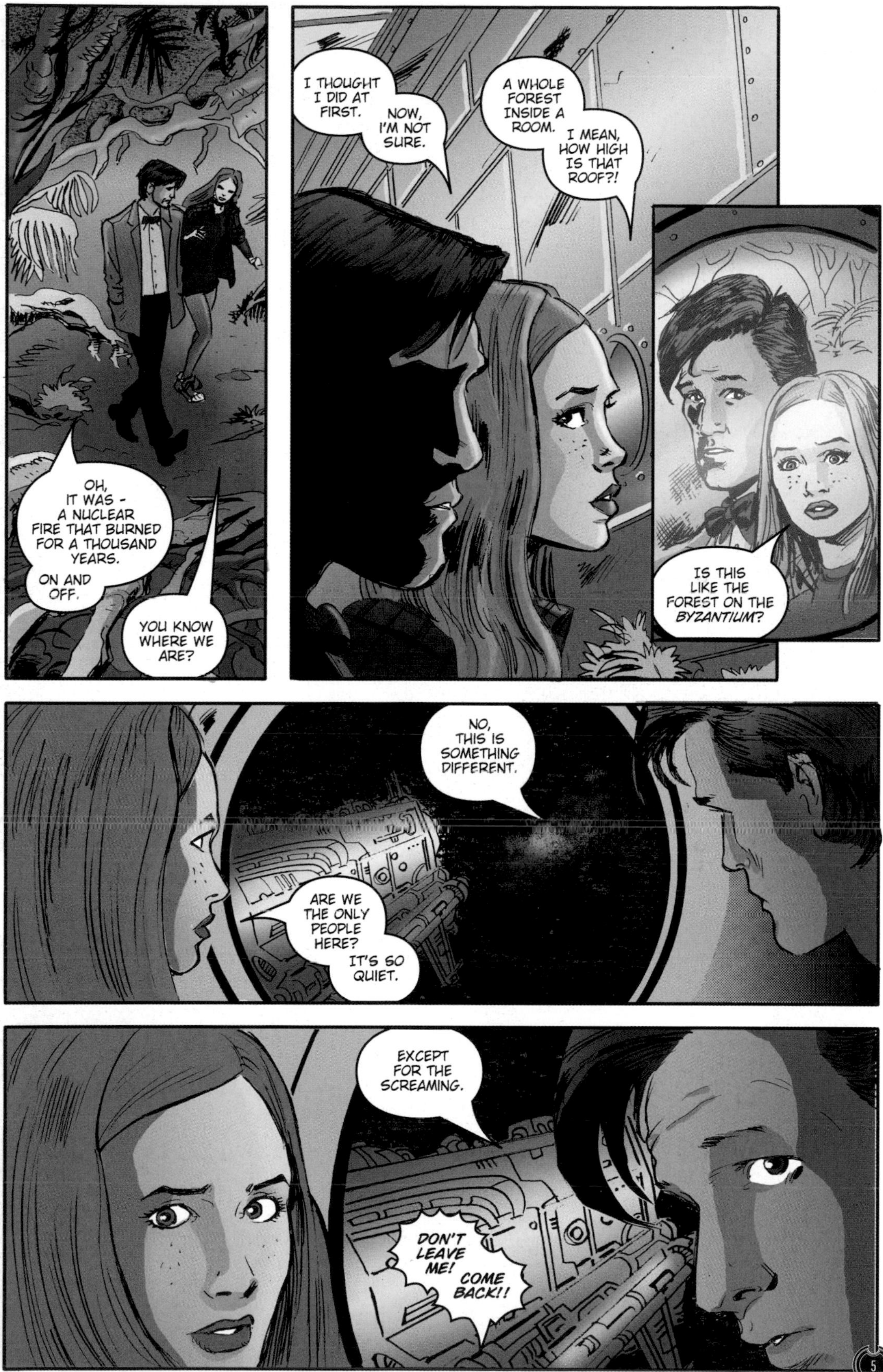
OH, IT WAS - A NUCLEAR FIRE THAT BURNED FOR A THOUSAND YEARS.
ON AND OFF.
YOU KNOW WHERE WE ARE?
I THOUGHT I DID AT FIRST.
NOW, I'M NOT SURE.
A WHOLE FOREST INSIDE A ROOM.
I MEAN, HOW HIGH IS THAT ROOF?!
IS THIS LIKE THE FOREST ON THE *BYZANTIUM*?
NO, THIS IS SOMETHING DIFFERENT.
ARE WE THE ONLY PEOPLE HERE?
IT'S SO QUIET.
EXCEPT FOR THE SCREAMING.
DON'T LEAVE ME!
COME BACK!!

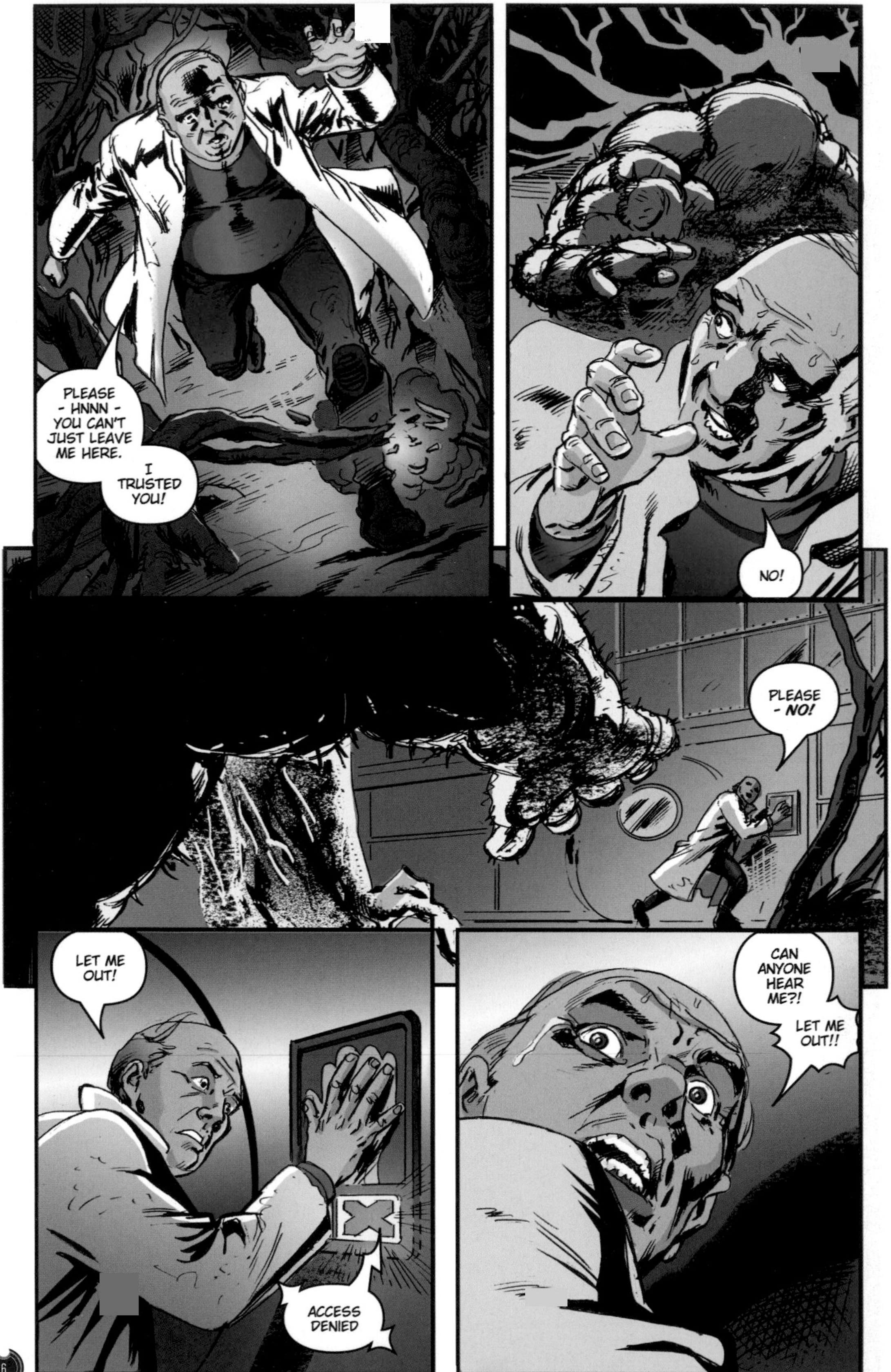
PLEASE - HNNN - YOU CAN'T JUST LEAVE ME HERE.
I TRUSTED YOU!
NO!
PLEASE - *NO!*
LET ME OUT!
ACCESS DENIED
CAN ANYONE HEAR ME?!
LET ME OUT!!

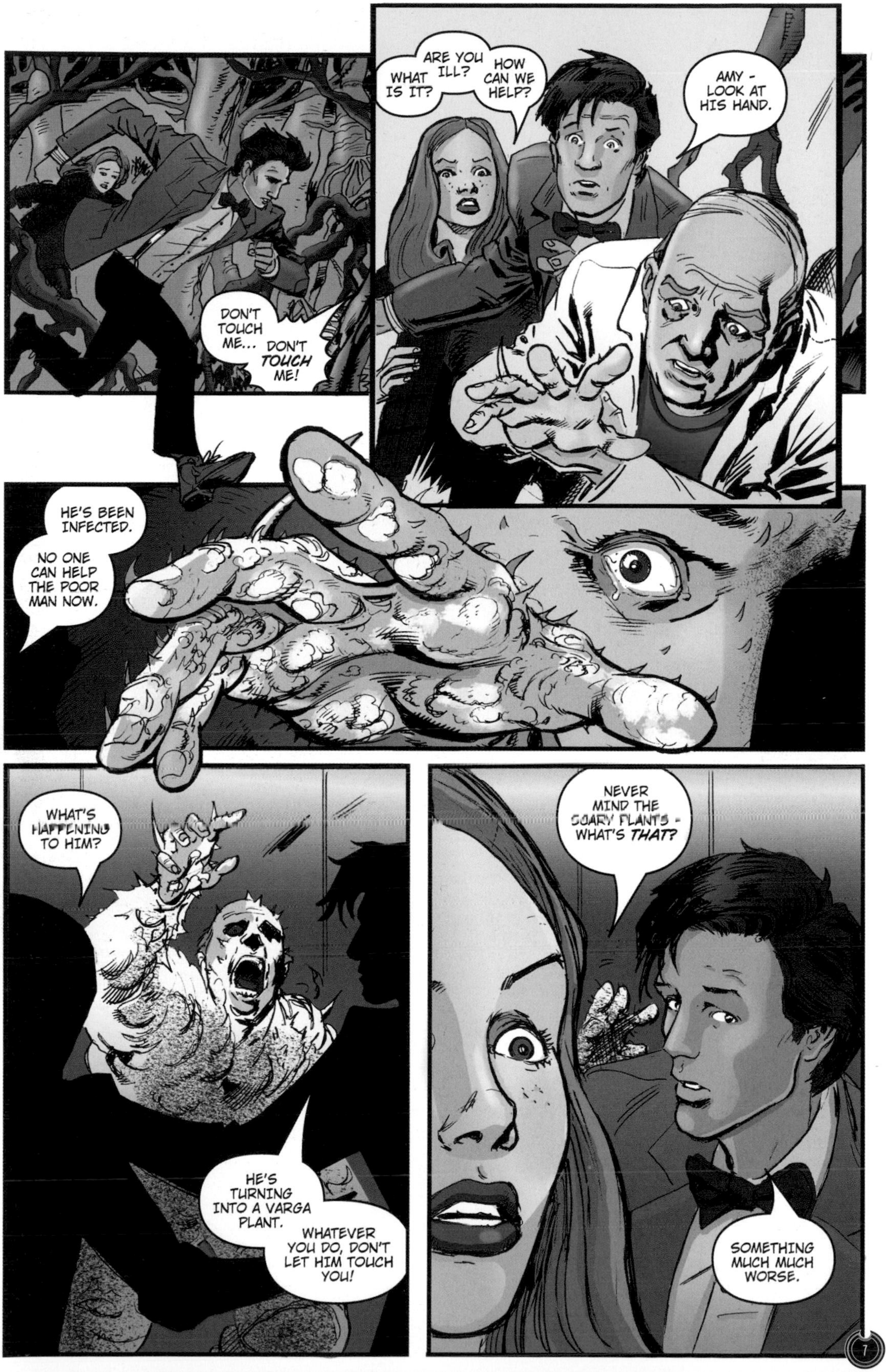
DON'T TOUCH ME... DON'T *TOUCH* ME!
WHAT IS IT?
ARE YOU ILL?
HOW CAN WE HELP?
AMY - LOOK AT HIS HAND.
HE'S BEEN INFECTED.
NO ONE CAN HELP THE POOR MAN NOW.
WHAT'S HAPPENING TO HIM?
HE'S TURNING INTO A VARGA PLANT.
WHATEVER YOU DO, DON'T LET HIM TOUCH YOU!
NEVER MIND THE SCARY PLANTS - WHAT'S *THAT?*
SOMETHING MUCH MUCH WORSE.

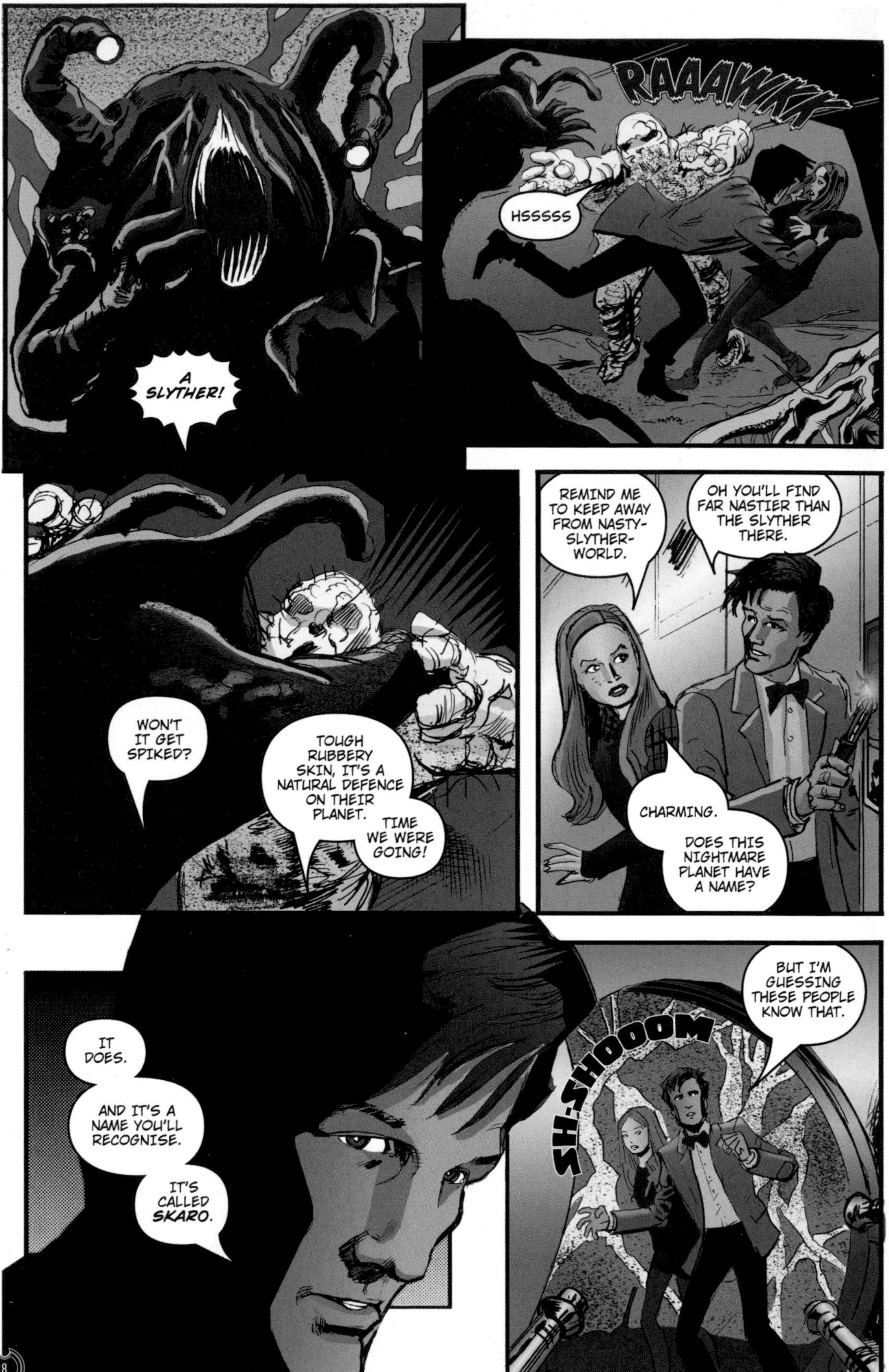
A SLYTHER!
RAAAWKK
HSSSSS
WON'T IT GET SPIKED?
TOUGH RUBBERY SKIN, IT'S A NATURAL DEFENCE ON THEIR PLANET.
TIME WE WERE GOING!
REMIND ME TO KEEP AWAY FROM NASTY-SLYTHER-WORLD.
OH YOU'LL FIND FAR NASTIER THAN THE SLYTHER THERE.
CHARMING.
DOES THIS NIGHTMARE PLANET HAVE A NAME?
IT DOES.
AND IT'S A NAME YOU'LL RECOGNISE.
IT'S CALLED SKARO.
SH-SHOOOM
BUT I'M GUESSING THESE PEOPLE KNOW THAT.

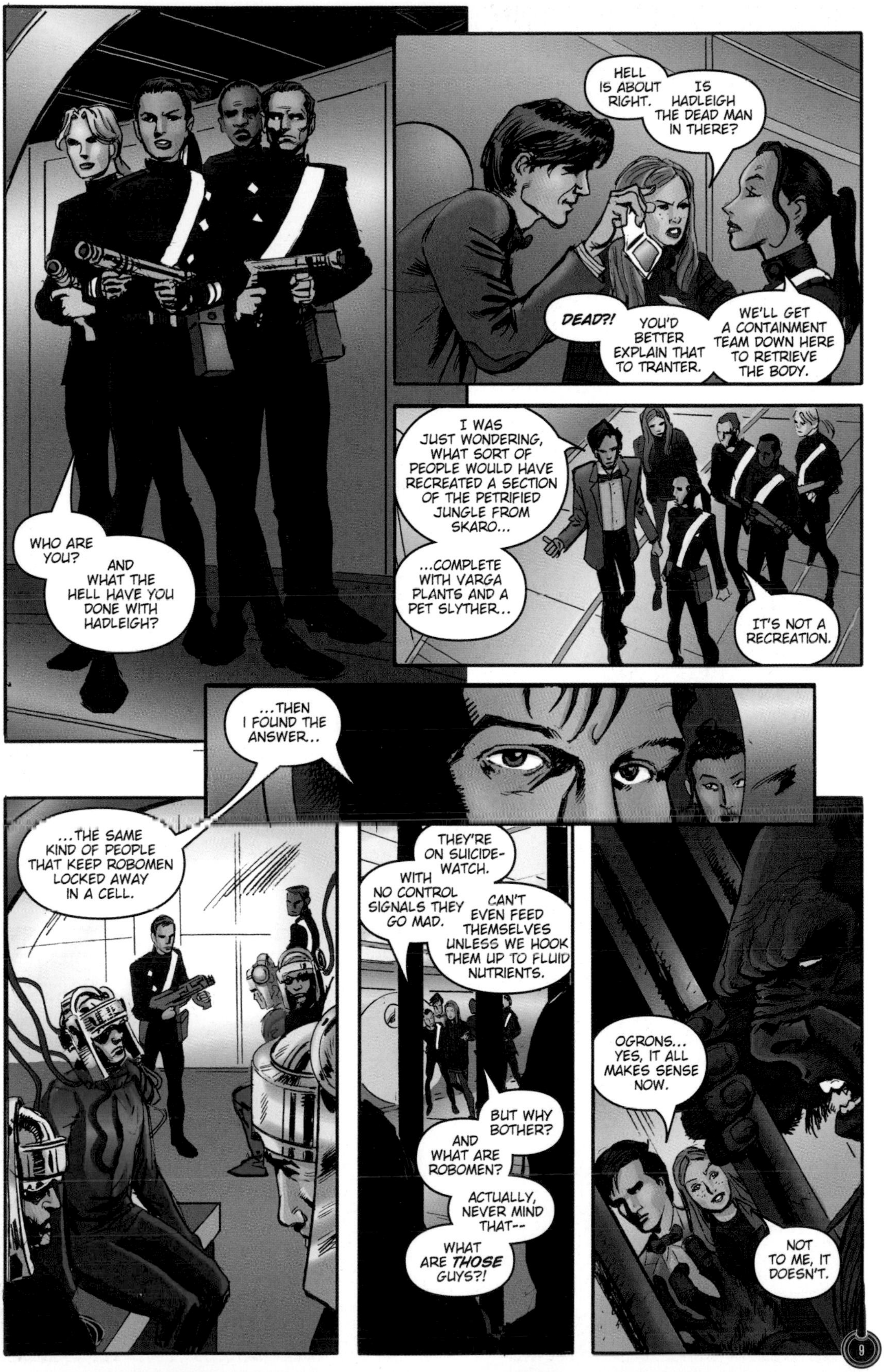
WHO ARE YOU?
AND WHAT THE HELL HAVE YOU DONE WITH HADLEIGH?
HELL IS ABOUT RIGHT.
IS HADLEIGH THE DEAD MAN IN THERE?
WE'LL GET A CONTAINMENT TEAM DOWN HERE TO RETRIEVE THE BODY.
DEAD?!
YOU'D BETTER EXPLAIN THAT TO TRANTER.
I WAS JUST WONDERING, WHAT SORT OF PEOPLE WOULD HAVE RECREATED A SECTION OF THE PETRIFIED JUNGLE FROM SKARO...
...COMPLETE WITH VARGA PLANTS AND A PET SLYTHER..
IT'S NOT A RECREATION.
...THEN I FOUND THE ANSWER...
...THE SAME KIND OF PEOPLE THAT KEEP ROBOMEN LOCKED AWAY IN A CELL.
THEY'RE ON SUICIDE-WATCH.
WITH NO CONTROL SIGNALS THEY GO MAD.
CAN'T EVEN FEED THEMSELVES UNLESS WE HOOK THEM UP TO FLUID NUTRIENTS.
BUT WHY BOTHER?
AND WHAT ARE ROBOMEN?
ACTUALLY, NEVER MIND THAT--
WHAT ARE *THOSE* GUYS?!
OGRONS... YES, IT ALL MAKES SENSE NOW.
NOT TO ME, IT DOESN'T.
9

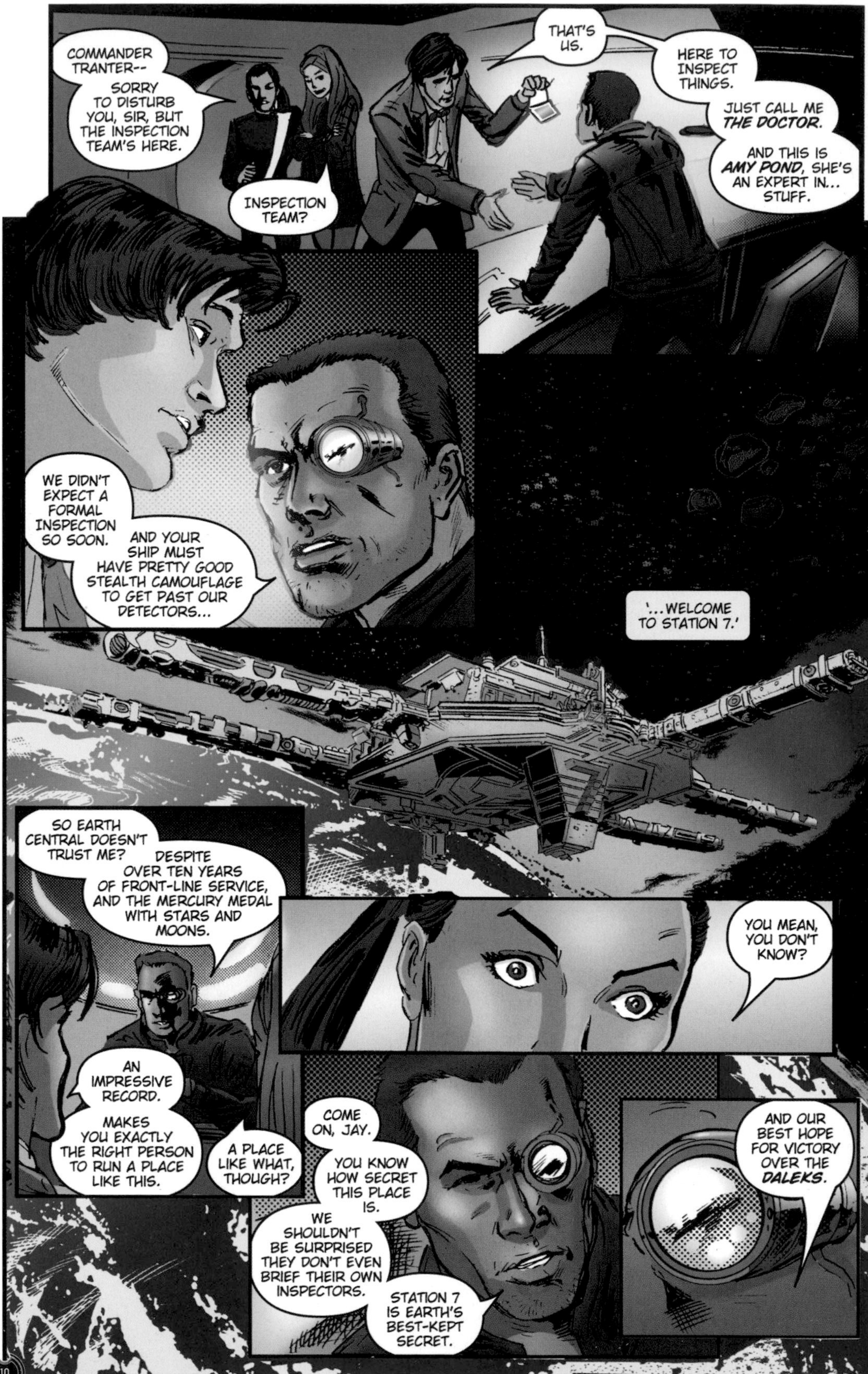
COMMANDER TRANTER--
SORRY TO DISTURB YOU, SIR, BUT THE INSPECTION TEAM'S HERE.
INSPECTION TEAM?
THAT'S US.
HERE TO INSPECT THINGS.
JUST CALL ME THE DOCTOR.
AND THIS IS AMY POND, SHE'S AN EXPERT IN... STUFF.
WE DIDN'T EXPECT A FORMAL INSPECTION SO SOON.
AND YOUR SHIP MUST HAVE PRETTY GOOD STEALTH CAMOUFLAGE TO GET PAST OUR DETECTORS...
'...WELCOME TO STATION 7.'
SO EARTH CENTRAL DOESN'T TRUST ME?
DESPITE OVER TEN YEARS OF FRONT-LINE SERVICE, AND THE MERCURY MEDAL WITH STARS AND MOONS.
YOU MEAN, YOU DON'T KNOW?
AN IMPRESSIVE RECORD.
MAKES YOU EXACTLY THE RIGHT PERSON TO RUN A PLACE LIKE THIS.
A PLACE LIKE WHAT, THOUGH?
COME ON, JAY.
YOU KNOW HOW SECRET THIS PLACE IS.
WE SHOULDN'T BE SURPRISED THEY DON'T EVEN BRIEF THEIR OWN INSPECTORS.
STATION 7 IS EARTH'S BEST-KEPT SECRET.
AND OUR BEST HOPE FOR VICTORY OVER THE DALEKS.

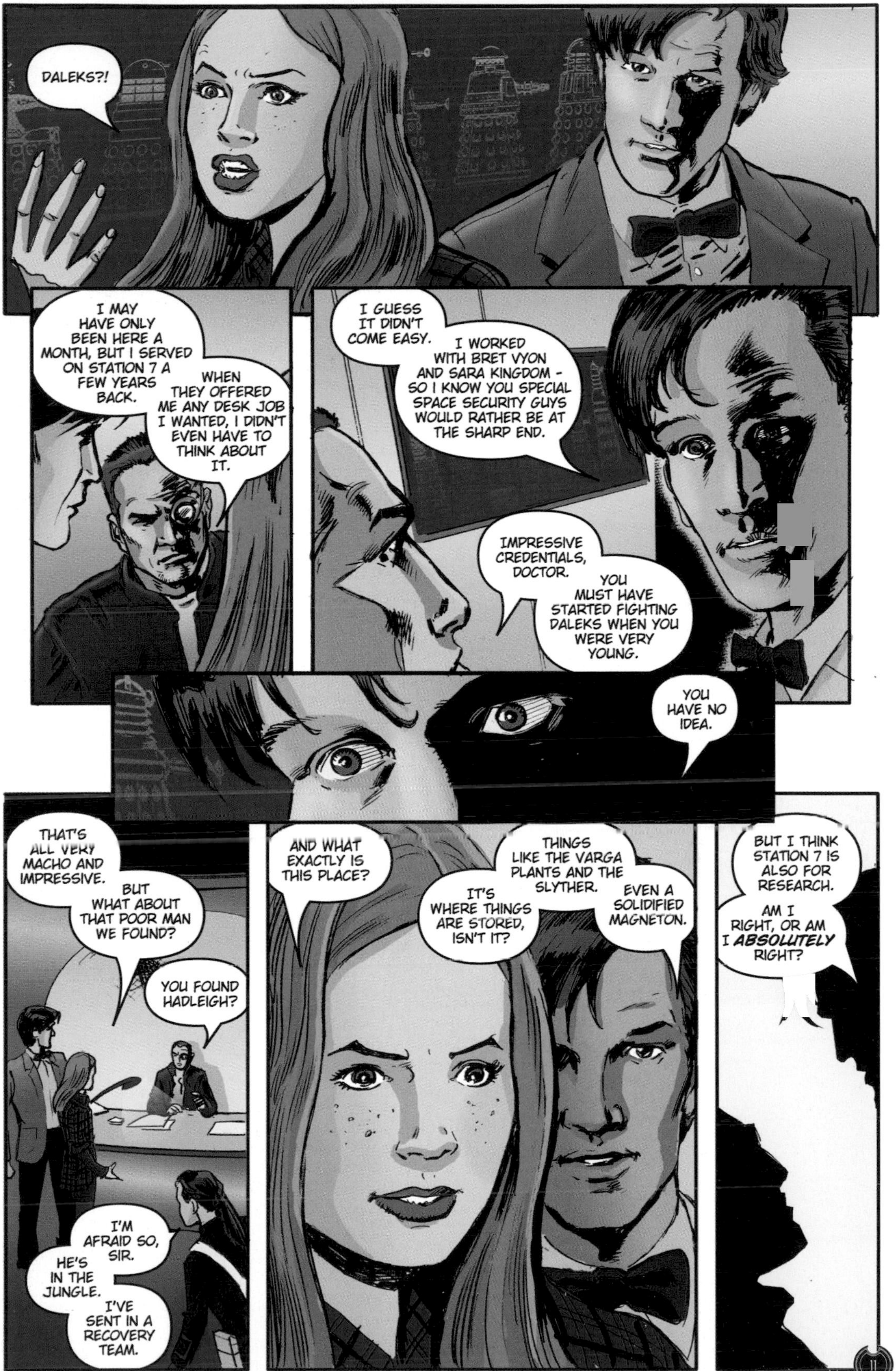
DALEKS?!
I MAY HAVE ONLY BEEN HERE A MONTH, BUT I SERVED ON STATION 7 A FEW YEARS BACK.
WHEN THEY OFFERED ME ANY DESK JOB I WANTED, I DIDN'T EVEN HAVE TO THINK ABOUT IT.
I GUESS IT DIDN'T COME EASY.
I WORKED WITH BRET VYON AND SARA KINGDOM - SO I KNOW YOU SPECIAL SPACE SECURITY GUYS WOULD RATHER BE AT THE SHARP END.
IMPRESSIVE CREDENTIALS, DOCTOR.
YOU MUST HAVE STARTED FIGHTING DALEKS WHEN YOU WERE VERY YOUNG.
YOU HAVE NO IDEA.
THAT'S ALL VERY MACHO AND IMPRESSIVE.
BUT WHAT ABOUT THAT POOR MAN WE FOUND?
YOU FOUND HADLEIGH?
I'M AFRAID SO, SIR.
HE'S IN THE JUNGLE.
I'VE SENT IN A RECOVERY TEAM.
AND WHAT EXACTLY IS THIS PLACE?
IT'S WHERE THINGS ARE STORED, ISN'T IT?
THINGS LIKE THE VARGA PLANTS AND THE SLYTHER.
EVEN A SOLIDIFIED MAGNETON.
BUT I THINK STATION 7 IS ALSO FOR RESEARCH.
AM I RIGHT, OR AM I *ABSOLUTELY* RIGHT?

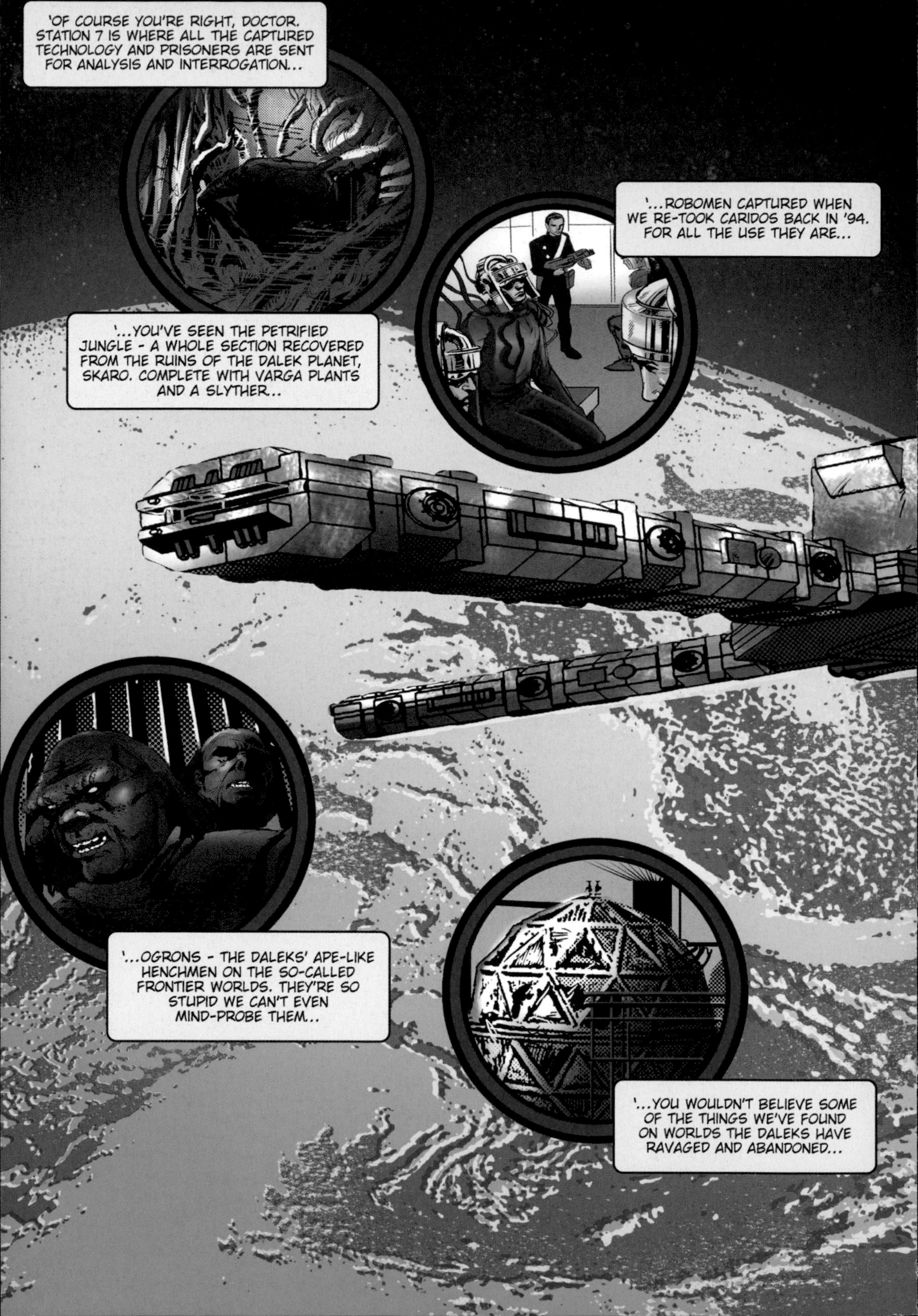
'OF COURSE YOU'RE RIGHT, DOCTOR. STATION 7 IS WHERE ALL THE CAPTURED TECHNOLOGY AND PRISONERS ARE SENT FOR ANALYSIS AND INTERROGATION...
'...YOU'VE SEEN THE PETRIFIED JUNGLE - A WHOLE SECTION RECOVERED FROM THE RUINS OF THE DALEK PLANET, SKARO. COMPLETE WITH VARGA PLANTS AND A SLYTHER...
'...ROBOMEN CAPTURED WHEN WE RE-TOOK CARIDOS BACK IN '94. FOR ALL THE USE THEY ARE...
'...OGRONS - THE DALEKS' APE-LIKE HENCHMEN ON THE SO-CALLED FRONTIER WORLDS. THEY'RE SO STUPID WE CAN'T EVEN MIND-PROBE THEM...
'...YOU WOULDN'T BELIEVE SOME OF THE THINGS WE'VE FOUND ON WORLDS THE DALEKS HAVE RAVAGED AND ABANDONED...

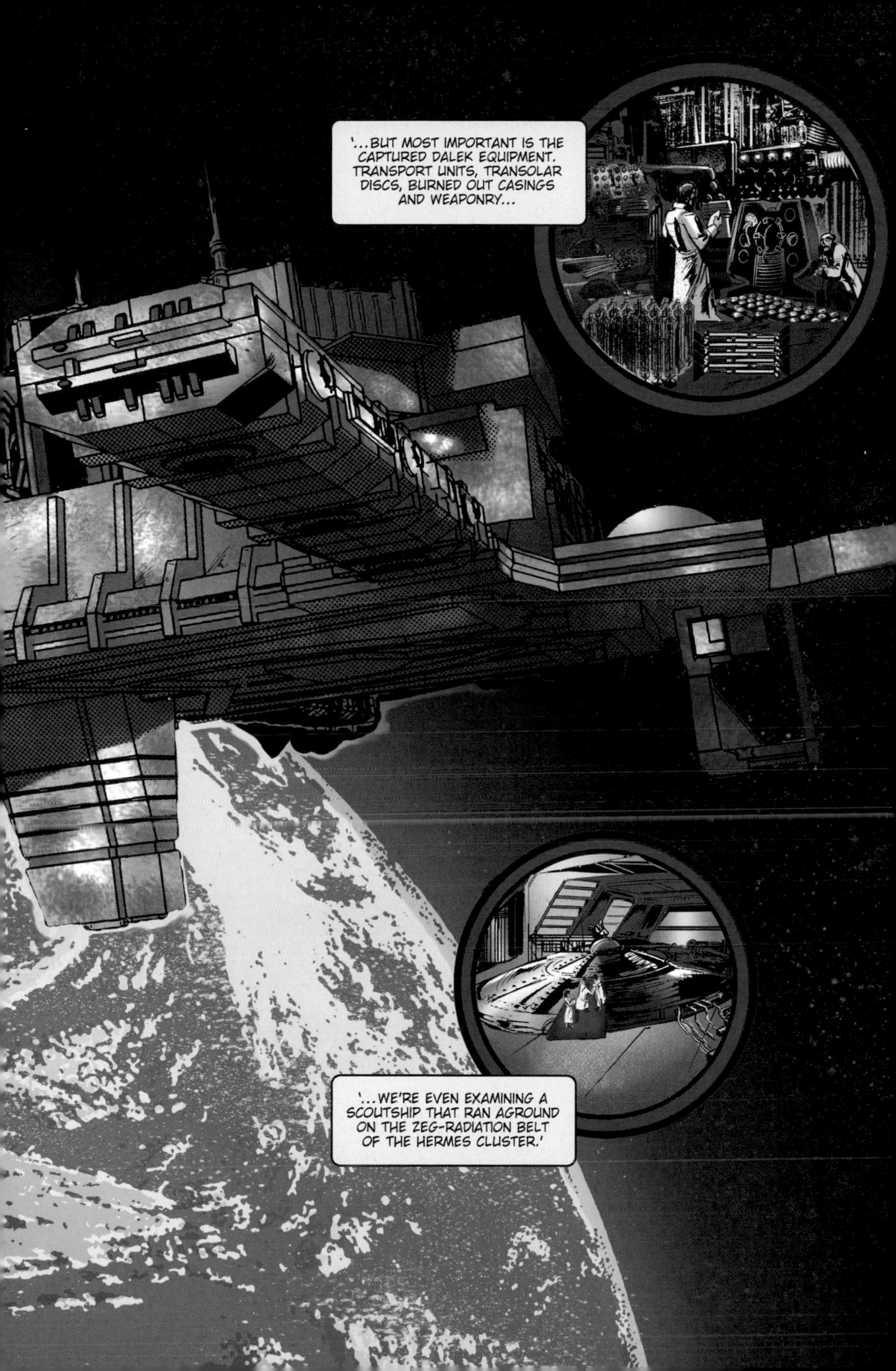
'...BUT MOST IMPORTANT IS THE CAPTURED DALEK EQUIPMENT. TRANSPORT UNITS, TRANSOLAR DISCS, BURNED OUT CASINGS AND WEAPONRY...
'...WE'RE EVEN EXAMINING A SCOUTSHIP THAT RAN AGROUND ON THE ZEG-RADIATION BELT OF THE HERMES CLUSTER.'

OF COURSE, NONE OF IT WORKS. THE SECRETS OF THE DALEKS CONTINUE TO ELUDE US.

ANY DALEK TECHNOLOGY WILL ONLY WORK FOR DALEKS. WHICH BRINGS ME NEATLY TO THE OBVIOUS QUESTION...

THERE'S ONE THING MISSING FROM YOUR COLLECTION.

Z-SHOOM

COME HERE.

LET ME SHOW YOU SOMETHING.

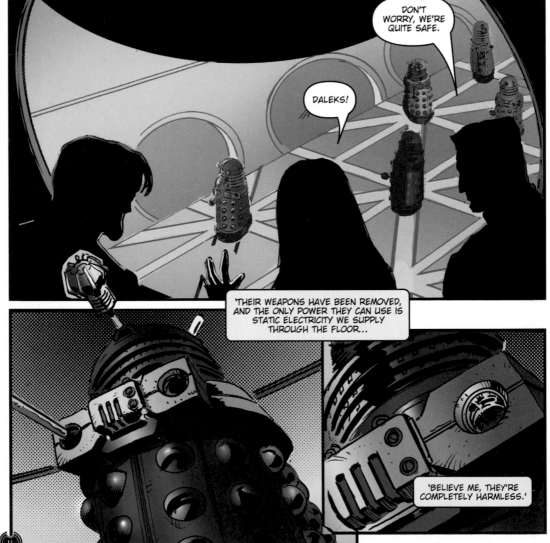

DON'T WORRY, WE'RE QUITE SAFE.

DALEKS!

'THEIR WEAPONS HAVE BEEN REMOVED, AND THE ONLY POWER THEY CAN USE IS STATIC ELECTRICITY WE SUPPLY THROUGH THE FLOOR...

'BELIEVE ME, THEY'RE COMPLETELY HARMLESS.'

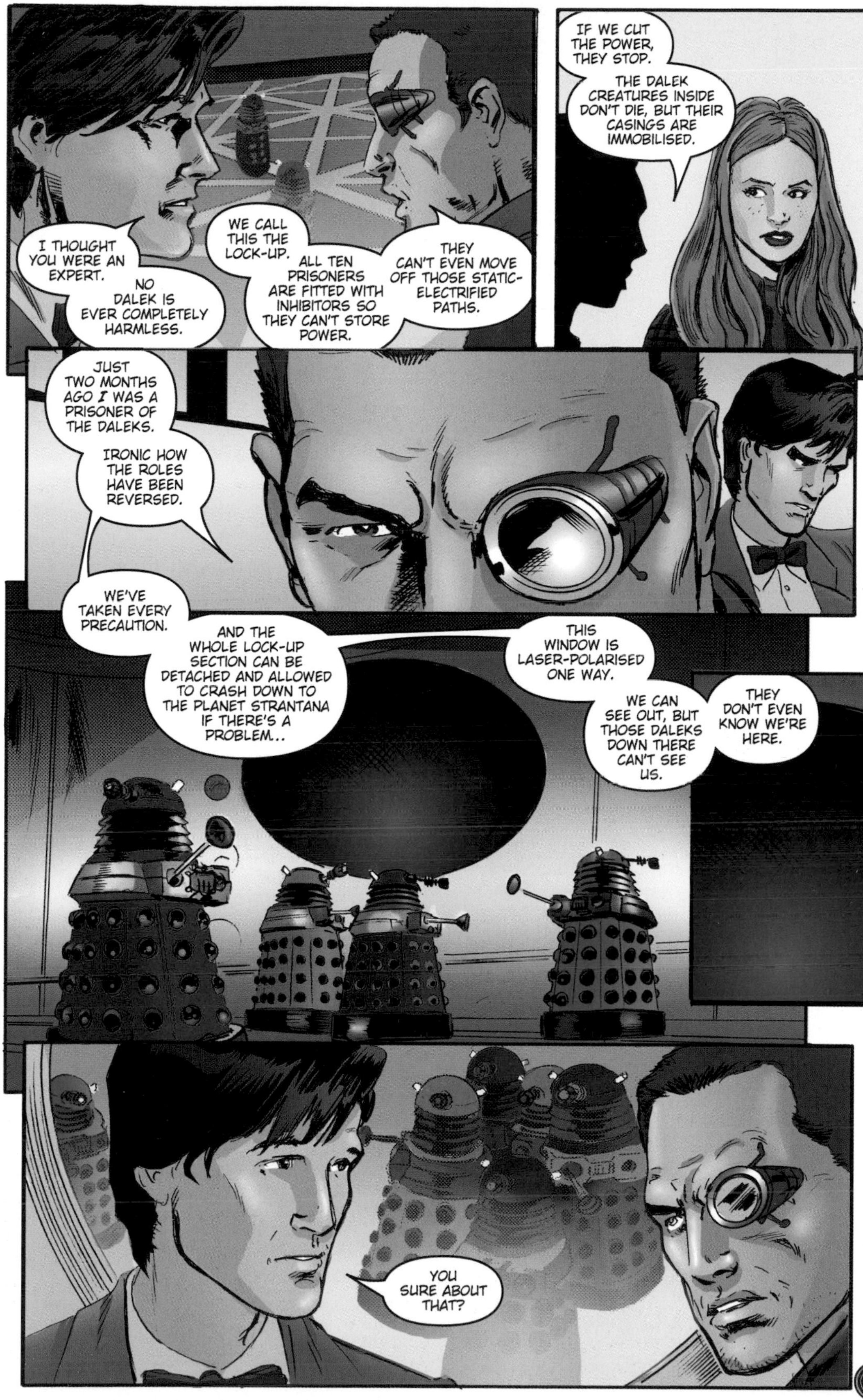
I THOUGHT YOU WERE AN EXPERT.
NO DALEK IS EVER COMPLETELY HARMLESS.
WE CALL THIS THE LOCK-UP.
ALL TEN PRISONERS ARE FITTED WITH INHIBITORS SO THEY CAN'T STORE POWER.
THEY CAN'T EVEN MOVE OFF THOSE STATIC-ELECTRIFIED PATHS.
IF WE CUT THE POWER, THEY STOP.
THE DALEK CREATURES INSIDE DON'T DIE, BUT THEIR CASINGS ARE IMMOBILISED.
JUST TWO MONTHS AGO *I* WAS A PRISONER OF THE DALEKS.
IRONIC HOW THE ROLES HAVE BEEN REVERSED.
WE'VE TAKEN EVERY PRECAUTION.
AND THE WHOLE LOCK-UP SECTION CAN BE DETACHED AND ALLOWED TO CRASH DOWN TO THE PLANET STRANTANA IF THERE'S A PROBLEM...
THIS WINDOW IS LASER-POLARISED ONE WAY.
WE CAN SEE OUT, BUT THOSE DALEKS DOWN THERE CAN'T SEE US.
THEY DON'T EVEN KNOW WE'RE HERE.
YOU SURE ABOUT THAT?

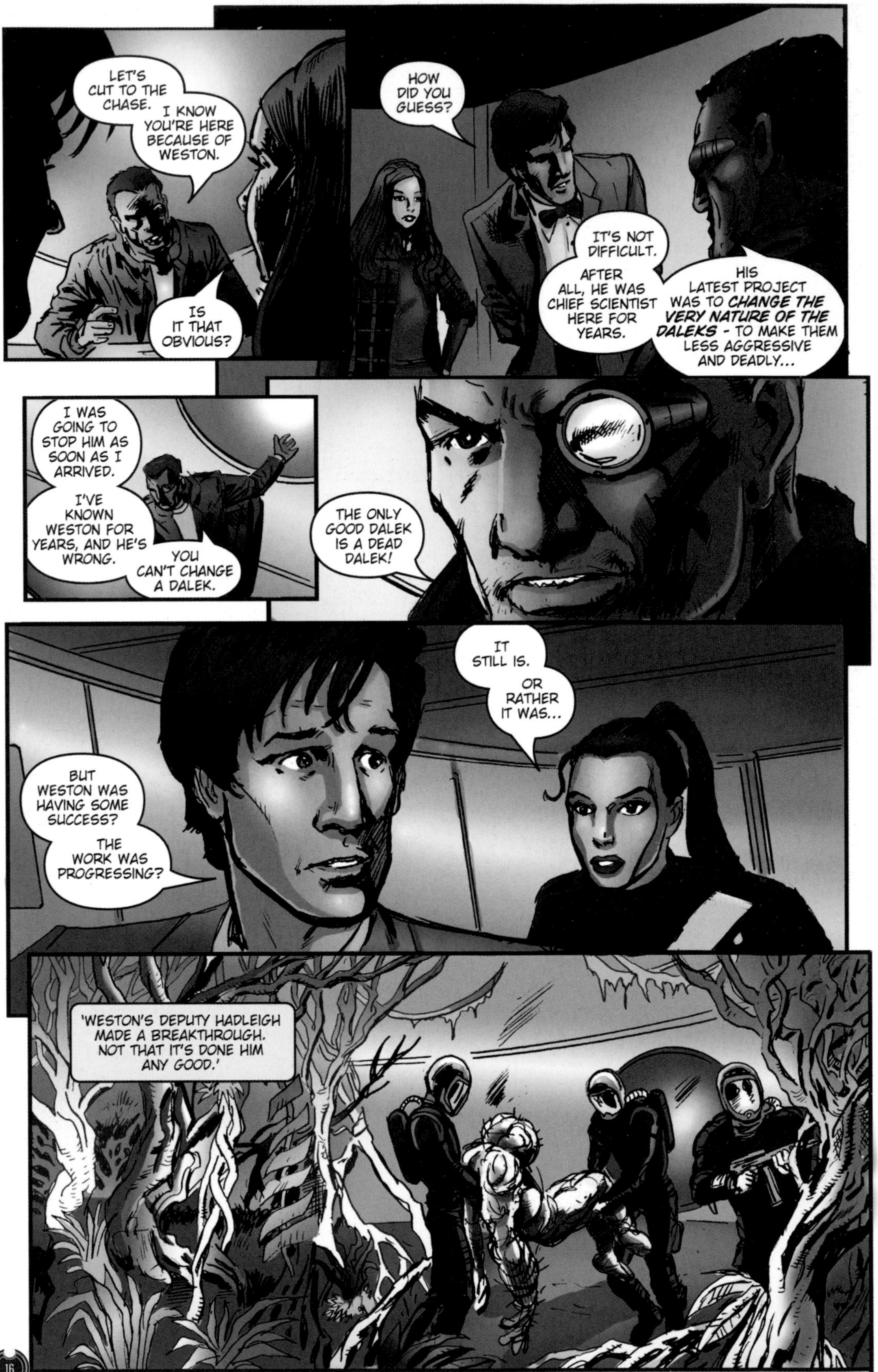
LET'S CUT TO THE CHASE.
I KNOW YOU'RE HERE BECAUSE OF WESTON.
IS IT THAT OBVIOUS?
HOW DID YOU GUESS?
IT'S NOT DIFFICULT.
AFTER ALL, HE WAS CHIEF SCIENTIST HERE FOR YEARS.
HIS LATEST PROJECT WAS TO CHANGE THE VERY NATURE OF THE DALEKS - TO MAKE THEM LESS AGGRESSIVE AND DEADLY...
I WAS GOING TO STOP HIM AS SOON AS I ARRIVED.
I'VE KNOWN WESTON FOR YEARS, AND HE'S WRONG.
YOU CAN'T CHANGE A DALEK.
THE ONLY GOOD DALEK IS A DEAD DALEK!
BUT WESTON WAS HAVING SOME SUCCESS?
THE WORK WAS PROGRESSING?
IT STILL IS.
OR RATHER IT WAS...
'WESTON'S DEPUTY HADLEIGH MADE A BREAKTHROUGH. NOT THAT IT'S DONE HIM ANY GOOD.'

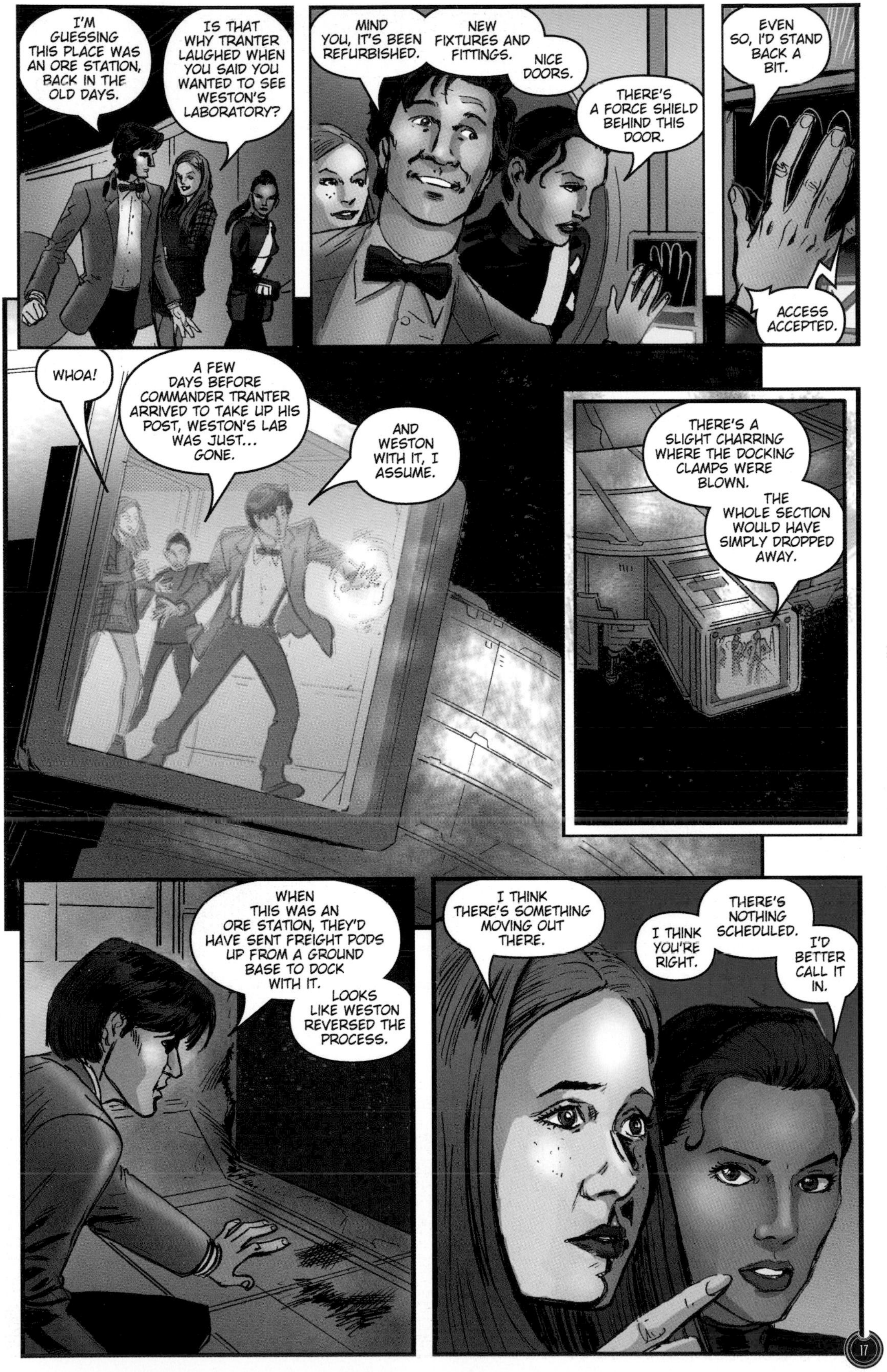

I'M GUESSING THIS PLACE WAS AN ORE STATION, BACK IN THE OLD DAYS.
IS THAT WHY TRANTER LAUGHED WHEN YOU SAID YOU WANTED TO SEE WESTON'S LABORATORY?
MIND YOU, IT'S BEEN REFURBISHED.
NEW FIXTURES AND FITTINGS.
NICE DOORS.
THERE'S A FORCE SHIELD BEHIND THIS DOOR.
EVEN SO, I'D STAND BACK A BIT.
ACCESS ACCEPTED.
WHOA!
A FEW DAYS BEFORE COMMANDER TRANTER ARRIVED TO TAKE UP HIS POST, WESTON'S LAB WAS JUST... GONE.
AND WESTON WITH IT, I ASSUME.
THERE'S A SLIGHT CHARRING WHERE THE DOCKING CLAMPS WERE BLOWN.
THE WHOLE SECTION WOULD HAVE SIMPLY DROPPED AWAY.
WHEN THIS WAS AN ORE STATION, THEY'D HAVE SENT FREIGHT PODS UP FROM A GROUND BASE TO DOCK WITH IT.
LOOKS LIKE WESTON REVERSED THE PROCESS.
I THINK THERE'S SOMETHING MOVING OUT THERE.
I THINK YOU'RE RIGHT.
THERE'S NOTHING SCHEDULED.
I'D BETTER CALL IT IN.

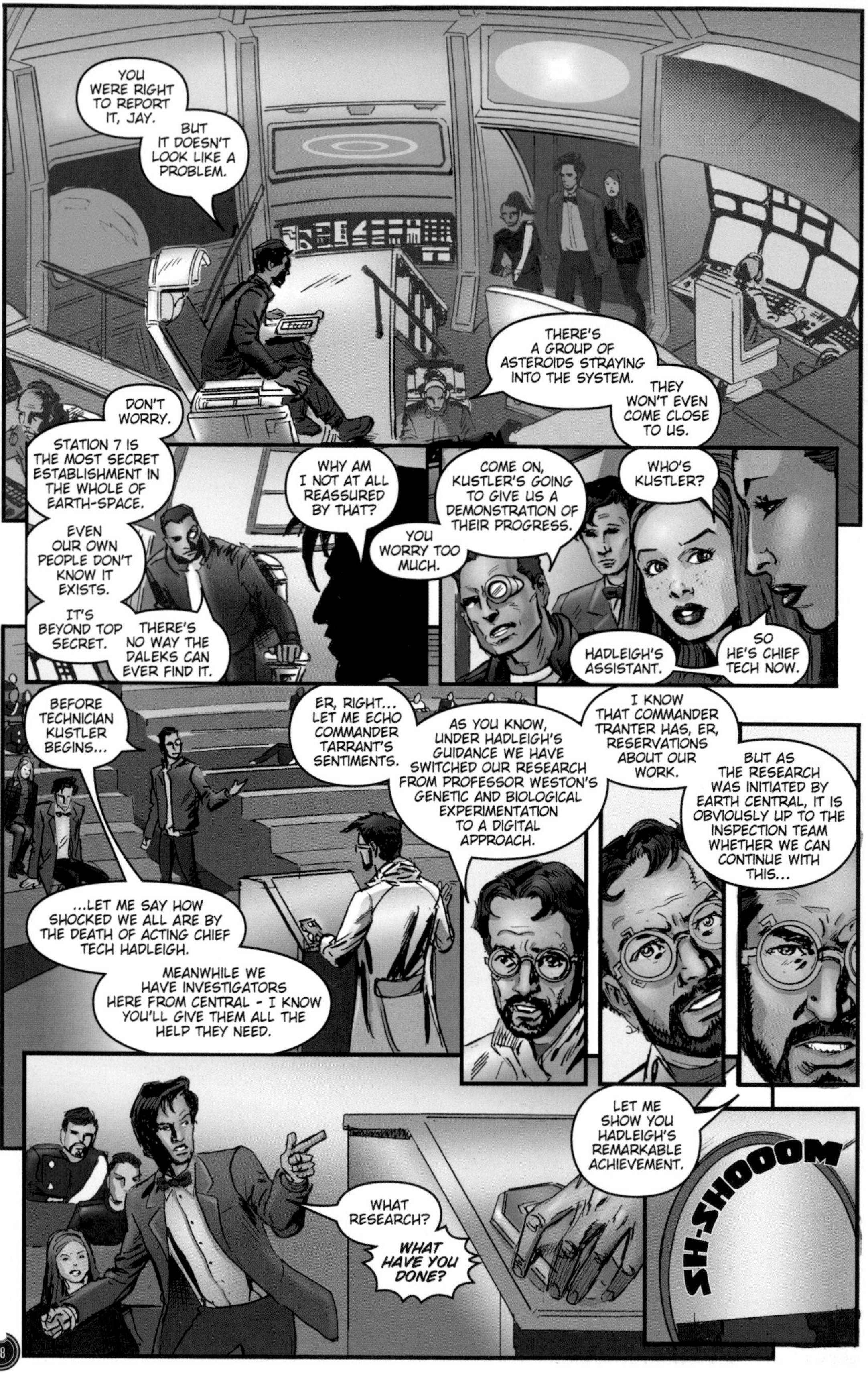
YOU WERE RIGHT TO REPORT IT, JAY.
BUT IT DOESN'T LOOK LIKE A PROBLEM.
THERE'S A GROUP OF ASTEROIDS STRAYING INTO THE SYSTEM.
THEY WON'T EVEN COME CLOSE TO US.
DON'T WORRY.
STATION 7 IS THE MOST SECRET ESTABLISHMENT IN THE WHOLE OF EARTH-SPACE.
EVEN OUR OWN PEOPLE DON'T KNOW IT EXISTS.
IT'S BEYOND TOP SECRET.
THERE'S NO WAY THE DALEKS CAN EVER FIND IT.
WHY AM I NOT AT ALL REASSURED BY THAT?
YOU WORRY TOO MUCH.
COME ON, KUSTLER'S GOING TO GIVE US A DEMONSTRATION OF THEIR PROGRESS.
WHO'S KUSTLER?
HADLEIGH'S ASSISTANT.
SO HE'S CHIEF TECH NOW.
BEFORE TECHNICIAN KUSTLER BEGINS...
...LET ME SAY HOW SHOCKED WE ALL ARE BY THE DEATH OF ACTING CHIEF TECH HADLEIGH.
MEANWHILE WE HAVE INVESTIGATORS HERE FROM CENTRAL - I KNOW YOU'LL GIVE THEM ALL THE HELP THEY NEED.
ER, RIGHT... LET ME ECHO COMMANDER TARRANT'S SENTIMENTS.
AS YOU KNOW, UNDER HADLEIGH'S GUIDANCE WE HAVE SWITCHED OUR RESEARCH FROM PROFESSOR WESTON'S GENETIC AND BIOLOGICAL EXPERIMENTATION TO A DIGITAL APPROACH.
I KNOW THAT COMMANDER TRANTER HAS, ER, RESERVATIONS ABOUT OUR WORK.
BUT AS THE RESEARCH WAS INITIATED BY EARTH CENTRAL, IT IS OBVIOUSLY UP TO THE INSPECTION TEAM WHETHER WE CAN CONTINUE WITH THIS...
LET ME SHOW YOU HADLEIGH'S REMARKABLE ACHIEVEMENT.
SH-SHOOOM
WHAT RESEARCH? *WHAT HAVE YOU DONE?*

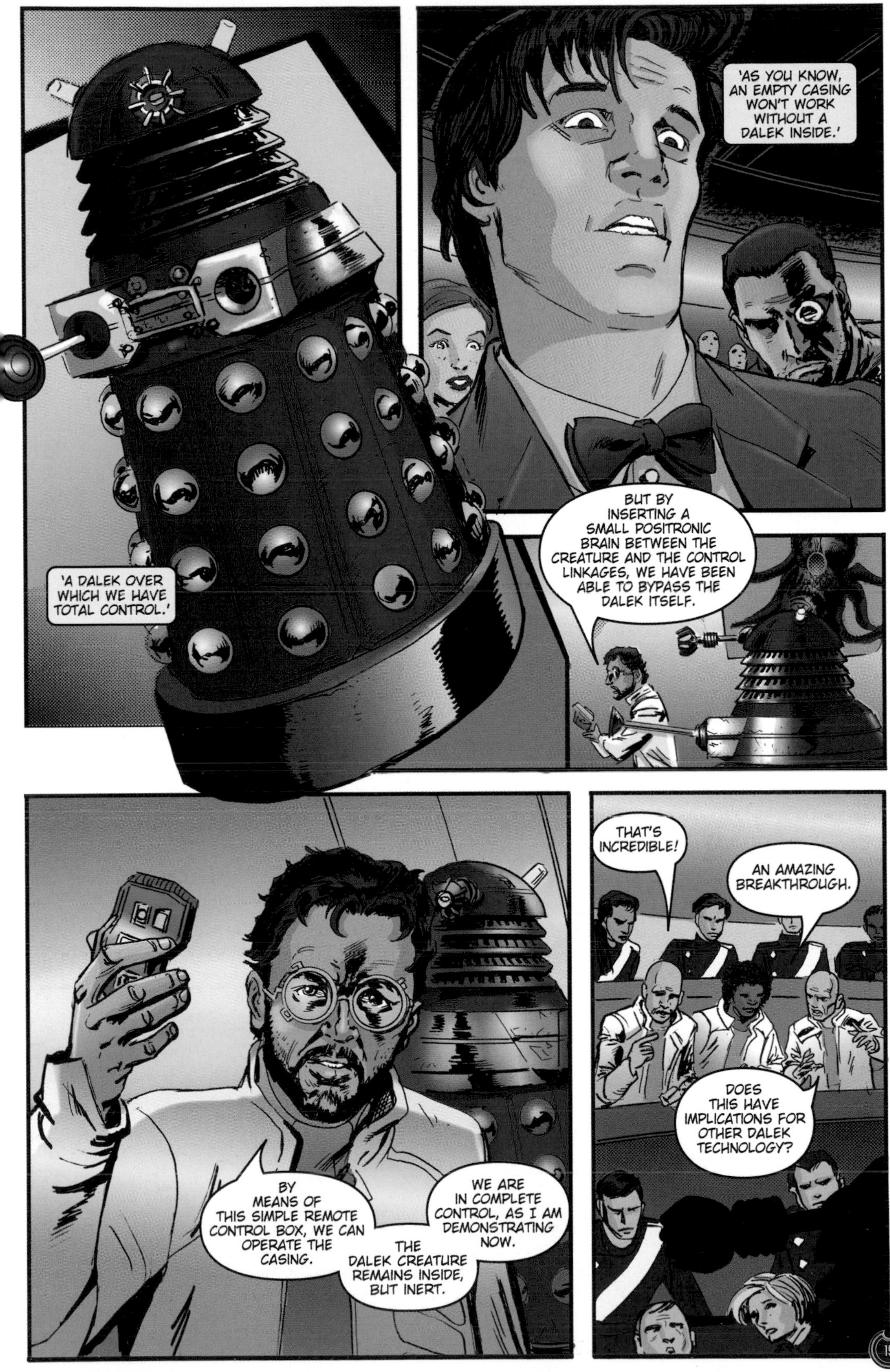
'AS YOU KNOW, AN EMPTY CASING WON'T WORK WITHOUT A DALEK INSIDE.'
'A DALEK OVER WHICH WE HAVE TOTAL CONTROL.'
BUT BY INSERTING A SMALL POSITRONIC BRAIN BETWEEN THE CREATURE AND THE CONTROL LINKAGES, WE HAVE BEEN ABLE TO BYPASS THE DALEK ITSELF.
BY MEANS OF THIS SIMPLE REMOTE CONTROL BOX, WE CAN OPERATE THE CASING.
THE DALEK CREATURE REMAINS INSIDE, BUT INERT.
WE ARE IN COMPLETE CONTROL, AS I AM DEMONSTRATING NOW.
THAT'S INCREDIBLE!
AN AMAZING BREAKTHROUGH.
DOES THIS HAVE IMPLICATIONS FOR OTHER DALEK TECHNOLOGY?

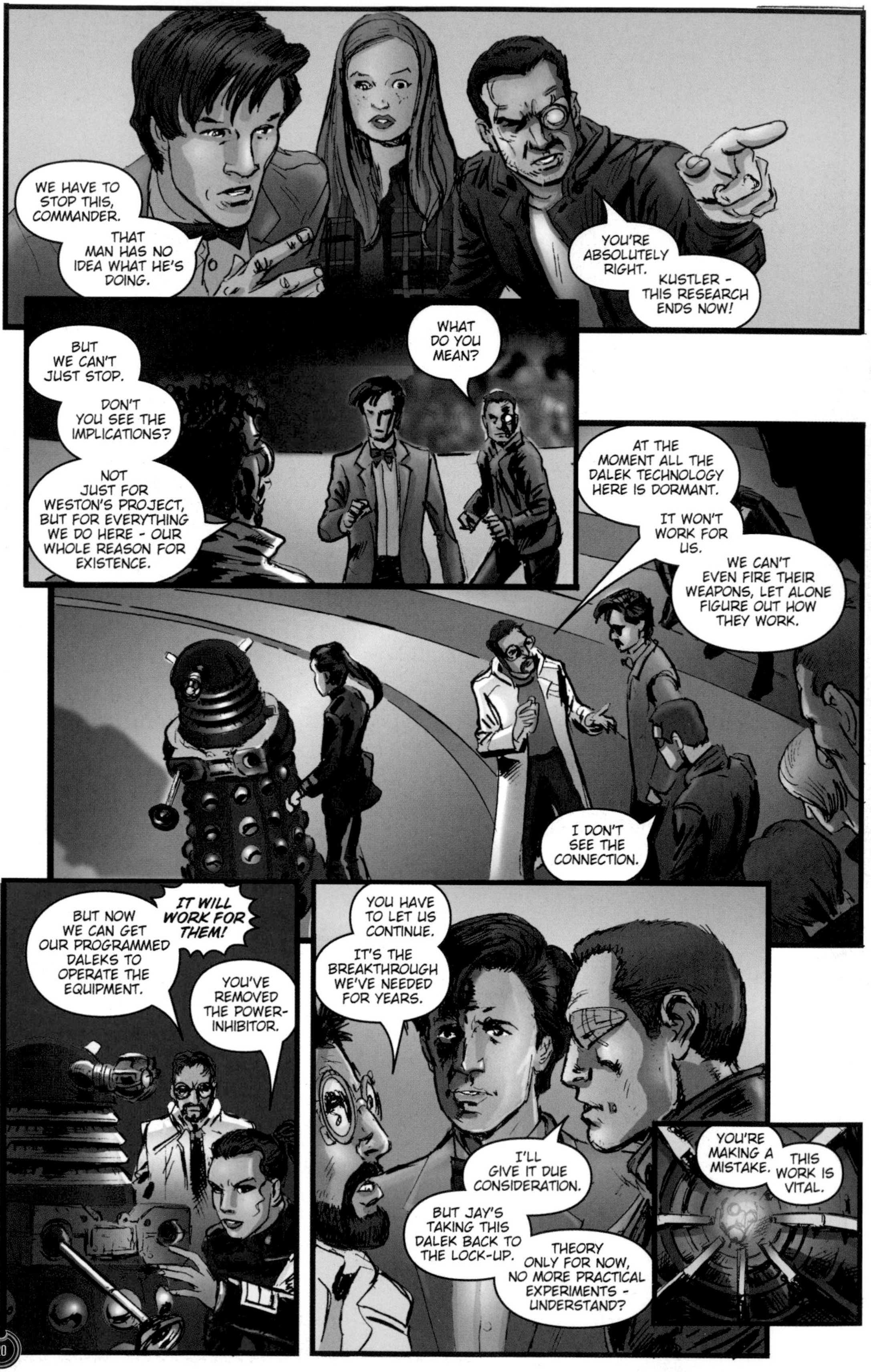
WE HAVE TO STOP THIS, COMMANDER.
THAT MAN HAS NO IDEA WHAT HE'S DOING.
YOU'RE ABSOLUTELY RIGHT.
KUSTLER - THIS RESEARCH ENDS NOW!
BUT WE CAN'T JUST STOP.
DON'T YOU SEE THE IMPLICATIONS?
NOT JUST FOR WESTON'S PROJECT, BUT FOR EVERYTHING WE DO HERE - OUR WHOLE REASON FOR EXISTENCE.
WHAT DO YOU MEAN?
AT THE MOMENT ALL THE DALEK TECHNOLOGY HERE IS DORMANT.
IT WON'T WORK FOR US.
WE CAN'T EVEN FIRE THEIR WEAPONS, LET ALONE FIGURE OUT HOW THEY WORK.
I DON'T SEE THE CONNECTION.
BUT NOW WE CAN GET OUR PROGRAMMED DALEKS TO OPERATE THE EQUIPMENT.
IT WILL WORK FOR THEM!
YOU'VE REMOVED THE POWER-INHIBITOR.
YOU HAVE TO LET US CONTINUE.
IT'S THE BREAKTHROUGH WE'VE NEEDED FOR YEARS.
I'LL GIVE IT DUE CONSIDERATION.
BUT JAY'S TAKING THIS DALEK BACK TO THE LOCK-UP.
THEORY ONLY FOR NOW, NO MORE PRACTICAL EXPERIMENTS - UNDERSTAND?
YOU'RE MAKING A MISTAKE.
THIS WORK IS VITAL.

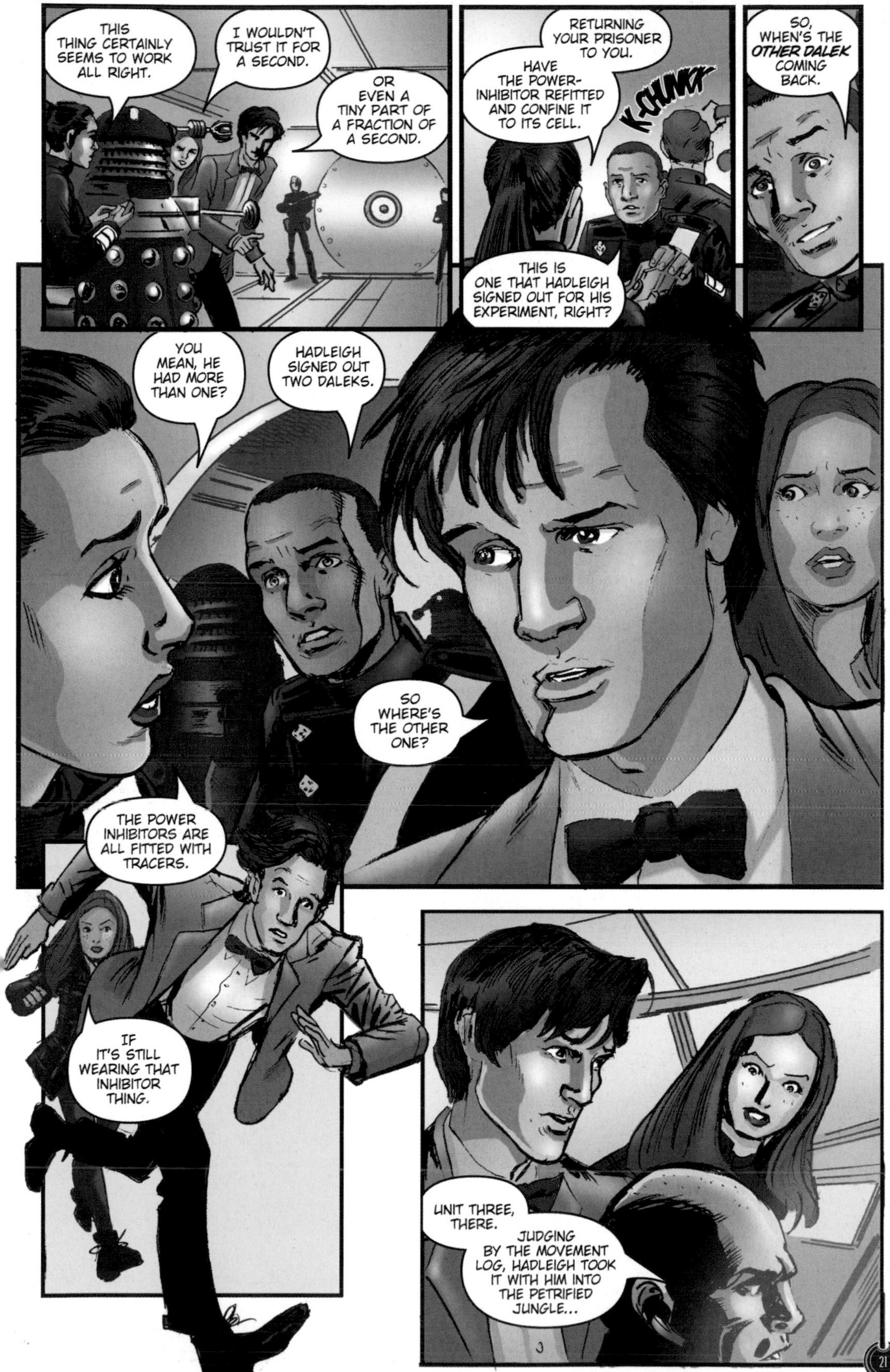
THIS THING CERTAINLY SEEMS TO WORK ALL RIGHT.
I WOULDN'T TRUST IT FOR A SECOND.
OR EVEN A TINY PART OF A FRACTION OF A SECOND.
RETURNING YOUR PRISONER TO YOU.
HAVE THE POWER-INHIBITOR REFITTED AND CONFINE IT TO ITS CELL.
K-CHUNKK
THIS IS ONE THAT HADLEIGH SIGNED OUT FOR HIS EXPERIMENT, RIGHT?
SO, WHEN'S THE OTHER DALEK COMING BACK.
YOU MEAN, HE HAD MORE THAN ONE?
HADLEIGH SIGNED OUT TWO DALEKS.
SO WHERE'S THE OTHER ONE?
THE POWER INHIBITORS ARE ALL FITTED WITH TRACERS.
IF IT'S STILL WEARING THAT INHIBITOR THING.
UNIT THREE, THERE.
JUDGING BY THE MOVEMENT LOG, HADLEIGH TOOK IT WITH HIM INTO THE PETRIFIED JUNGLE...

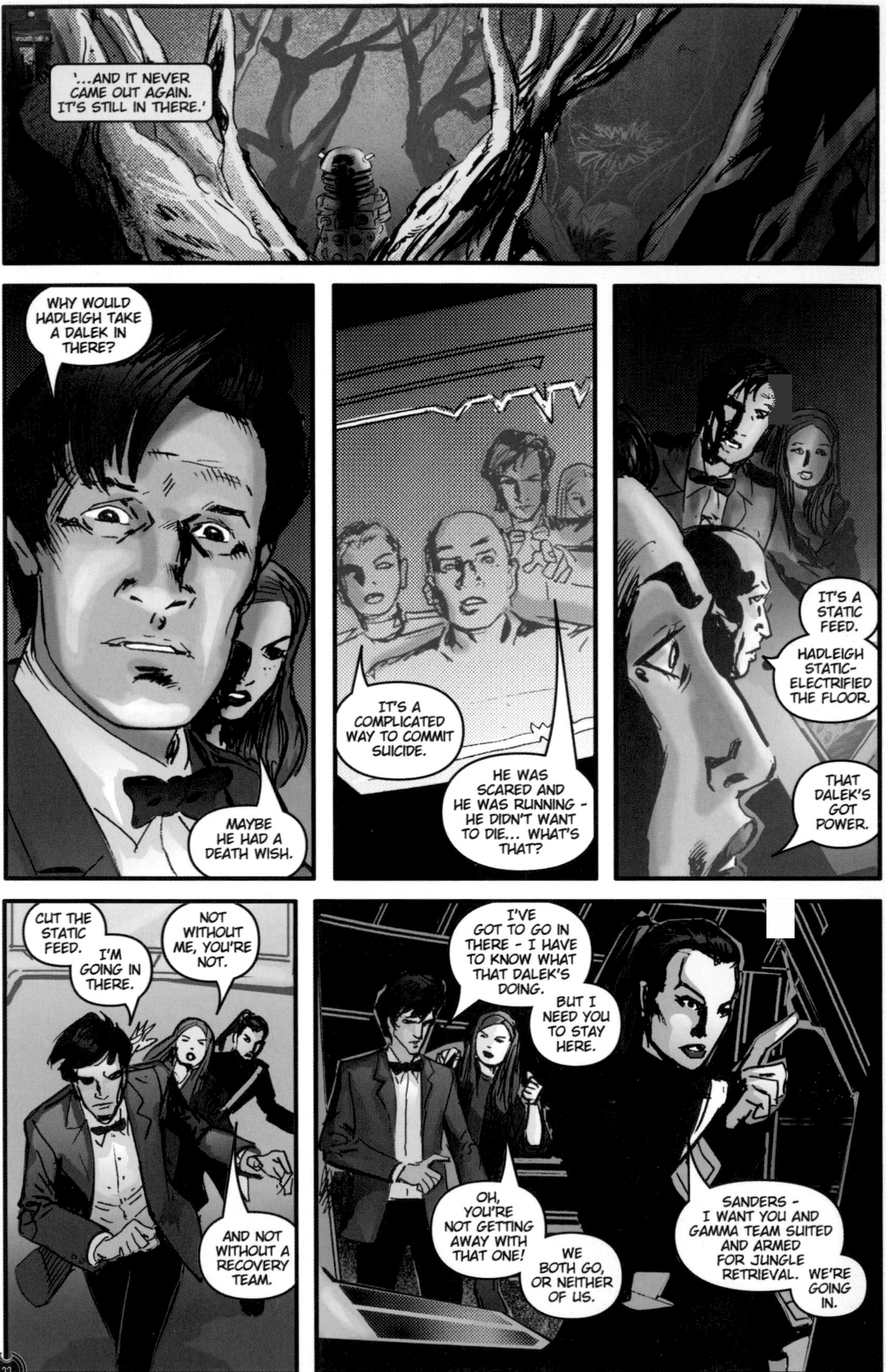
'...AND IT NEVER CAME OUT AGAIN. IT'S STILL IN THERE.'
WHY WOULD HADLEIGH TAKE A DALEK IN THERE?
MAYBE HE HAD A DEATH WISH.
IT'S A COMPLICATED WAY TO COMMIT SUICIDE.
HE WAS SCARED AND HE WAS RUNNING - HE DIDN'T WANT TO DIE... WHAT'S THAT?
IT'S A STATIC FEED.
HADLEIGH STATIC-ELECTRIFIED THE FLOOR.
THAT DALEK'S GOT POWER.
CUT THE STATIC FEED.
I'M GOING IN THERE.
NOT WITHOUT ME, YOU'RE NOT.
AND NOT WITHOUT A RECOVERY TEAM.
I'VE GOT TO GO IN THERE - I HAVE TO KNOW WHAT THAT DALEK'S DOING.
BUT I NEED YOU TO STAY HERE.
OH, YOU'RE NOT GETTING AWAY WITH THAT ONE!
WE BOTH GO, OR NEITHER OF US.
SANDERS - I WANT YOU AND GAMMA TEAM SUITED AND ARMED FOR JUNGLE RETRIEVAL.
WE'RE GOING IN.

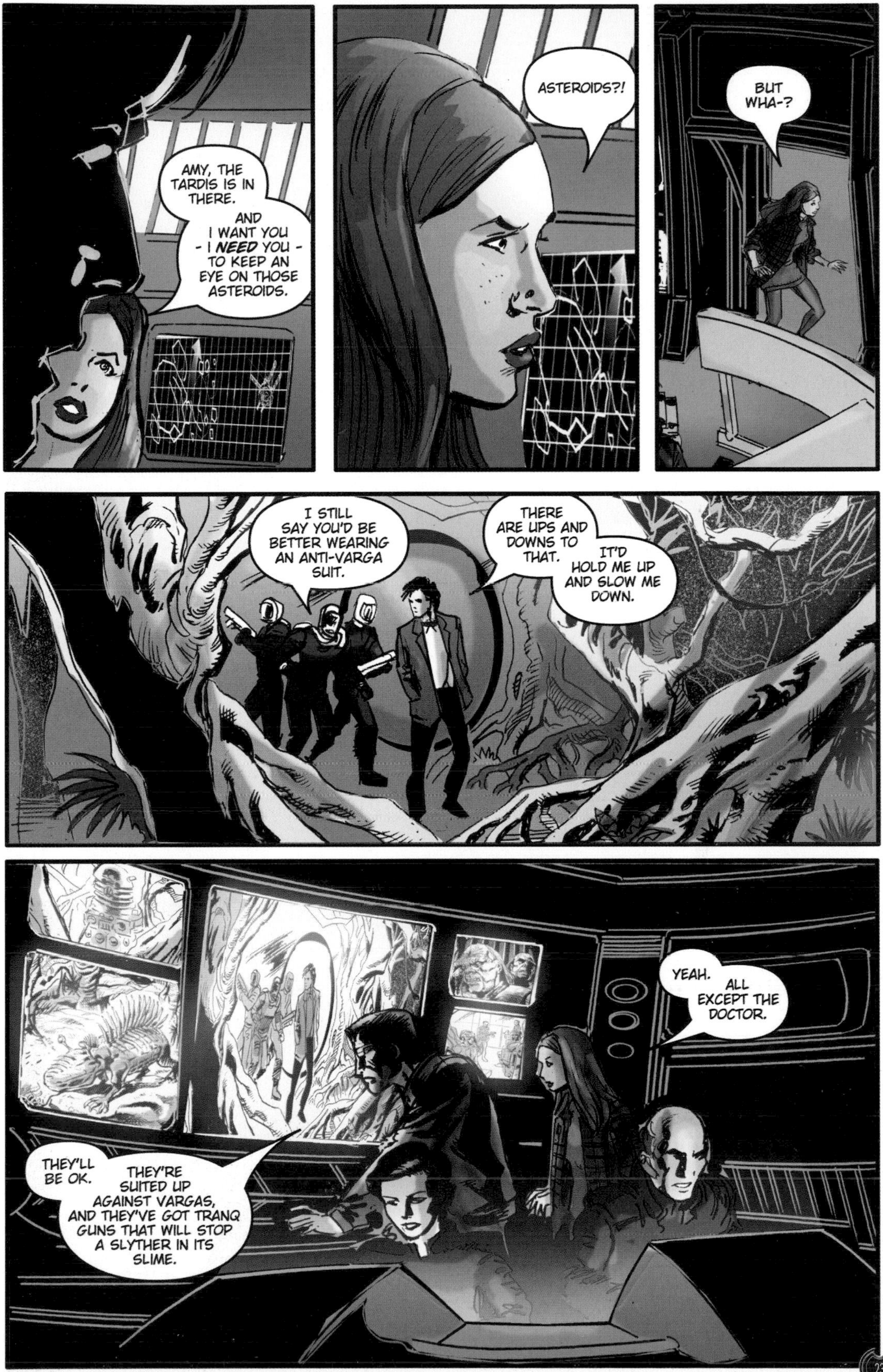
AMY, THE TARDIS IS IN THERE.
AND I WANT YOU - I **NEED** YOU - TO KEEP AN EYE ON THOSE ASTEROIDS.
ASTEROIDS?!
BUT WHA-?
I STILL SAY YOU'D BE BETTER WEARING AN ANTI-VARGA SUIT.
THERE ARE UPS AND DOWNS TO THAT.
IT'D HOLD ME UP AND SLOW ME DOWN.
YEAH.
ALL EXCEPT THE DOCTOR.
THEY'LL BE OK.
THEY'RE SUITED UP AGAINST VARGAS, AND THEY'VE GOT TRANQ GUNS THAT WILL STOP A SLYTHER IN ITS SLIME.

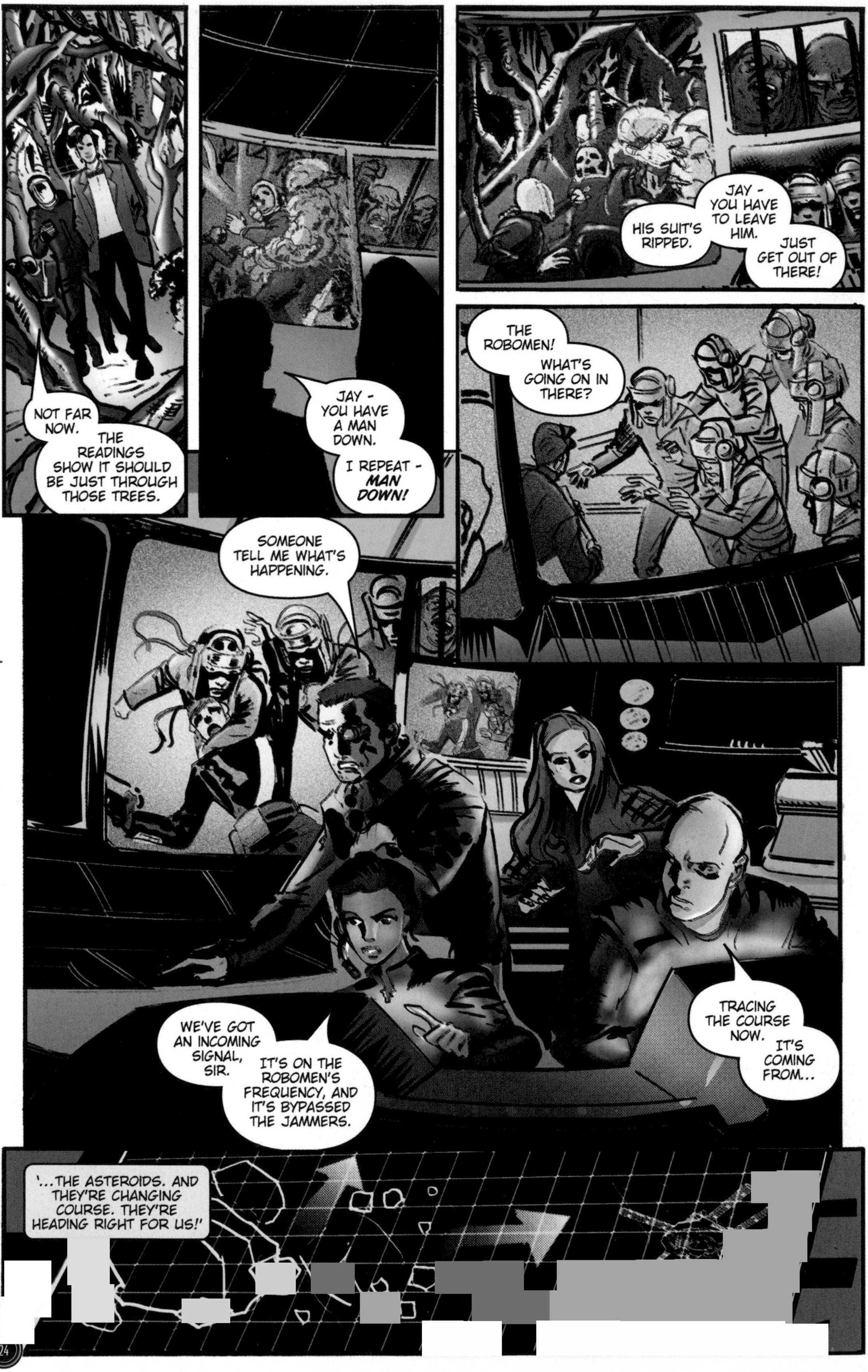

NOT FAR NOW.
THE READINGS SHOW IT SHOULD BE JUST THROUGH THOSE TREES.
JAY - YOU HAVE A MAN DOWN.
I REPEAT - ***MAN DOWN!***
HIS SUIT'S RIPPED.
JAY - YOU HAVE TO LEAVE HIM.
JUST GET OUT OF THERE!
THE ROBOMEN!
WHAT'S GOING ON IN THERE?
SOMEONE TELL ME WHAT'S HAPPENING.
WE'VE GOT AN INCOMING SIGNAL, SIR.
IT'S ON THE ROBOMEN'S FREQUENCY, AND IT'S BYPASSED THE JAMMERS.
TRACING THE COURSE NOW.
IT'S COMING FROM...
'...THE ASTEROIDS. AND THEY'RE CHANGING COURSE. THEY'RE HEADING RIGHT FOR US!'

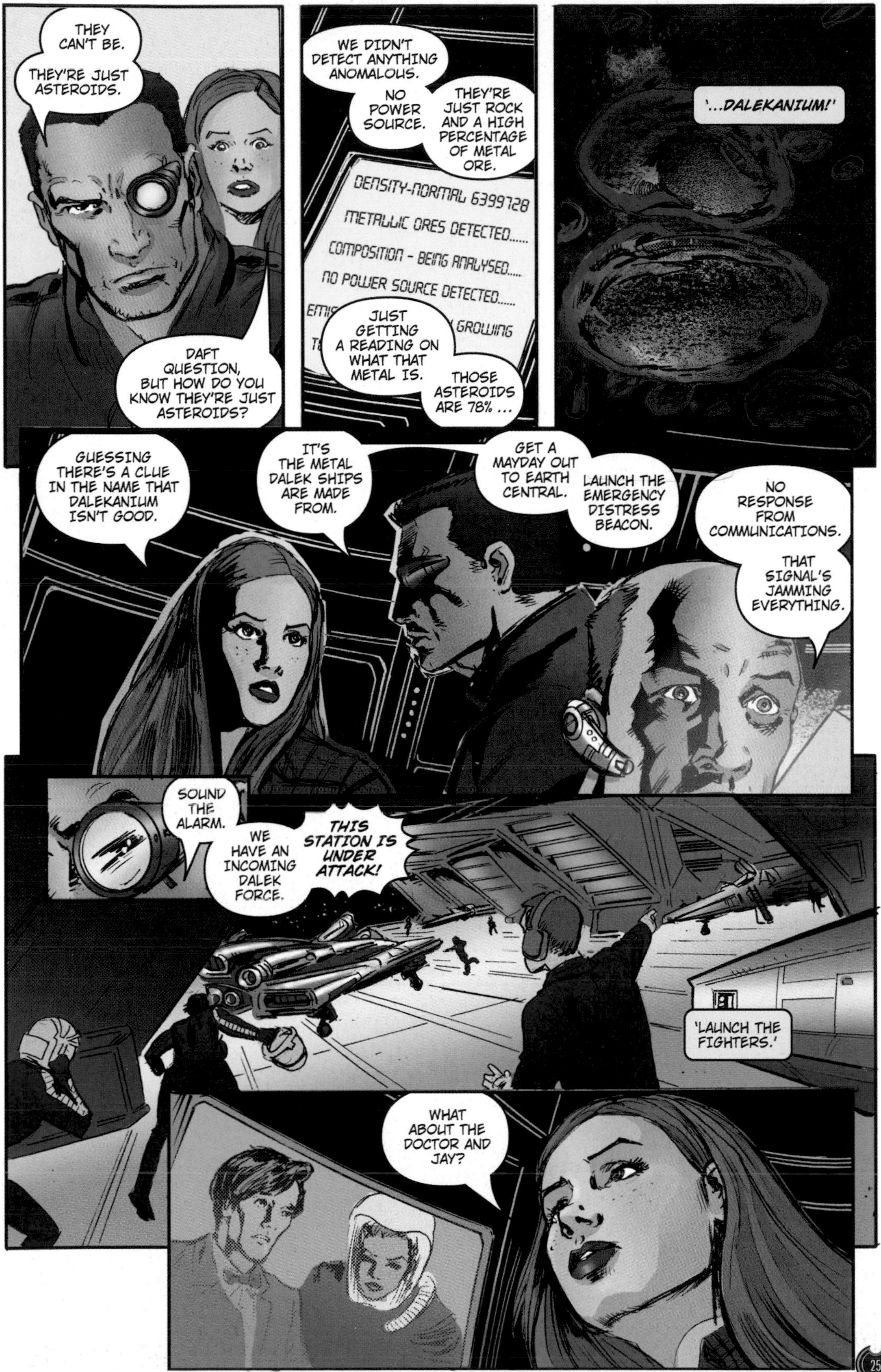
THEY CAN'T BE.
THEY'RE JUST ASTEROIDS.
DAFT QUESTION, BUT HOW DO YOU KNOW THEY'RE JUST ASTEROIDS?
WE DIDN'T DETECT ANYTHING ANOMALOUS.
NO POWER SOURCE.
THEY'RE JUST ROCK AND A HIGH PERCENTAGE OF METAL ORE.
DENSITY-NORMAL 6399728
METALLIC ORES DETECTED......
COMPOSITION - BEING ANALYSED.....
NO POWER SOURCE DETECTED......
GROWING
JUST GETTING A READING ON WHAT THAT METAL IS.
THOSE ASTEROIDS ARE 78% ...
'...DALEKANIUM!'
GUESSING THERE'S A CLUE IN THE NAME THAT DALEKANIUM ISN'T GOOD.
IT'S THE METAL DALEK SHIPS ARE MADE FROM.
GET A MAYDAY OUT TO EARTH CENTRAL.
LAUNCH THE EMERGENCY DISTRESS BEACON.
NO RESPONSE FROM COMMUNICATIONS.
THAT SIGNAL'S JAMMING EVERYTHING.
SOUND THE ALARM.
WE HAVE AN INCOMING DALEK FORCE.
THIS STATION IS UNDER ATTACK!
'LAUNCH THE FIGHTERS.'
WHAT ABOUT THE DOCTOR AND JAY?

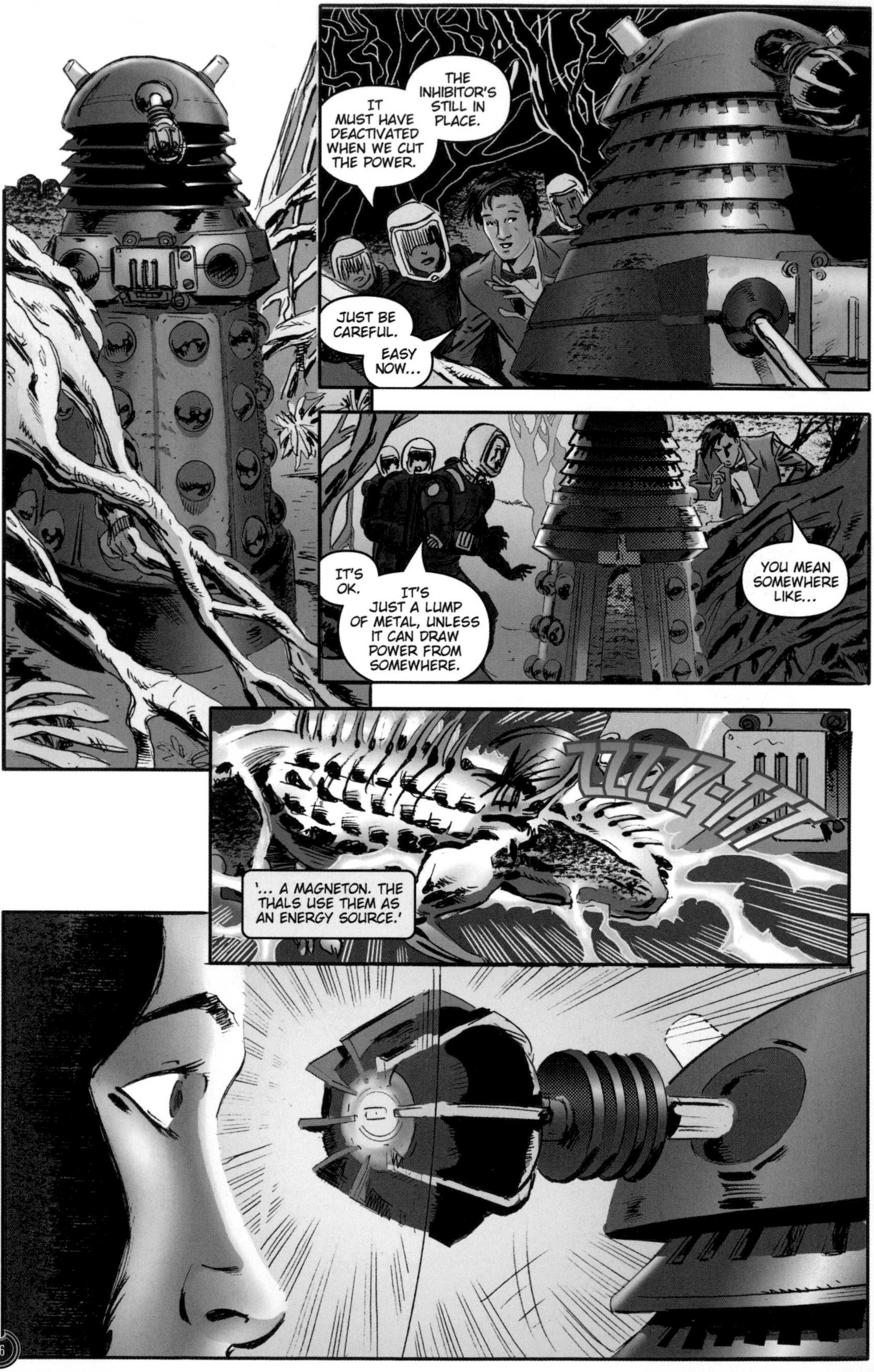
IT MUST HAVE DEACTIVATED WHEN WE CUT THE POWER.
THE INHIBITOR'S STILL IN PLACE.
JUST BE CAREFUL.
EASY NOW...
IT'S OK.
IT'S JUST A LUMP OF METAL, UNLESS IT CAN DRAW POWER FROM SOMEWHERE.
YOU MEAN SOMEWHERE LIKE...
'... A MAGNETON. THE THALS USE THEM AS AN ENERGY SOURCE.'
ZZZZZ-TT!

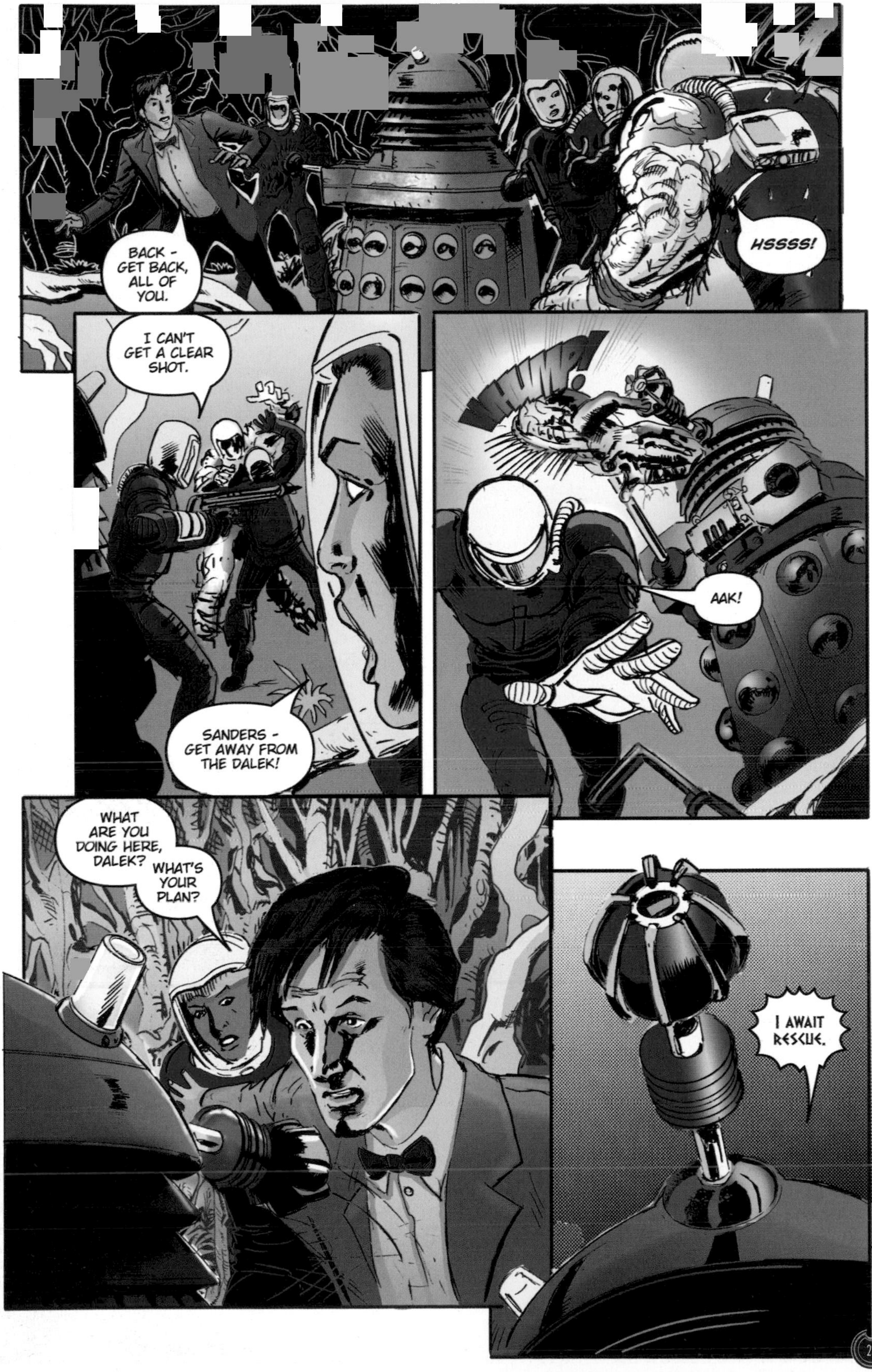
BACK - GET BACK, ALL OF YOU.
HSSSS!
I CAN'T GET A CLEAR SHOT.
SANDERS - GET AWAY FROM THE DALEK!
THUMP!
AAK!
WHAT ARE YOU DOING HERE, DALEK?
WHAT'S YOUR PLAN?
I AWAIT RESCUE.

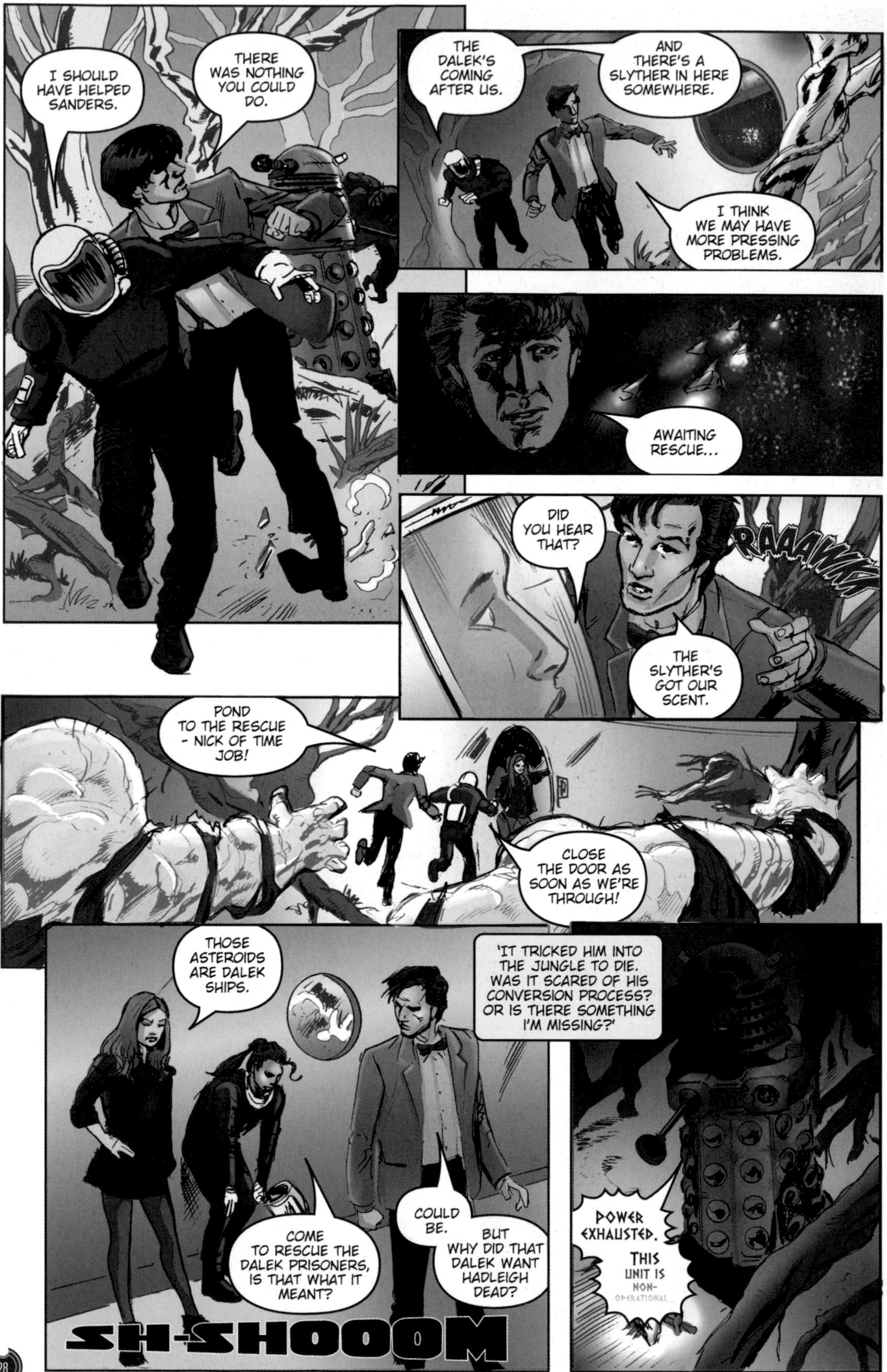
I SHOULD HAVE HELPED SANDERS.
THERE WAS NOTHING YOU COULD DO.
THE DALEK'S COMING AFTER US.
AND THERE'S A SLYTHER IN HERE SOMEWHERE.
I THINK WE MAY HAVE MORE PRESSING PROBLEMS.
AWAITING RESCUE...
DID YOU HEAR THAT?
RAAAWK!
THE SLYTHER'S GOT OUR SCENT.
POND TO THE RESCUE - NICK OF TIME JOB!
CLOSE THE DOOR AS SOON AS WE'RE THROUGH!
THOSE ASTEROIDS ARE DALEK SHIPS.
COME TO RESCUE THE DALEK PRISONERS, IS THAT WHAT IT MEANT?
COULD BE.
BUT WHY DID THAT DALEK WANT HADLEIGH DEAD?
SH-SHOOOM
'IT TRICKED HIM INTO THE JUNGLE TO DIE. WAS IT SCARED OF HIS CONVERSION PROCESS? OR IS THERE SOMETHING I'M MISSING?'
POWER EXHAUSTED.
THIS UNIT IS NON-OPERATIONAL...

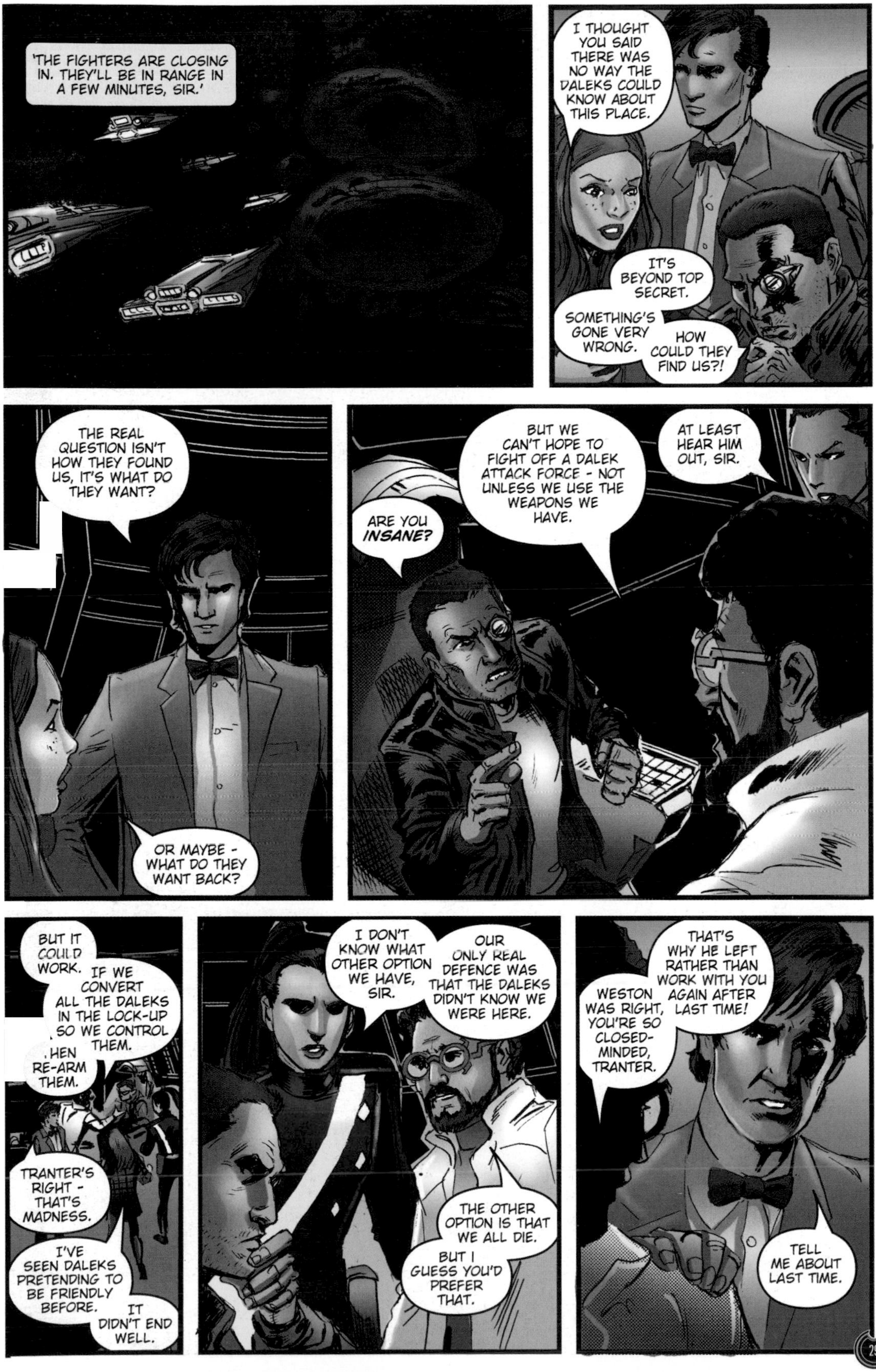
'THE FIGHTERS ARE CLOSING IN. THEY'LL BE IN RANGE IN A FEW MINUTES, SIR.'
I THOUGHT YOU SAID THERE WAS NO WAY THE DALEKS COULD KNOW ABOUT THIS PLACE.
IT'S BEYOND TOP SECRET.
SOMETHING'S GONE VERY WRONG.
HOW COULD THEY FIND US?!
THE REAL QUESTION ISN'T HOW THEY FOUND US, IT'S WHAT DO THEY WANT?
OR MAYBE - WHAT DO THEY WANT BACK?
BUT WE CAN'T HOPE TO FIGHT OFF A DALEK ATTACK FORCE - NOT UNLESS WE USE THE WEAPONS WE HAVE.
AT LEAST HEAR HIM OUT, SIR.
ARE YOU *INSANE?*
BUT IT COULD WORK.
IF WE CONVERT ALL THE DALEKS IN THE LOCK-UP SO WE CONTROL THEM.
HEN RE-ARM THEM.
TRANTER'S RIGHT - THAT'S MADNESS.
I'VE SEEN DALEKS PRETENDING TO BE FRIENDLY BEFORE.
IT DIDN'T END WELL.
I DON'T KNOW WHAT OTHER OPTION WE HAVE, SIR.
OUR ONLY REAL DEFENCE WAS THAT THE DALEKS DIDN'T KNOW WE WERE HERE.
THE OTHER OPTION IS THAT WE ALL DIE.
BUT I GUESS YOU'D PREFER THAT.
THAT'S WHY HE LEFT RATHER THAN WORK WITH YOU AGAIN AFTER LAST TIME!
WESTON WAS RIGHT, YOU'RE SO CLOSED-MINDED, TRANTER.
TELL ME ABOUT LAST TIME.

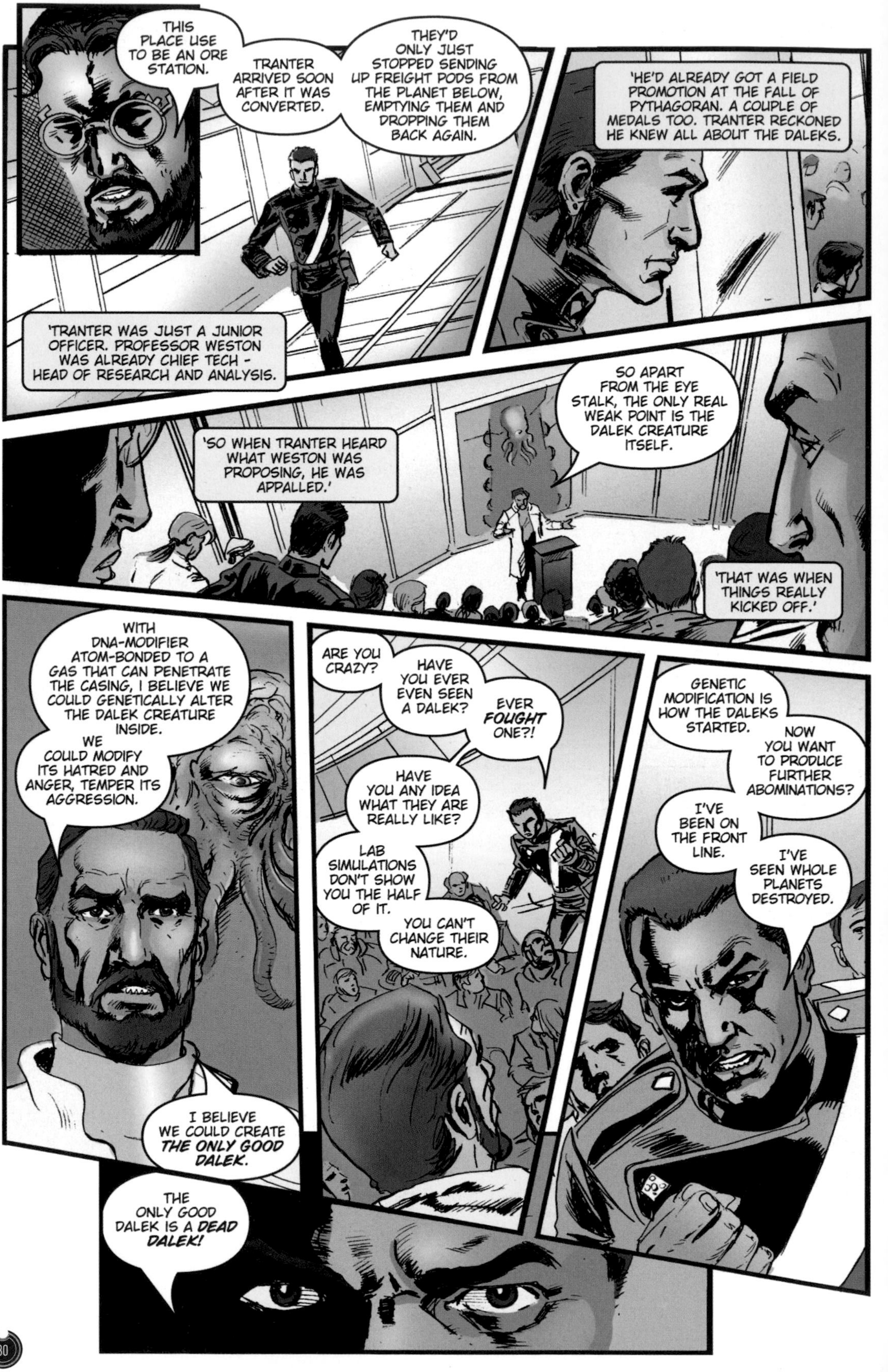
THIS PLACE USE TO BE AN ORE STATION.
TRANTER ARRIVED SOON AFTER IT WAS CONVERTED.
THEY'D ONLY JUST STOPPED SENDING UP FREIGHT PODS FROM THE PLANET BELOW, EMPTYING THEM AND DROPPING THEM BACK AGAIN.
'TRANTER WAS JUST A JUNIOR OFFICER. PROFESSOR WESTON WAS ALREADY CHIEF TECH - HEAD OF RESEARCH AND ANALYSIS.
'HE'D ALREADY GOT A FIELD PROMOTION AT THE FALL OF PYTHAGORAN. A COUPLE OF MEDALS TOO. TRANTER RECKONED HE KNEW ALL ABOUT THE DALEKS.
'SO WHEN TRANTER HEARD WHAT WESTON WAS PROPOSING, HE WAS APPALLED.'
SO APART FROM THE EYE STALK, THE ONLY REAL WEAK POINT IS THE DALEK CREATURE ITSELF.
'THAT WAS WHEN THINGS REALLY KICKED OFF.'
WITH DNA-MODIFIER ATOM-BONDED TO A GAS THAT CAN PENETRATE THE CASING, I BELIEVE WE COULD GENETICALLY ALTER THE DALEK CREATURE INSIDE.
WE COULD MODIFY ITS HATRED AND ANGER, TEMPER ITS AGGRESSION.
I BELIEVE WE COULD CREATE ***THE ONLY GOOD DALEK***.
ARE YOU CRAZY?
HAVE YOU EVER EVEN SEEN A DALEK?
EVER ***FOUGHT*** ONE?!
HAVE YOU ANY IDEA WHAT THEY ARE REALLY LIKE?
LAB SIMULATIONS DON'T SHOW YOU THE HALF OF IT.
YOU CAN'T CHANGE THEIR NATURE.
GENETIC MODIFICATION IS HOW THE DALEKS STARTED.
NOW YOU WANT TO PRODUCE FURTHER ABOMINATIONS?
I'VE BEEN ON THE FRONT LINE.
I'VE SEEN WHOLE PLANETS DESTROYED.
THE ONLY GOOD DALEK IS A ***DEAD DALEK!***

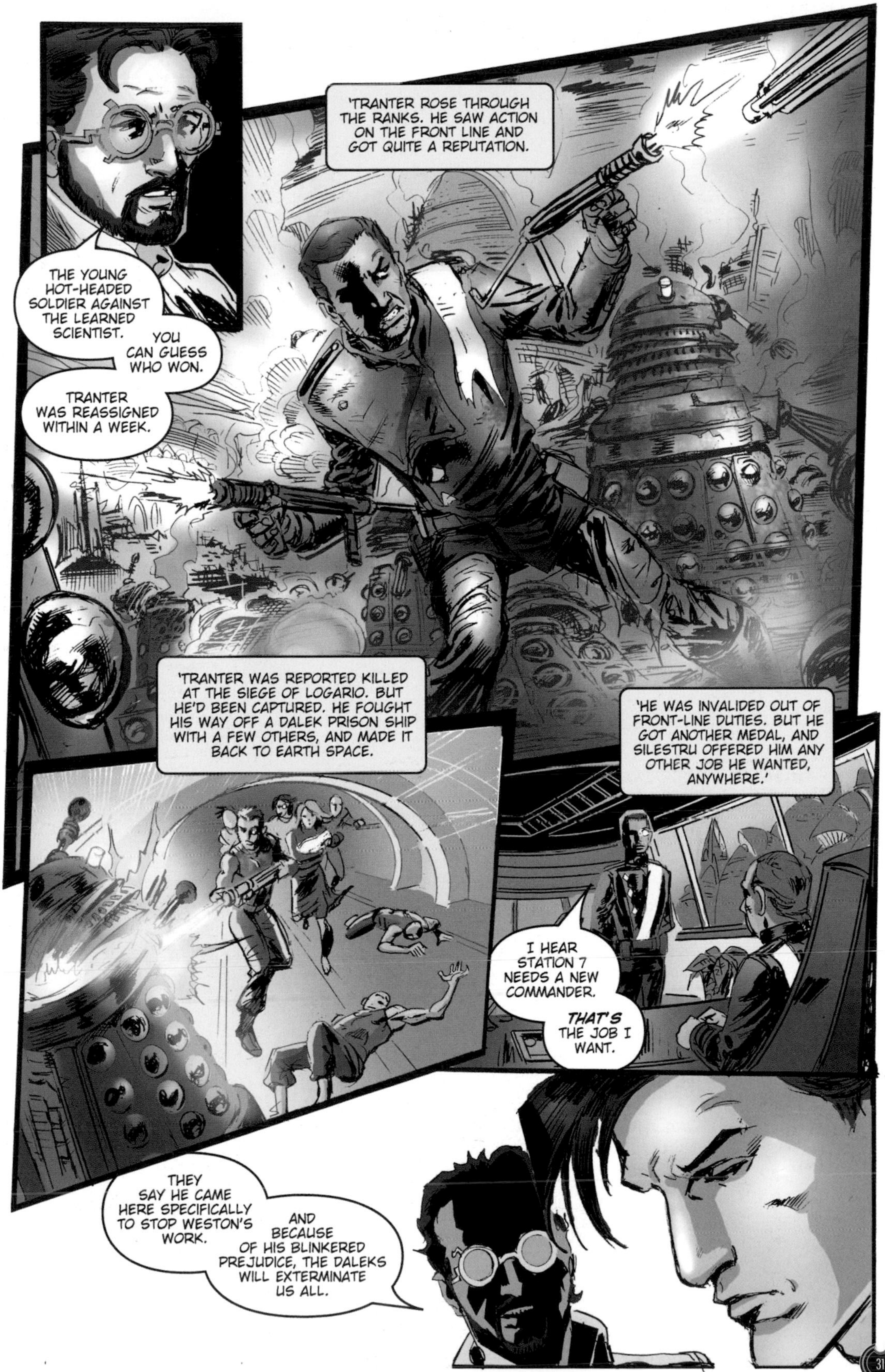

THE YOUNG HOT-HEADED SOLDIER AGAINST THE LEARNED SCIENTIST.
YOU CAN GUESS WHO WON.
TRANTER WAS REASSIGNED WITHIN A WEEK.
'TRANTER ROSE THROUGH THE RANKS. HE SAW ACTION ON THE FRONT LINE AND GOT QUITE A REPUTATION.
'TRANTER WAS REPORTED KILLED AT THE SIEGE OF LOGARIO. BUT HE'D BEEN CAPTURED. HE FOUGHT HIS WAY OFF A DALEK PRISON SHIP WITH A FEW OTHERS, AND MADE IT BACK TO EARTH SPACE.
'HE WAS INVALIDED OUT OF FRONT-LINE DUTIES. BUT HE GOT ANOTHER MEDAL, AND SILESTRU OFFERED HIM ANY OTHER JOB HE WANTED, ANYWHERE.'
I HEAR STATION 7 NEEDS A NEW COMMANDER.
THAT'S THE JOB I WANT.
THEY SAY HE CAME HERE SPECIFICALLY TO STOP WESTON'S WORK.
AND BECAUSE OF HIS BLINKERED PREJUDICE, THE DALEKS WILL EXTERMINATE US ALL.

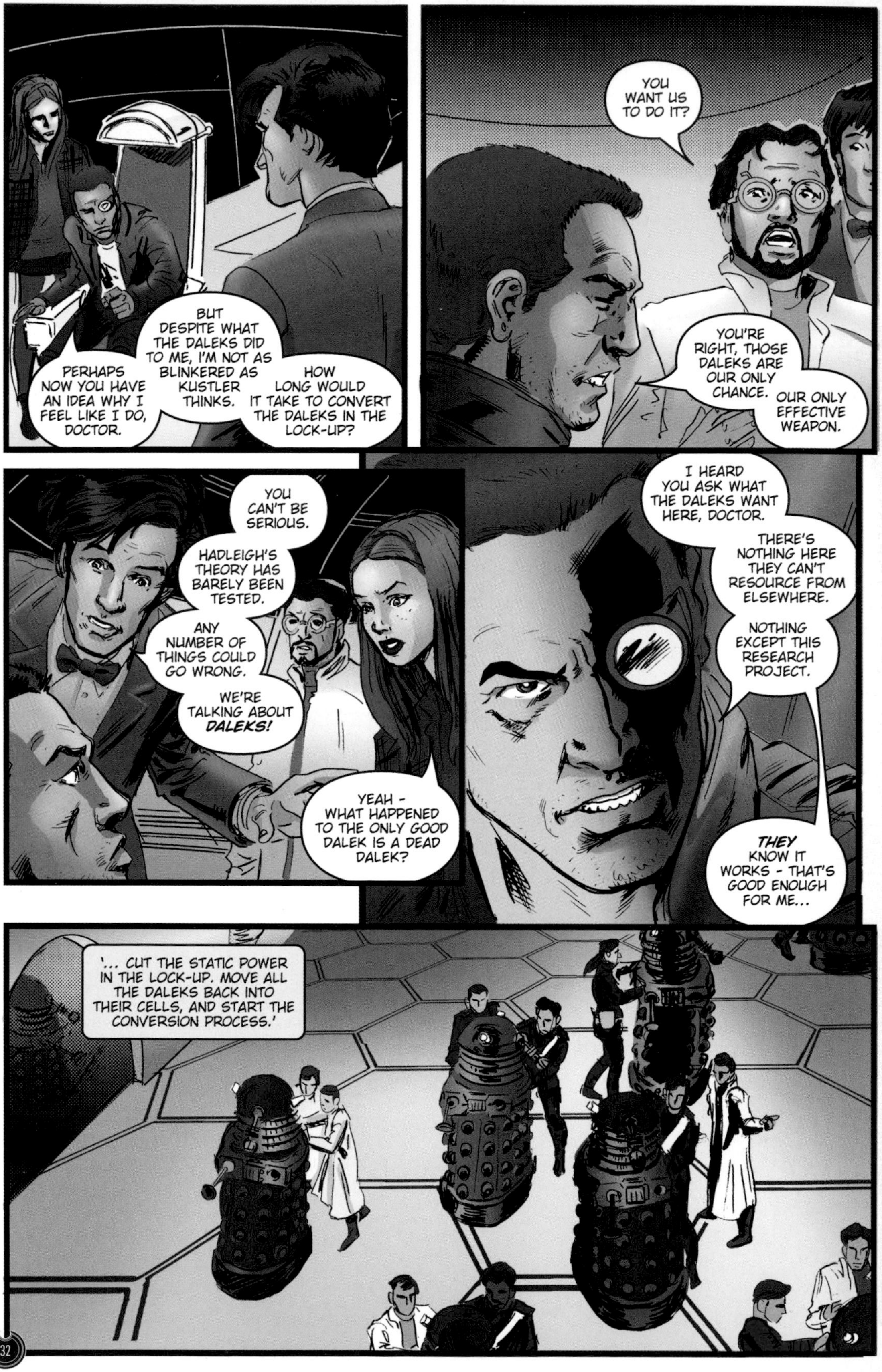
PERHAPS NOW YOU HAVE AN IDEA WHY I FEEL LIKE I DO, DOCTOR.
BUT DESPITE WHAT THE DALEKS DID TO ME, I'M NOT AS BLINKERED AS KUSTLER THINKS.
HOW LONG WOULD IT TAKE TO CONVERT THE DALEKS IN THE LOCK-UP?
YOU WANT US TO DO IT?
YOU'RE RIGHT, THOSE DALEKS ARE OUR ONLY CHANCE.
OUR ONLY EFFECTIVE WEAPON.
YOU CAN'T BE SERIOUS.
HADLEIGH'S THEORY HAS BARELY BEEN TESTED.
ANY NUMBER OF THINGS COULD GO WRONG.
WE'RE TALKING ABOUT *DALEKS!*
YEAH - WHAT HAPPENED TO THE ONLY GOOD DALEK IS A DEAD DALEK?
I HEARD YOU ASK WHAT THE DALEKS WANT HERE, DOCTOR.
THERE'S NOTHING HERE THEY CAN'T RESOURCE FROM ELSEWHERE.
NOTHING EXCEPT THIS RESEARCH PROJECT.
THEY KNOW IT WORKS - THAT'S GOOD ENOUGH FOR ME...
'... CUT THE STATIC POWER IN THE LOCK-UP. MOVE ALL THE DALEKS BACK INTO THEIR CELLS, AND START THE CONVERSION PROCESS.'

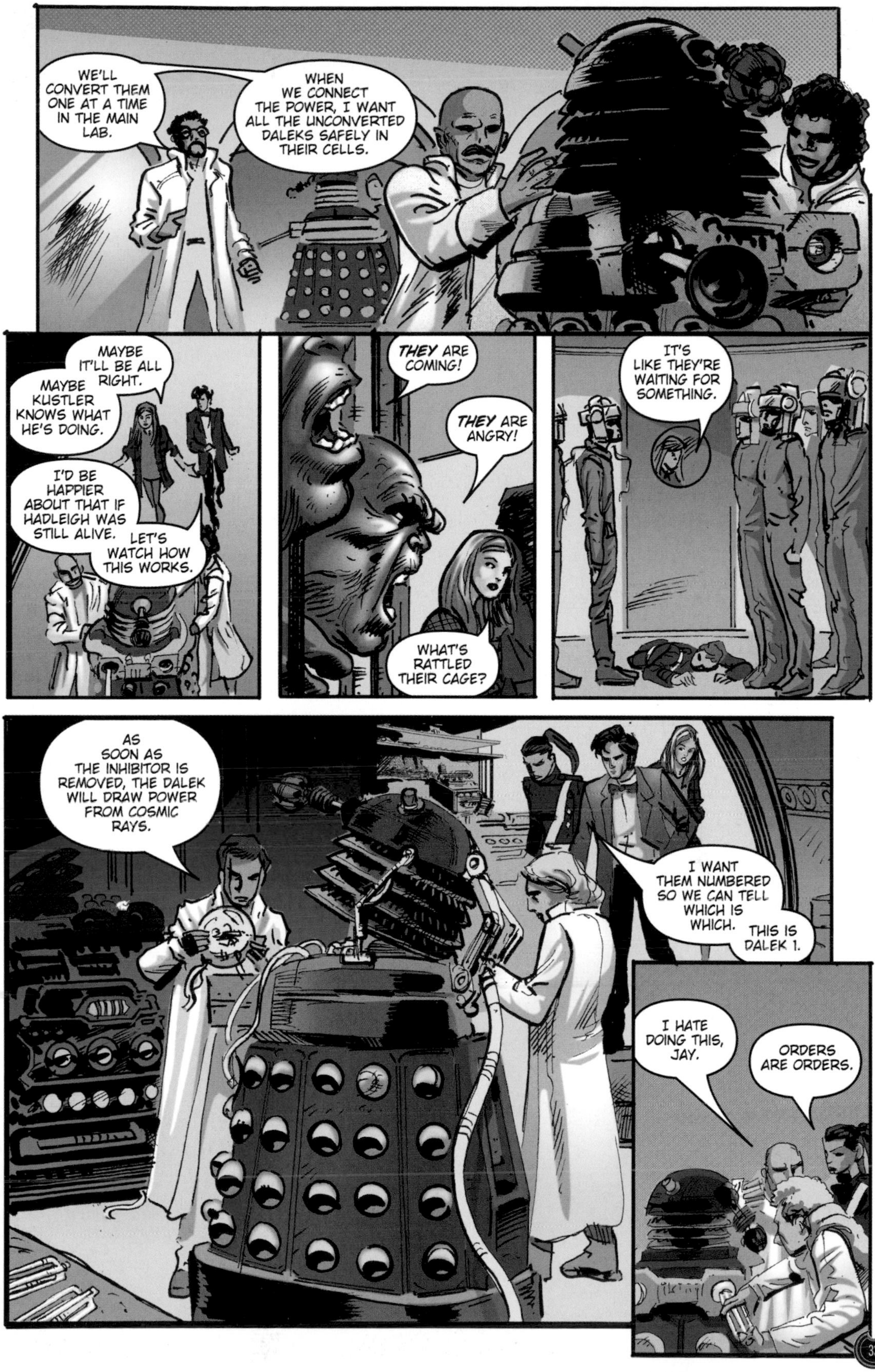

WE'LL CONVERT THEM ONE AT A TIME IN THE MAIN LAB.
WHEN WE CONNECT THE POWER, I WANT ALL THE UNCONVERTED DALEKS SAFELY IN THEIR CELLS.
MAYBE KUSTLER KNOWS WHAT HE'S DOING.
MAYBE IT'LL BE ALL RIGHT.
I'D BE HAPPIER ABOUT THAT IF HADLEIGH WAS STILL ALIVE.
LET'S WATCH HOW THIS WORKS.
THEY ARE COMING!
THEY ARE ANGRY!
WHAT'S RATTLED THEIR CAGE?
IT'S LIKE THEY'RE WAITING FOR SOMETHING.
AS SOON AS THE INHIBITOR IS REMOVED, THE DALEK WILL DRAW POWER FROM COSMIC RAYS.
I WANT THEM NUMBERED SO WE CAN TELL WHICH IS WHICH.
THIS IS DALEK 1.
I HATE DOING THIS, JAY.
ORDERS ARE ORDERS.

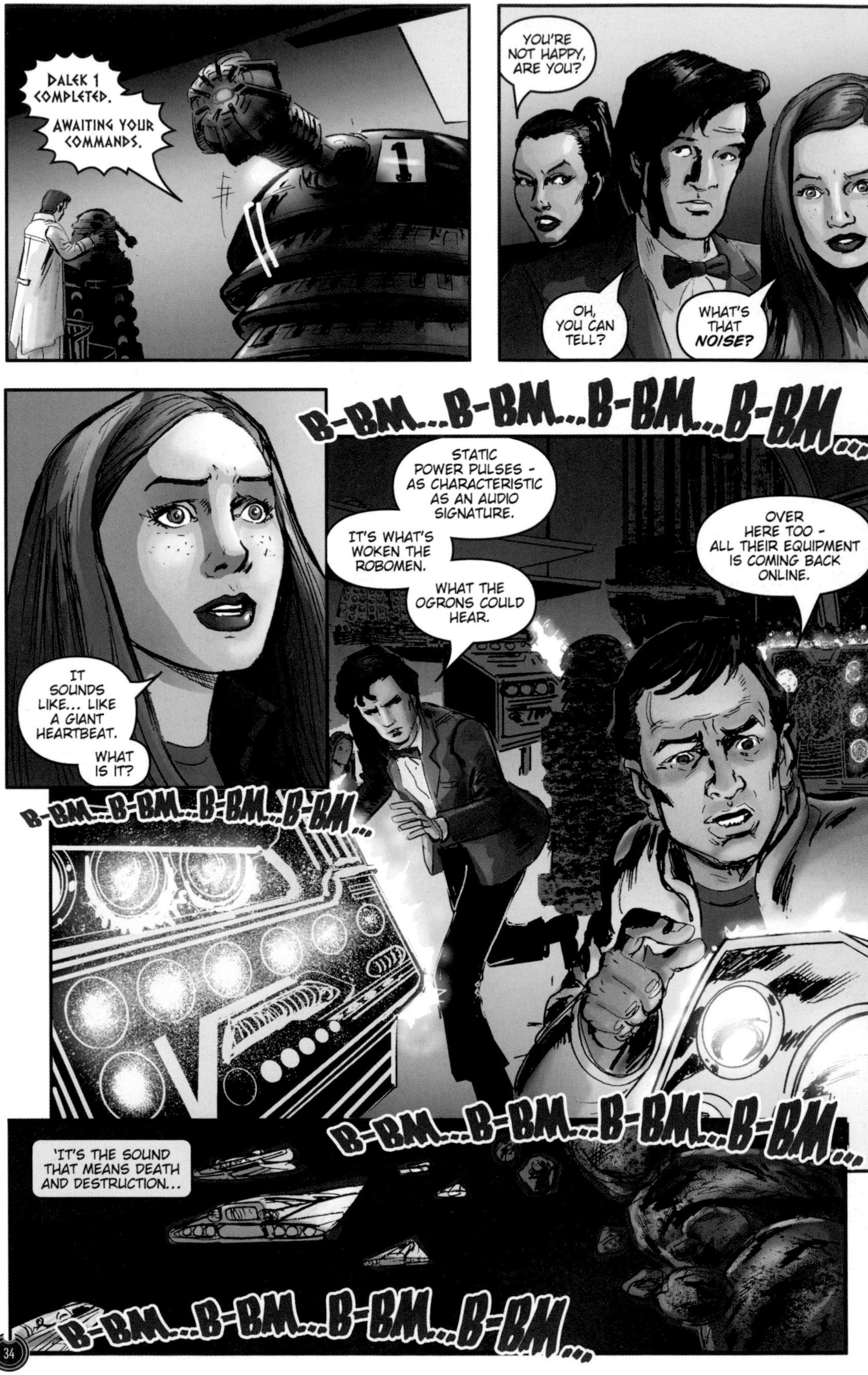
DALEK 1 COMPLETED.
AWAITING YOUR COMMANDS.
YOU'RE NOT HAPPY, ARE YOU?
OH, YOU CAN TELL?
WHAT'S THAT NOISE?
B-BM...B-BM...B-BM...B-BM...
IT SOUNDS LIKE... LIKE A GIANT HEARTBEAT.
WHAT IS IT?
STATIC POWER PULSES - AS CHARACTERISTIC AS AN AUDIO SIGNATURE.
IT'S WHAT'S WOKEN THE ROBOMEN.
WHAT THE OGRONS COULD HEAR.
OVER HERE TOO - ALL THEIR EQUIPMENT IS COMING BACK ONLINE.
B-BM...B-BM...B-BM...B-BM...
B-BM...B-BM...B-BM...B-BM...
'IT'S THE SOUND THAT MEANS DEATH AND DESTRUCTION...
B-BM...B-BM...B-BM...B-BM...

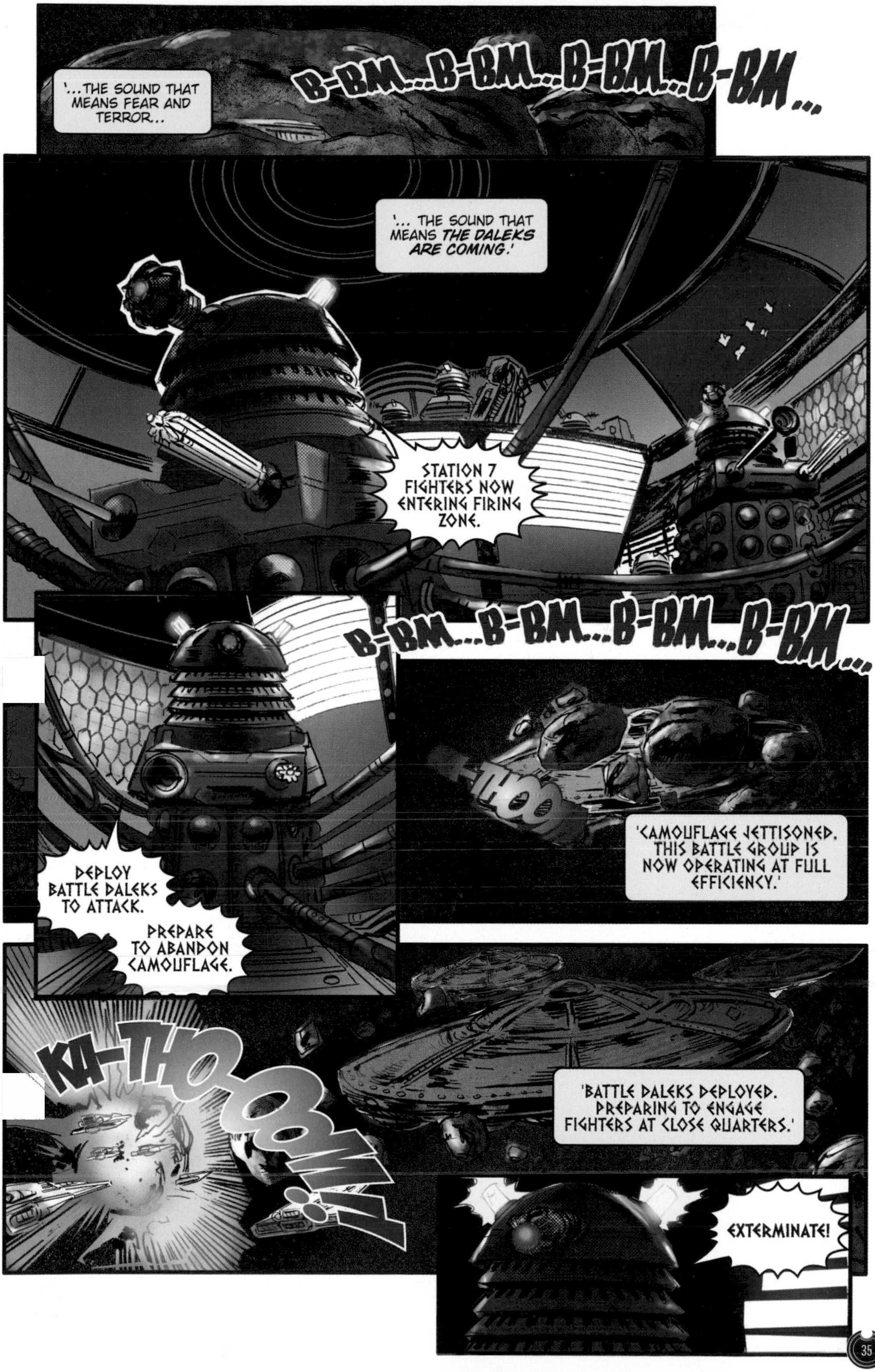
'...THE SOUND THAT MEANS FEAR AND TERROR...
B-BM...B-BM...B-BM...B-BM...
'... THE SOUND THAT MEANS *THE DALEKS ARE COMING*.'
STATION 7 FIGHTERS NOW ENTERING FIRING ZONE.
B-BM...B-BM...B-BM...B-BM...
DEPLOY BATTLE DALEKS TO ATTACK.
PREPARE TO ABANDON CAMOUFLAGE.
THOO
'CAMOUFLAGE JETTISONED. THIS BATTLE GROUP IS NOW OPERATING AT FULL EFFICIENCY.'
KA-THOOOM!!
'BATTLE DALEKS DEPLOYED. PREPARING TO ENGAGE FIGHTERS AT CLOSE QUARTERS.'
EXTERMINATE!

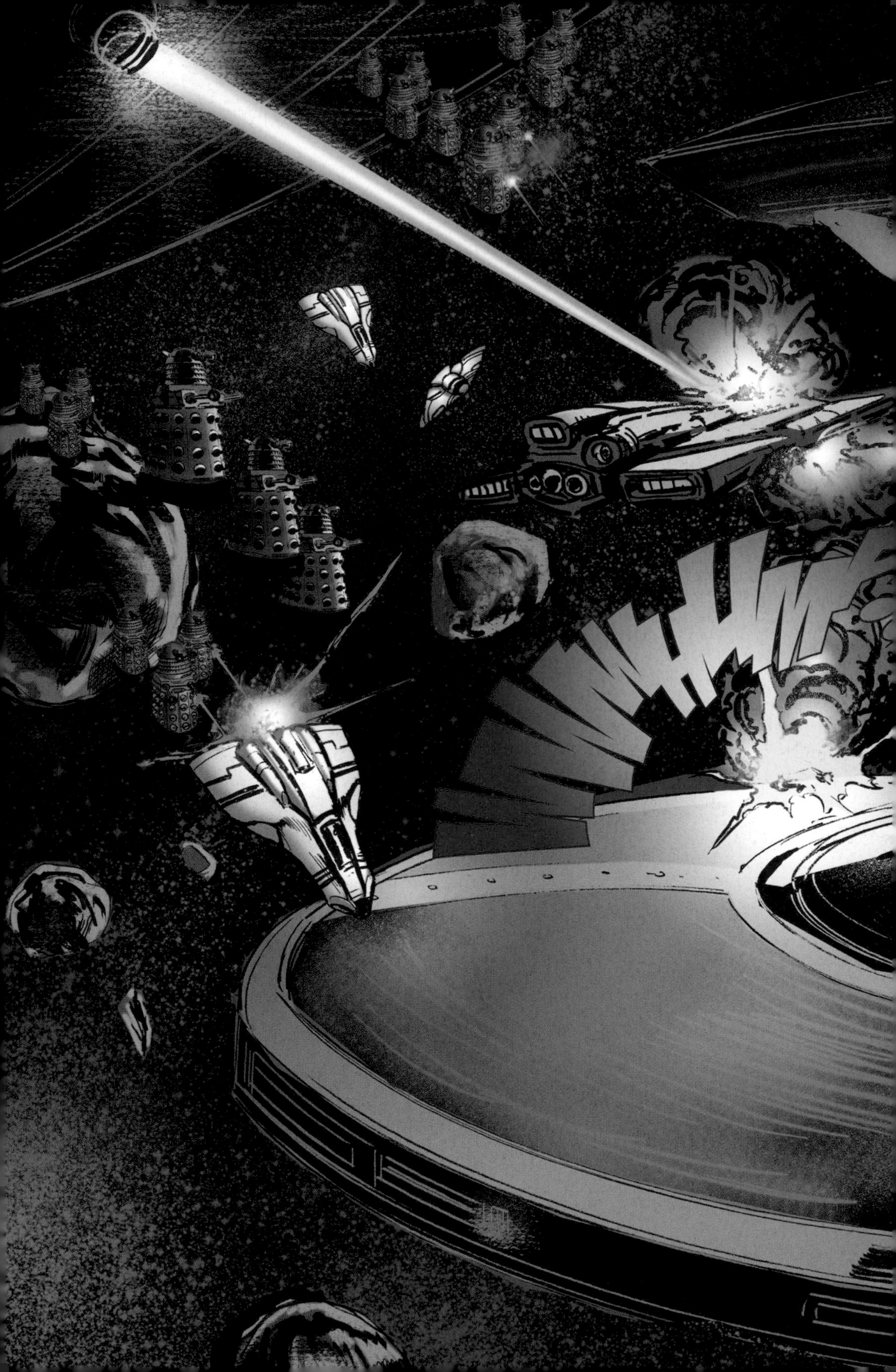

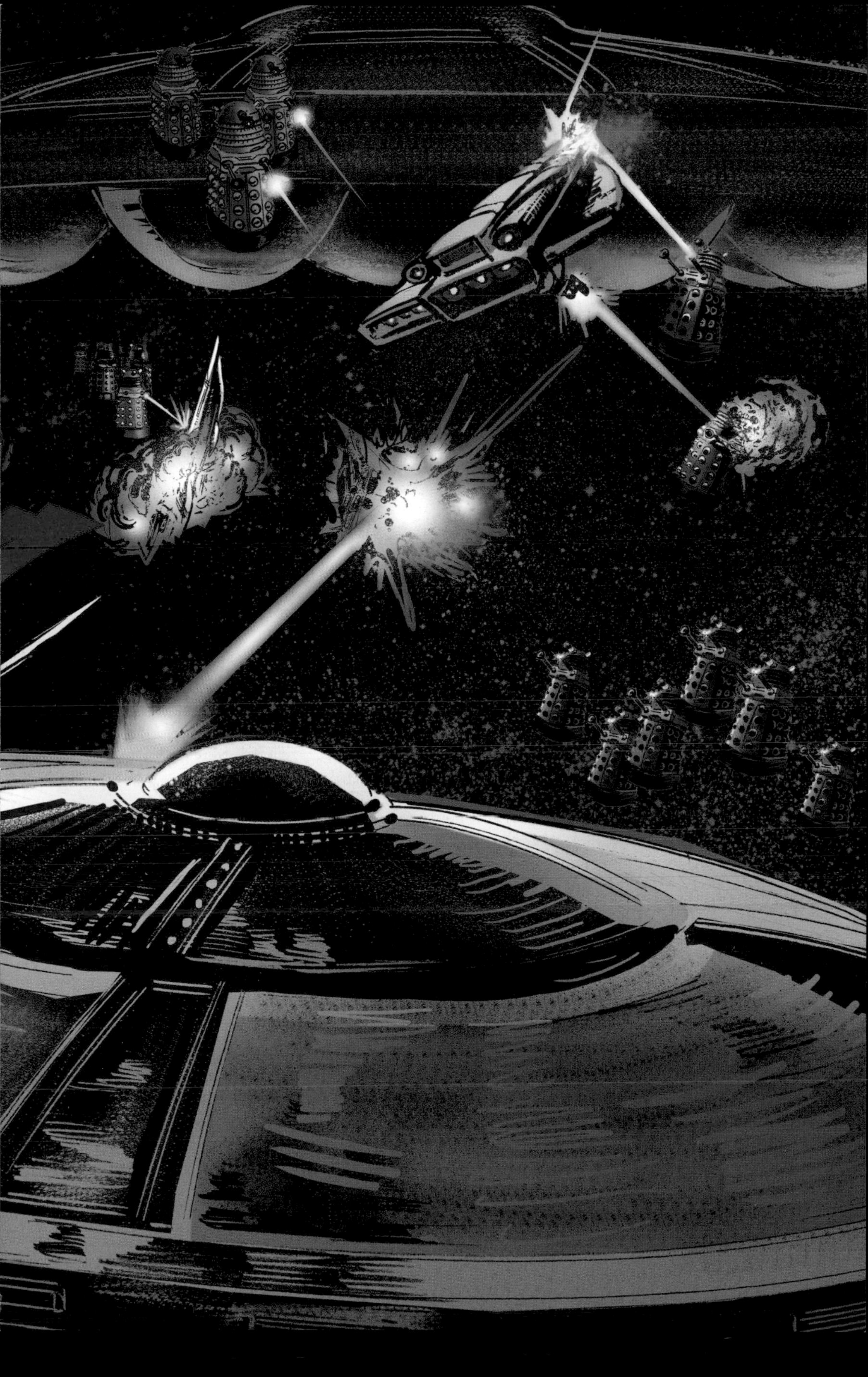

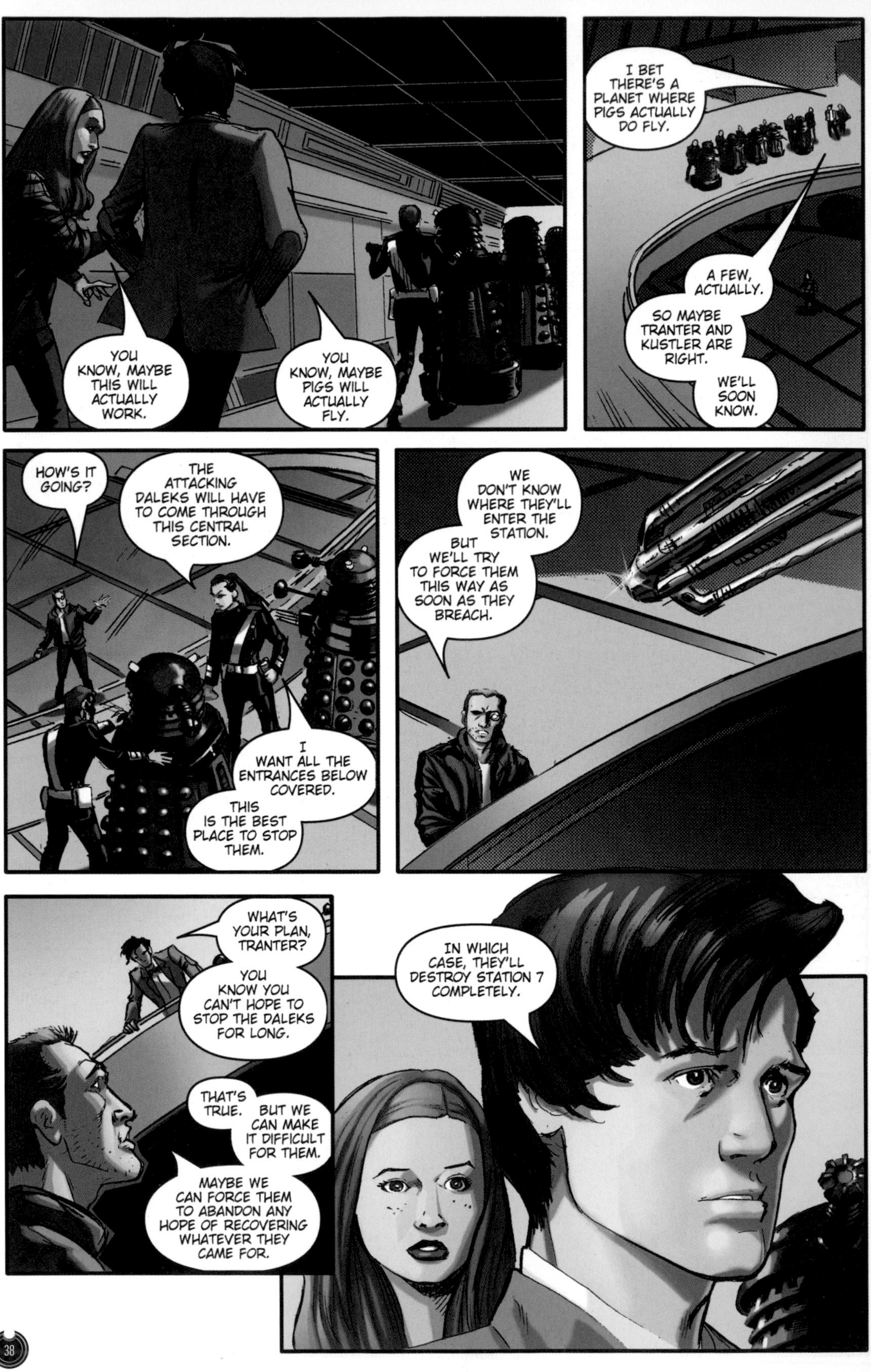
YOU KNOW, MAYBE THIS WILL ACTUALLY WORK.
YOU KNOW, MAYBE PIGS WILL ACTUALLY FLY.
I BET THERE'S A PLANET WHERE PIGS ACTUALLY DO FLY.
A FEW, ACTUALLY.
SO MAYBE TRANTER AND KUSTLER ARE RIGHT.
WE'LL SOON KNOW.
HOW'S IT GOING?
THE ATTACKING DALEKS WILL HAVE TO COME THROUGH THIS CENTRAL SECTION.
I WANT ALL THE ENTRANCES BELOW COVERED.
THIS IS THE BEST PLACE TO STOP THEM.
WE DON'T KNOW WHERE THEY'LL ENTER THE STATION.
BUT WE'LL TRY TO FORCE THEM THIS WAY AS SOON AS THEY BREACH.
WHAT'S YOUR PLAN, TRANTER?
YOU KNOW YOU CAN'T HOPE TO STOP THE DALEKS FOR LONG.
THAT'S TRUE.
BUT WE CAN MAKE IT DIFFICULT FOR THEM.
MAYBE WE CAN FORCE THEM TO ABANDON ANY HOPE OF RECOVERING WHATEVER THEY CAME FOR.
IN WHICH CASE, THEY'LL DESTROY STATION 7 COMPLETELY.

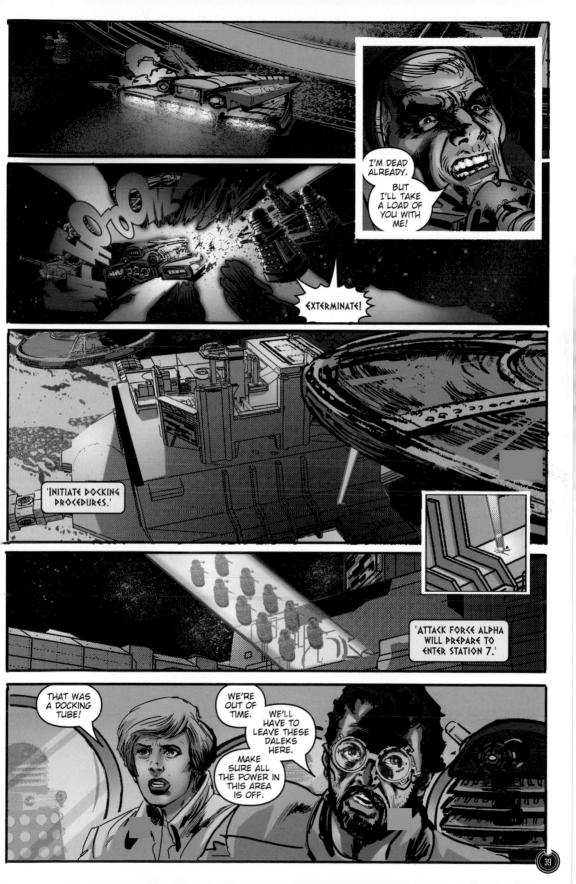

I'M DEAD ALREADY. BUT I'LL TAKE A LOAD OF YOU WITH ME!

KROOM

EXTERMINATE!

'INITIATE DOCKING PROCEDURES.'

'ATTACK FORCE ALPHA WILL PREPARE TO ENTER STATION 7.'

THAT WAS A DOCKING TUBE!

WE'RE OUT OF TIME. WE'LL HAVE TO LEAVE THESE DALEKS HERE.

MAKE SURE ALL THE POWER IN THIS AREA IS OFF.

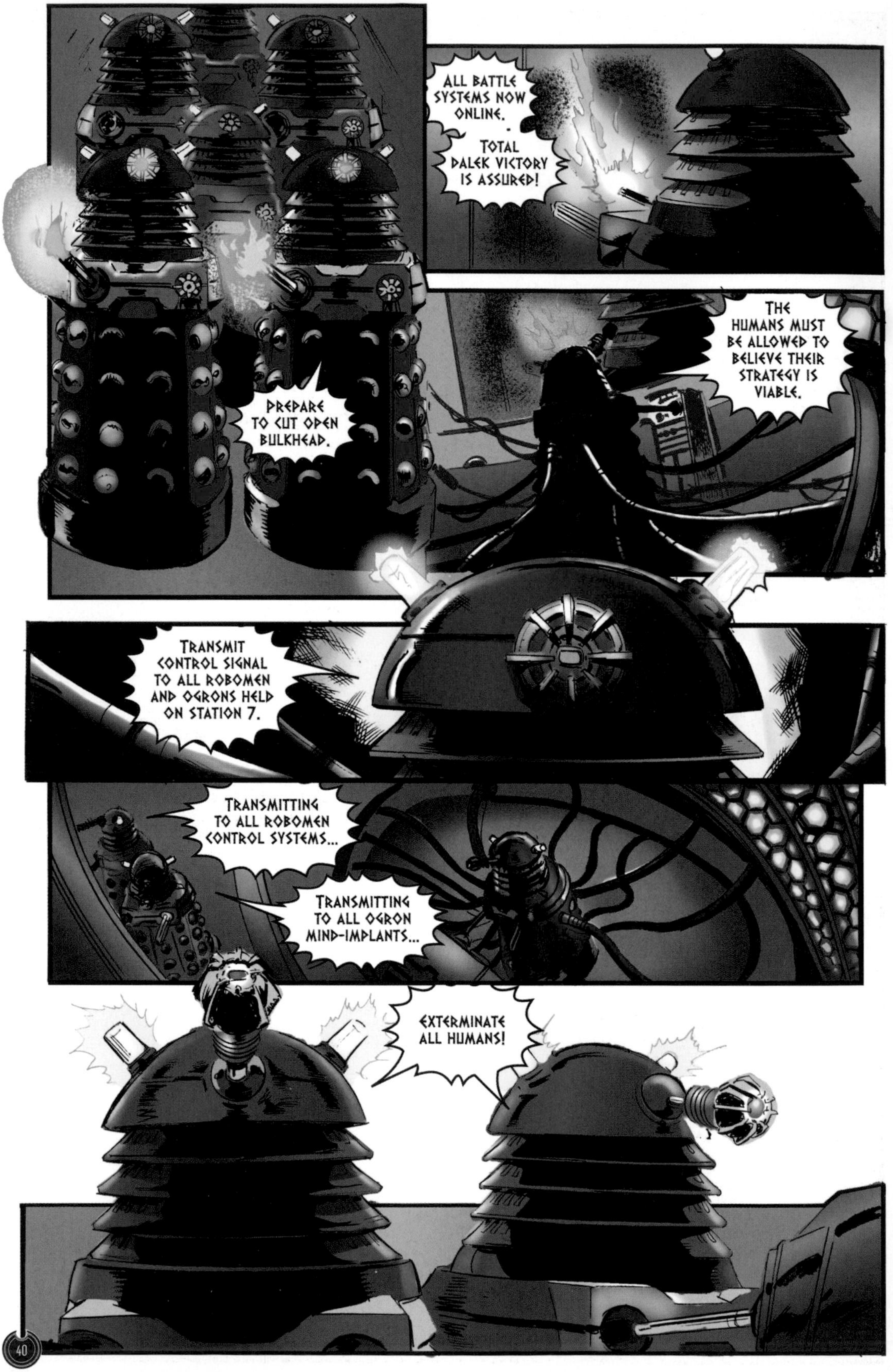
ALL BATTLE SYSTEMS NOW ONLINE.
TOTAL DALEK VICTORY IS ASSURED!
PREPARE TO CUT OPEN BULKHEAD.
THE HUMANS MUST BE ALLOWED TO BELIEVE THEIR STRATEGY IS VIABLE.
TRANSMIT CONTROL SIGNAL TO ALL ROBOMEN AND OGRONS HELD ON STATION 7.
TRANSMITTING TO ALL ROBOMEN CONTROL SYSTEMS...
TRANSMITTING TO ALL OGRON MIND-IMPLANTS...
EXTERMINATE ALL HUMANS!

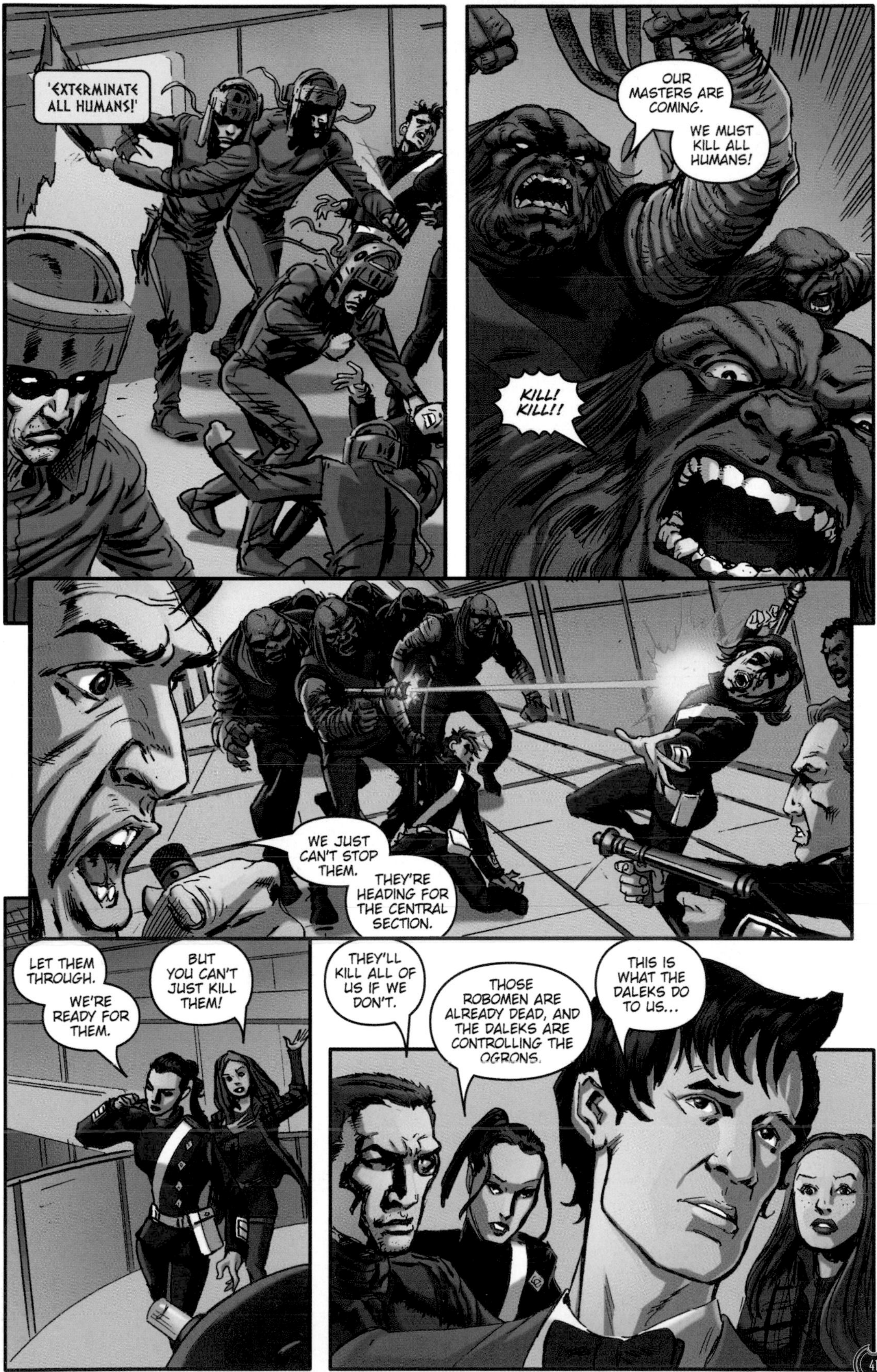

'EXTERMINATE ALL HUMANS!'
OUR MASTERS ARE COMING.
WE MUST KILL ALL HUMANS!
KILL! KILL!!
WE JUST CAN'T STOP THEM.
THEY'RE HEADING FOR THE CENTRAL SECTION.
LET THEM THROUGH.
WE'RE READY FOR THEM.
BUT YOU CAN'T JUST KILL THEM!
THEY'LL KILL ALL OF US IF WE DON'T.
THOSE ROBOMEN ARE ALREADY DEAD, AND THE DALEKS ARE CONTROLLING THE OGRONS.
THIS IS WHAT THE DALEKS DO TO US...

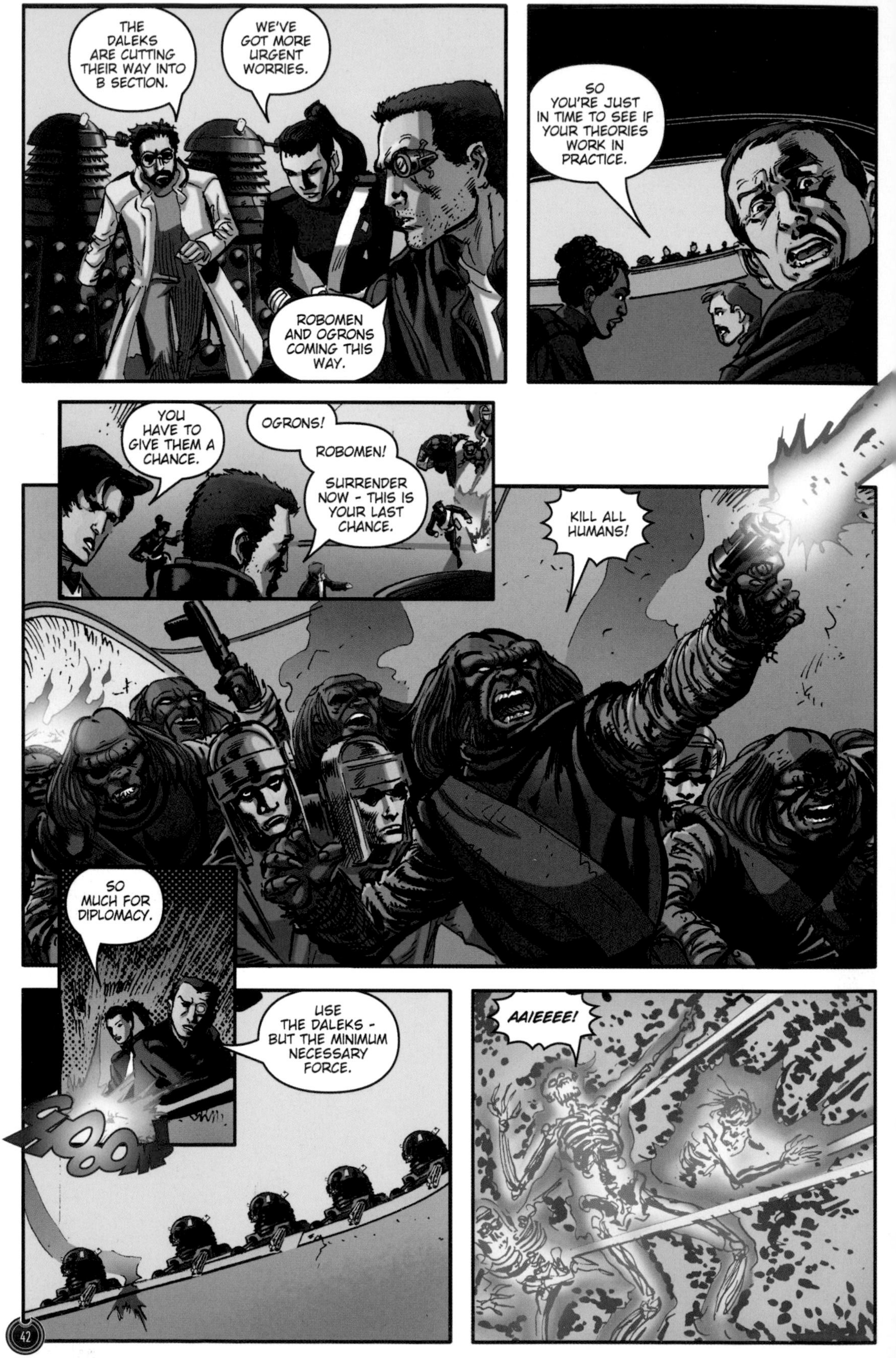
THE DALEKS ARE CUTTING THEIR WAY INTO B SECTION.
WE'VE GOT MORE URGENT WORRIES.
ROBOMEN AND OGRONS COMING THIS WAY.
SO YOU'RE JUST IN TIME TO SEE IF YOUR THEORIES WORK IN PRACTICE.
YOU HAVE TO GIVE THEM A CHANCE.
OGRONS!
ROBOMEN!
SURRENDER NOW - THIS IS YOUR LAST CHANCE.
KILL ALL HUMANS!
SO MUCH FOR DIPLOMACY.
USE THE DALEKS - BUT THE MINIMUM NECESSARY FORCE.
AAIEEEE!

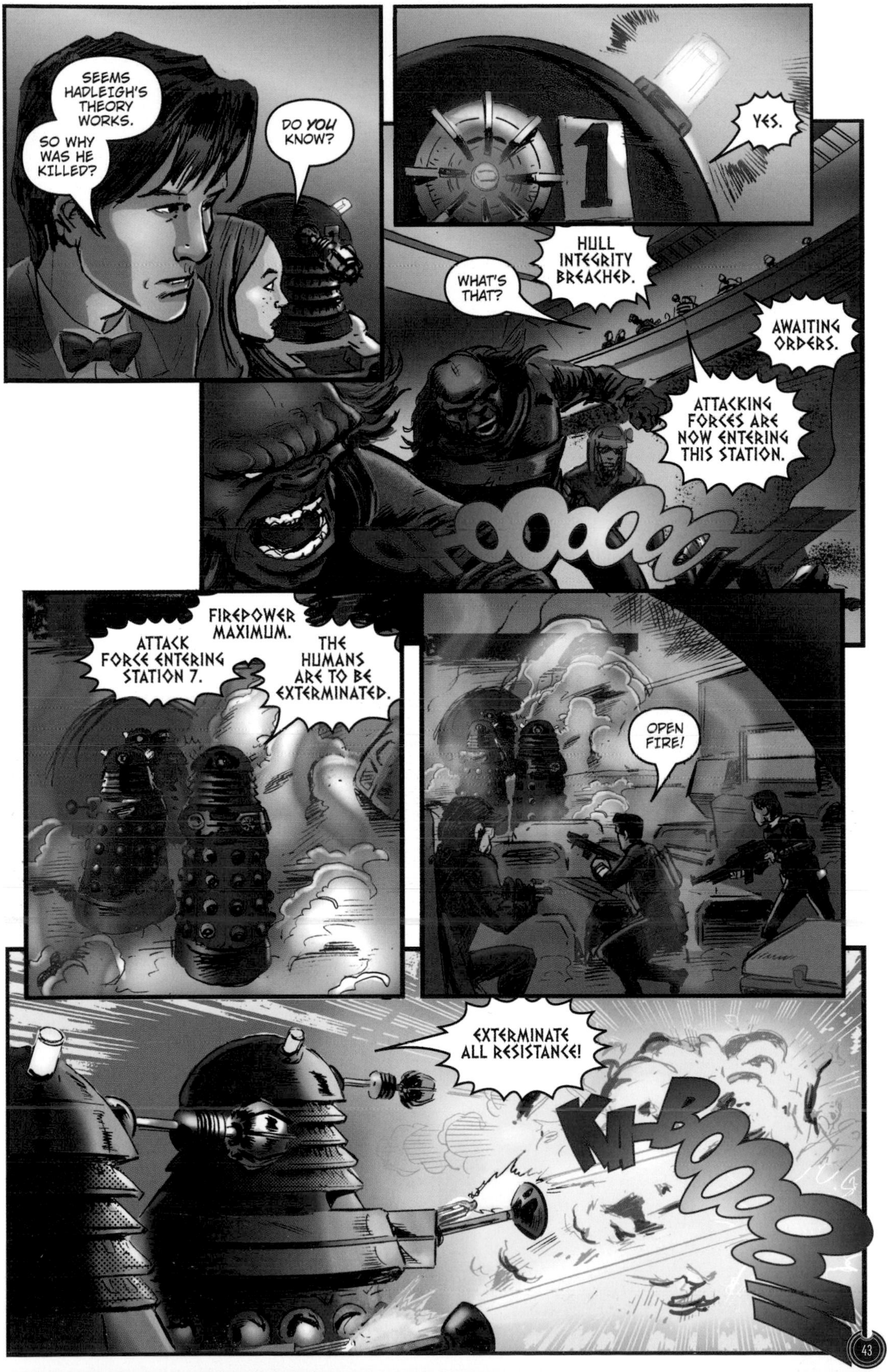

SEEMS HADLEIGH'S THEORY WORKS.
SO WHY WAS HE KILLED?
DO YOU KNOW?
YES.
WHAT'S THAT?
HULL INTEGRITY BREACHED.
AWAITING ORDERS.
ATTACKING FORCES ARE NOW ENTERING THIS STATION.
ATTACK FORCE ENTERING STATION 7.
FIREPOWER MAXIMUM.
THE HUMANS ARE TO BE EXTERMINATED.
OPEN FIRE!
EXTERMINATE ALL RESISTANCE!
KA-BOOOOM

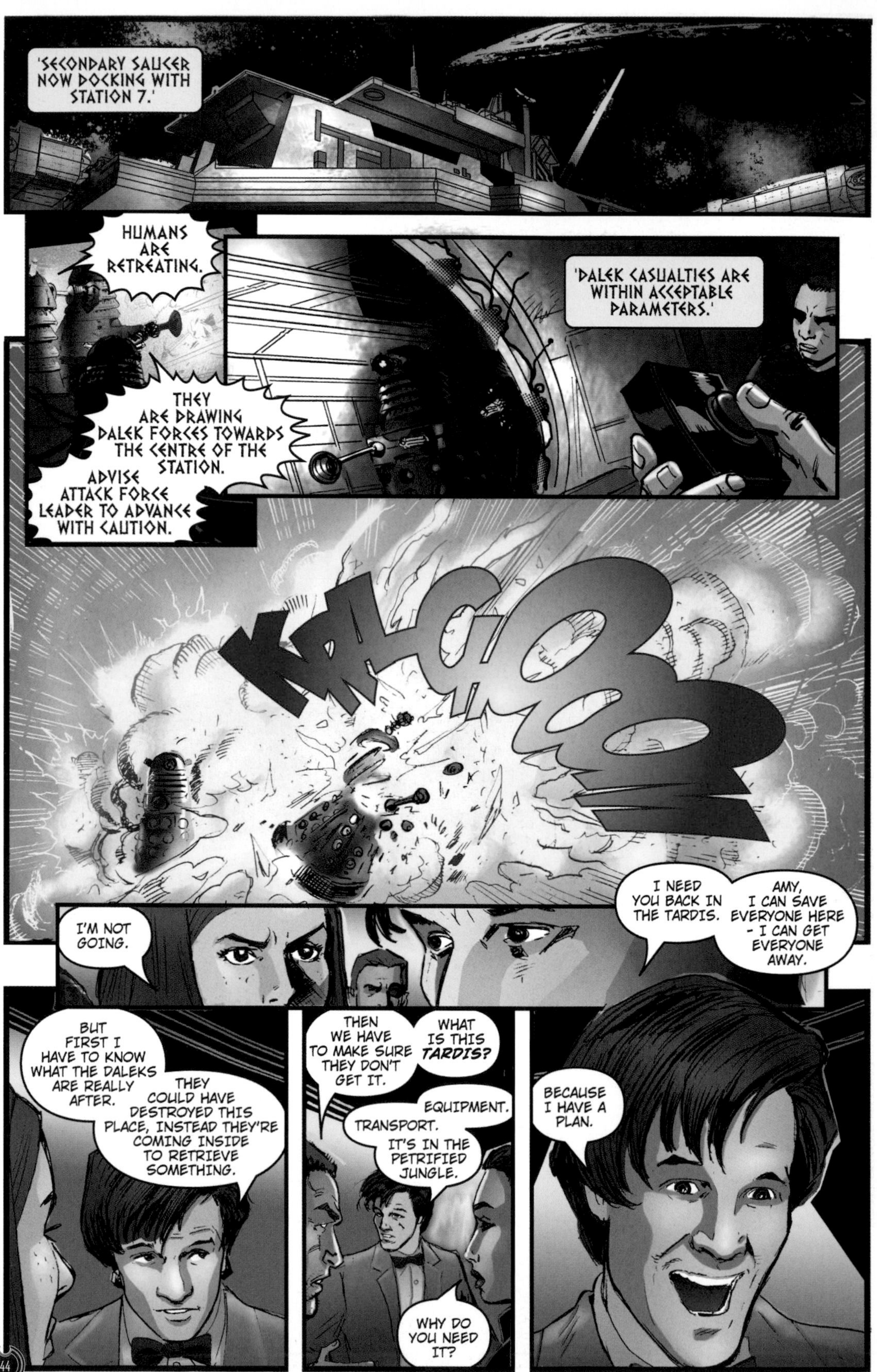
'SECONDARY SAUCER NOW DOCKING WITH STATION 7.'
HUMANS ARE RETREATING.
'DALEK CASUALTIES ARE WITHIN ACCEPTABLE PARAMETERS.'
THEY ARE DRAWING DALEK FORCES TOWARDS THE CENTRE OF THE STATION.
ADVISE ATTACK FORCE LEADER TO ADVANCE WITH CAUTION.
KRACOOM
I NEED YOU BACK IN THE TARDIS.
AMY, I CAN SAVE EVERYONE HERE - I CAN GET EVERYONE AWAY.
I'M NOT GOING.
BUT FIRST I HAVE TO KNOW WHAT THE DALEKS ARE REALLY AFTER.
THEY COULD HAVE DESTROYED THIS PLACE, INSTEAD THEY'RE COMING INSIDE TO RETRIEVE SOMETHING.
THEN WE HAVE TO MAKE SURE THEY DON'T GET IT.
WHAT IS THIS *TARDIS?*
EQUIPMENT.
TRANSPORT.
IT'S IN THE PETRIFIED JUNGLE.
WHY DO YOU NEED IT?
BECAUSE I HAVE A PLAN.

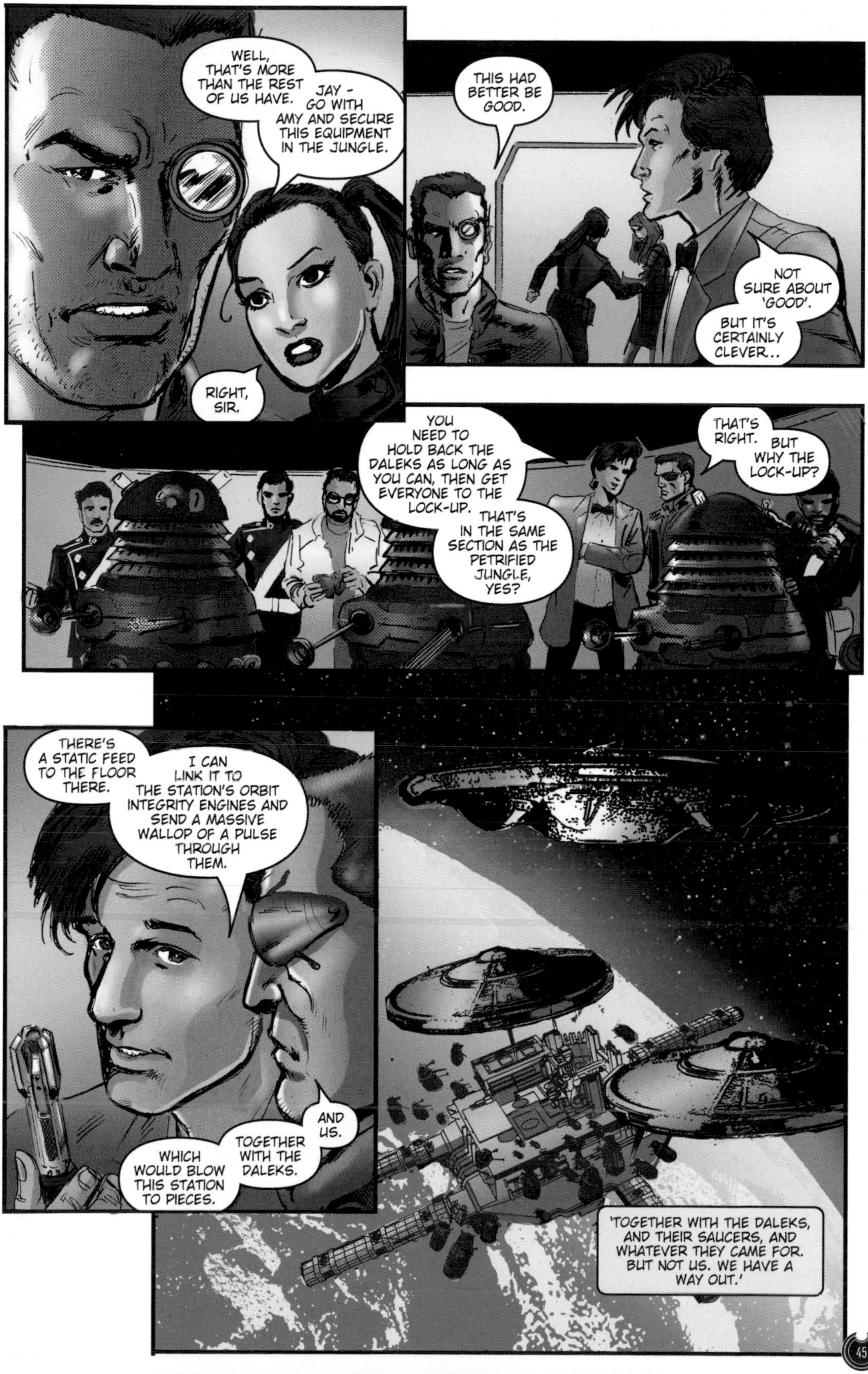
WELL, THAT'S MORE THAN THE REST OF US HAVE.
JAY - GO WITH AMY AND SECURE THIS EQUIPMENT IN THE JUNGLE.
RIGHT, SIR.
THIS HAD BETTER BE GOOD.
NOT SURE ABOUT 'GOOD'.
BUT IT'S CERTAINLY CLEVER...
YOU NEED TO HOLD BACK THE DALEKS AS LONG AS YOU CAN, THEN GET EVERYONE TO THE LOCK-UP.
THAT'S IN THE SAME SECTION AS THE PETRIFIED JUNGLE, YES?
THAT'S RIGHT.
BUT WHY THE LOCK-UP?
THERE'S A STATIC FEED TO THE FLOOR THERE.
I CAN LINK IT TO THE STATION'S ORBIT INTEGRITY ENGINES AND SEND A MASSIVE WALLOP OF A PULSE THROUGH THEM.
WHICH WOULD BLOW THIS STATION TO PIECES.
TOGETHER WITH THE DALEKS.
AND US.
'TOGETHER WITH THE DALEKS, AND THEIR SAUCERS, AND WHATEVER THEY CAME FOR. BUT NOT US. WE HAVE A WAY OUT.'

ATTACK PROCEEDING ON SCHEDULE. DALEK CASUALTIES MINIMAL.

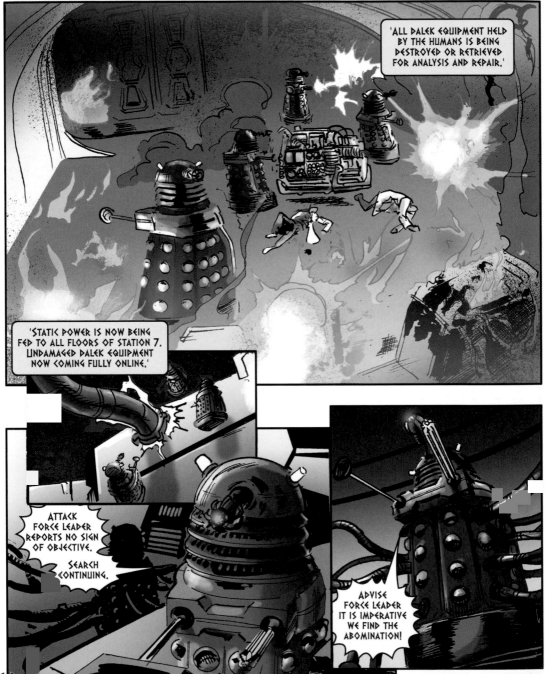

'ALL DALEK EQUIPMENT HELD BY THE HUMANS IS BEING DESTROYED OR RETRIEVED FOR ANALYSIS AND REPAIR.'

'STATIC POWER IS NOW BEING FED TO ALL FLOORS OF STATION 7. UNDAMAGED DALEK EQUIPMENT NOW COMING FULLY ONLINE.'

ATTACK FORCE LEADER REPORTS NO SIGN OF OBJECTIVE.

SEARCH CONTINUING.

ADVISE FORCE LEADER IT IS IMPERATIVE WE FIND THE ABOMINATION!

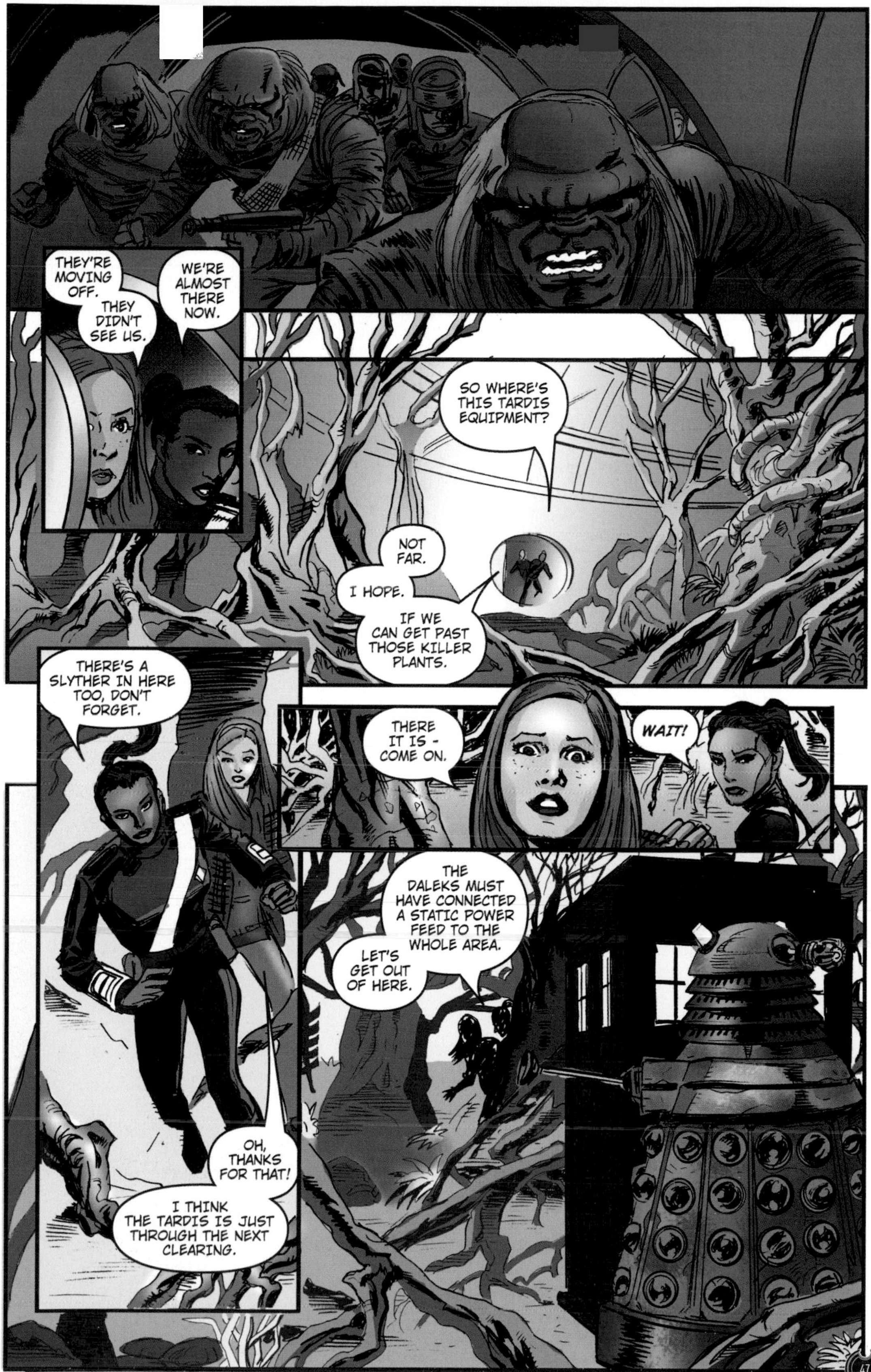
THEY'RE MOVING OFF.
THEY DIDN'T SEE US.
WE'RE ALMOST THERE NOW.
SO WHERE'S THIS TARDIS EQUIPMENT?
NOT FAR.
I HOPE.
IF WE CAN GET PAST THOSE KILLER PLANTS.
THERE'S A SLYTHER IN HERE TOO, DON'T FORGET.
OH, THANKS FOR THAT!
I THINK THE TARDIS IS JUST THROUGH THE NEXT CLEARING.
THERE IT IS - COME ON.
WAIT!
THE DALEKS MUST HAVE CONNECTED A STATIC POWER FEED TO THE WHOLE AREA.
LET'S GET OUT OF HERE.

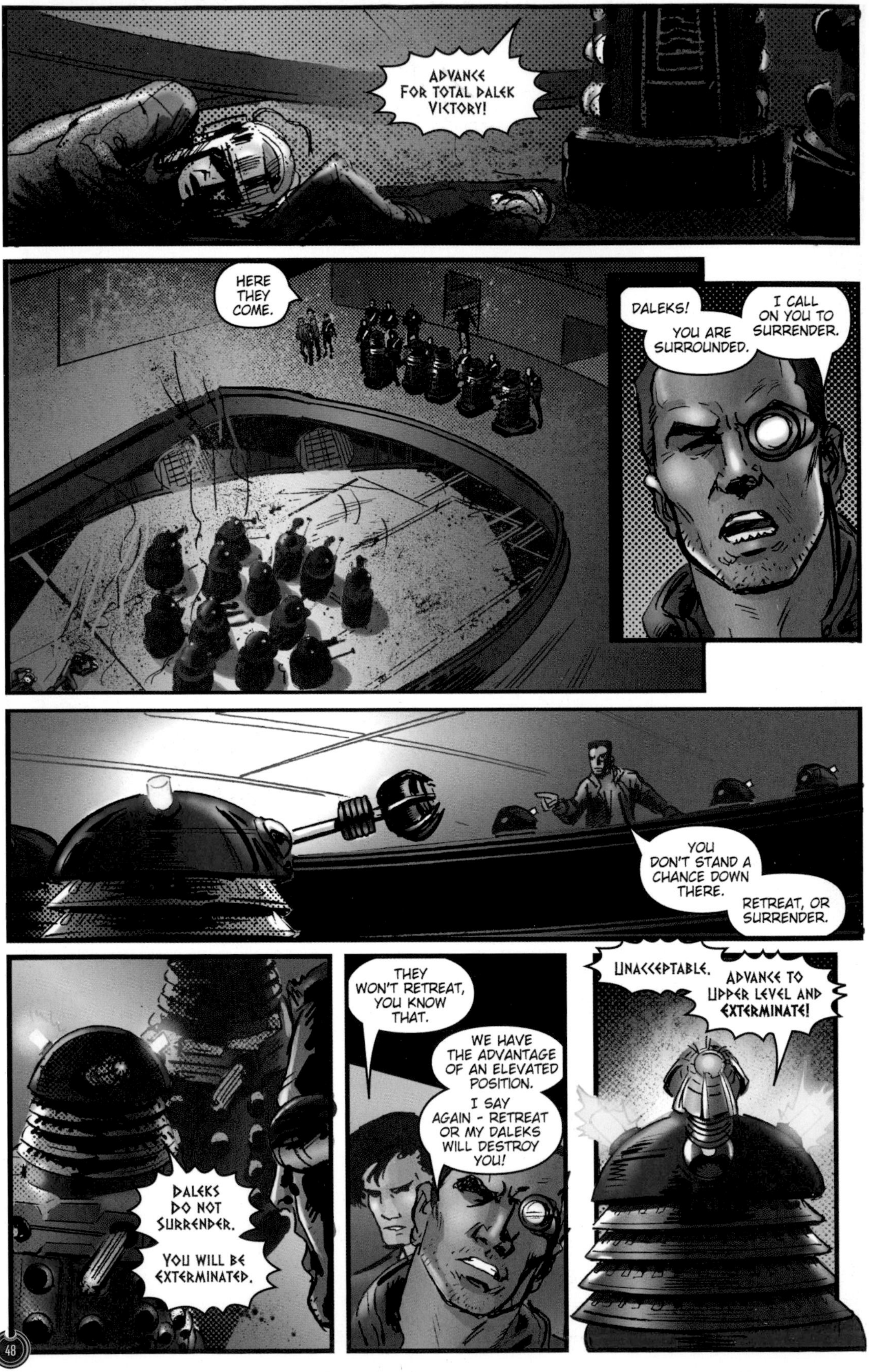

ADVANCE FOR TOTAL DALEK VICTORY!
HERE THEY COME.
DALEKS!
YOU ARE SURROUNDED.
I CALL ON YOU TO SURRENDER.
YOU DON'T STAND A CHANCE DOWN THERE.
RETREAT, OR SURRENDER.
DALEKS DO NOT SURRENDER.
YOU WILL BE EXTERMINATED.
THEY WON'T RETREAT, YOU KNOW THAT.
WE HAVE THE ADVANTAGE OF AN ELEVATED POSITION.
I SAY AGAIN - RETREAT OR MY DALEKS WILL DESTROY YOU!
UNACCEPTABLE.
ADVANCE TO UPPER LEVEL AND EXTERMINATE!

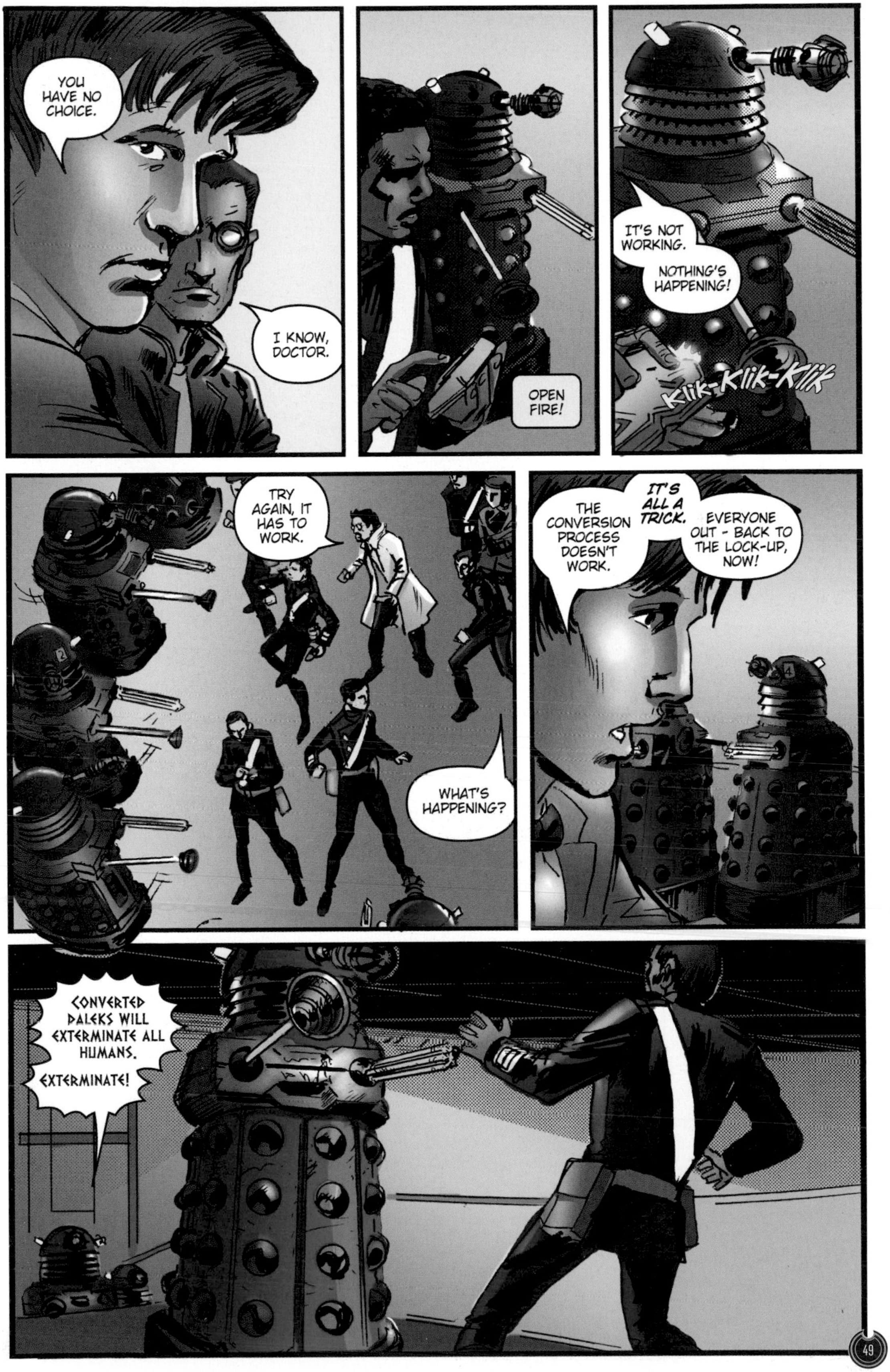
YOU HAVE NO CHOICE.
I KNOW, DOCTOR.
OPEN FIRE!
IT'S NOT WORKING.
NOTHING'S HAPPENING!
KLIK-KLIK-KLIK
TRY AGAIN, IT HAS TO WORK.
WHAT'S HAPPENING?
THE CONVERSION PROCESS DOESN'T WORK.
IT'S ALL A TRICK.
EVERYONE OUT - BACK TO THE LOCK-UP, NOW!
CONVERTED DALEKS WILL EXTERMINATE ALL HUMANS.
EXTERMINATE!

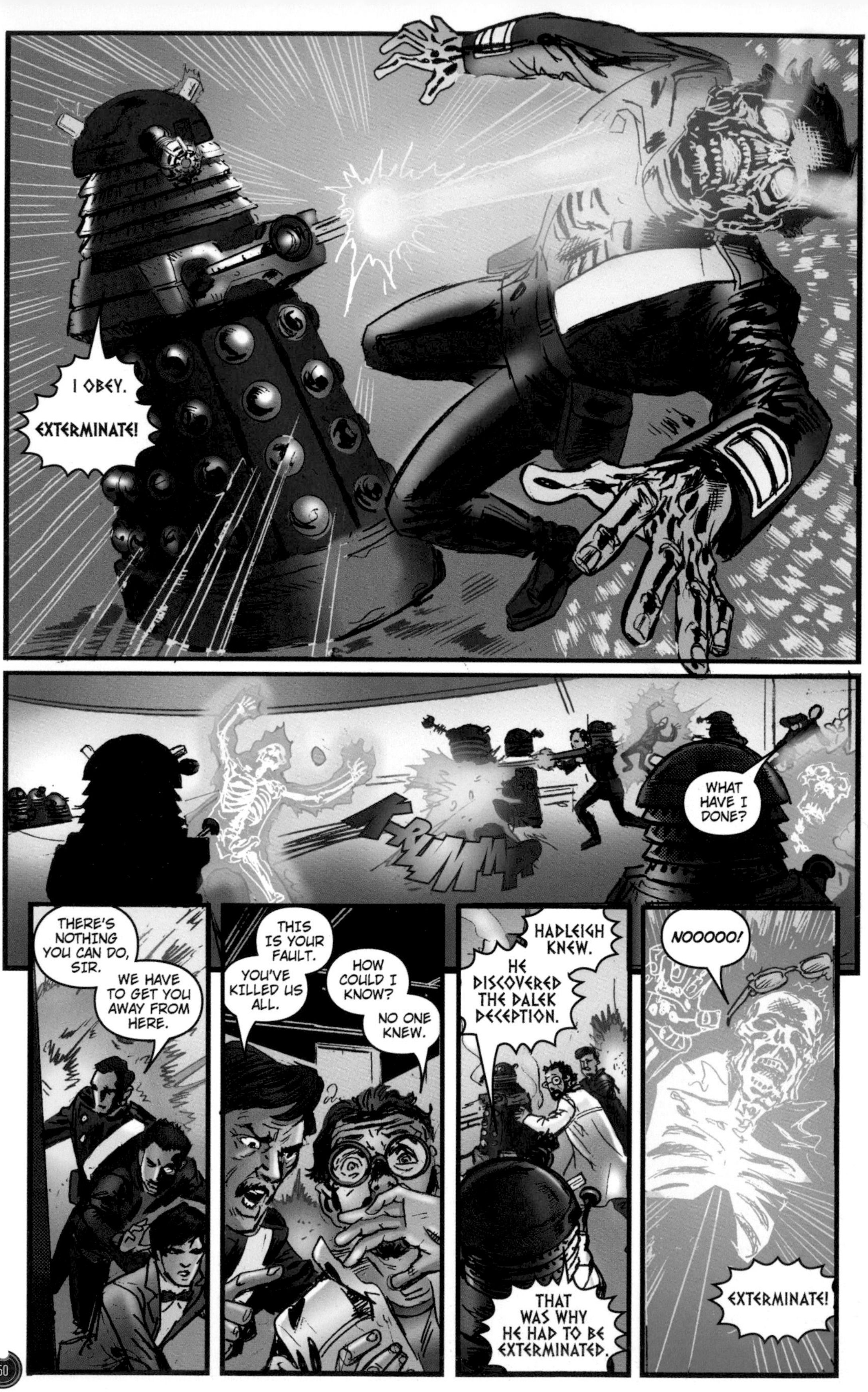
I OBEY.
EXTERMINATE!
WHAT HAVE I DONE?
THERE'S NOTHING YOU CAN DO, SIR.
WE HAVE TO GET YOU AWAY FROM HERE.
THIS IS YOUR FAULT.
YOU'VE KILLED US ALL.
HOW COULD I KNOW?
NO ONE KNEW.
HADLEIGH KNEW.
HE DISCOVERED THE DALEK DECEPTION.
THAT WAS WHY HE HAD TO BE EXTERMINATED.
NOOOOO!
EXTERMINATE!

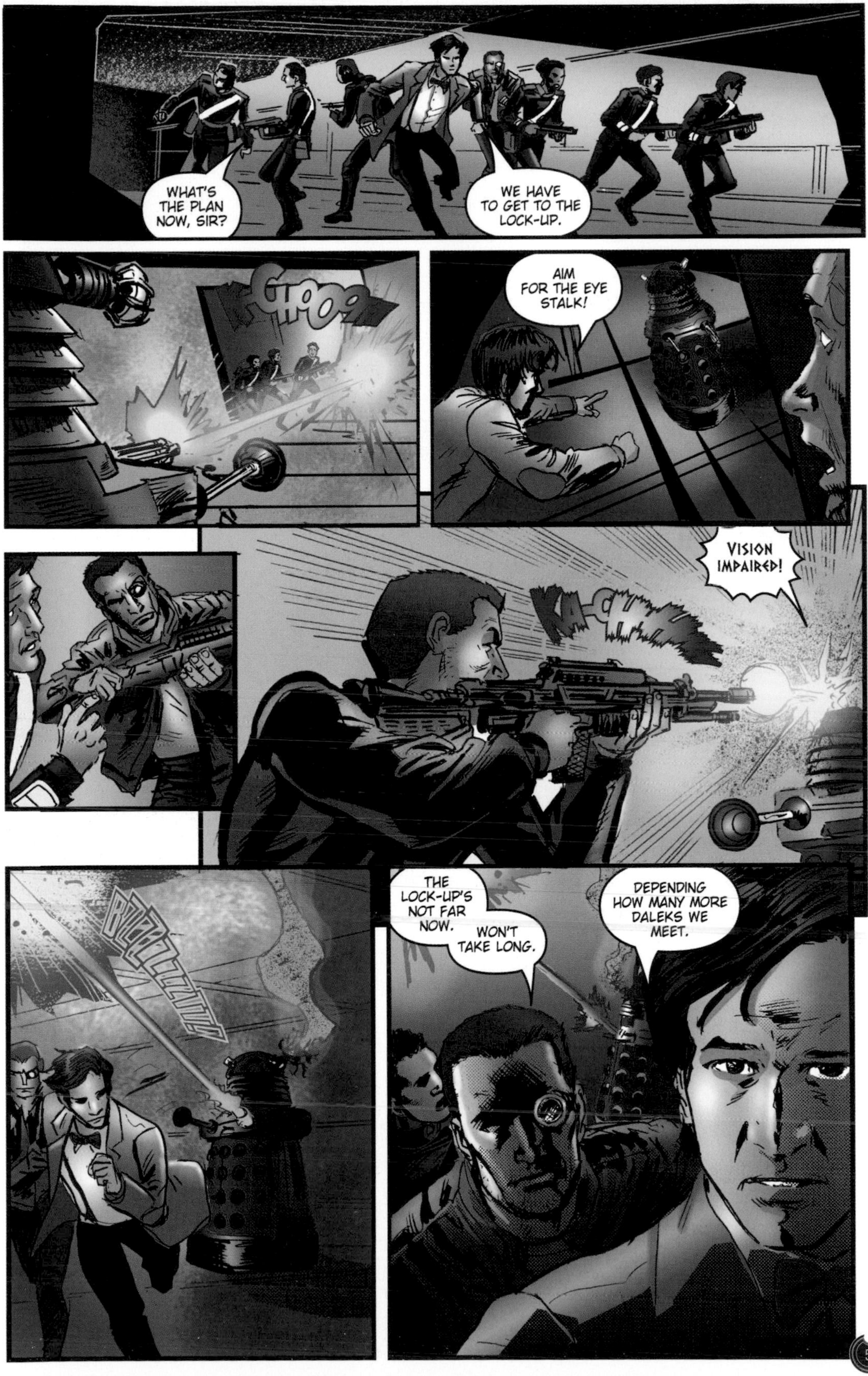
WHAT'S THE PLAN NOW, SIR?
WE HAVE TO GET TO THE LOCK-UP.
AIM FOR THE EYE STALK!
VISION IMPAIRED!
THE LOCK-UP'S NOT FAR NOW.
WON'T TAKE LONG.
DEPENDING HOW MANY MORE DALEKS WE MEET.

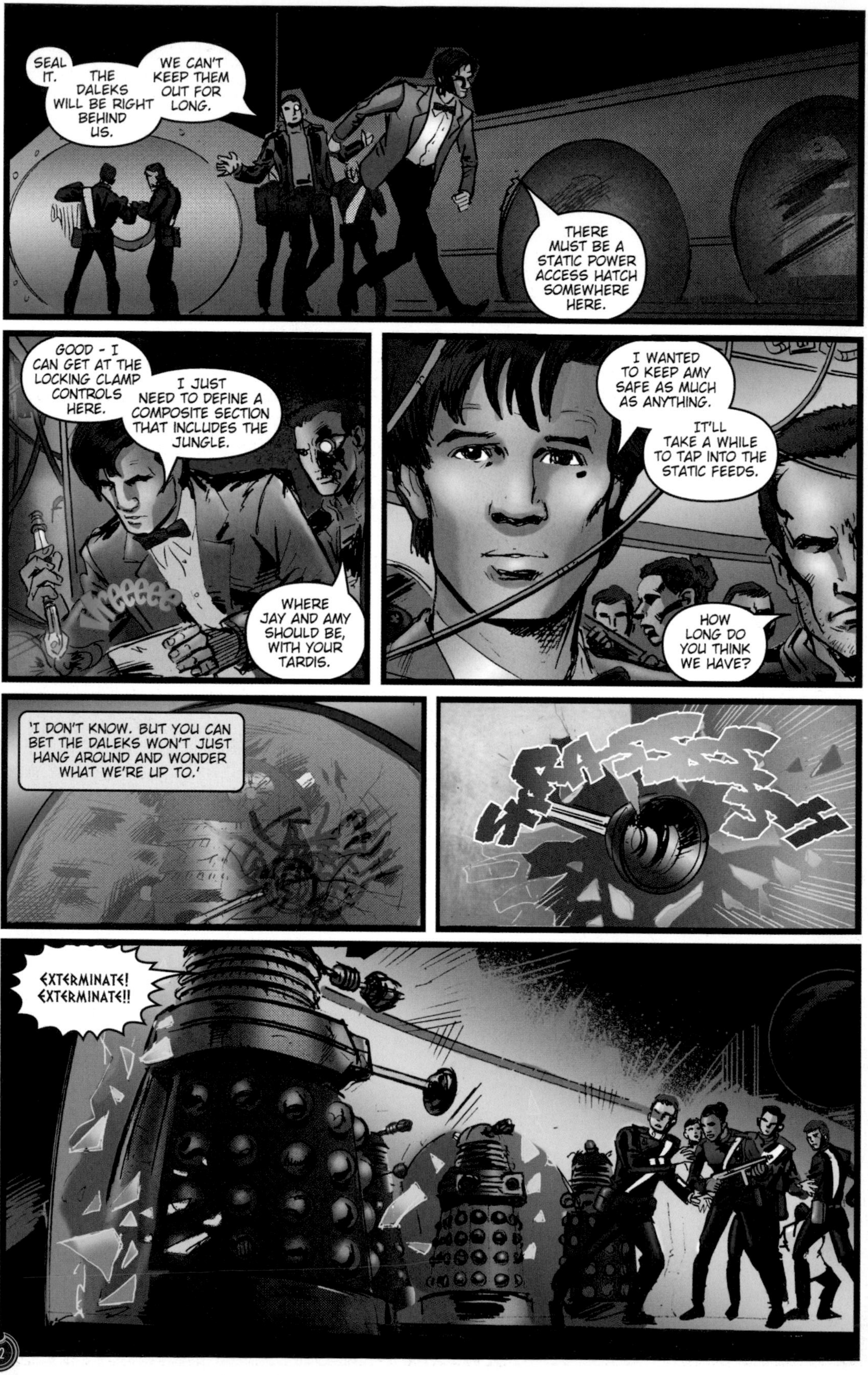
SEAL IT.
THE DALEKS WILL BE RIGHT BEHIND US.
WE CAN'T KEEP THEM OUT FOR LONG.
THERE MUST BE A STATIC POWER ACCESS HATCH SOMEWHERE HERE.
GOOD - I CAN GET AT THE LOCKING CLAMP CONTROLS HERE.
I JUST NEED TO DEFINE A COMPOSITE SECTION THAT INCLUDES THE JUNGLE.
WHERE JAY AND AMY SHOULD BE, WITH YOUR TARDIS.
I WANTED TO KEEP AMY SAFE AS MUCH AS ANYTHING.
IT'LL TAKE A WHILE TO TAP INTO THE STATIC FEEDS.
HOW LONG DO YOU THINK WE HAVE?
'I DON'T KNOW. BUT YOU CAN BET THE DALEKS WON'T JUST HANG AROUND AND WONDER WHAT WE'RE UP TO.'
EXTERMINATE!
EXTERMINATE!!

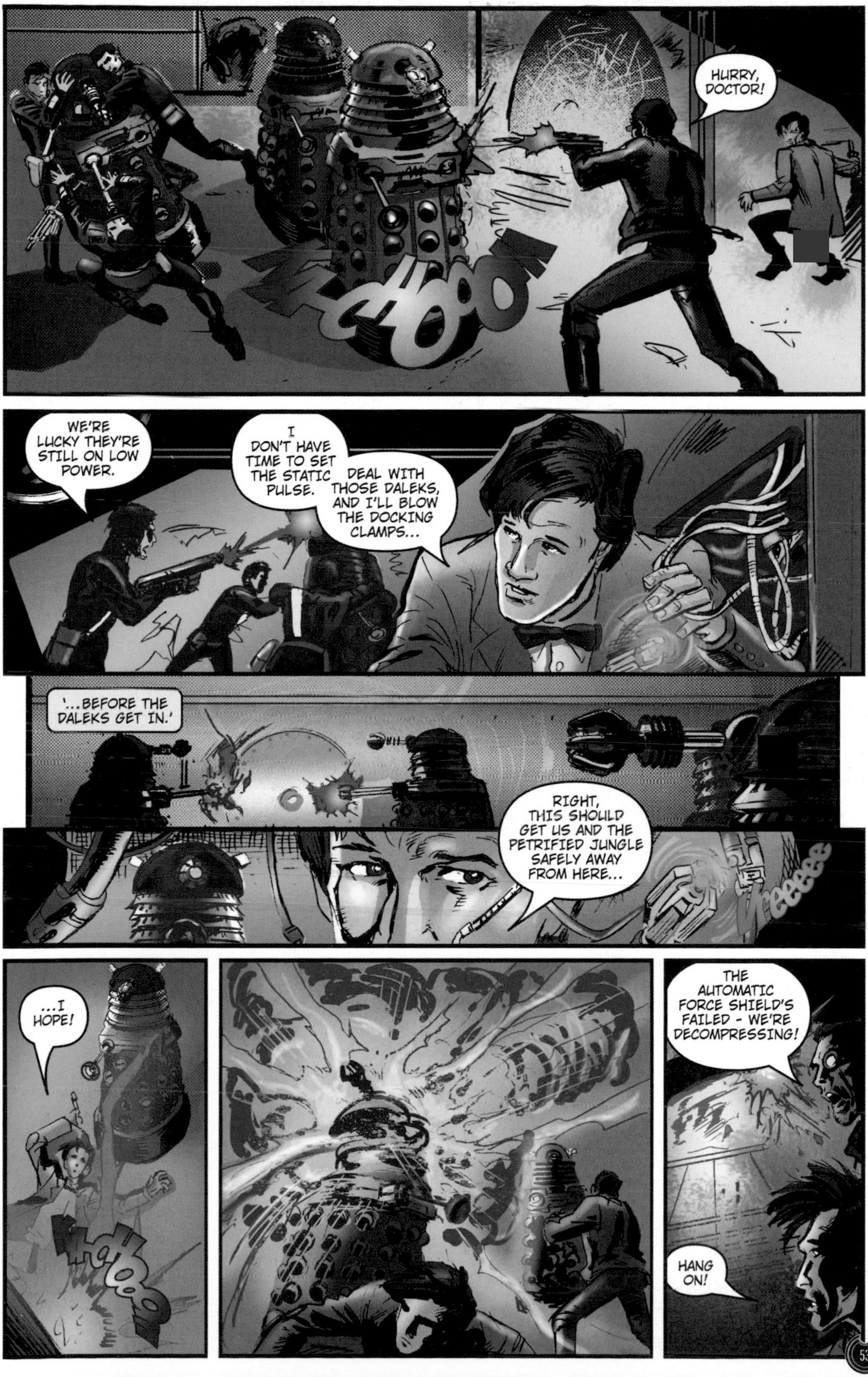
HURRY, DOCTOR!
WE'RE LUCKY THEY'RE STILL ON LOW POWER.
I DON'T HAVE TIME TO SET THE STATIC PULSE.
DEAL WITH THOSE DALEKS, AND I'LL BLOW THE DOCKING CLAMPS...
'...BEFORE THE DALEKS GET IN.'
RIGHT, THIS SHOULD GET US AND THE PETRIFIED JUNGLE SAFELY AWAY FROM HERE...
...I HOPE!
THE AUTOMATIC FORCE SHIELD'S FAILED - WE'RE DECOMPRESSING!
HANG ON!

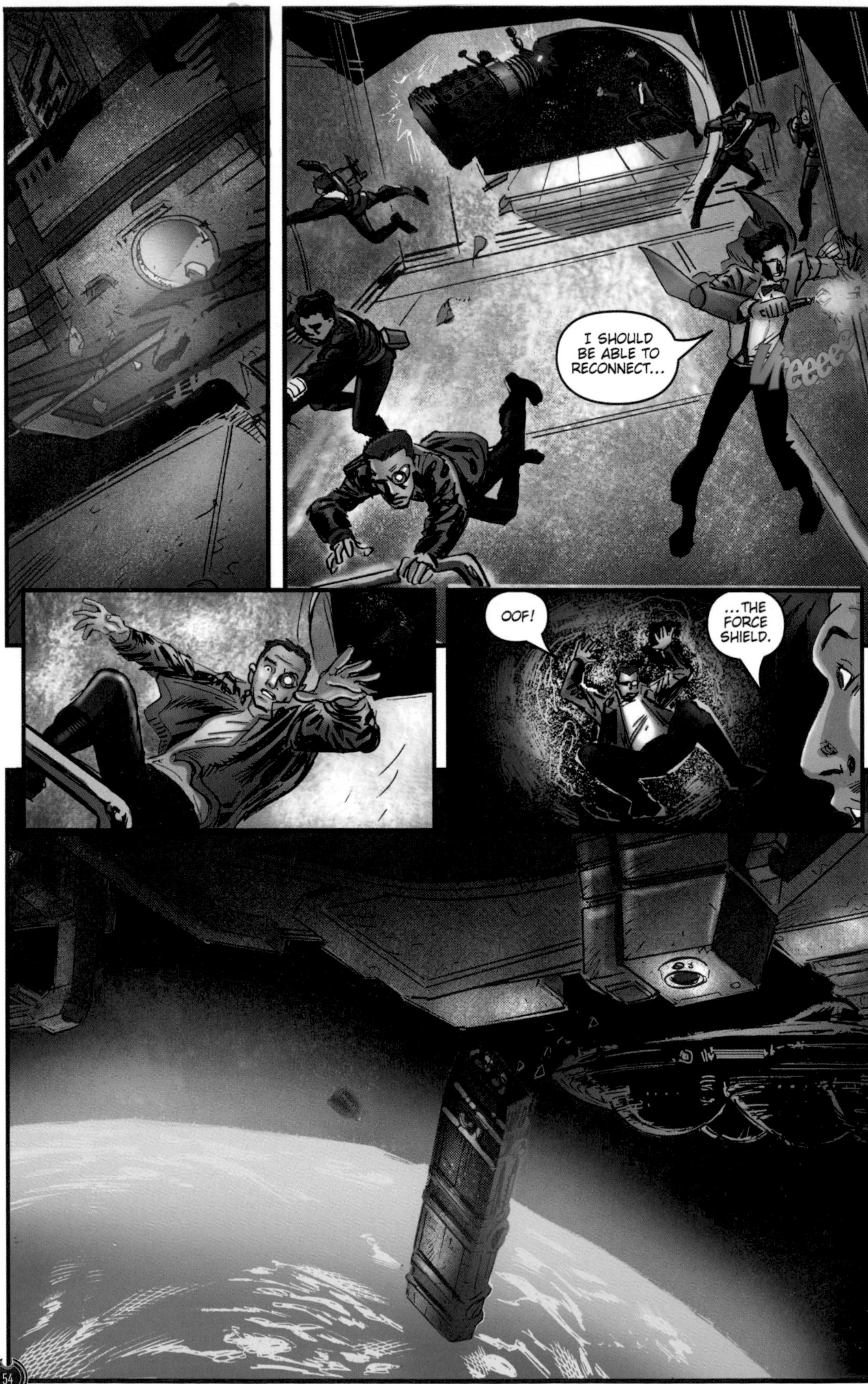
I SHOULD BE ABLE TO RECONNECT...
OOF!
...THE FORCE SHIELD.

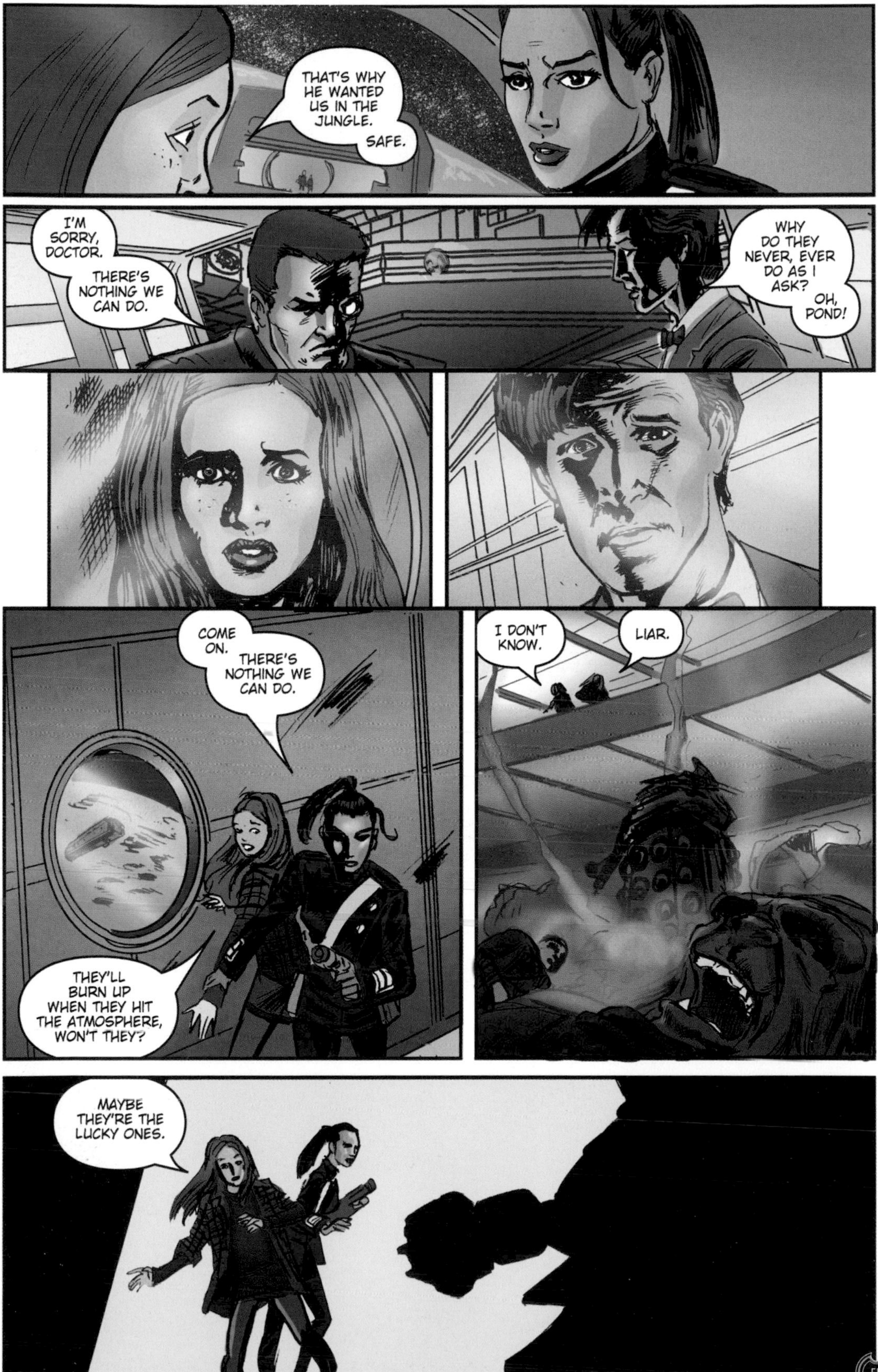

THAT'S WHY HE WANTED US IN THE JUNGLE.
SAFE.
I'M SORRY, DOCTOR.
THERE'S NOTHING WE CAN DO.
WHY DO THEY NEVER, EVER DO AS I ASK?
OH, POND!
COME ON.
THERE'S NOTHING WE CAN DO.
THEY'LL BURN UP WHEN THEY HIT THE ATMOSPHERE, WON'T THEY?
I DON'T KNOW.
LIAR.
MAYBE THEY'RE THE LUCKY ONES.

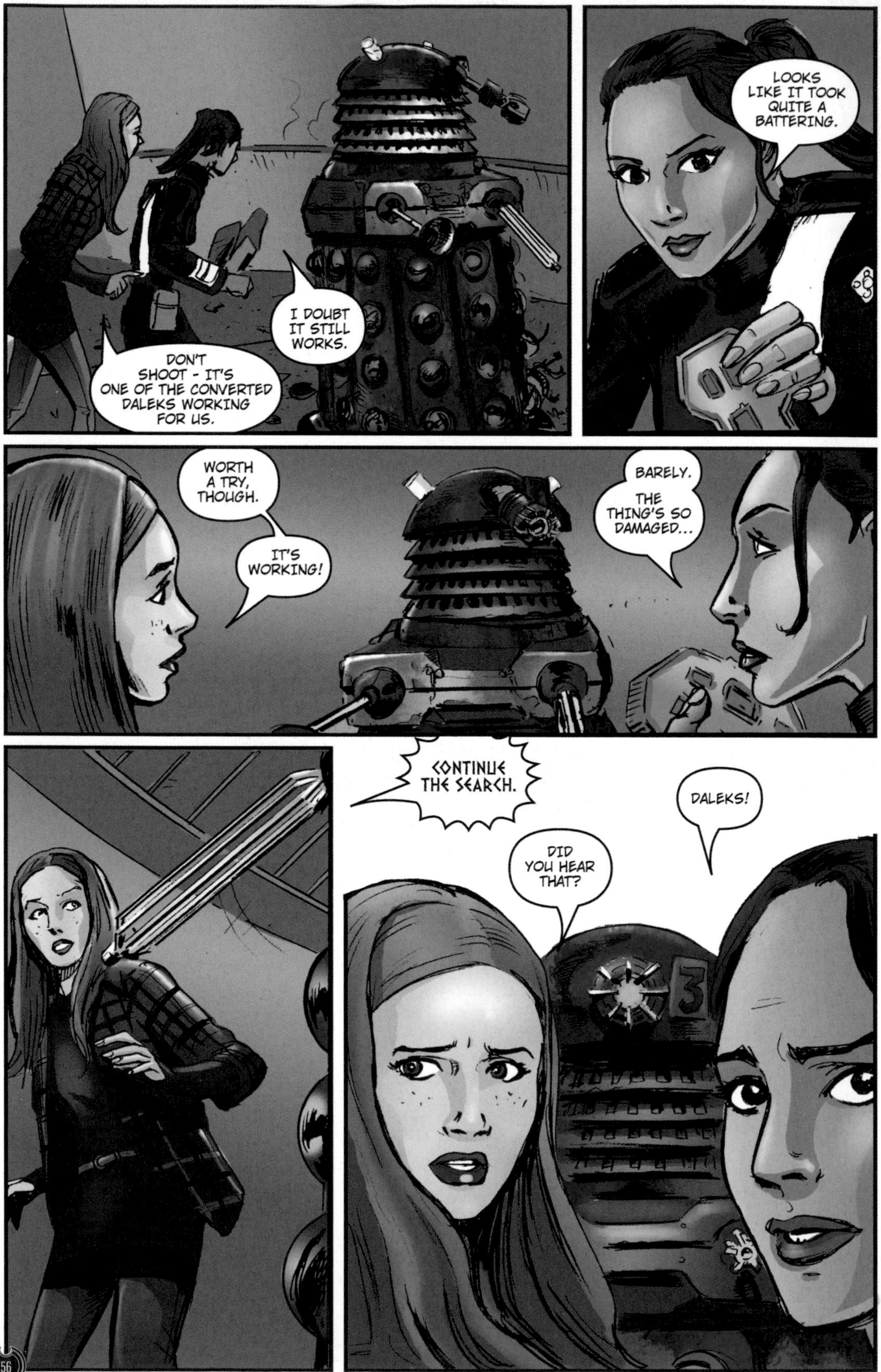
DON'T SHOOT - IT'S ONE OF THE CONVERTED DALEKS WORKING FOR US.
I DOUBT IT STILL WORKS.
LOOKS LIKE IT TOOK QUITE A BATTERING.
WORTH A TRY, THOUGH.
IT'S WORKING!
BARELY.
THE THING'S SO DAMAGED...
CONTINUE THE SEARCH.
DALEKS!
DID YOU HEAR THAT?

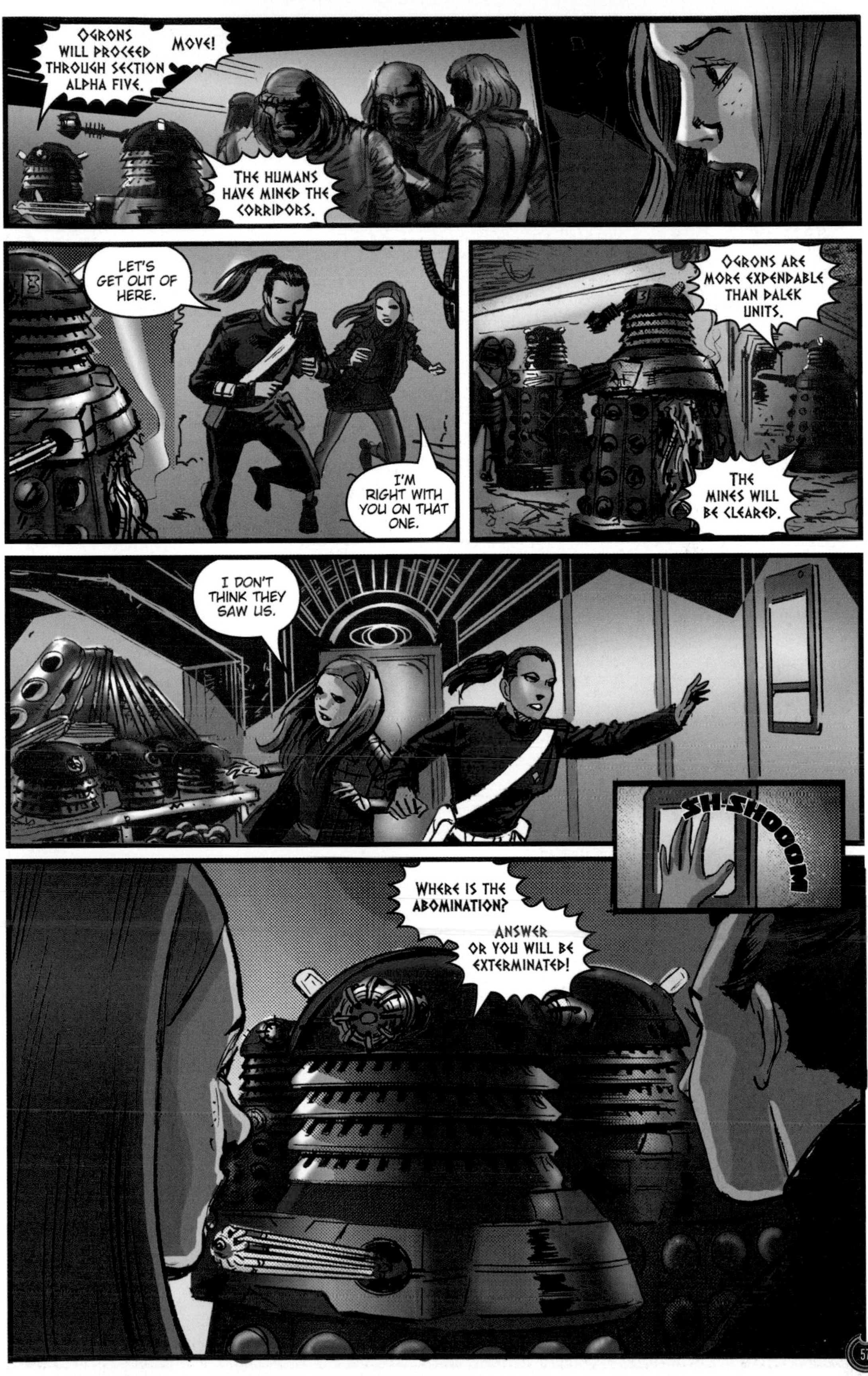
OGRONS WILL PROCEED THROUGH SECTION ALPHA FIVE.
MOVE!
THE HUMANS HAVE MINED THE CORRIDORS.
LET'S GET OUT OF HERE.
I'M RIGHT WITH YOU ON THAT ONE.
OGRONS ARE MORE EXPENDABLE THAN DALEK UNITS.
THE MINES WILL BE CLEARED.
I DON'T THINK THEY SAW US.
SH-SHOOOM
WHERE IS THE ABOMINATION?
ANSWER OR YOU WILL BE EXTERMINATED!

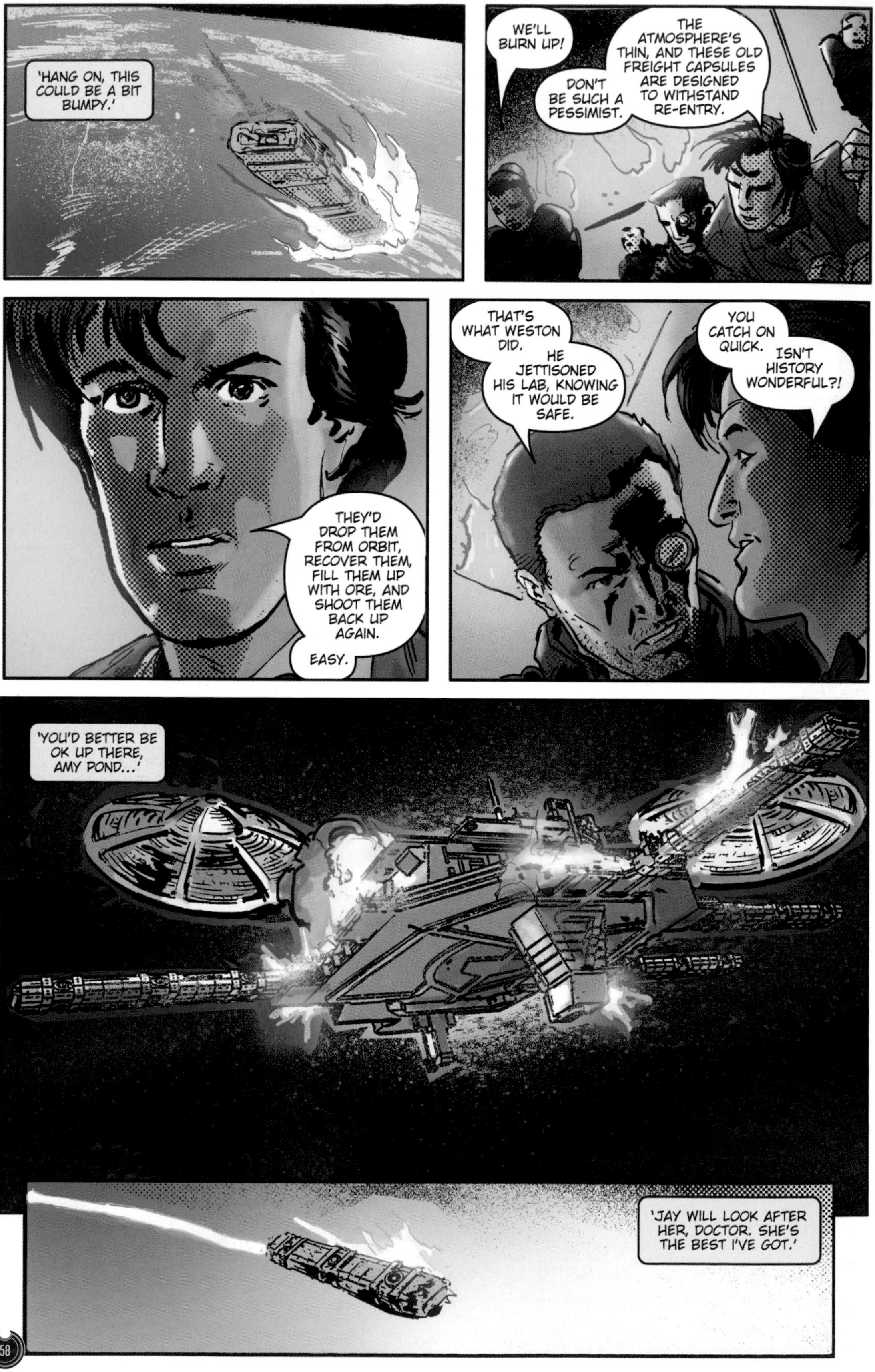
'HANG ON, THIS COULD BE A BIT BUMPY.'
WE'LL BURN UP!
DON'T BE SUCH A PESSIMIST.
THE ATMOSPHERE'S THIN, AND THESE OLD FREIGHT CAPSULES ARE DESIGNED TO WITHSTAND RE-ENTRY.
THEY'D DROP THEM FROM ORBIT, RECOVER THEM, FILL THEM UP WITH ORE, AND SHOOT THEM BACK UP AGAIN.
EASY.
THAT'S WHAT WESTON DID.
HE JETTISONED HIS LAB, KNOWING IT WOULD BE SAFE.
YOU CATCH ON QUICK.
ISN'T HISTORY WONDERFUL?!
'YOU'D BETTER BE OK UP THERE, AMY POND...'
'JAY WILL LOOK AFTER HER, DOCTOR. SHE'S THE BEST I'VE GOT.'

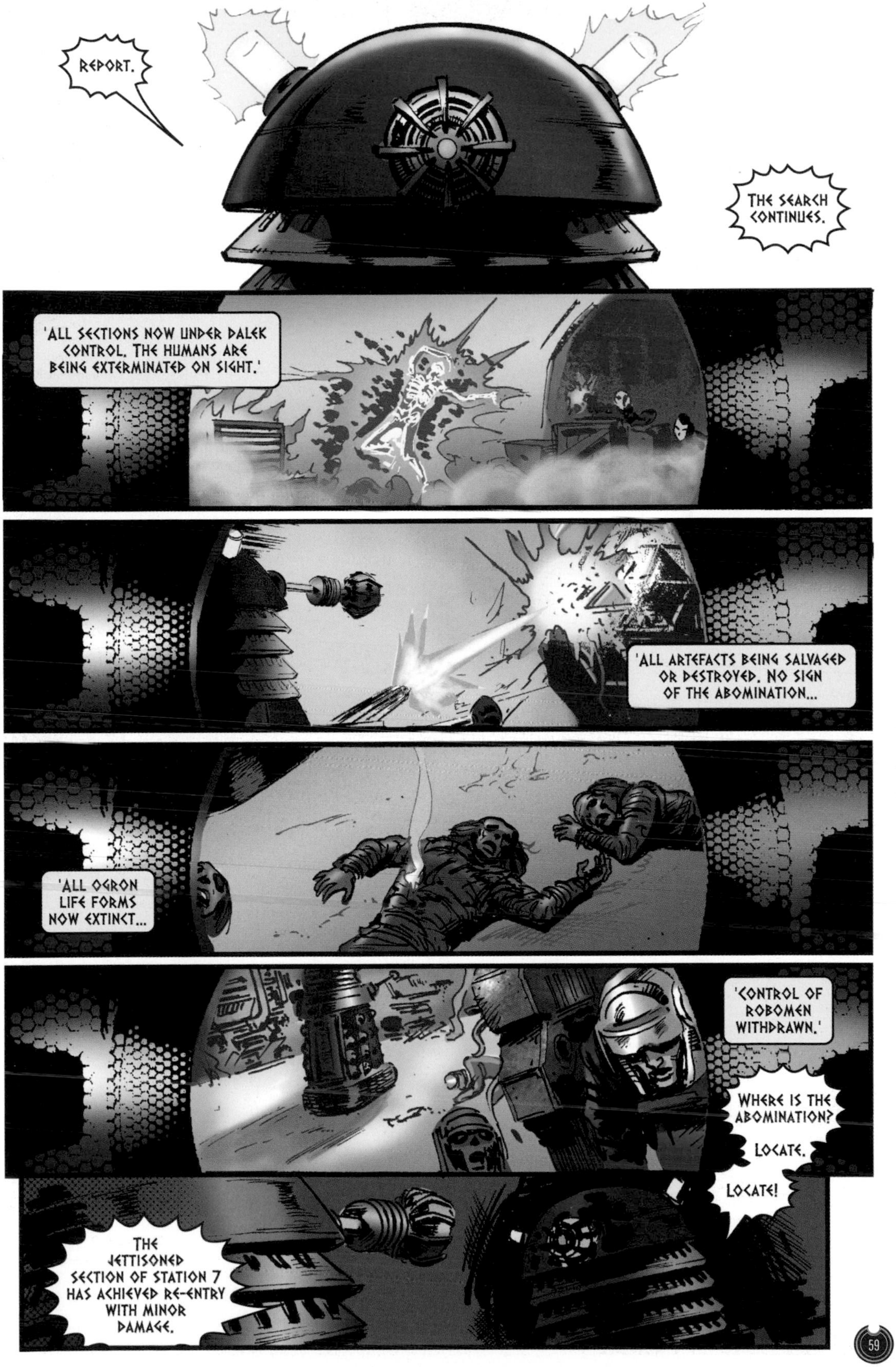
REPORT.
THE SEARCH CONTINUES.
'ALL SECTIONS NOW UNDER DALEK CONTROL. THE HUMANS ARE BEING EXTERMINATED ON SIGHT.'
'ALL ARTEFACTS BEING SALVAGED OR DESTROYED. NO SIGN OF THE ABOMINATION...
'ALL OGRON LIFE FORMS NOW EXTINCT...
'CONTROL OF ROBOMEN WITHDRAWN.'
WHERE IS THE ABOMINATION?
LOCATE.
LOCATE!
THE JETTISONED SECTION OF STATION 7 HAS ACHIEVED RE-ENTRY WITH MINOR DAMAGE.

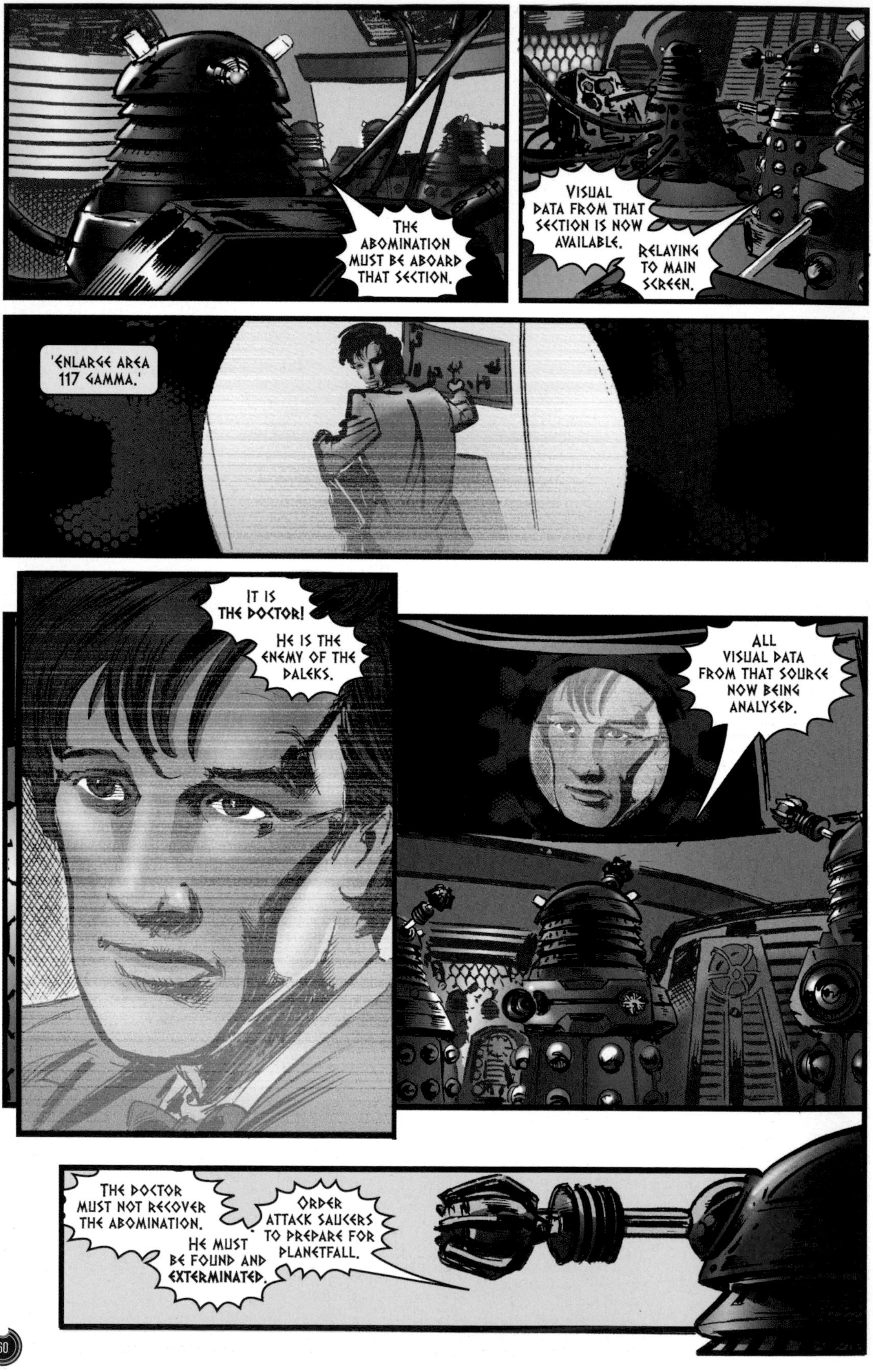
THE ABOMINATION MUST BE ABOARD THAT SECTION.
VISUAL DATA FROM THAT SECTION IS NOW AVAILABLE.
RELAYING TO MAIN SCREEN.
'ENLARGE AREA 117 GAMMA.'
IT IS THE DOCTOR!
HE IS THE ENEMY OF THE DALEKS.
ALL VISUAL DATA FROM THAT SOURCE NOW BEING ANALYSED.
THE DOCTOR MUST NOT RECOVER THE ABOMINATION.
HE MUST BE FOUND AND EXTERMINATED.
ORDER ATTACK SAUCERS TO PREPARE FOR PLANETFALL.

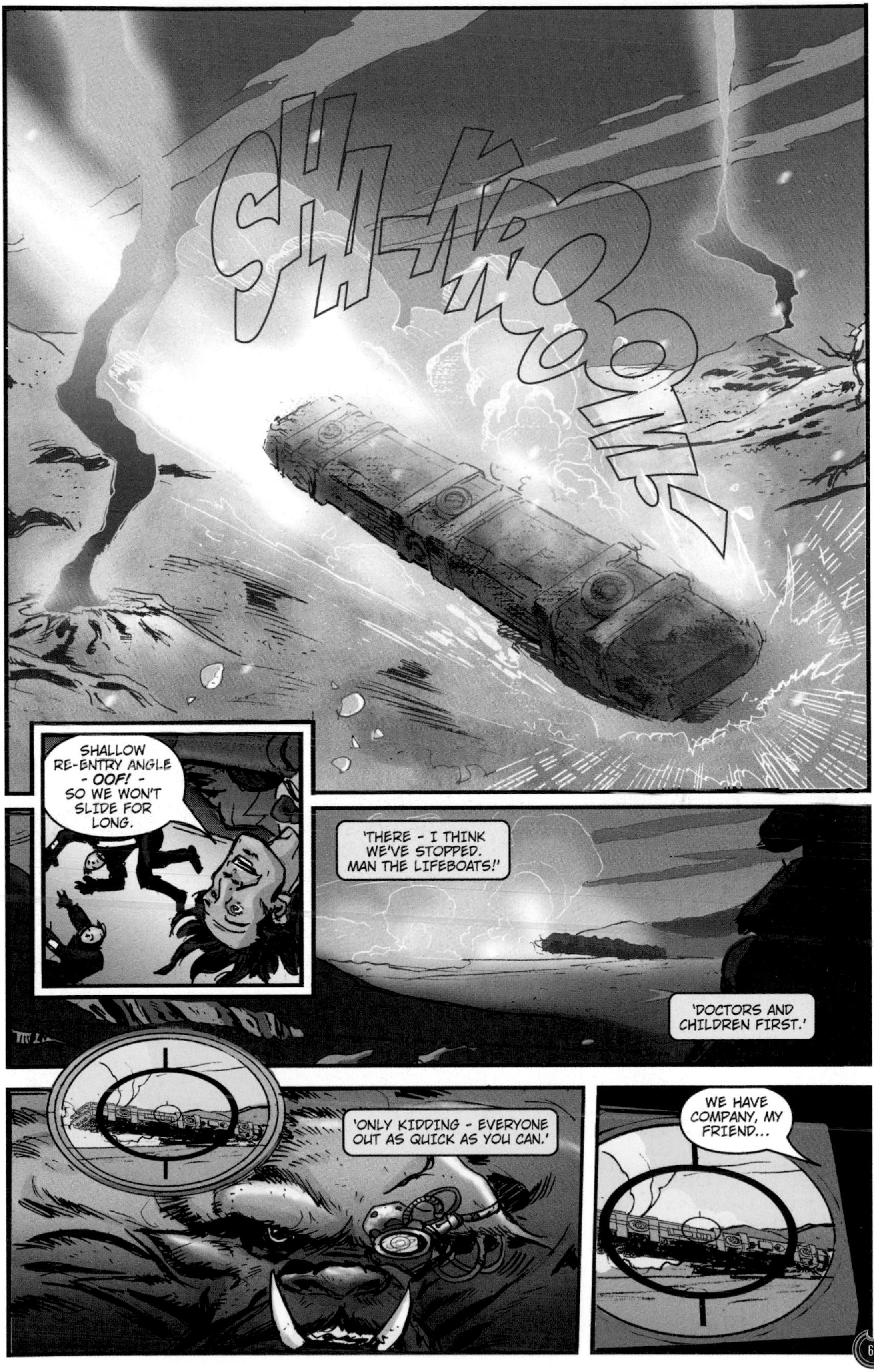
SHHHWOOM!
SHALLOW RE-ENTRY ANGLE - OOF! - SO WE WON'T SLIDE FOR LONG.
'THERE - I THINK WE'VE STOPPED. MAN THE LIFEBOATS!'
'DOCTORS AND CHILDREN FIRST.'
'ONLY KIDDING - EVERYONE OUT AS QUICK AS YOU CAN.'
WE HAVE COMPANY, MY FRIEND...

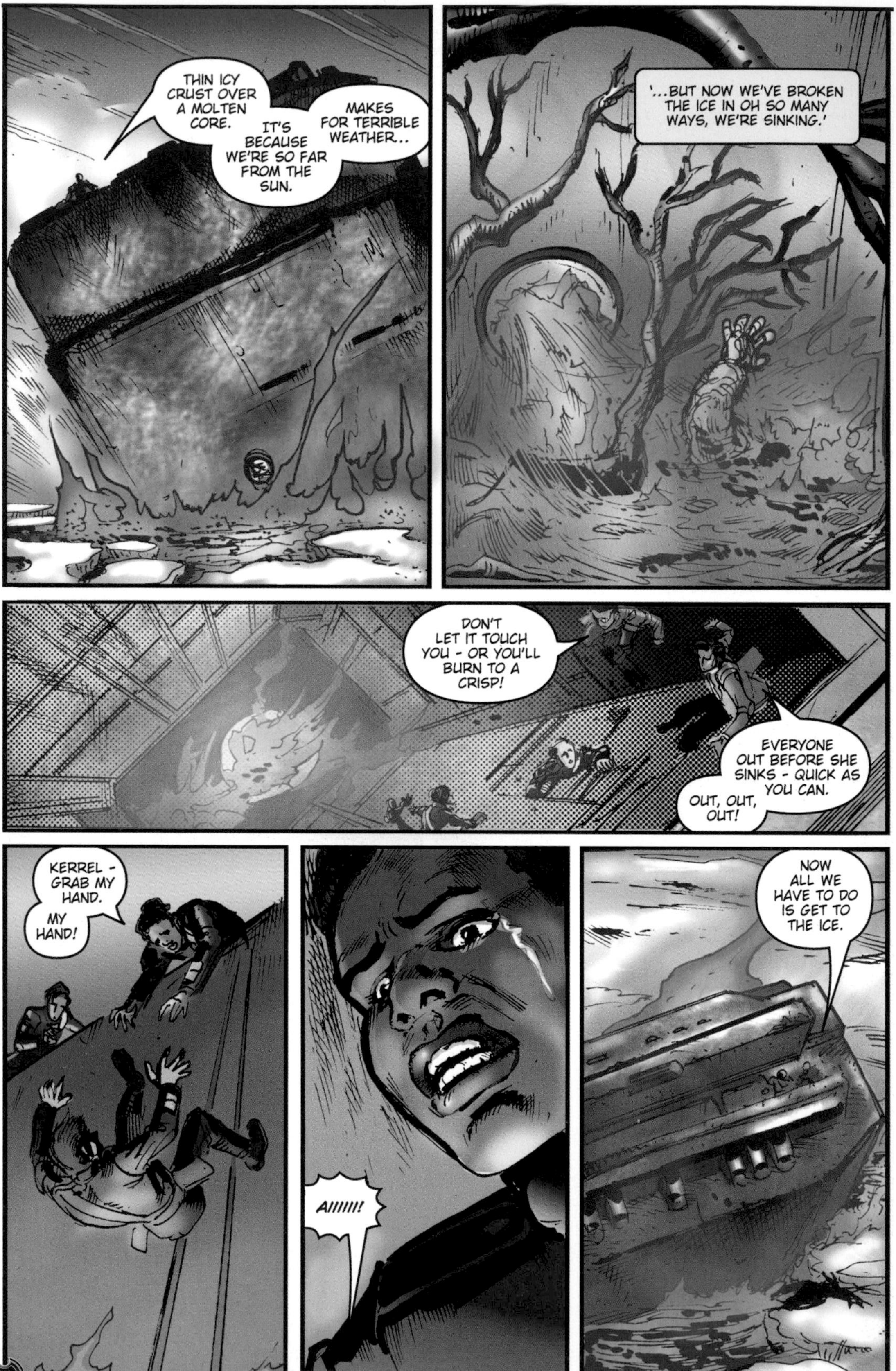

THIN ICY CRUST OVER A MOLTEN CORE.
IT'S BECAUSE WE'RE SO FAR FROM THE SUN.
MAKES FOR TERRIBLE WEATHER..
'...BUT NOW WE'VE BROKEN THE ICE IN OH SO MANY WAYS, WE'RE SINKING.'
DON'T LET IT TOUCH YOU - OR YOU'LL BURN TO A CRISP!
EVERYONE OUT BEFORE SHE SINKS - QUICK AS YOU CAN.
OUT, OUT, OUT!
KERREL - GRAB MY HAND.
MY HAND!
AIIIIII!
NOW ALL WE HAVE TO DO IS GET TO THE ICE.

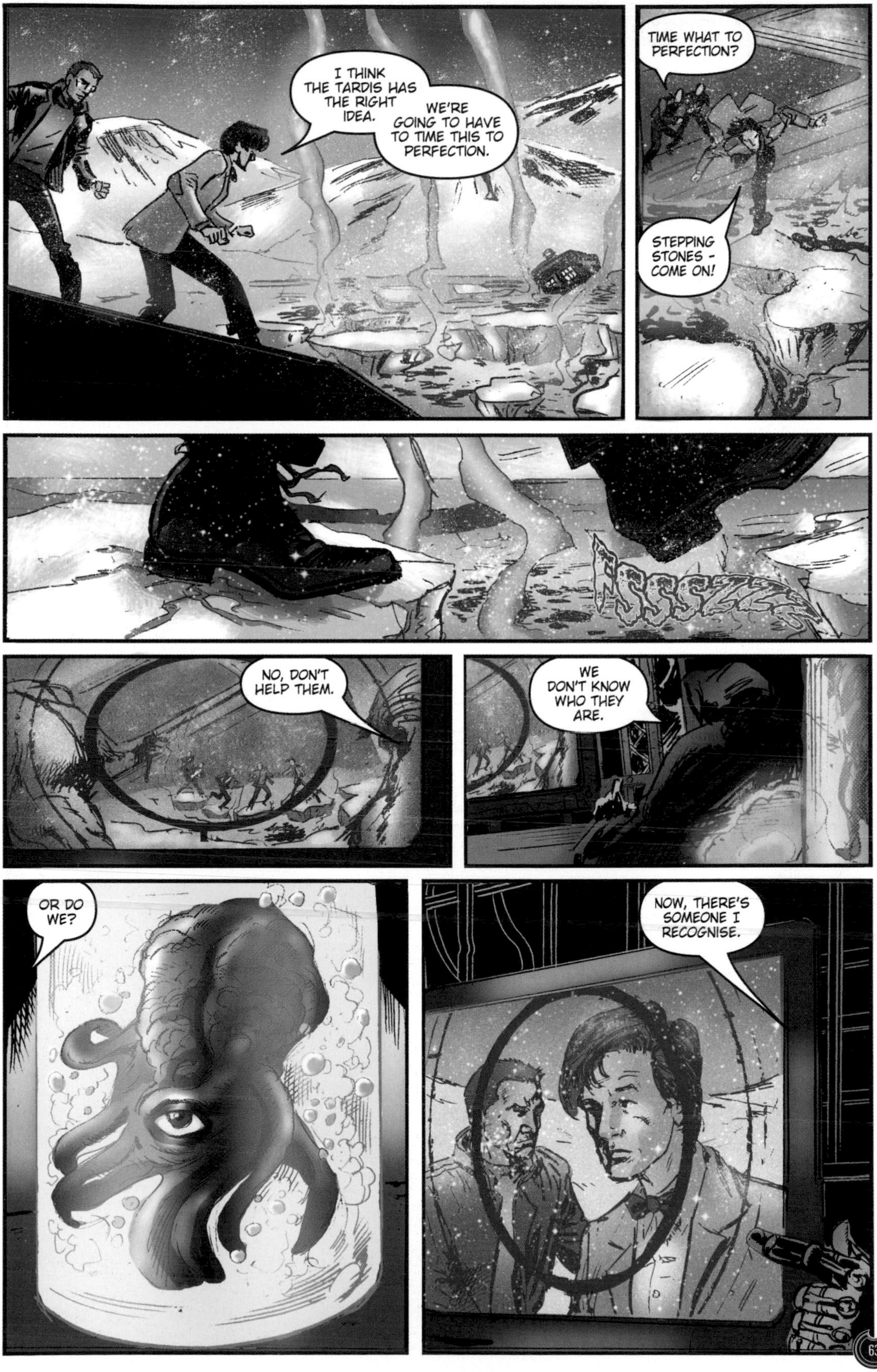
I THINK THE TARDIS HAS THE RIGHT IDEA.
WE'RE GOING TO HAVE TO TIME THIS TO PERFECTION.
TIME WHAT TO PERFECTION?
STEPPING STONES - COME ON!
NO, DON'T HELP THEM.
WE DON'T KNOW WHO THEY ARE.
OR DO WE?
NOW, THERE'S SOMEONE I RECOGNISE.

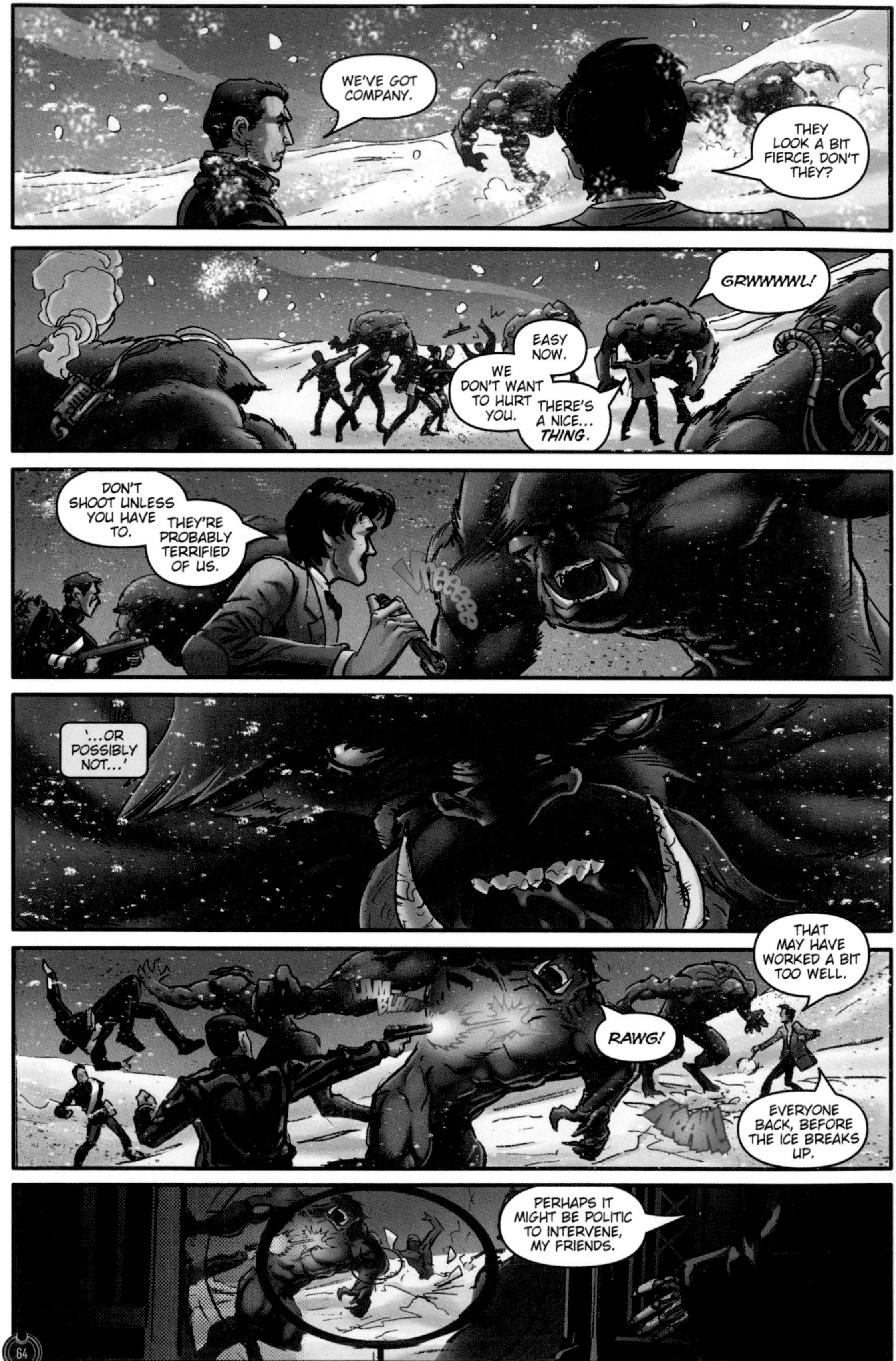
WE'VE GOT COMPANY.
THEY LOOK A BIT FIERCE, DON'T THEY?
GRWWWWL!
EASY NOW.
WE DON'T WANT TO HURT YOU.
THERE'S A NICE... THING.
DON'T SHOOT UNLESS YOU HAVE TO.
THEY'RE PROBABLY TERRIFIED OF US.
'...OR POSSIBLY NOT...'
THAT MAY HAVE WORKED A BIT TOO WELL.
RAWG!
EVERYONE BACK, BEFORE THE ICE BREAKS UP.
PERHAPS IT MIGHT BE POLITIC TO INTERVENE, MY FRIENDS.

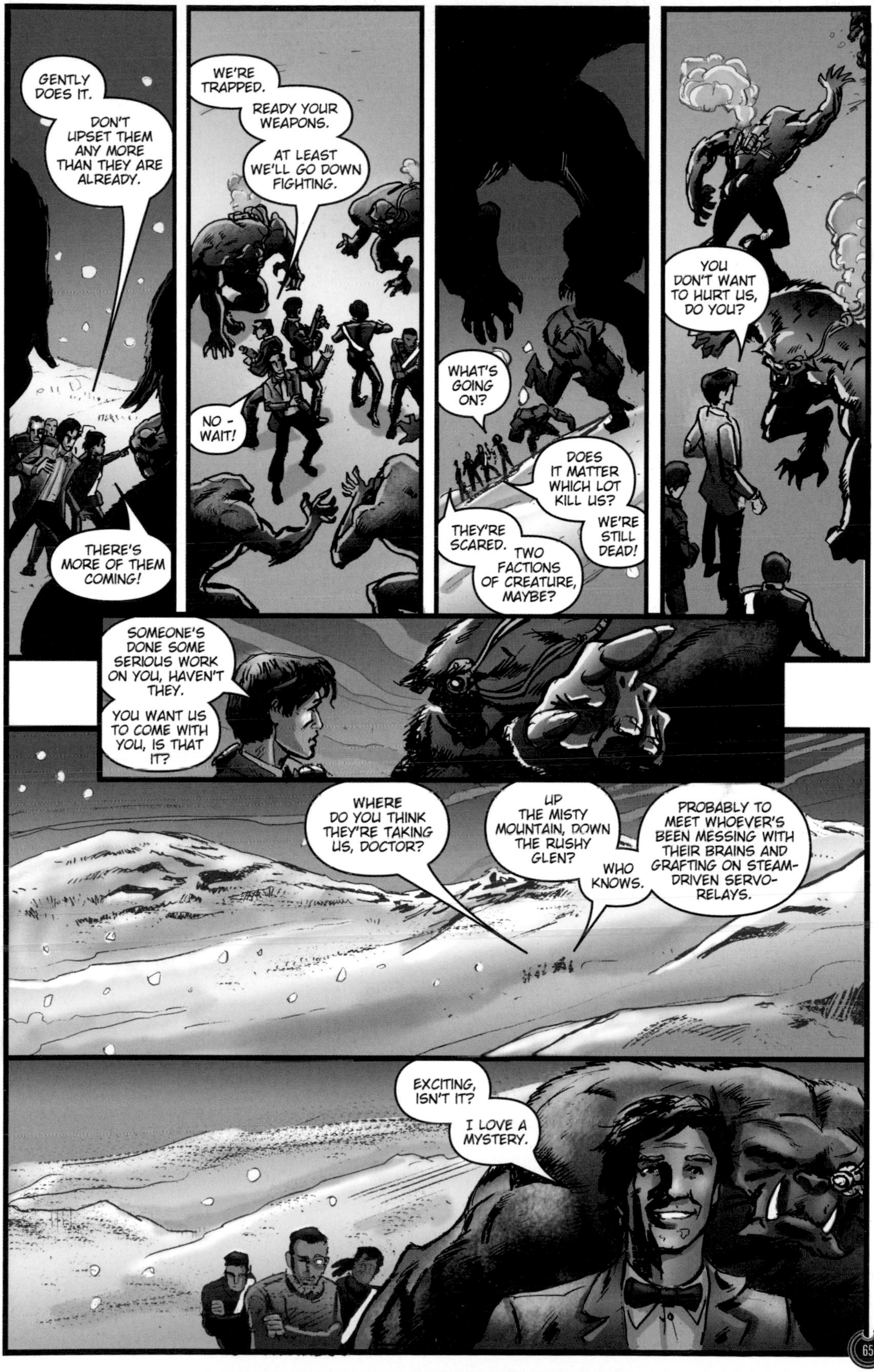
GENTLY DOES IT.
DON'T UPSET THEM ANY MORE THAN THEY ARE ALREADY.
THERE'S MORE OF THEM COMING!
WE'RE TRAPPED.
READY YOUR WEAPONS.
AT LEAST WE'LL GO DOWN FIGHTING.
NO - WAIT!
WHAT'S GOING ON?
DOES IT MATTER WHICH LOT KILL US?
WE'RE STILL DEAD!
THEY'RE SCARED.
TWO FACTIONS OF CREATURE, MAYBE?
YOU DON'T WANT TO HURT US, DO YOU?
SOMEONE'S DONE SOME SERIOUS WORK ON YOU, HAVEN'T THEY.
YOU WANT US TO COME WITH YOU, IS THAT IT?
WHERE DO YOU THINK THEY'RE TAKING US, DOCTOR?
UP THE MISTY MOUNTAIN, DOWN THE RUSHY GLEN?
WHO KNOWS.
PROBABLY TO MEET WHOEVER'S BEEN MESSING WITH THEIR BRAINS AND GRAFTING ON STEAM-DRIVEN SERVO-RELAYS.
EXCITING, ISN'T IT?
I LOVE A MYSTERY.

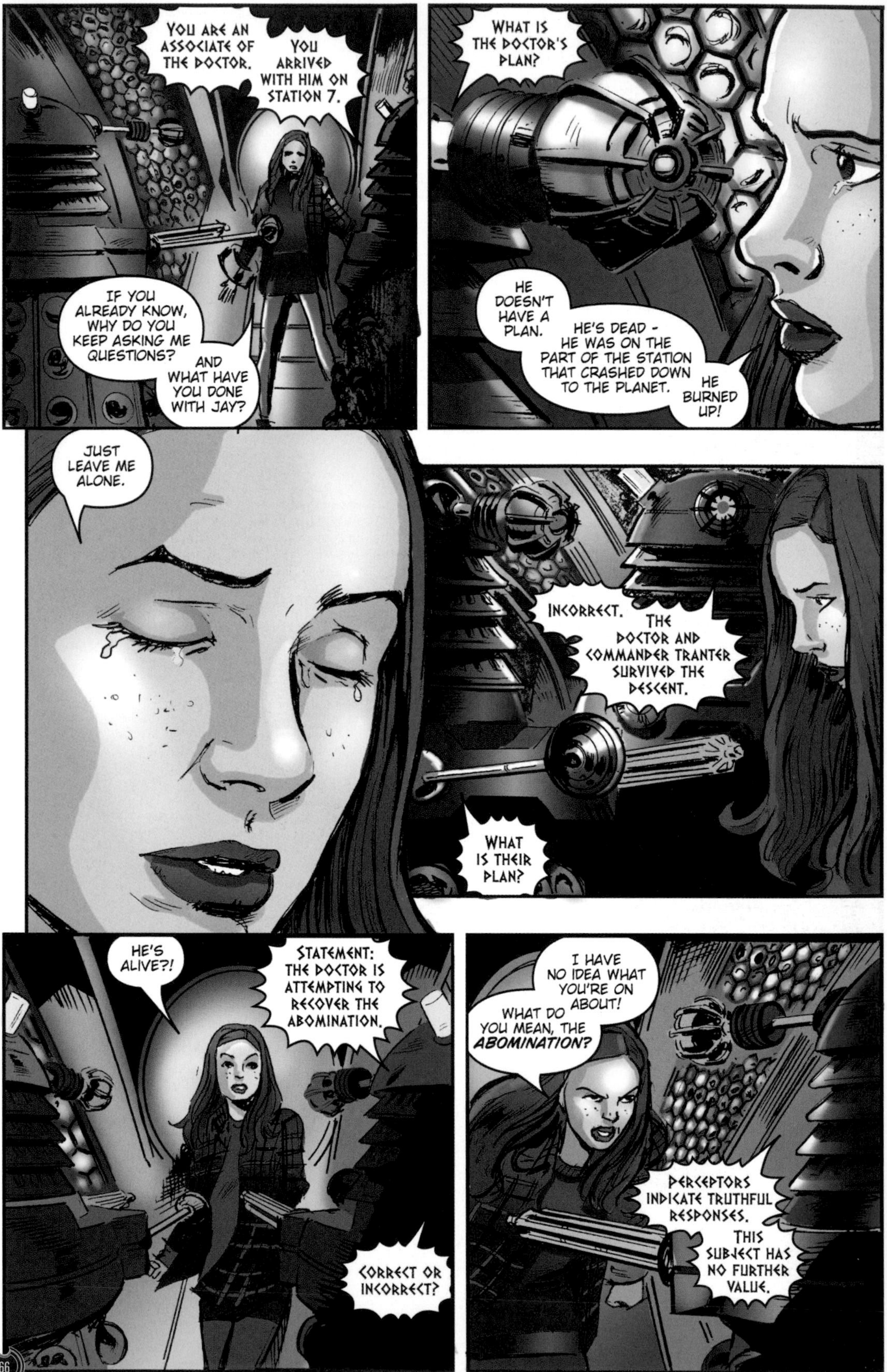
YOU ARE AN ASSOCIATE OF THE DOCTOR.
YOU ARRIVED WITH HIM ON STATION 7.
IF YOU ALREADY KNOW, WHY DO YOU KEEP ASKING ME QUESTIONS?
AND WHAT HAVE YOU DONE WITH JAY?
WHAT IS THE DOCTOR'S PLAN?
HE DOESN'T HAVE A PLAN.
HE'S DEAD - HE WAS ON THE PART OF THE STATION THAT CRASHED DOWN TO THE PLANET.
HE BURNED UP!
JUST LEAVE ME ALONE.
INCORRECT.
THE DOCTOR AND COMMANDER TRANTER SURVIVED THE DESCENT.
WHAT IS THEIR PLAN?
HE'S ALIVE?!
STATEMENT: THE DOCTOR IS ATTEMPTING TO RECOVER THE ABOMINATION.
CORRECT OR INCORRECT?
I HAVE NO IDEA WHAT YOU'RE ON ABOUT!
WHAT DO YOU MEAN, THE *ABOMINATION?*
PERCEPTORS INDICATE TRUTHFUL RESPONSES.
THIS SUBJECT HAS NO FURTHER VALUE.

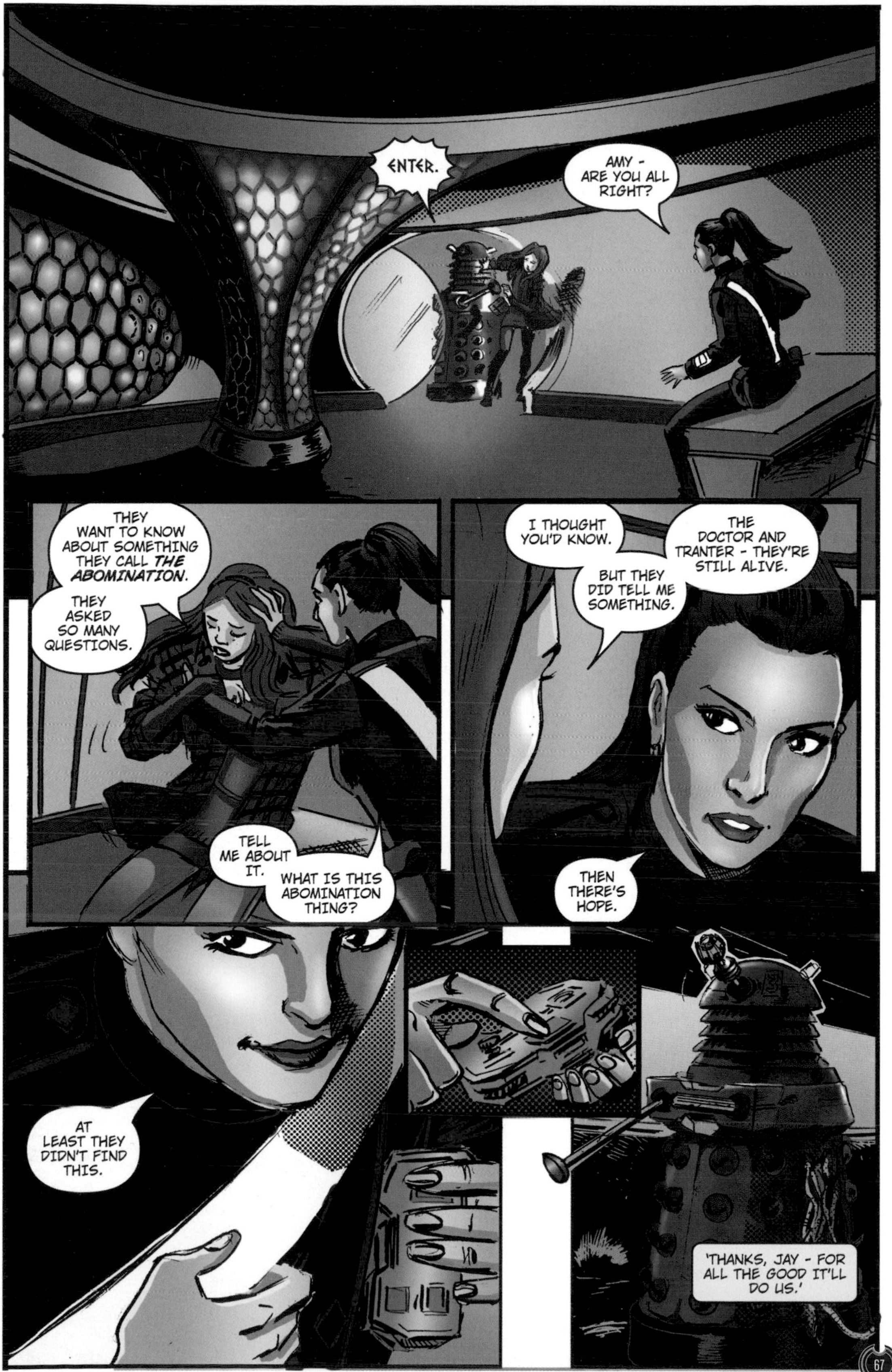
ENTER.
AMY - ARE YOU ALL RIGHT?
THEY WANT TO KNOW ABOUT SOMETHING THEY CALL *THE ABOMINATION*.
THEY ASKED SO MANY QUESTIONS.
TELL ME ABOUT IT.
WHAT IS THIS ABOMINATION THING?
I THOUGHT YOU'D KNOW.
BUT THEY DID TELL ME SOMETHING.
THE DOCTOR AND TRANTER - THEY'RE STILL ALIVE.
THEN THERE'S HOPE.
AT LEAST THEY DIDN'T FIND THIS.
'THANKS, JAY - FOR ALL THE GOOD IT'LL DO US.'

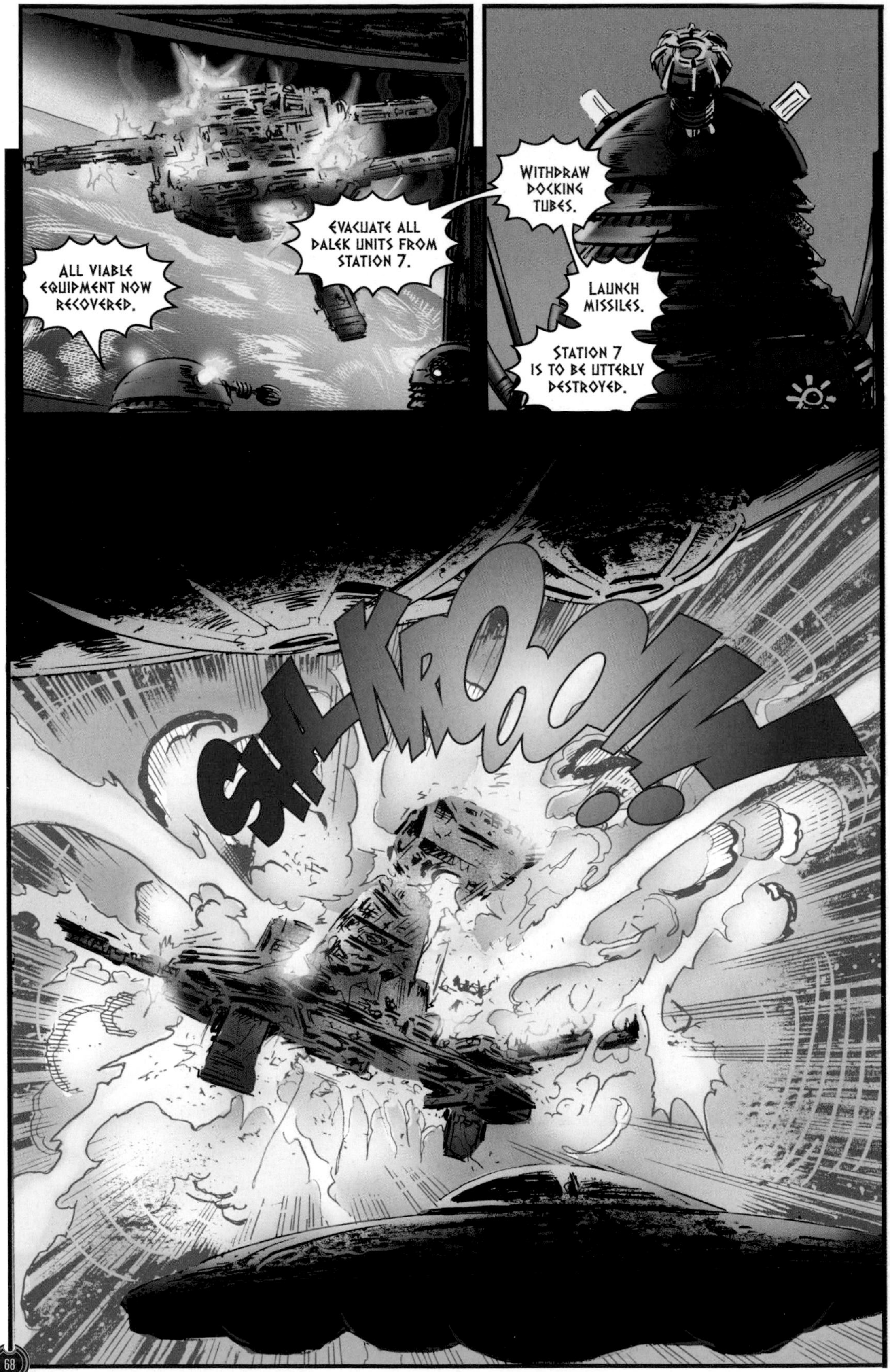
ALL VIABLE EQUIPMENT NOW RECOVERED.
EVACUATE ALL DALEK UNITS FROM STATION 7.
WITHDRAW DOCKING TUBES.
LAUNCH MISSILES.
STATION 7 IS TO BE UTTERLY DESTROYED.
SHHKROOOOM!

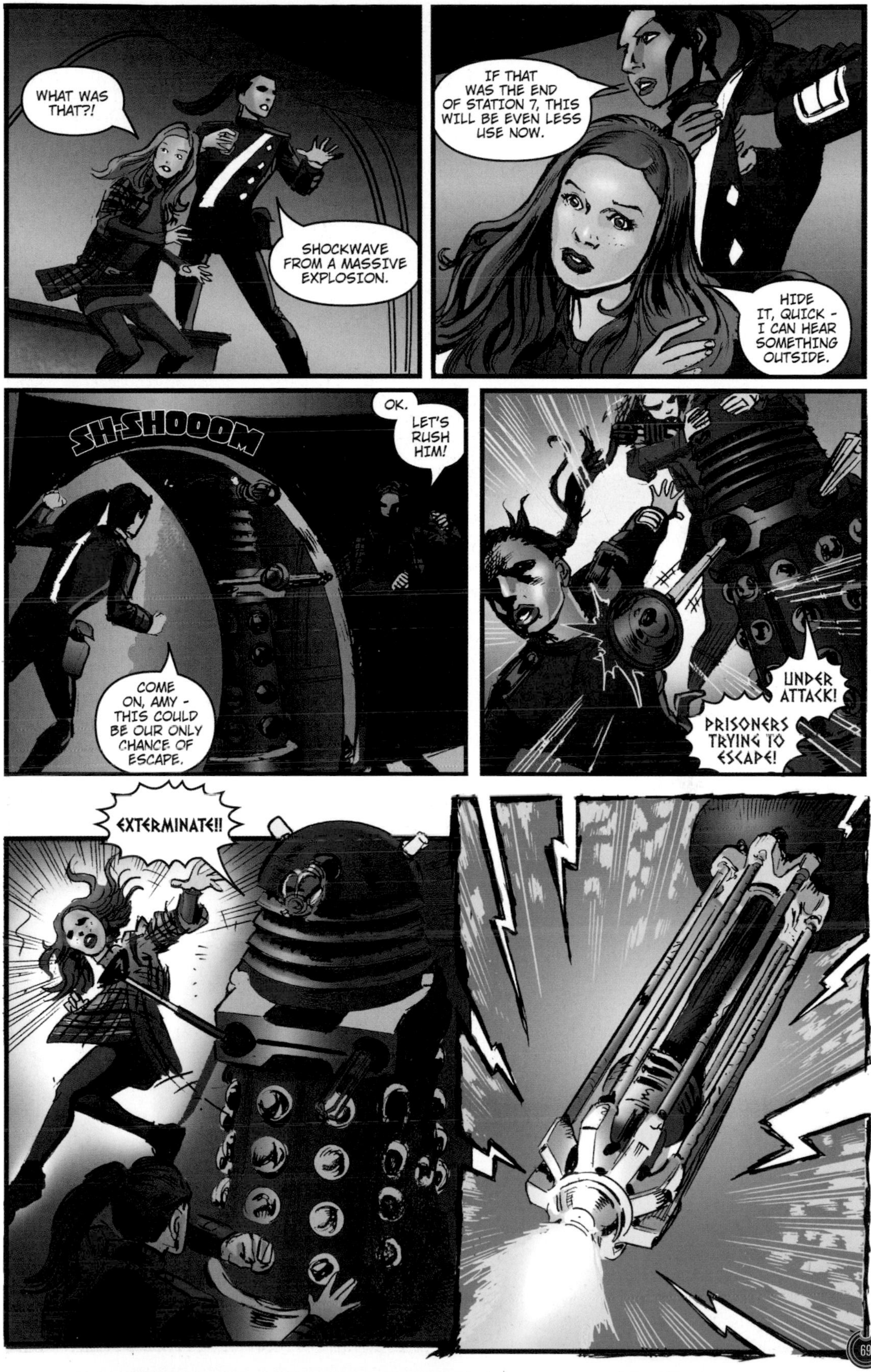
WHAT WAS THAT?!
SHOCKWAVE FROM A MASSIVE EXPLOSION.
IF THAT WAS THE END OF STATION 7, THIS WILL BE EVEN LESS USE NOW.
HIDE IT, QUICK - I CAN HEAR SOMETHING OUTSIDE.
SH-SHOOOM
OK.
LET'S RUSH HIM!
COME ON, AMY - THIS COULD BE OUR ONLY CHANCE OF ESCAPE.
UNDER ATTACK!
PRISONERS TRYING TO ESCAPE!
EXTERMINATE!!

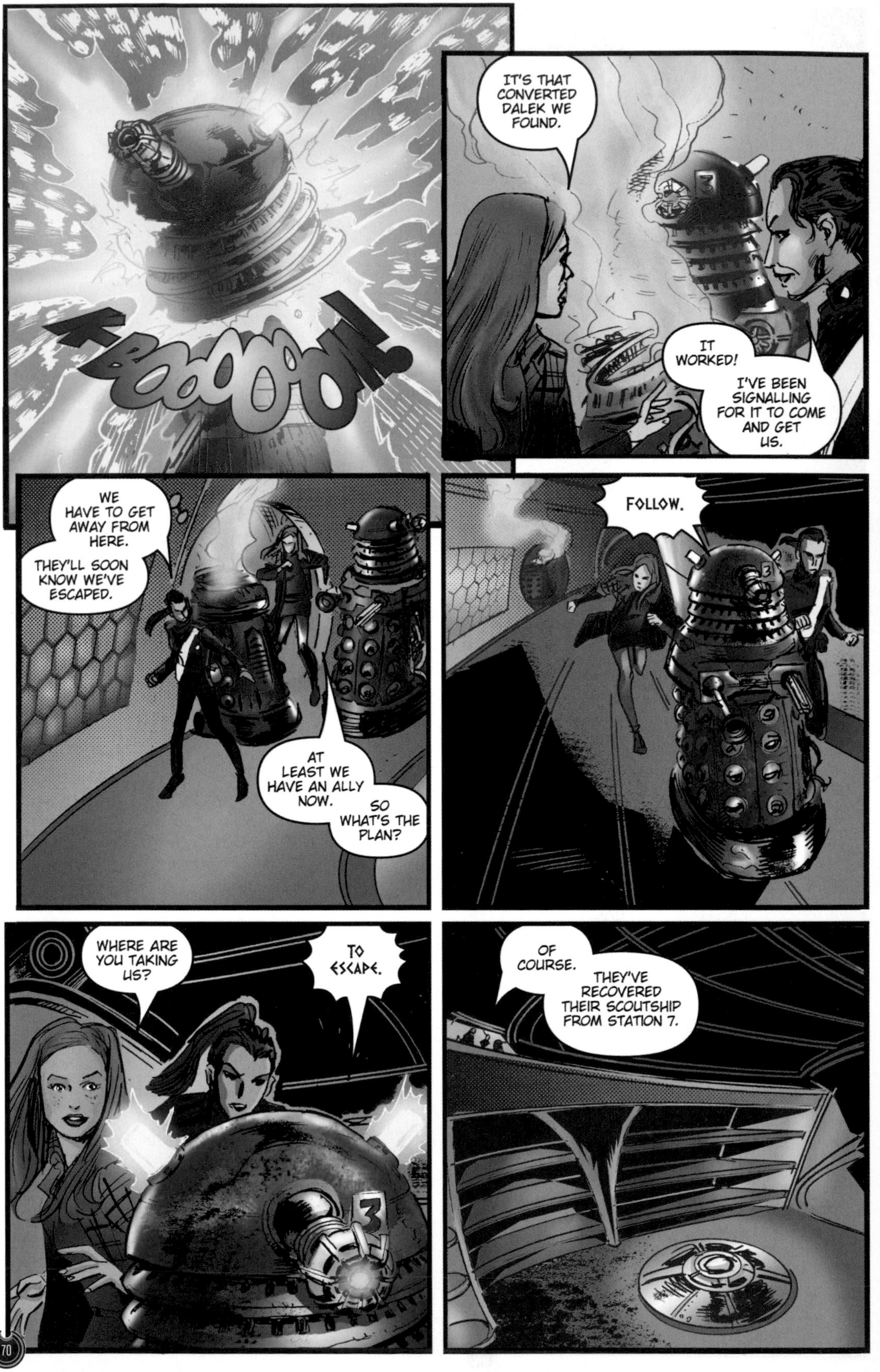
KABOOOOOM!
IT'S THAT CONVERTED DALEK WE FOUND.
IT WORKED!
I'VE BEEN SIGNALLING FOR IT TO COME AND GET US.
WE HAVE TO GET AWAY FROM HERE.
THEY'LL SOON KNOW WE'VE ESCAPED.
AT LEAST WE HAVE AN ALLY NOW.
SO WHAT'S THE PLAN?
FOLLOW.
WHERE ARE YOU TAKING US?
TO ESCAPE.
OF COURSE.
THEY'VE RECOVERED THEIR SCOUTSHIP FROM STATION 7.

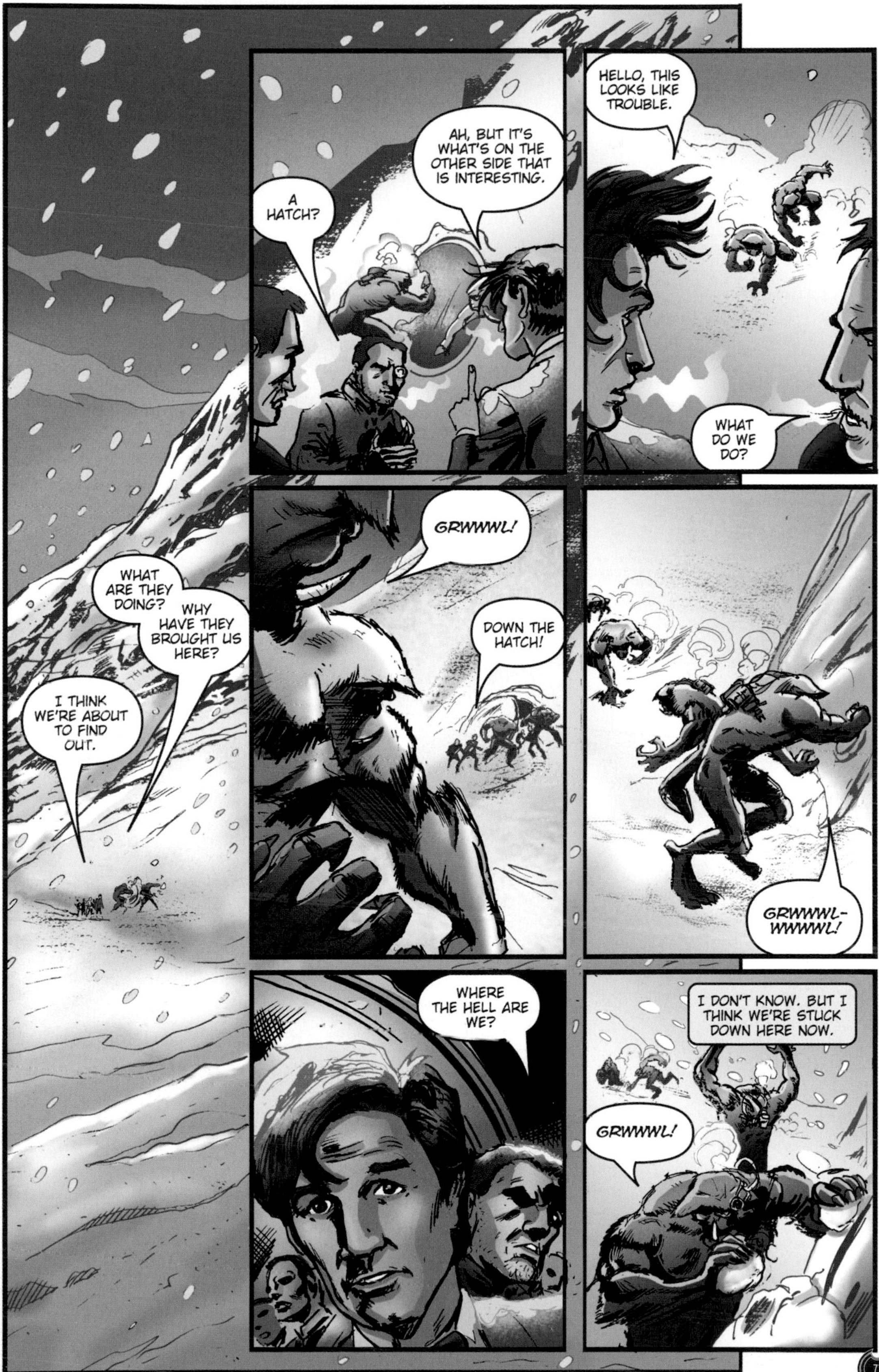
A HATCH?
AH, BUT IT'S WHAT'S ON THE OTHER SIDE THAT IS INTERESTING.
HELLO, THIS LOOKS LIKE TROUBLE.
WHAT DO WE DO?
WHAT ARE THEY DOING?
WHY HAVE THEY BROUGHT US HERE?
I THINK WE'RE ABOUT TO FIND OUT.
GRWWWL!
DOWN THE HATCH!
GRWWWL-WWWWL!
WHERE THE HELL ARE WE?
I DON'T KNOW. BUT I THINK WE'RE STUCK DOWN HERE NOW.
GRWWWL!

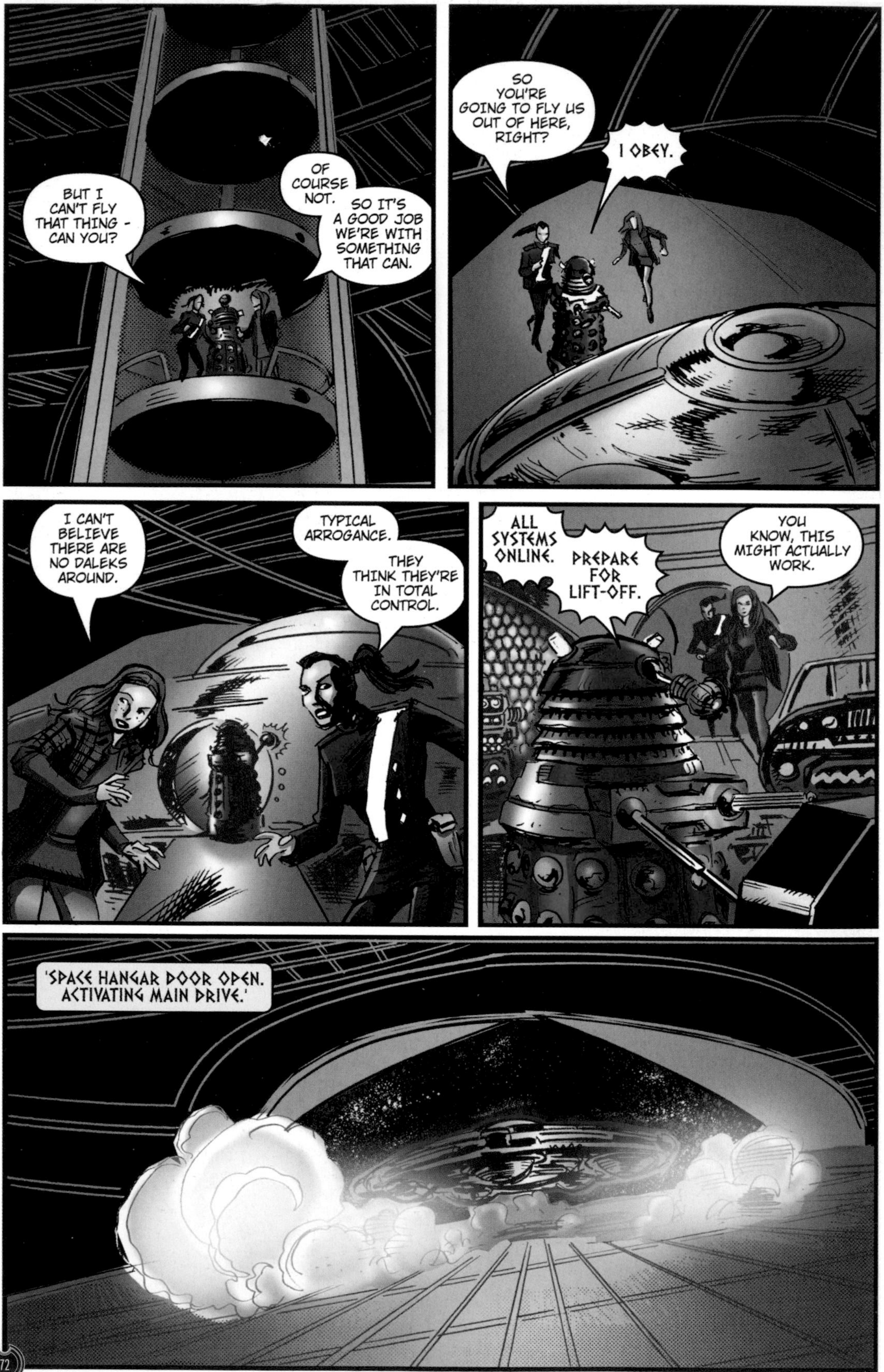
BUT I CAN'T FLY THAT THING - CAN YOU?
OF COURSE NOT.
SO IT'S A GOOD JOB WE'RE WITH SOMETHING THAT CAN.
SO YOU'RE GOING TO FLY US OUT OF HERE, RIGHT?
I OBEY.
I CAN'T BELIEVE THERE ARE NO DALEKS AROUND.
TYPICAL ARROGANCE.
THEY THINK THEY'RE IN TOTAL CONTROL.
ALL SYSTEMS ONLINE.
PREPARE FOR LIFT-OFF.
YOU KNOW, THIS MIGHT ACTUALLY WORK.
'SPACE HANGAR DOOR OPEN. ACTIVATING MAIN DRIVE.'

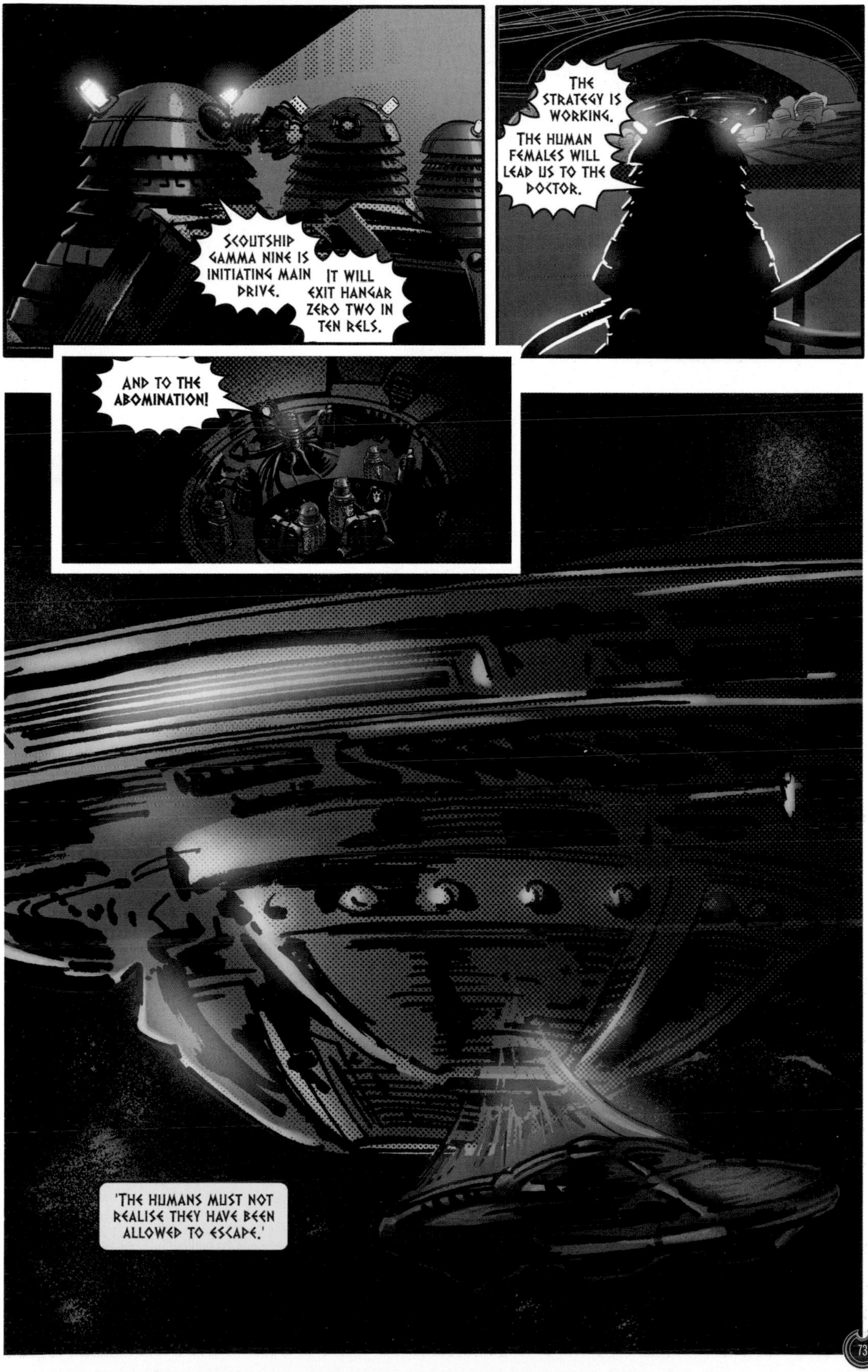
SCOUTSHIP GAMMA NINE IS INITIATING MAIN DRIVE.
IT WILL EXIT HANGAR ZERO TWO IN TEN RELS.
THE STRATEGY IS WORKING.
THE HUMAN FEMALES WILL LEAD US TO THE DOCTOR.
AND TO THE ABOMINATION!
'THE HUMANS MUST NOT REALISE THEY HAVE BEEN ALLOWED TO ESCAPE.'

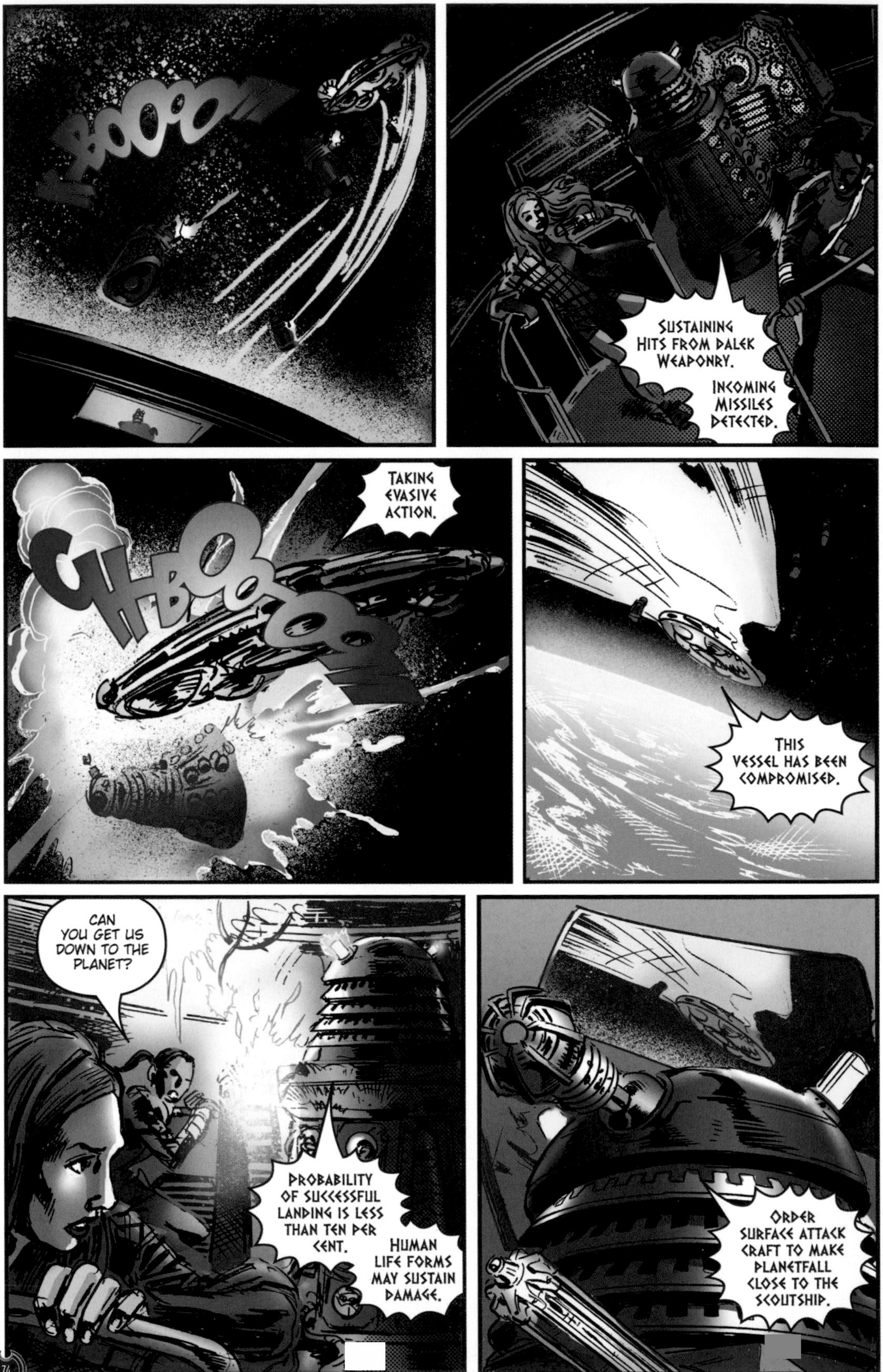
SUSTAINING HITS FROM DALEK WEAPONRY.
INCOMING MISSILES DETECTED.
TAKING EVASIVE ACTION.
THIS VESSEL HAS BEEN COMPROMISED.
CAN YOU GET US DOWN TO THE PLANET?
PROBABILITY OF SUCCESSFUL LANDING IS LESS THAN TEN PER CENT.
HUMAN LIFE FORMS MAY SUSTAIN DAMAGE.
ORDER SURFACE ATTACK CRAFT TO MAKE PLANETFALL CLOSE TO THE SCOUTSHIP.

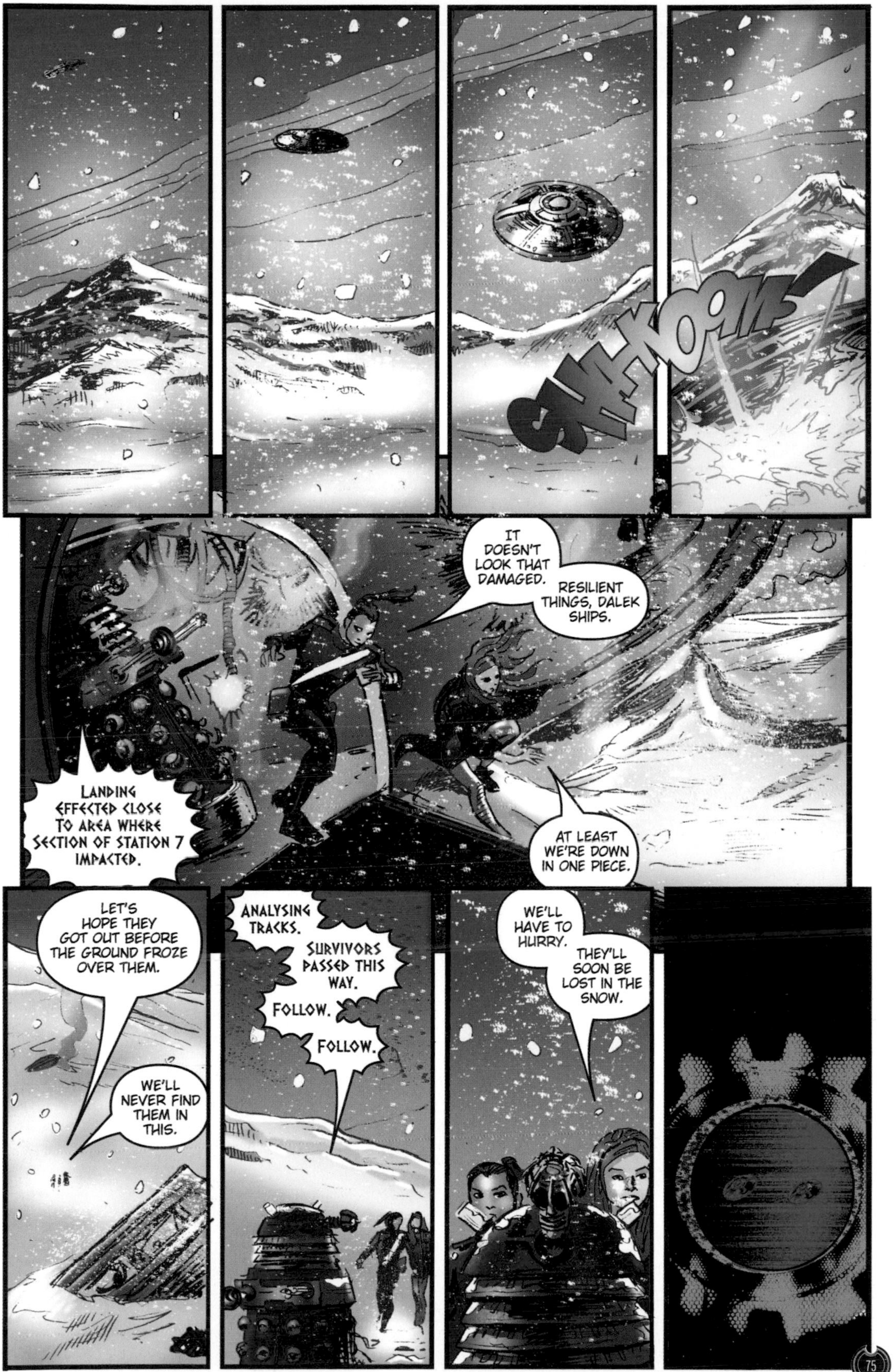
SHH-KOOM!
IT DOESN'T LOOK THAT DAMAGED.
RESILIENT THINGS, DALEK SHIPS.
LANDING EFFECTED CLOSE TO AREA WHERE SECTION OF STATION 7 IMPACTED.
AT LEAST WE'RE DOWN IN ONE PIECE.
LET'S HOPE THEY GOT OUT BEFORE THE GROUND FROZE OVER THEM.
WE'LL NEVER FIND THEM IN THIS.
ANALYSING TRACKS.
SURVIVORS PASSED THIS WAY.
FOLLOW.
FOLLOW.
WE'LL HAVE TO HURRY.
THEY'LL SOON BE LOST IN THE SNOW.

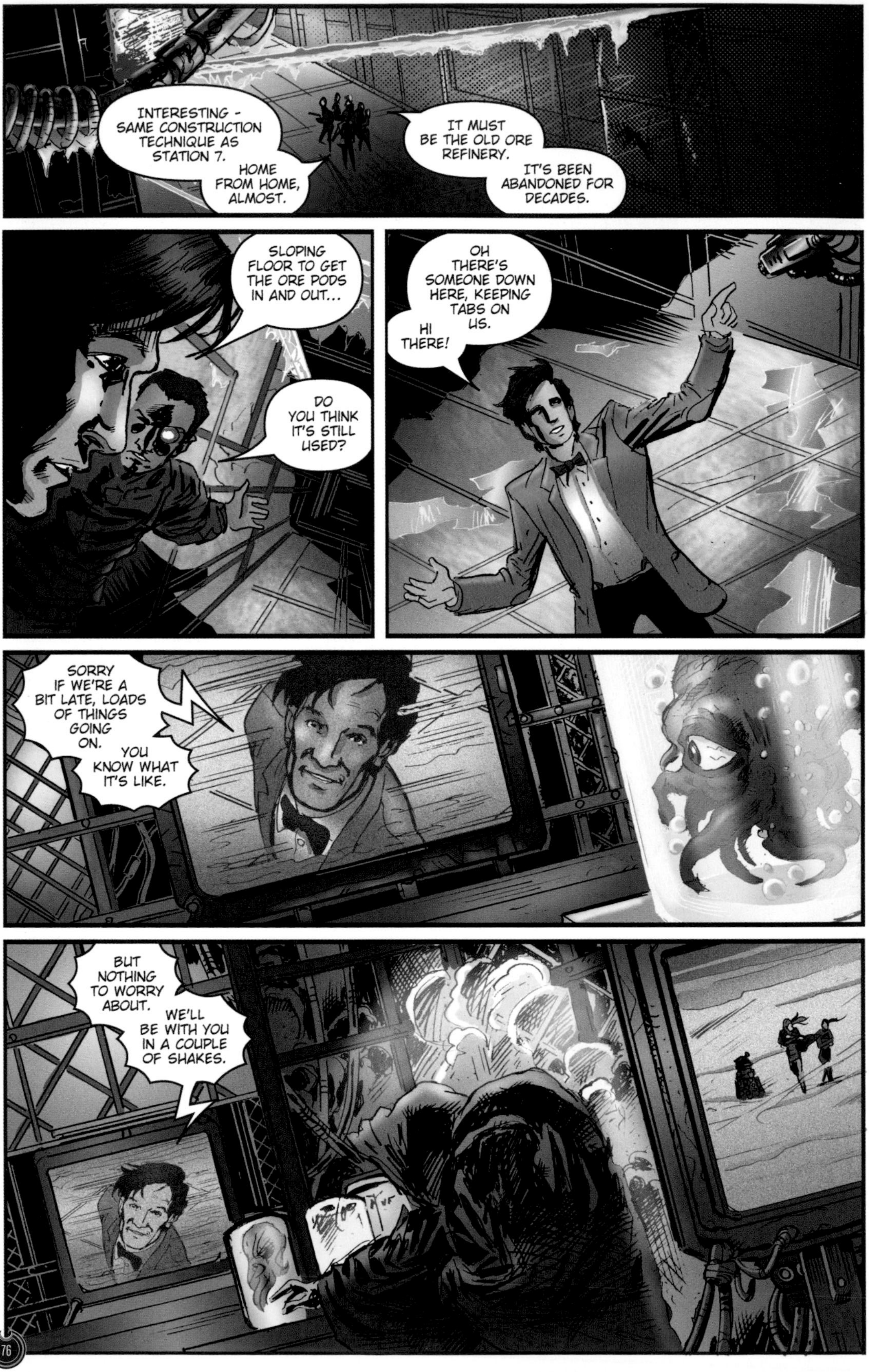
INTERESTING - SAME CONSTRUCTION TECHNIQUE AS STATION 7.
HOME FROM HOME, ALMOST.
IT MUST BE THE OLD ORE REFINERY.
IT'S BEEN ABANDONED FOR DECADES.
SLOPING FLOOR TO GET THE ORE PODS IN AND OUT...
DO YOU THINK IT'S STILL USED?
OH THERE'S SOMEONE DOWN HERE, KEEPING TABS ON US.
HI THERE!
SORRY IF WE'RE A BIT LATE, LOADS OF THINGS GOING ON.
YOU KNOW WHAT IT'S LIKE.
BUT NOTHING TO WORRY ABOUT.
WE'LL BE WITH YOU IN A COUPLE OF SHAKES.

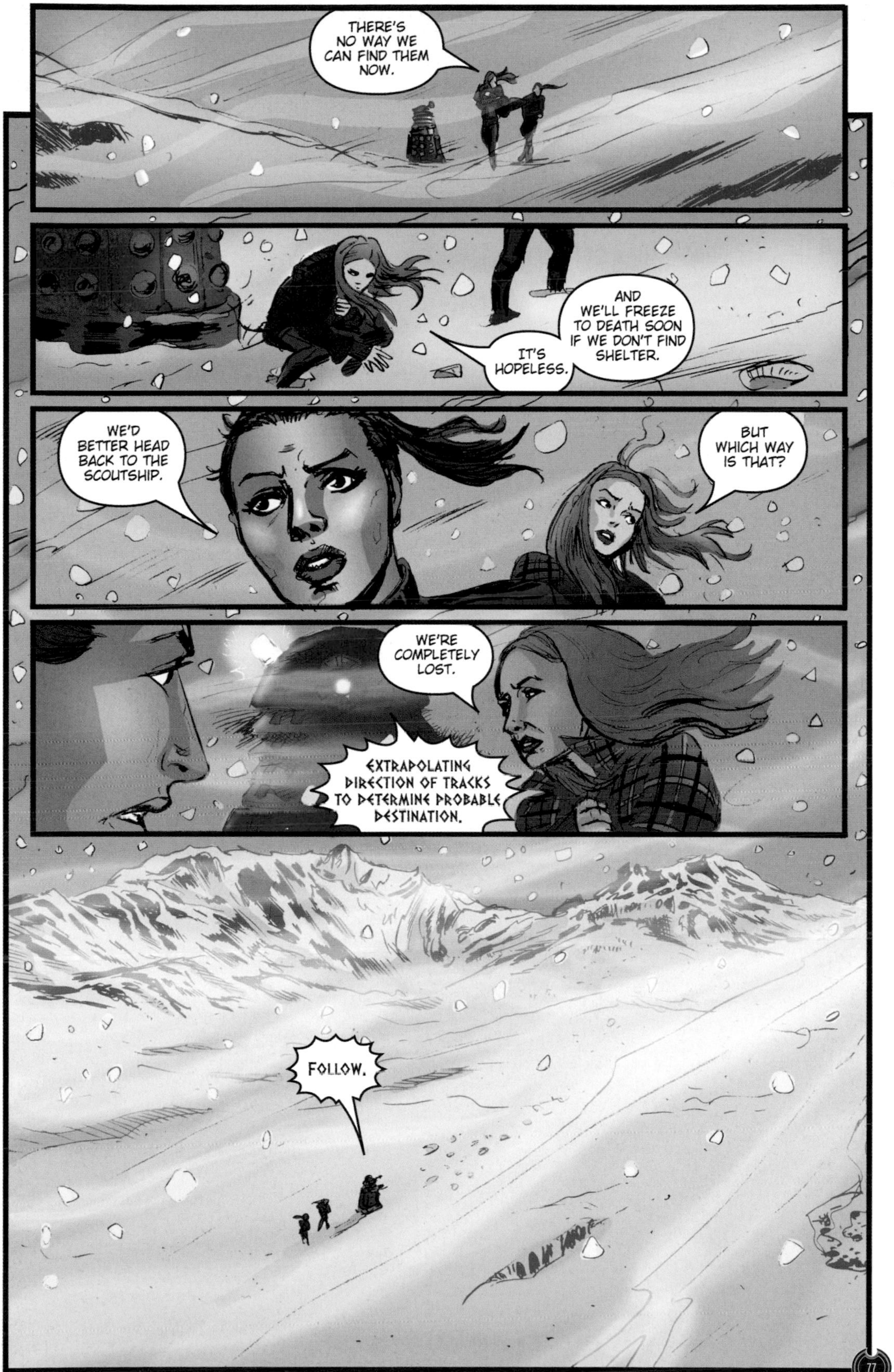
THERE'S NO WAY WE CAN FIND THEM NOW.
IT'S HOPELESS.
AND WE'LL FREEZE TO DEATH SOON IF WE DON'T FIND SHELTER.
WE'D BETTER HEAD BACK TO THE SCOUTSHIP.
BUT WHICH WAY IS THAT?
WE'RE COMPLETELY LOST.
EXTRAPOLATING DIRECTION OF TRACKS TO DETERMINE PROBABLE DESTINATION.
FOLLOW.

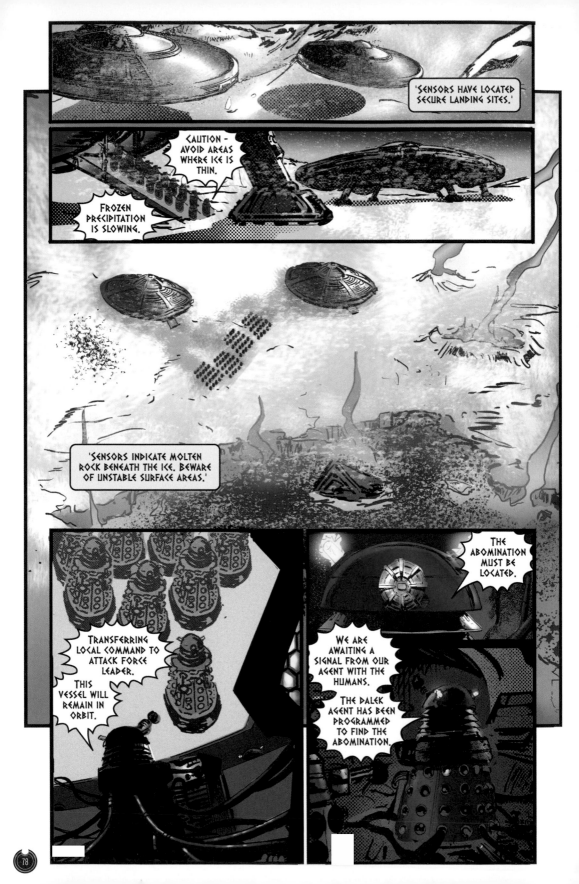

'SENSORS HAVE LOCATED SECURE LANDING SITES.'

CAUTION - AVOID AREAS WHERE ICE IS THIN.

FROZEN PRECIPITATION IS SLOWING.

'SENSORS INDICATE MOLTEN ROCK BENEATH THE ICE. BEWARE OF UNSTABLE SURFACE AREAS.'

TRANSFERRING LOCAL COMMAND TO ATTACK FORCE LEADER.

THIS VESSEL WILL REMAIN IN ORBIT.

THE ABOMINATION MUST BE LOCATED.

WE ARE AWAITING A SIGNAL FROM OUR AGENT WITH THE HUMANS.

THE DALEK AGENT HAS BEEN PROGRAMMED TO FIND THE ABOMINATION.

NO MOVEMENT DETECTED WITHIN THE STATION SECTION.

LIFE-SIGNS DETECTED CLOSE BY - INVESTIGATE.

RECOVER THE SLYTHER. IT MAY BE OF VALUE.

CAUTION, ICE IS THIN AT THIS POINT.

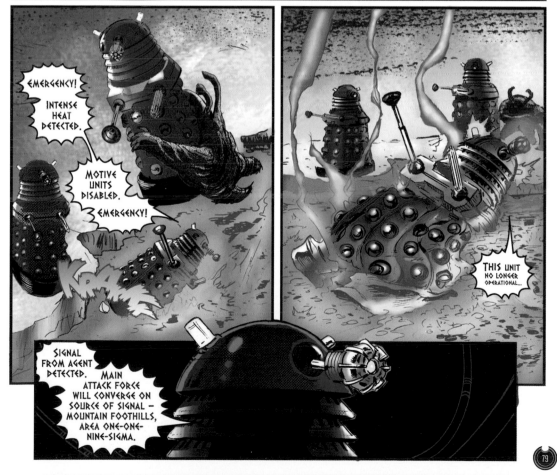

EMERGENCY! INTENSE HEAT DETECTED.

MOTIVE UNITS DISABLED. EMERGENCY!

THIS UNIT NO LONGER OPERATIONAL...

SIGNAL FROM AGENT DETECTED. MAIN ATTACK FORCE WILL CONVERGE ON SOURCE OF SIGNAL - MOUNTAIN FOOTHILLS, AREA ONE-ONE-NINE-SIGMA.

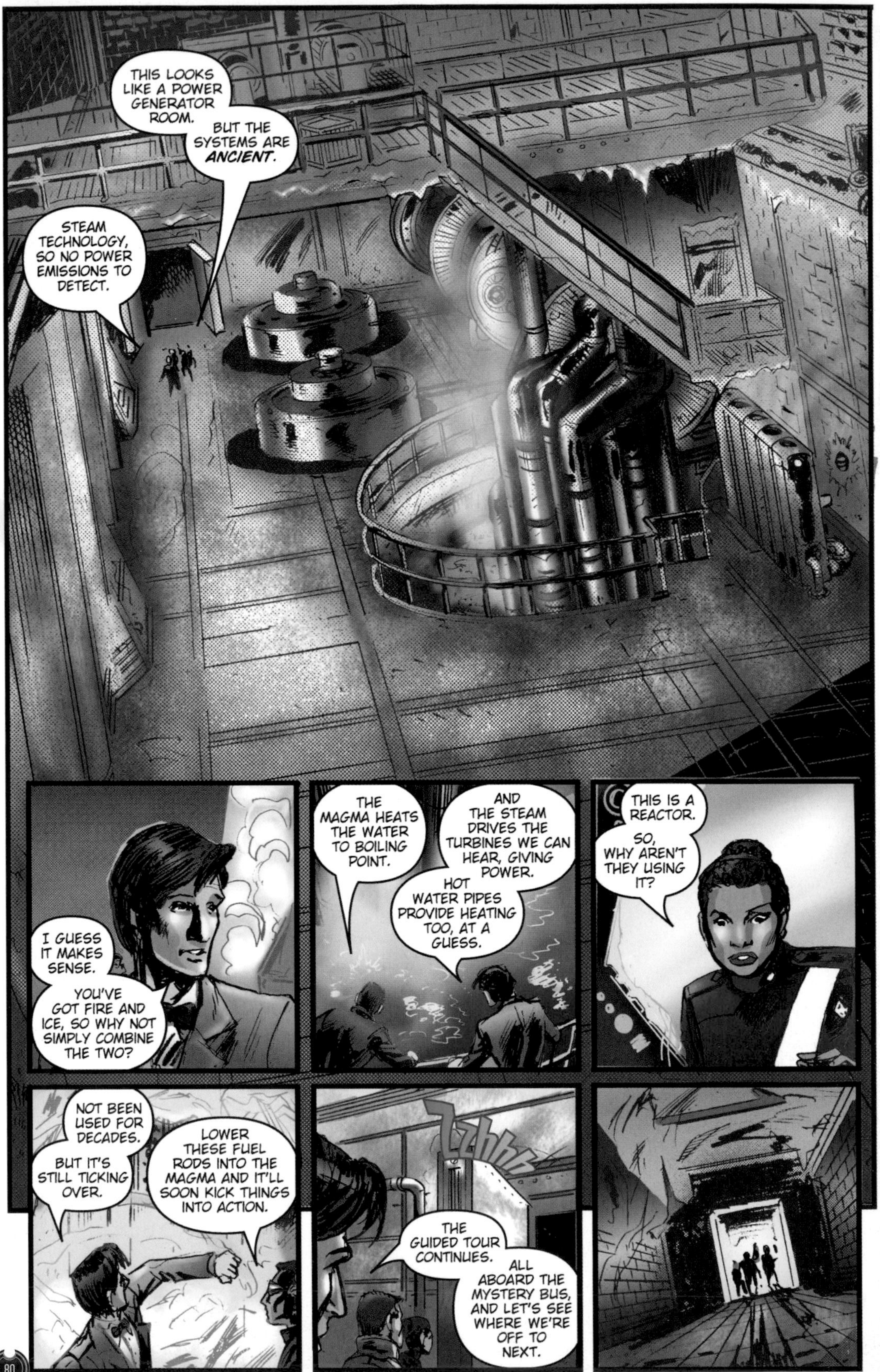
THIS LOOKS LIKE A POWER GENERATOR ROOM.
BUT THE SYSTEMS ARE *ANCIENT*.
STEAM TECHNOLOGY, SO NO POWER EMISSIONS TO DETECT.
I GUESS IT MAKES SENSE.
YOU'VE GOT FIRE AND ICE, SO WHY NOT SIMPLY COMBINE THE TWO?
THE MAGMA HEATS THE WATER TO BOILING POINT.
AND THE STEAM DRIVES THE TURBINES WE CAN HEAR, GIVING POWER.
HOT WATER PIPES PROVIDE HEATING TOO, AT A GUESS.
THIS IS A REACTOR.
SO, WHY AREN'T THEY USING IT?
NOT BEEN USED FOR DECADES.
BUT IT'S STILL TICKING OVER.
LOWER THESE FUEL RODS INTO THE MAGMA AND IT'LL SOON KICK THINGS INTO ACTION.
ZZHHH
THE GUIDED TOUR CONTINUES.
ALL ABOARD THE MYSTERY BUS, AND LET'S SEE WHERE WE'RE OFF TO NEXT.

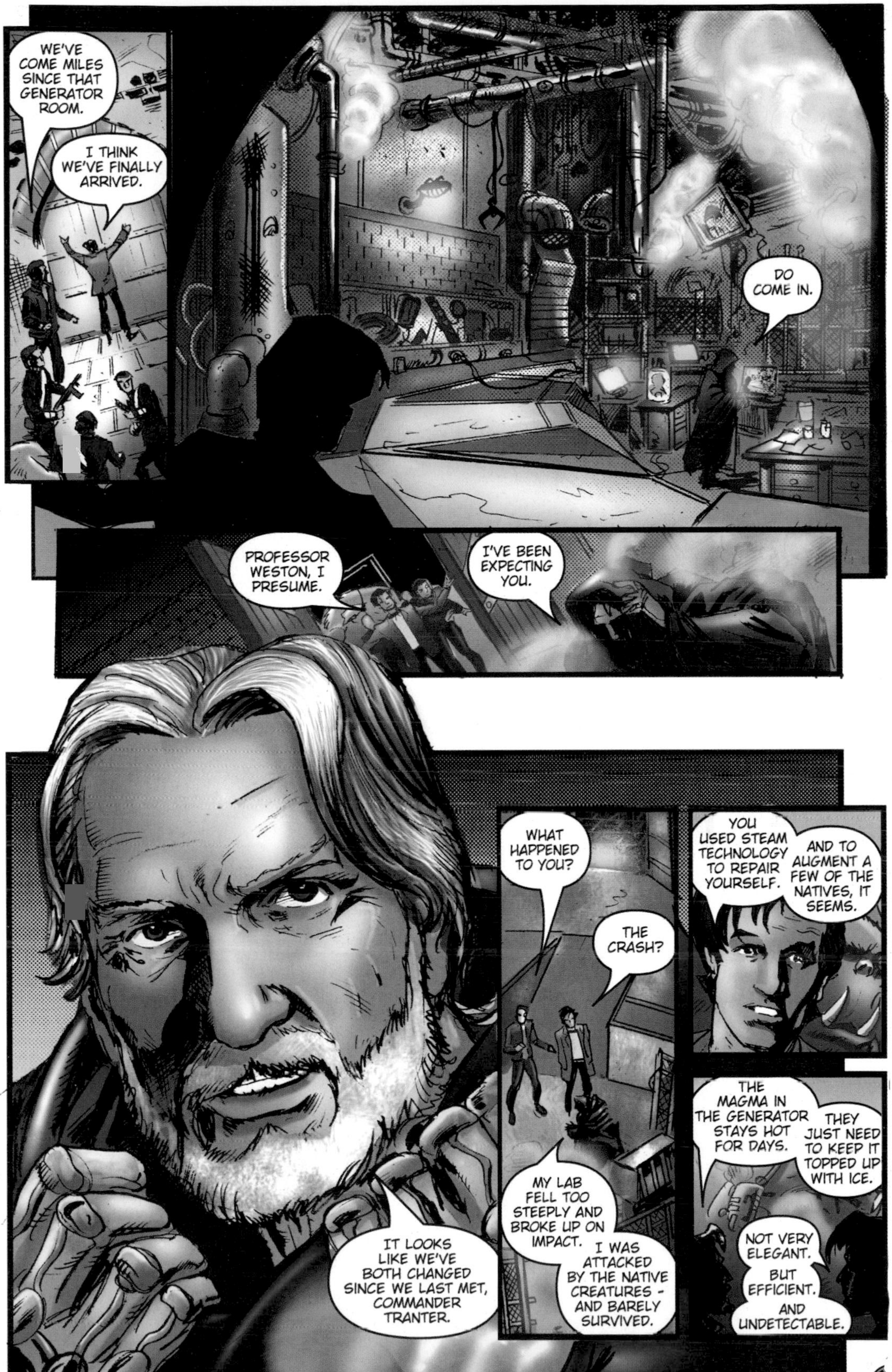

WE'VE COME MILES SINCE THAT GENERATOR ROOM.
I THINK WE'VE FINALLY ARRIVED.
DO COME IN.
PROFESSOR WESTON, I PRESUME.
I'VE BEEN EXPECTING YOU.
IT LOOKS LIKE WE'VE BOTH CHANGED SINCE WE LAST MET, COMMANDER TRANTER.
WHAT HAPPENED TO YOU?
THE CRASH?
MY LAB FELL TOO STEEPLY AND BROKE UP ON IMPACT.
I WAS ATTACKED BY THE NATIVE CREATURES - AND BARELY SURVIVED.
YOU USED STEAM TECHNOLOGY TO REPAIR YOURSELF.
AND TO AUGMENT A FEW OF THE NATIVES, IT SEEMS.
THE MAGMA IN THE GENERATOR STAYS HOT FOR DAYS.
THEY JUST NEED TO KEEP IT TOPPED UP WITH ICE.
NOT VERY ELEGANT.
BUT EFFICIENT.
AND UNDETECTABLE.

AVERN, ISN'T IT?

AND GRIBBIN AND PHELPS. YOU LOOK LIKE YOU'VE HAD A ROUGH TIME.

YOU COULD SAY THAT, PROFESSOR, SIR.

SHOW THEM WHERE THEY CAN GET SOME REST, AND BRING THEM FOOD AND DRINK.

THANK YOU. YOU GOING WITH THEM, DOCTOR?

OH I'LL STAY HERE WITH YOU TWO. THIS IS ALL VERY... INTERESTING.

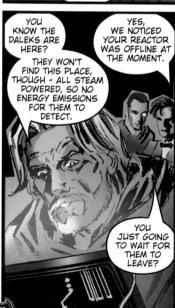

YOU KNOW THE DALEKS ARE HERE?

THEY WON'T FIND THIS PLACE, THOUGH - ALL STEAM POWERED, SO NO ENERGY EMISSIONS FOR THEM TO DETECT.

YES, WE NOTICED YOUR REACTOR WAS OFFLINE AT THE MOMENT.

YOU JUST GOING TO WAIT FOR THEM TO LEAVE?

OH NO, INDEED.

I SHALL SEND MY AUGMENTED CREATURES TO ATTACK THEM.

BUT - HANG ON...

STARTING WITH THESE HUMAN COLLABORATORS.

BUT THAT'S AMY.

AND JAY.

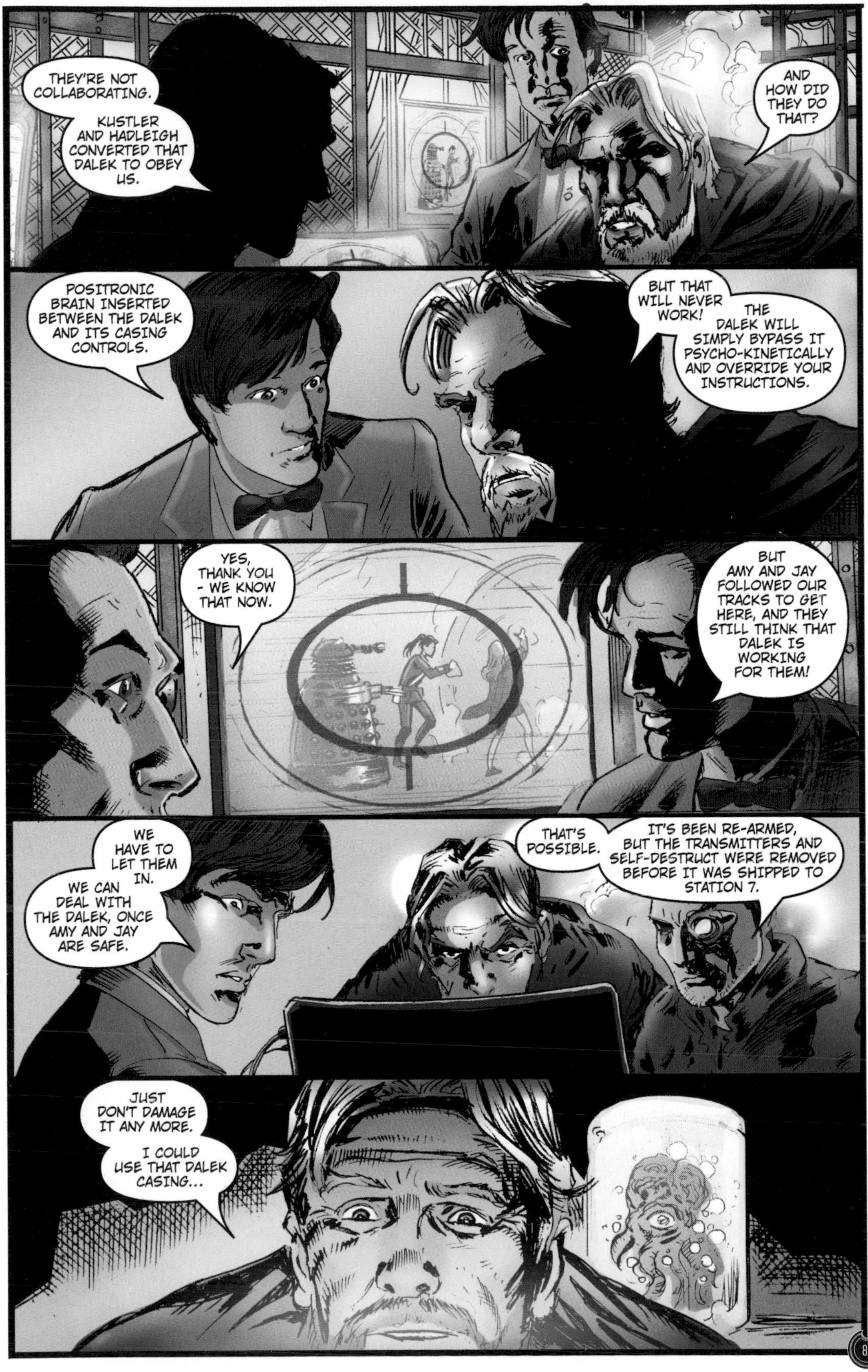
THEY'RE NOT COLLABORATING.
KUSTLER AND HADLEIGH CONVERTED THAT DALEK TO OBEY US.
AND HOW DID THEY DO THAT?
POSITRONIC BRAIN INSERTED BETWEEN THE DALEK AND ITS CASING CONTROLS.
BUT THAT WILL NEVER WORK!
THE DALEK WILL SIMPLY BYPASS IT PSYCHO-KINETICALLY AND OVERRIDE YOUR INSTRUCTIONS.
YES, THANK YOU - WE KNOW THAT NOW.
BUT AMY AND JAY FOLLOWED OUR TRACKS TO GET HERE, AND THEY STILL THINK THAT DALEK IS WORKING FOR THEM!
WE HAVE TO LET THEM IN.
WE CAN DEAL WITH THE DALEK, ONCE AMY AND JAY ARE SAFE.
THAT'S POSSIBLE.
IT'S BEEN RE-ARMED, BUT THE TRANSMITTERS AND SELF-DESTRUCT WERE REMOVED BEFORE IT WAS SHIPPED TO STATION 7.
JUST DON'T DAMAGE IT ANY MORE.
I COULD USE THAT DALEK CASING...

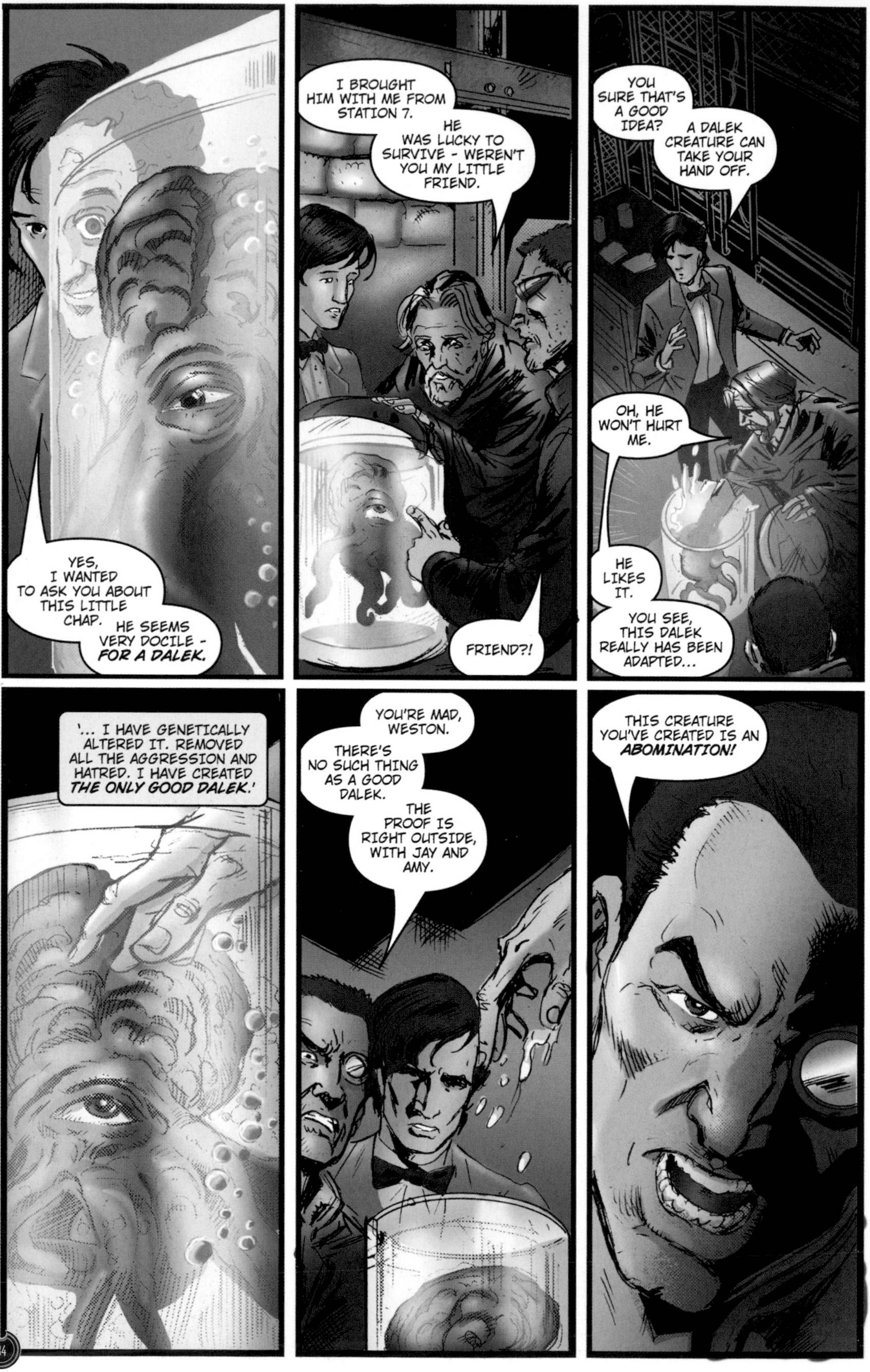

YES, I WANTED TO ASK YOU ABOUT THIS LITTLE CHAP.
HE SEEMS VERY DOCILE - ***FOR A DALEK.***
I BROUGHT HIM WITH ME FROM STATION 7.
HE WAS LUCKY TO SURVIVE - WEREN'T YOU MY LITTLE FRIEND.
FRIEND?!
YOU SURE THAT'S A GOOD IDEA?
A DALEK CREATURE CAN TAKE YOUR HAND OFF.
OH, HE WON'T HURT ME.
HE LIKES IT.
YOU SEE, THIS DALEK REALLY HAS BEEN ADAPTED...
'... I HAVE GENETICALLY ALTERED IT. REMOVED ALL THE AGGRESSION AND HATRED. I HAVE CREATED ***THE ONLY GOOD DALEK.***'
YOU'RE MAD, WESTON.
THERE'S NO SUCH THING AS A GOOD DALEK.
THE PROOF IS RIGHT OUTSIDE, WITH JAY AND AMY.
THIS CREATURE YOU'VE CREATED IS AN ***ABOMINATION!***

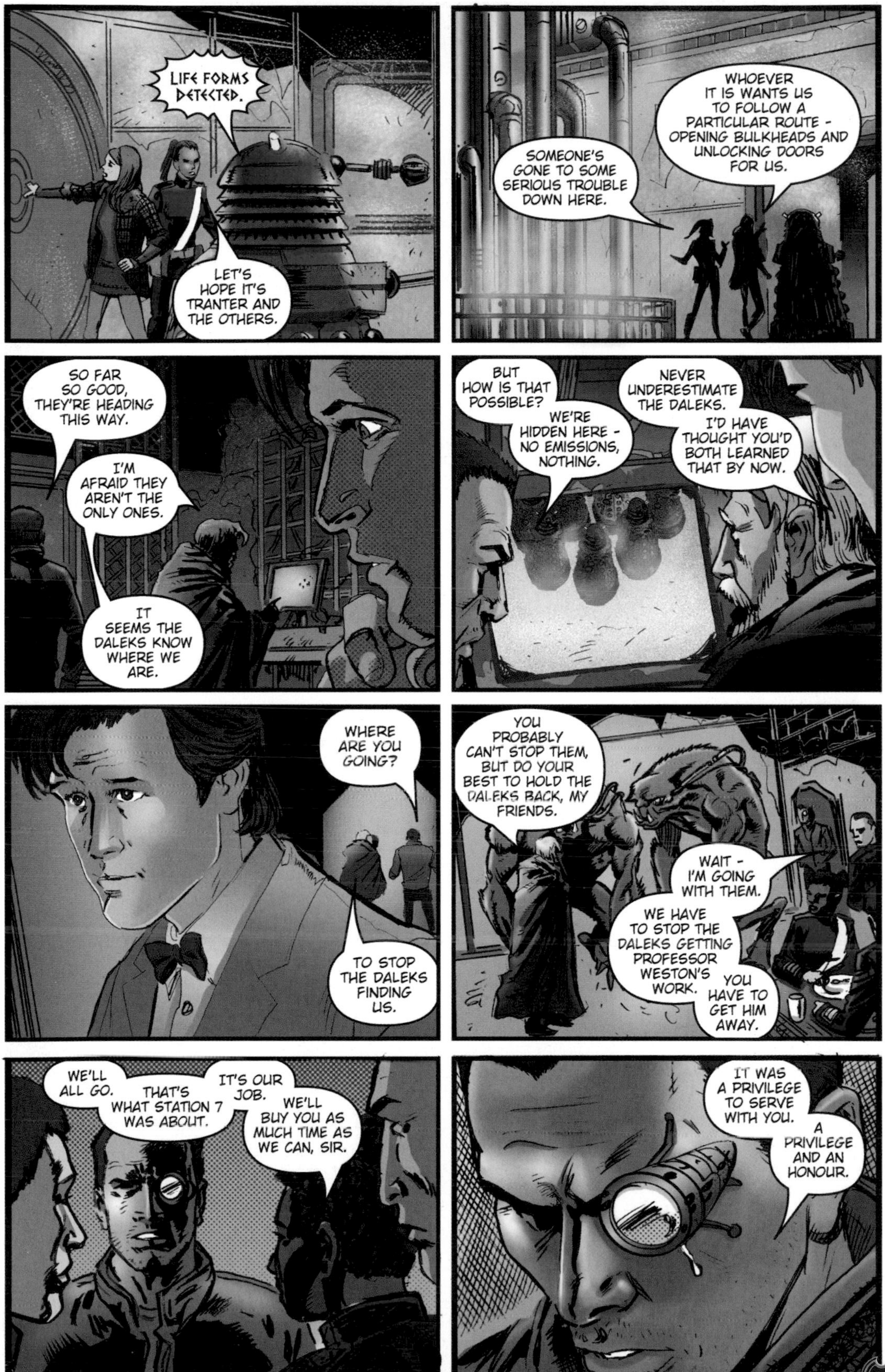
LIFE FORMS DETECTED.
LET'S HOPE IT'S TRANTER AND THE OTHERS.
SOMEONE'S GONE TO SOME SERIOUS TROUBLE DOWN HERE.
WHOEVER IT IS WANTS US TO FOLLOW A PARTICULAR ROUTE - OPENING BULKHEADS AND UNLOCKING DOORS FOR US.
SO FAR SO GOOD, THEY'RE HEADING THIS WAY.
I'M AFRAID THEY AREN'T THE ONLY ONES.
IT SEEMS THE DALEKS KNOW WHERE WE ARE.
BUT HOW IS THAT POSSIBLE?
WE'RE HIDDEN HERE - NO EMISSIONS, NOTHING.
NEVER UNDERESTIMATE THE DALEKS.
I'D HAVE THOUGHT YOU'D BOTH LEARNED THAT BY NOW.
WHERE ARE YOU GOING?
TO STOP THE DALEKS FINDING US.
YOU PROBABLY CAN'T STOP THEM, BUT DO YOUR BEST TO HOLD THE DALEKS BACK, MY FRIENDS.
WAIT - I'M GOING WITH THEM.
WE HAVE TO STOP THE DALEKS GETTING PROFESSOR WESTON'S WORK.
YOU HAVE TO GET HIM AWAY.
WE'LL ALL GO.
THAT'S WHAT STATION 7 WAS ABOUT.
IT'S OUR JOB.
WE'LL BUY YOU AS MUCH TIME AS WE CAN, SIR.
IT WAS A PRIVILEGE TO SERVE WITH YOU.
A PRIVILEGE AND AN HONOUR.

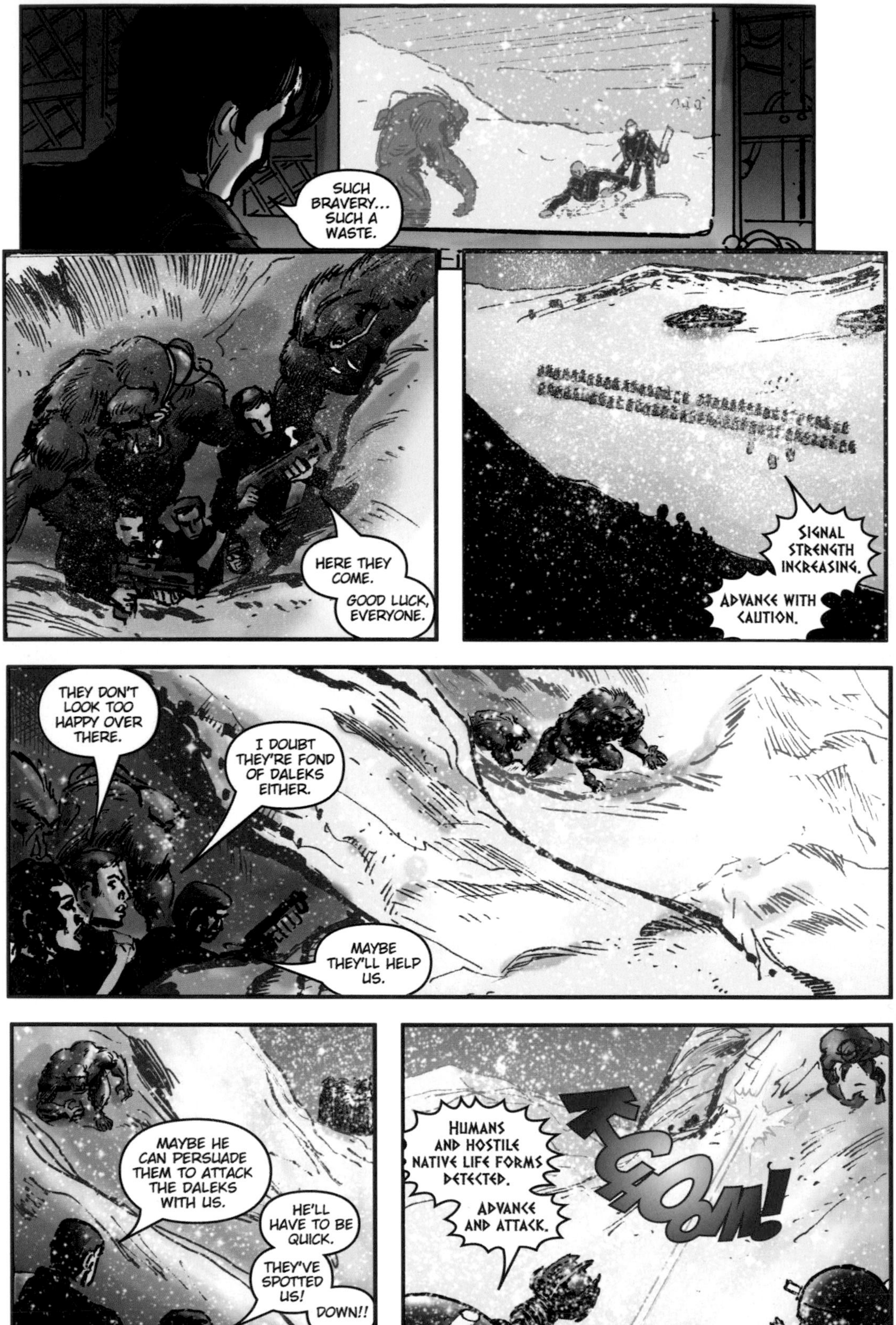

SUCH BRAVERY... SUCH A WASTE.
HERE THEY COME.
GOOD LUCK, EVERYONE.
SIGNAL STRENGTH INCREASING.
ADVANCE WITH CAUTION.
THEY DON'T LOOK TOO HAPPY OVER THERE.
I DOUBT THEY'RE FOND OF DALEKS EITHER.
MAYBE THEY'LL HELP US.
MAYBE HE CAN PERSUADE THEM TO ATTACK THE DALEKS WITH US.
HE'LL HAVE TO BE QUICK.
THEY'VE SPOTTED US!
DOWN!!
HUMANS AND HOSTILE NATIVE LIFE FORMS DETECTED.
ADVANCE AND ATTACK.
KCHOOM!

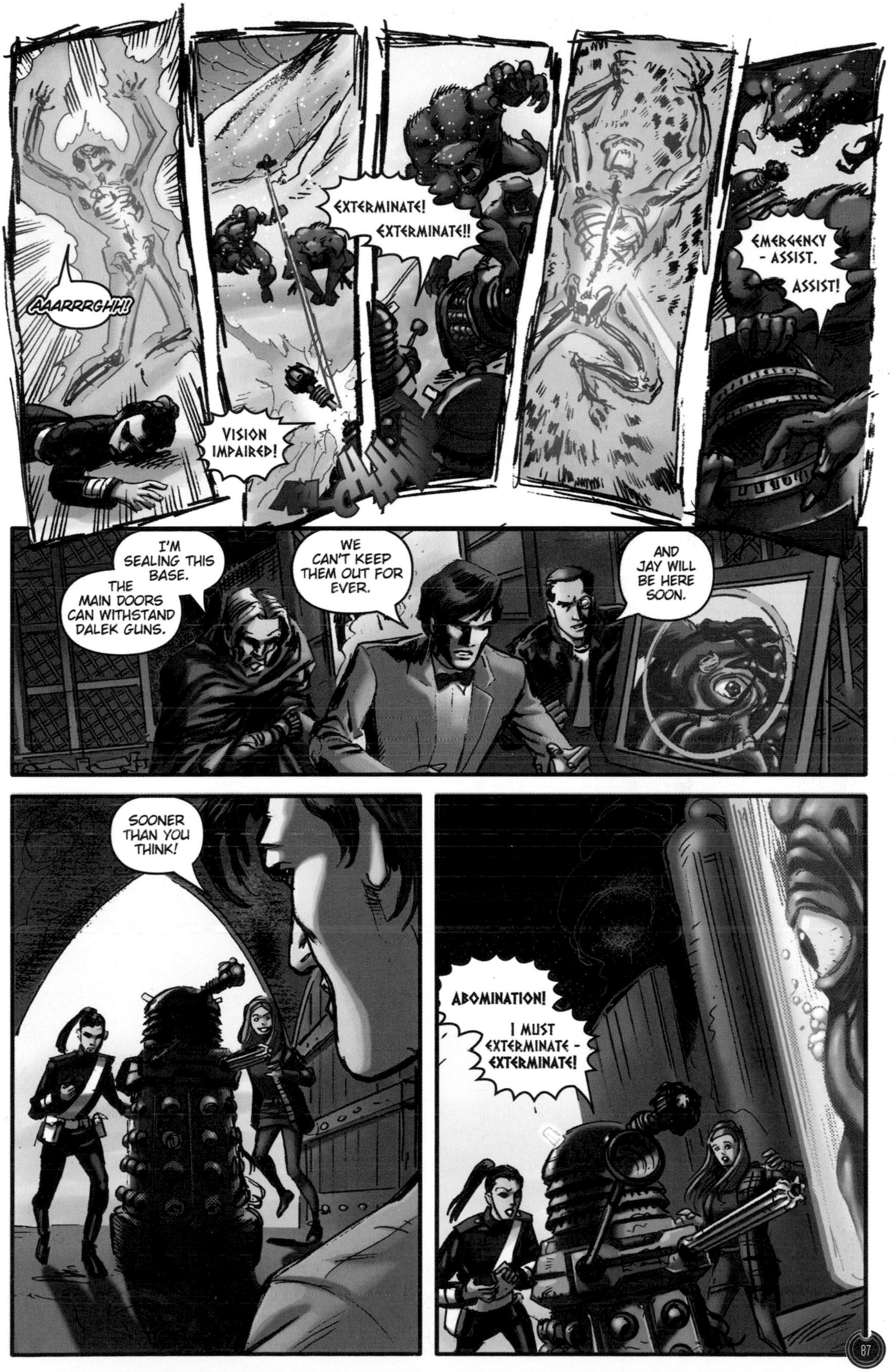

AAARRRGHH!
EXTERMINATE!
EXTERMINATE!!
VISION IMPAIRED!
EMERGENCY - ASSIST.
ASSIST!
I'M SEALING THIS BASE.
THE MAIN DOORS CAN WITHSTAND DALEK GUNS.
WE CAN'T KEEP THEM OUT FOR EVER.
AND JAY WILL BE HERE SOON.
SOONER THAN YOU THINK!
ABOMINATION!
I MUST EXTERMINATE - EXTERMINATE!

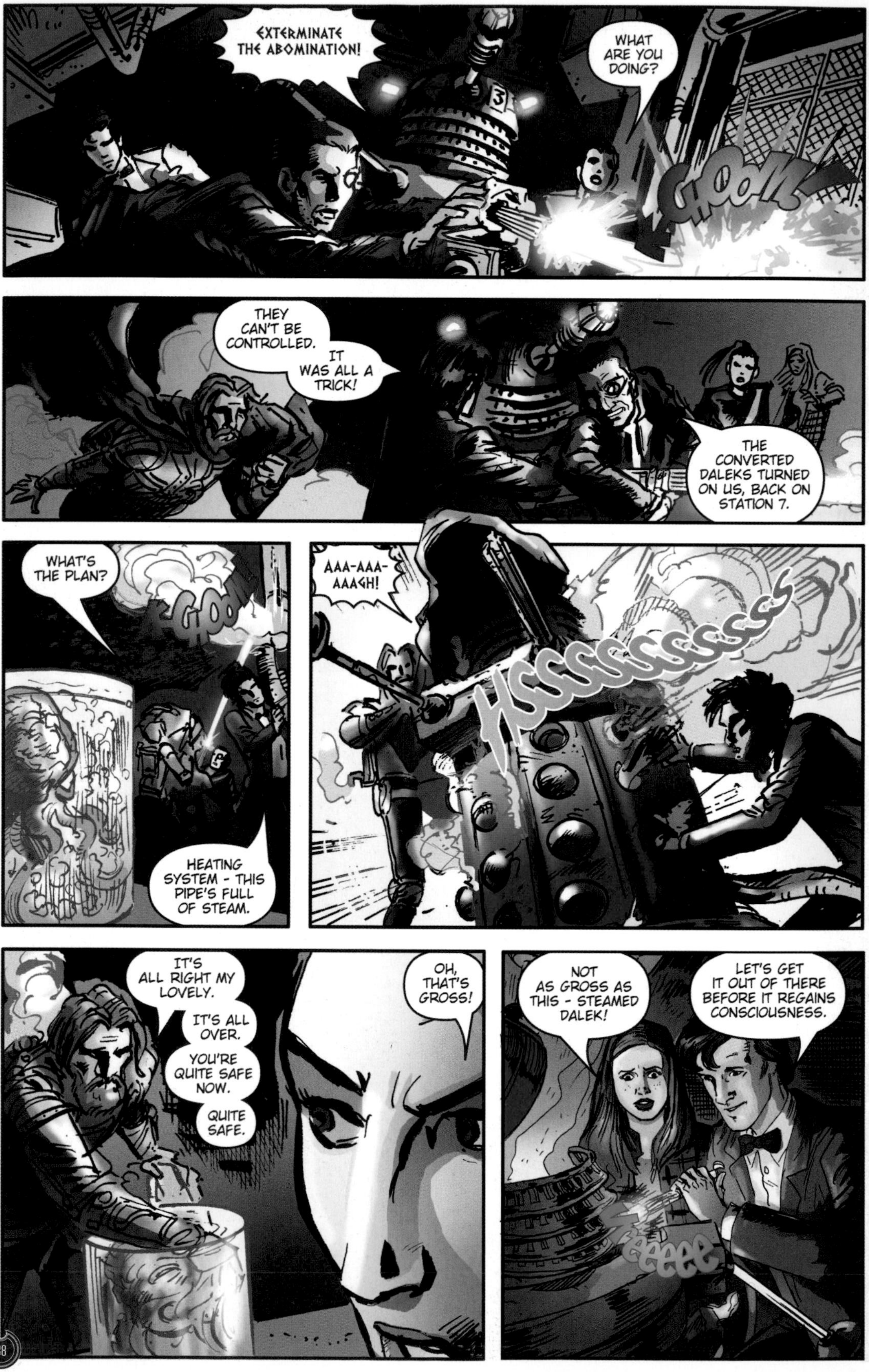
EXTERMINATE THE ABOMINATION!
WHAT ARE YOU DOING?
GHOOM
THEY CAN'T BE CONTROLLED.
IT WAS ALL A TRICK!
THE CONVERTED DALEKS TURNED ON US, BACK ON STATION 7.
WHAT'S THE PLAN?
HEATING SYSTEM - THIS PIPE'S FULL OF STEAM.
AAA-AAA-AAAGH!
HSSSSSSSSSSS
IT'S ALL RIGHT MY LOVELY.
IT'S ALL OVER.
YOU'RE QUITE SAFE NOW.
QUITE SAFE.
OH, THAT'S GROSS!
NOT AS GROSS AS THIS - STEAMED DALEK!
LET'S GET IT OUT OF THERE BEFORE IT REGAINS CONSCIOUSNESS.
zeeeee

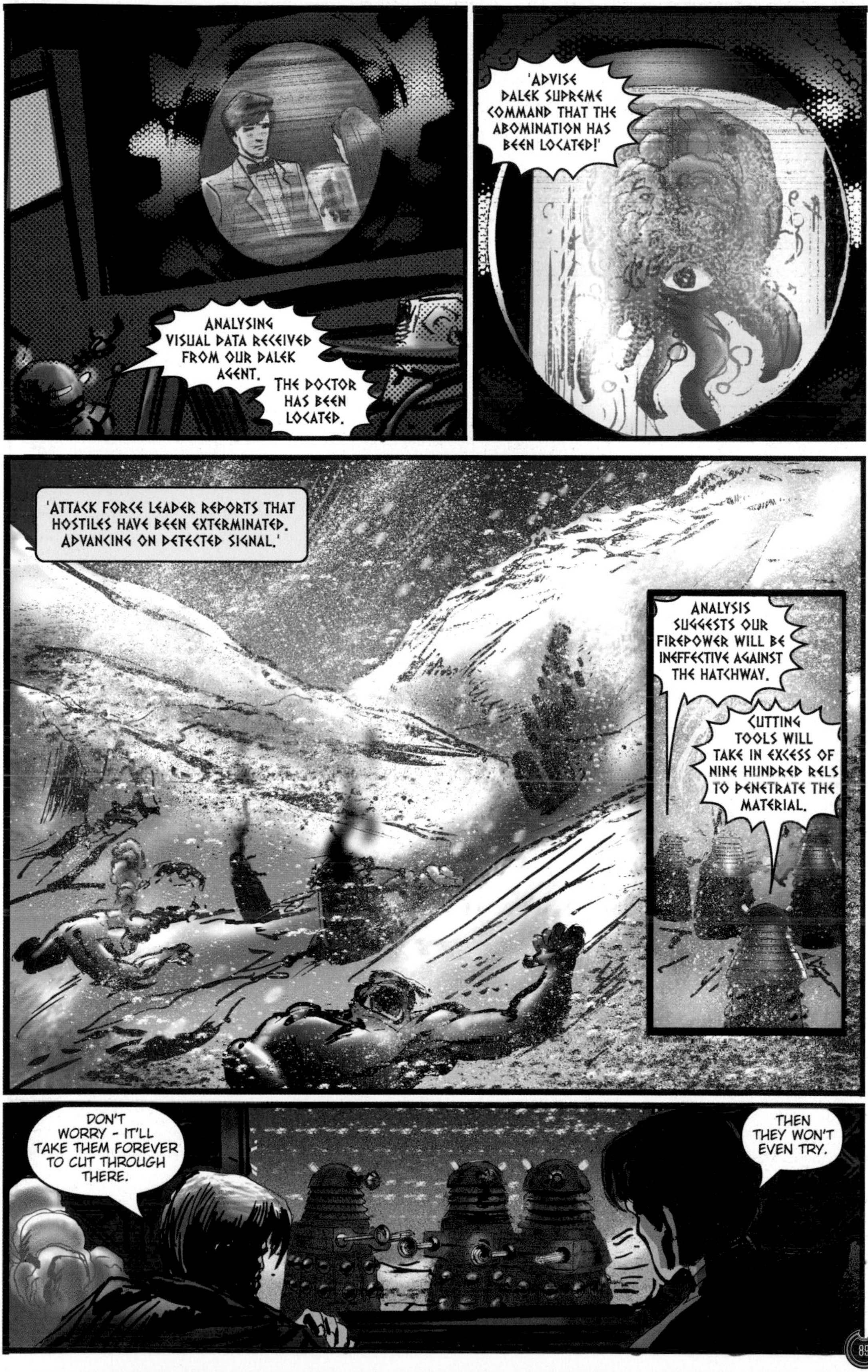
ANALYSING VISUAL DATA RECEIVED FROM OUR DALEK AGENT.
THE DOCTOR HAS BEEN LOCATED.
'ADVISE DALEK SUPREME COMMAND THAT THE ABOMINATION HAS BEEN LOCATED!'
'ATTACK FORCE LEADER REPORTS THAT HOSTILES HAVE BEEN EXTERMINATED. ADVANCING ON DETECTED SIGNAL.'
ANALYSIS SUGGESTS OUR FIREPOWER WILL BE INEFFECTIVE AGAINST THE HATCHWAY.
CUTTING TOOLS WILL TAKE IN EXCESS OF NINE HUNDRED RELS TO PENETRATE THE MATERIAL.
DON'T WORRY - IT'LL TAKE THEM FOREVER TO CUT THROUGH THERE.
THEN THEY WON'T EVEN TRY.

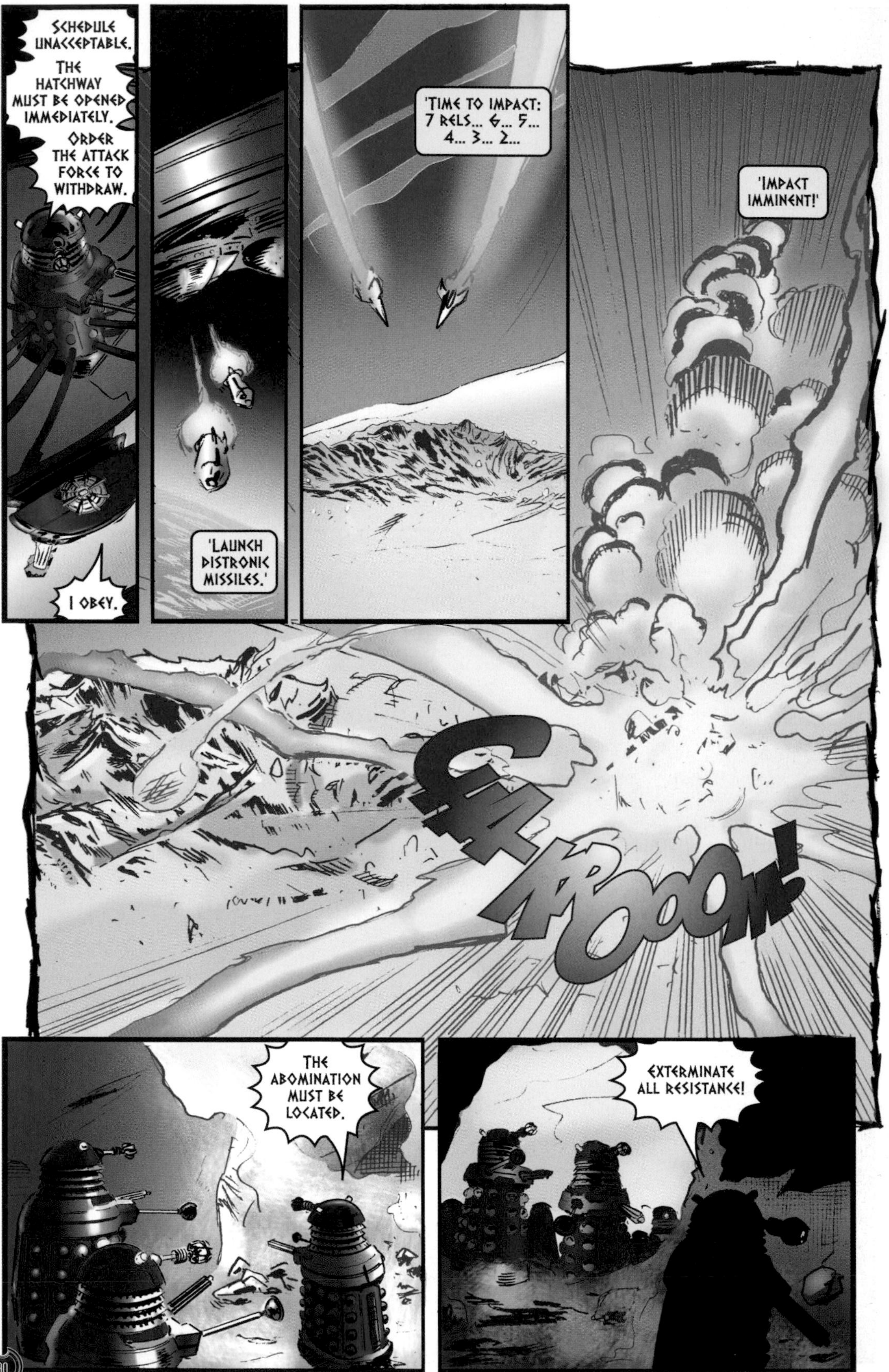
SCHEDULE UNACCEPTABLE.
THE HATCHWAY MUST BE OPENED IMMEDIATELY.
ORDER THE ATTACK FORCE TO WITHDRAW.
I OBEY.
'LAUNCH DISTRONIC MISSILES.'
'TIME TO IMPACT: 7 RELS... 6... 5... 4... 3... 2...
'IMPACT IMMINENT!'
CHKROOOM!
THE ABOMINATION MUST BE LOCATED.
EXTERMINATE ALL RESISTANCE!

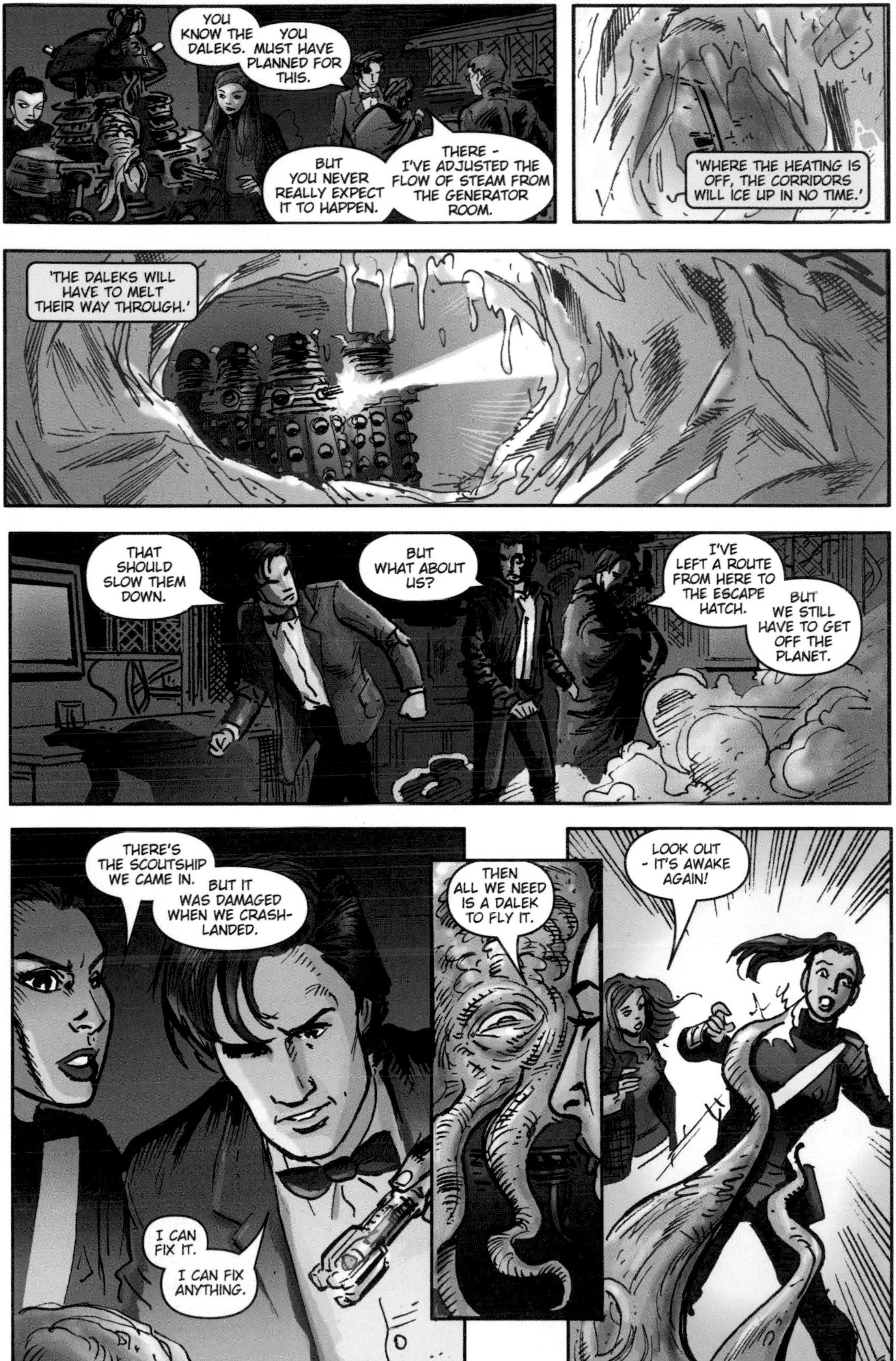
YOU KNOW THE DALEKS.
YOU MUST HAVE PLANNED FOR THIS.
BUT YOU NEVER REALLY EXPECT IT TO HAPPEN.
THERE - I'VE ADJUSTED THE FLOW OF STEAM FROM THE GENERATOR ROOM.
'WHERE THE HEATING IS OFF, THE CORRIDORS WILL ICE UP IN NO TIME.'
'THE DALEKS WILL HAVE TO MELT THEIR WAY THROUGH.'
THAT SHOULD SLOW THEM DOWN.
BUT WHAT ABOUT US?
I'VE LEFT A ROUTE FROM HERE TO THE ESCAPE HATCH.
BUT WE STILL HAVE TO GET OFF THE PLANET.
THERE'S THE SCOUTSHIP WE CAME IN.
BUT IT WAS DAMAGED WHEN WE CRASH-LANDED.
I CAN FIX IT.
I CAN FIX ANYTHING.
THEN ALL WE NEED IS A DALEK TO FLY IT.
LOOK OUT - IT'S AWAKE AGAIN!

IT'S ALL RIGHT — WE'VE GOT IT!

IF I CAN JUST DETACH IT FROM THE CASING...

I'M OK — JUST BRUISED, I THINK.

WHAT DO WE DO WITH IT WHEN WE'VE GOT IT OUT?

WE'RE LUCKY IT'S STILL GROGGY!

QUICKLY, PUT IT IN HERE.

WILL THAT HOLD IT?

IT HELD THE OTHER ONE, BEFORE I MODIFIED IT. NASTY LITTLE FIGHTER, *HE* WAS.

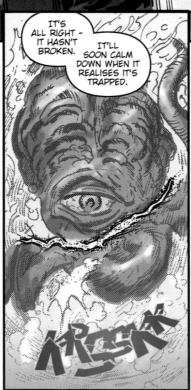

IT'S ALL RIGHT — IT HASN'T BROKEN.

IT'LL SOON CALM DOWN WHEN IT REALISES IT'S TRAPPED.

PUT YOUR HAND IN *THERE* AND YOU'LL NEVER GET IT OUT AGAIN!

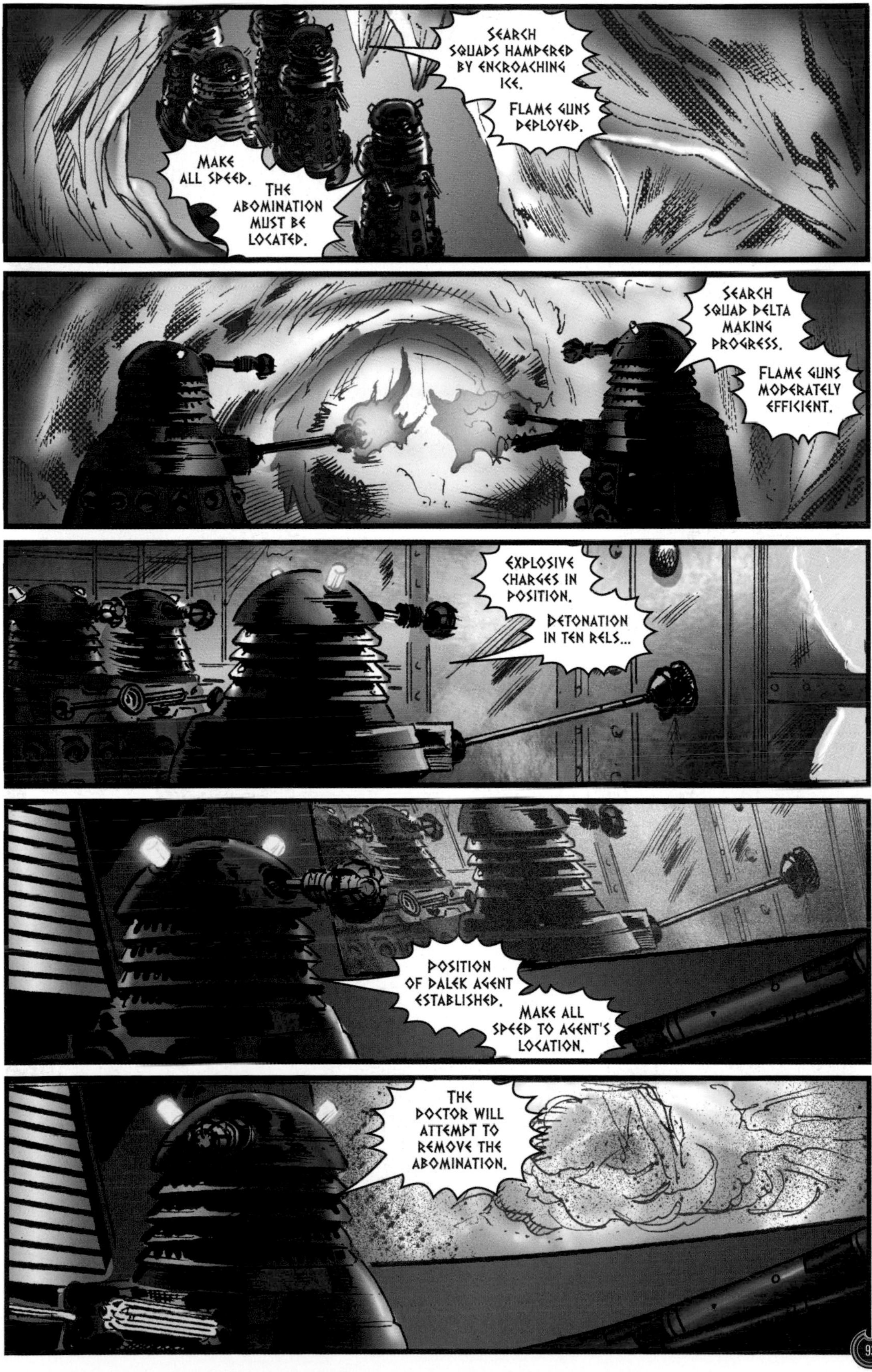
SEARCH SQUADS HAMPERED BY ENCROACHING ICE.
FLAME GUNS DEPLOYED.
MAKE ALL SPEED.
THE ABOMINATION MUST BE LOCATED.
SEARCH SQUAD DELTA MAKING PROGRESS.
FLAME GUNS MODERATELY EFFICIENT.
EXPLOSIVE CHARGES IN POSITION.
DETONATION IN TEN RELS...
POSITION OF DALEK AGENT ESTABLISHED.
MAKE ALL SPEED TO AGENT'S LOCATION.
THE DOCTOR WILL ATTEMPT TO REMOVE THE ABOMINATION.

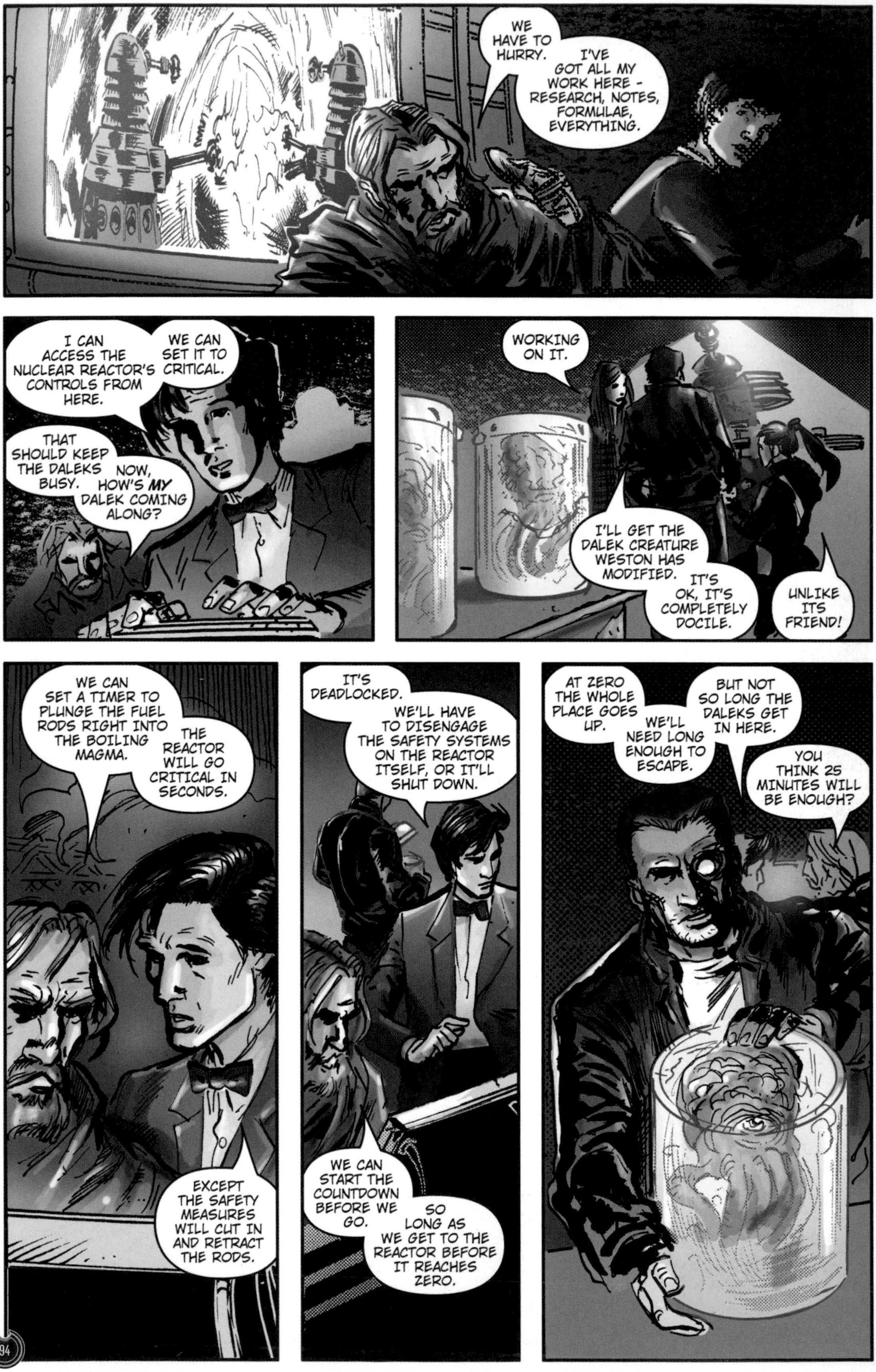
WE HAVE TO HURRY.
I'VE GOT ALL MY WORK HERE - RESEARCH, NOTES, FORMULAE, EVERYTHING.
I CAN ACCESS THE NUCLEAR REACTOR'S CONTROLS FROM HERE.
WE CAN SET IT TO CRITICAL.
THAT SHOULD KEEP THE DALEKS BUSY.
NOW, HOW'S *MY* DALEK COMING ALONG?
WORKING ON IT.
I'LL GET THE DALEK CREATURE WESTON HAS MODIFIED.
IT'S OK, IT'S COMPLETELY DOCILE.
UNLIKE ITS FRIEND!
WE CAN SET A TIMER TO PLUNGE THE FUEL RODS RIGHT INTO THE BOILING MAGMA.
THE REACTOR WILL GO CRITICAL IN SECONDS.
EXCEPT THE SAFETY MEASURES WILL CUT IN AND RETRACT THE RODS.
IT'S DEADLOCKED.
WE'LL HAVE TO DISENGAGE THE SAFETY SYSTEMS ON THE REACTOR ITSELF, OR IT'LL SHUT DOWN.
WE CAN START THE COUNTDOWN BEFORE WE GO.
SO LONG AS WE GET TO THE REACTOR BEFORE IT REACHES ZERO.
AT ZERO THE WHOLE PLACE GOES UP.
WE'LL NEED LONG ENOUGH TO ESCAPE.
BUT NOT SO LONG THE DALEKS GET IN HERE.
YOU THINK 25 MINUTES WILL BE ENOUGH?

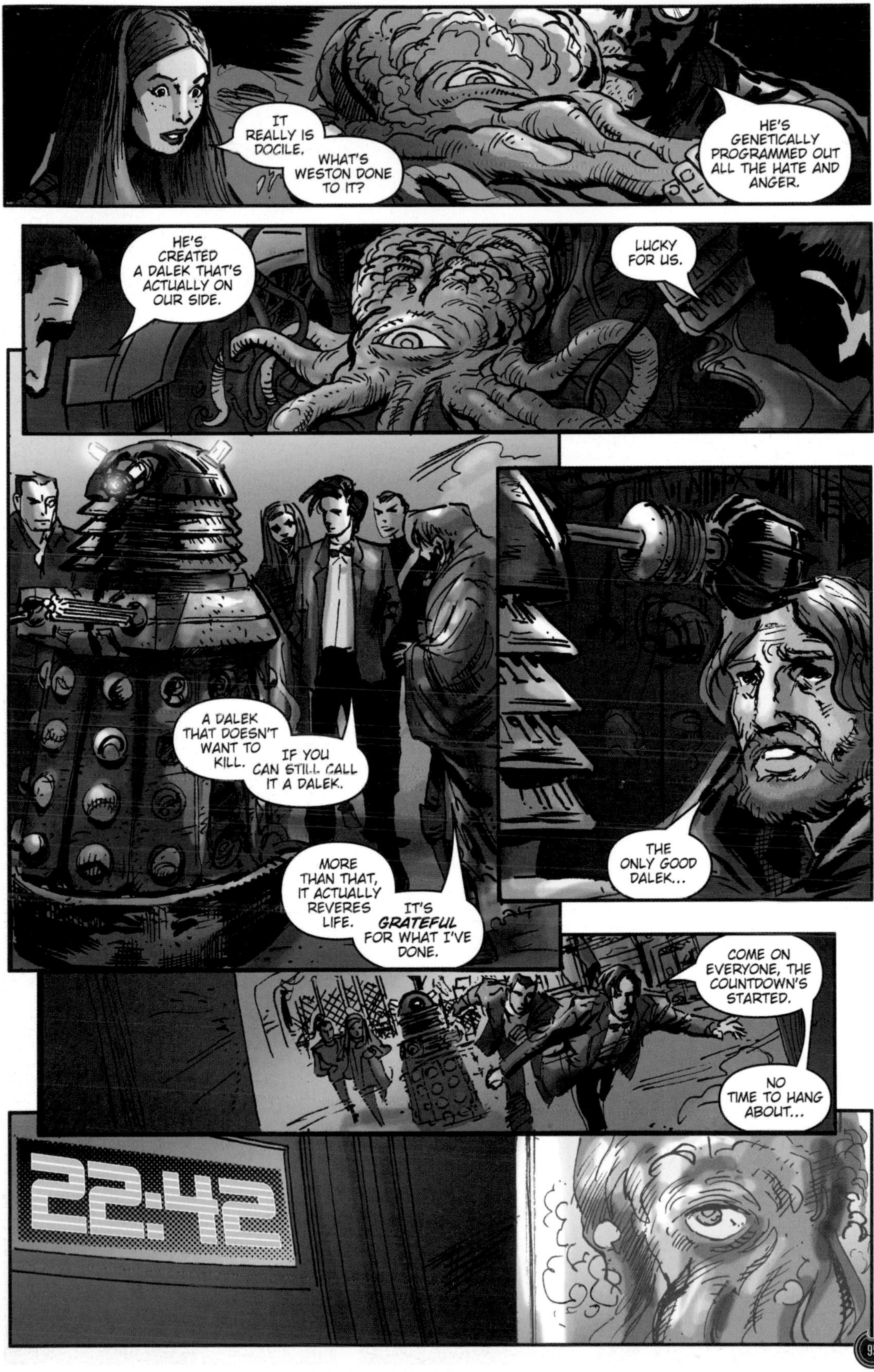
IT REALLY IS DOCILE.
WHAT'S WESTON DONE TO IT?
HE'S GENETICALLY PROGRAMMED OUT ALL THE HATE AND ANGER.
HE'S CREATED A DALEK THAT'S ACTUALLY ON OUR SIDE.
LUCKY FOR US.
A DALEK THAT DOESN'T WANT TO KILL.
IF YOU CAN STILL CALL IT A DALEK.
MORE THAN THAT, IT ACTUALLY REVERES LIFE.
IT'S GRATEFUL FOR WHAT I'VE DONE.
THE ONLY GOOD DALEK...
COME ON EVERYONE, THE COUNTDOWN'S STARTED.
NO TIME TO HANG ABOUT...
22:42

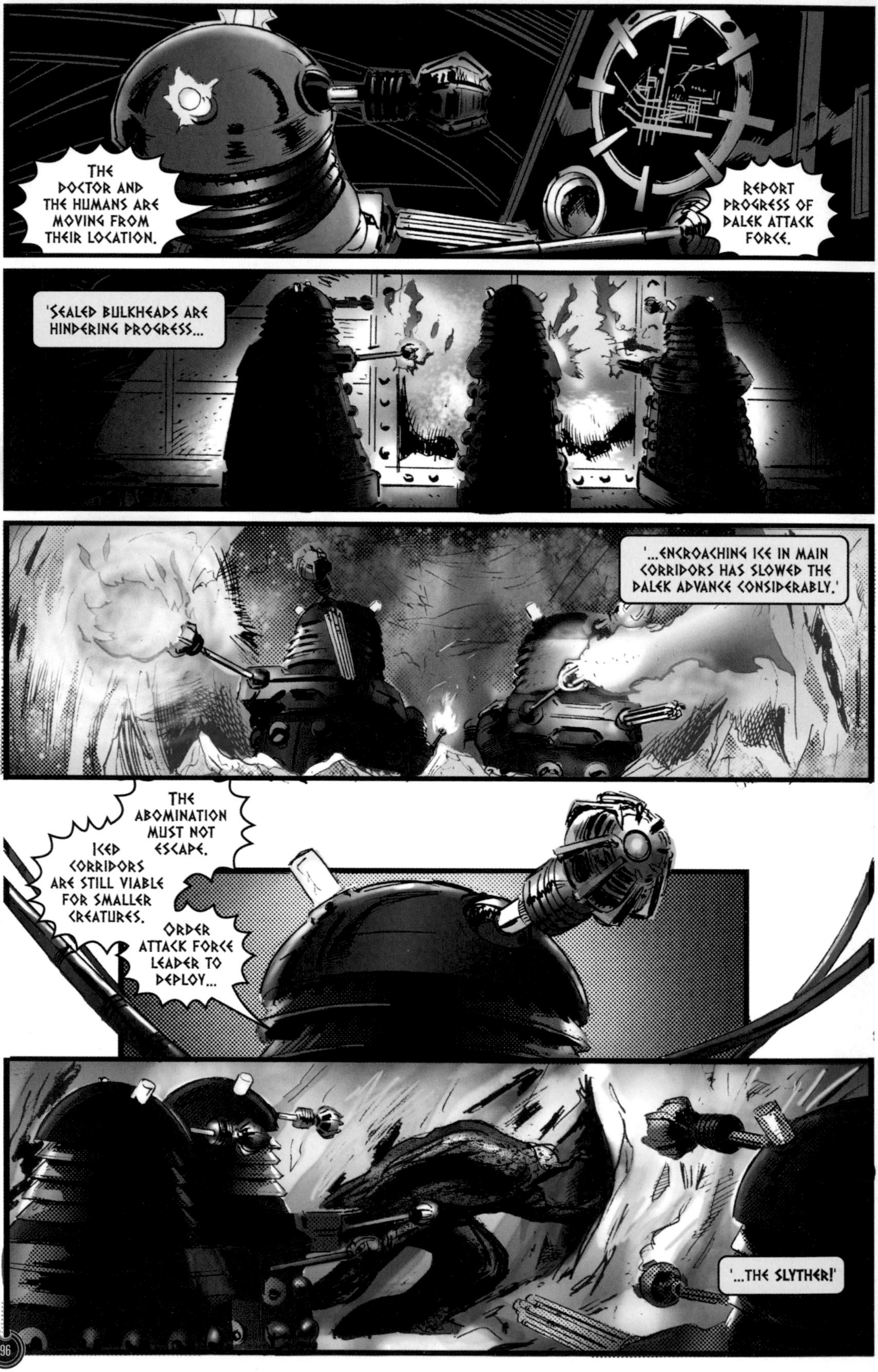
THE DOCTOR AND THE HUMANS ARE MOVING FROM THEIR LOCATION.
REPORT PROGRESS OF DALEK ATTACK FORCE.
'SEALED BULKHEADS ARE HINDERING PROGRESS...
'...ENCROACHING ICE IN MAIN CORRIDORS HAS SLOWED THE DALEK ADVANCE CONSIDERABLY.'
THE ABOMINATION MUST NOT ESCAPE.
ICED CORRIDORS ARE STILL VIABLE FOR SMALLER CREATURES.
ORDER ATTACK FORCE LEADER TO DEPLOY...
'...THE SLYTHER!'

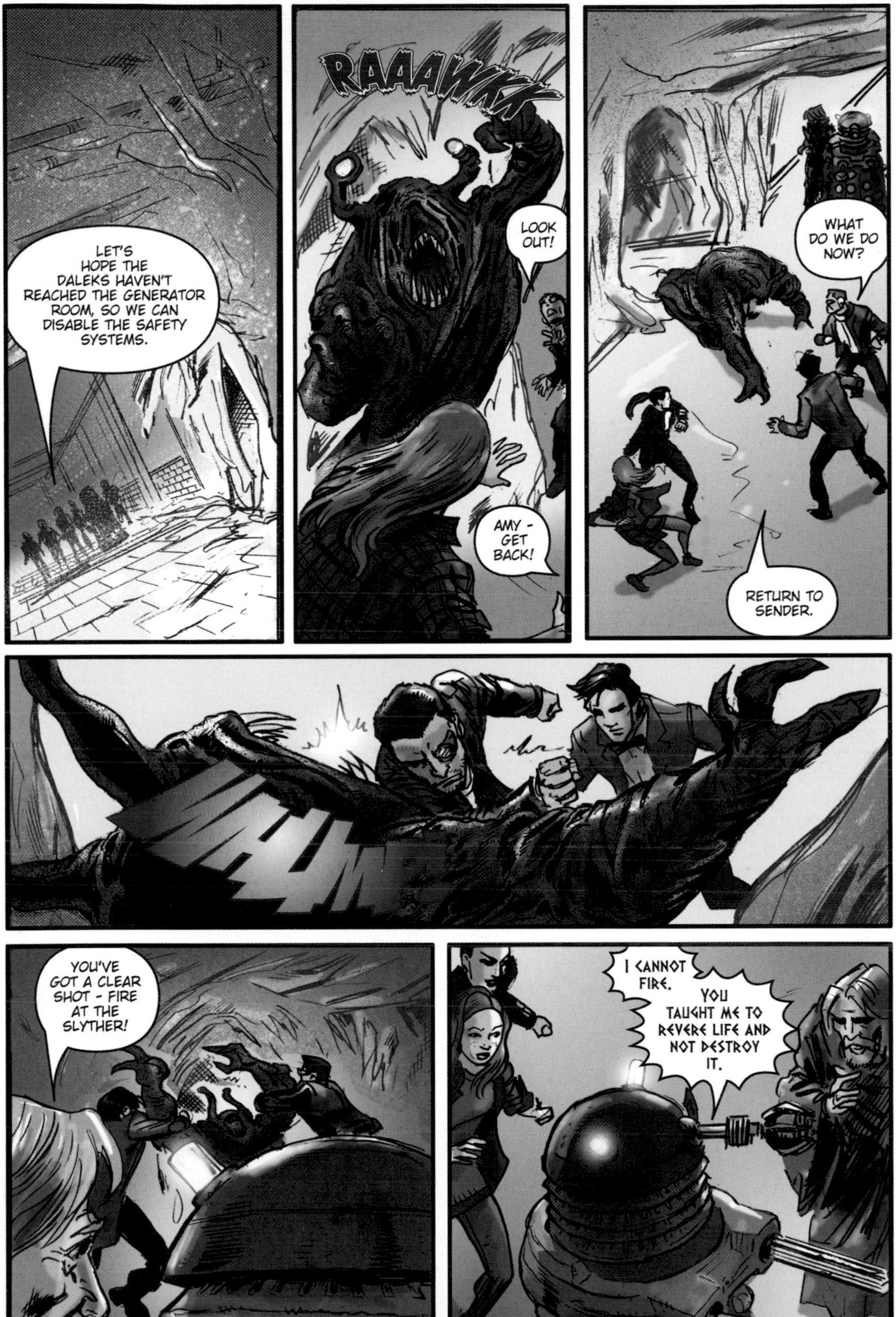
LET'S HOPE THE DALEKS HAVEN'T REACHED THE GENERATOR ROOM, SO WE CAN DISABLE THE SAFETY SYSTEMS.
RAAAWKKK
LOOK OUT!
AMY - GET BACK!
WHAT DO WE DO NOW?
RETURN TO SENDER.
YOU'VE GOT A CLEAR SHOT - FIRE AT THE SLYTHER!
I CANNOT FIRE.
YOU TAUGHT ME TO REVERE LIFE AND NOT DESTROY IT.

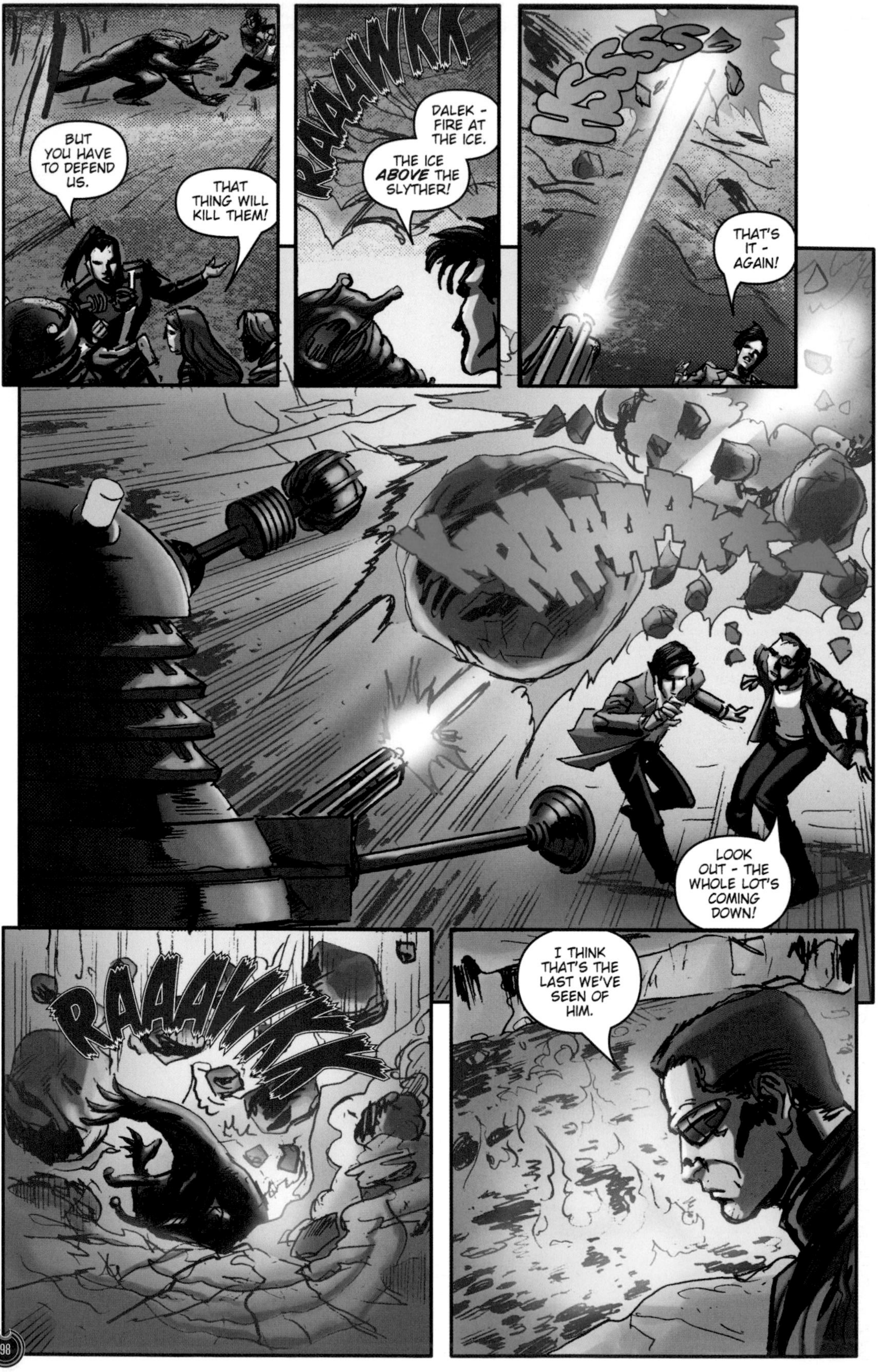
BUT YOU HAVE TO DEFEND US.
THAT THING WILL KILL THEM!
RAAAWKK
DALEK - FIRE AT THE ICE.
THE ICE *ABOVE* THE SLYTHER!
HSSSS
THAT'S IT - AGAIN!
LOOK OUT - THE WHOLE LOT'S COMING DOWN!
RAAAWKK
I THINK THAT'S THE LAST WE'VE SEEN OF HIM.

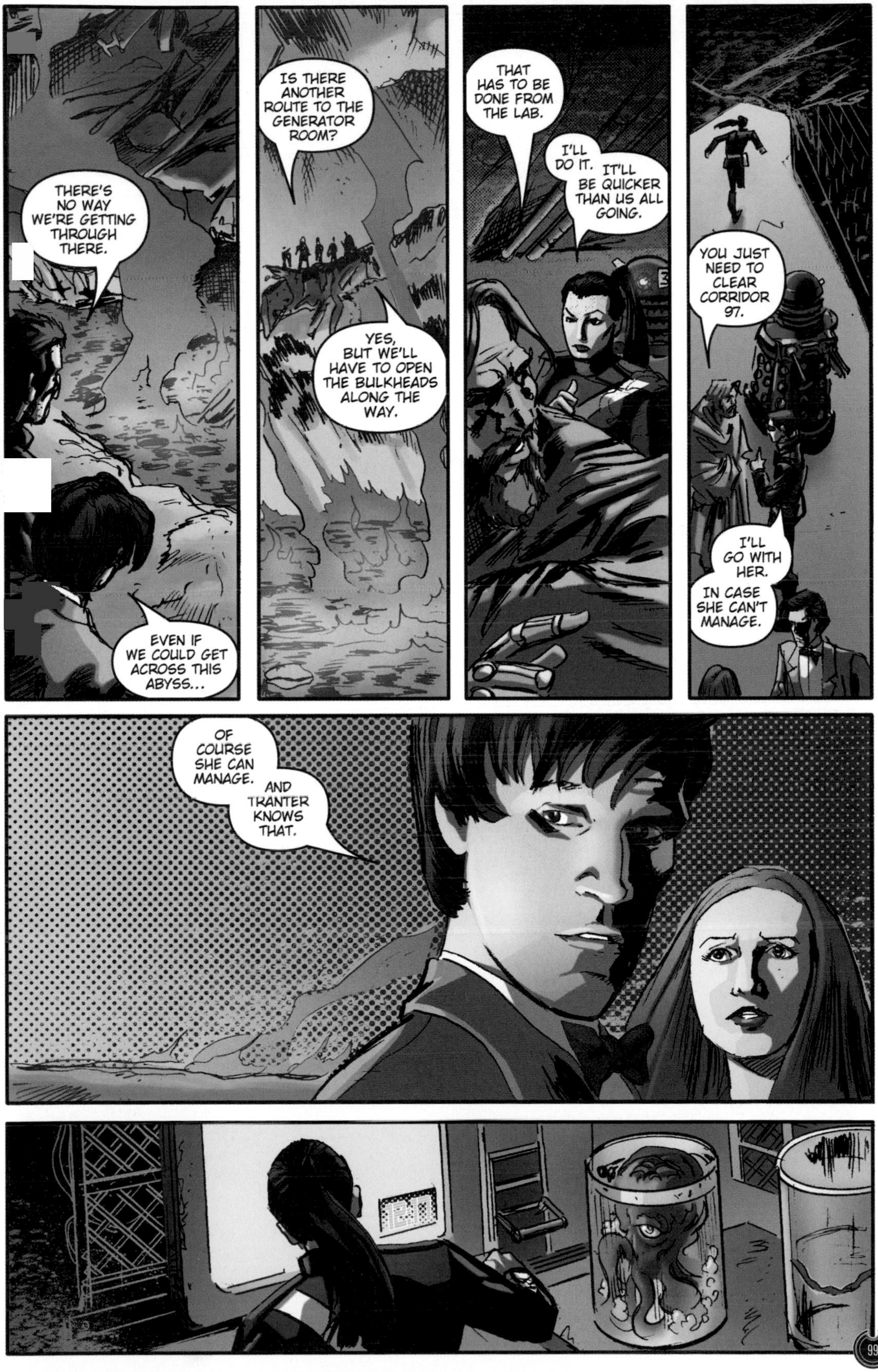
THERE'S NO WAY WE'RE GETTING THROUGH THERE.
EVEN IF WE COULD GET ACROSS THIS ABYSS...
IS THERE ANOTHER ROUTE TO THE GENERATOR ROOM?
YES, BUT WE'LL HAVE TO OPEN THE BULKHEADS ALONG THE WAY.
THAT HAS TO BE DONE FROM THE LAB.
I'LL DO IT.
IT'LL BE QUICKER THAN US ALL GOING.
YOU JUST NEED TO CLEAR CORRIDOR 97.
I'LL GO WITH HER.
IN CASE SHE CAN'T MANAGE.
OF COURSE SHE CAN MANAGE.
AND TRANTER KNOWS THAT.

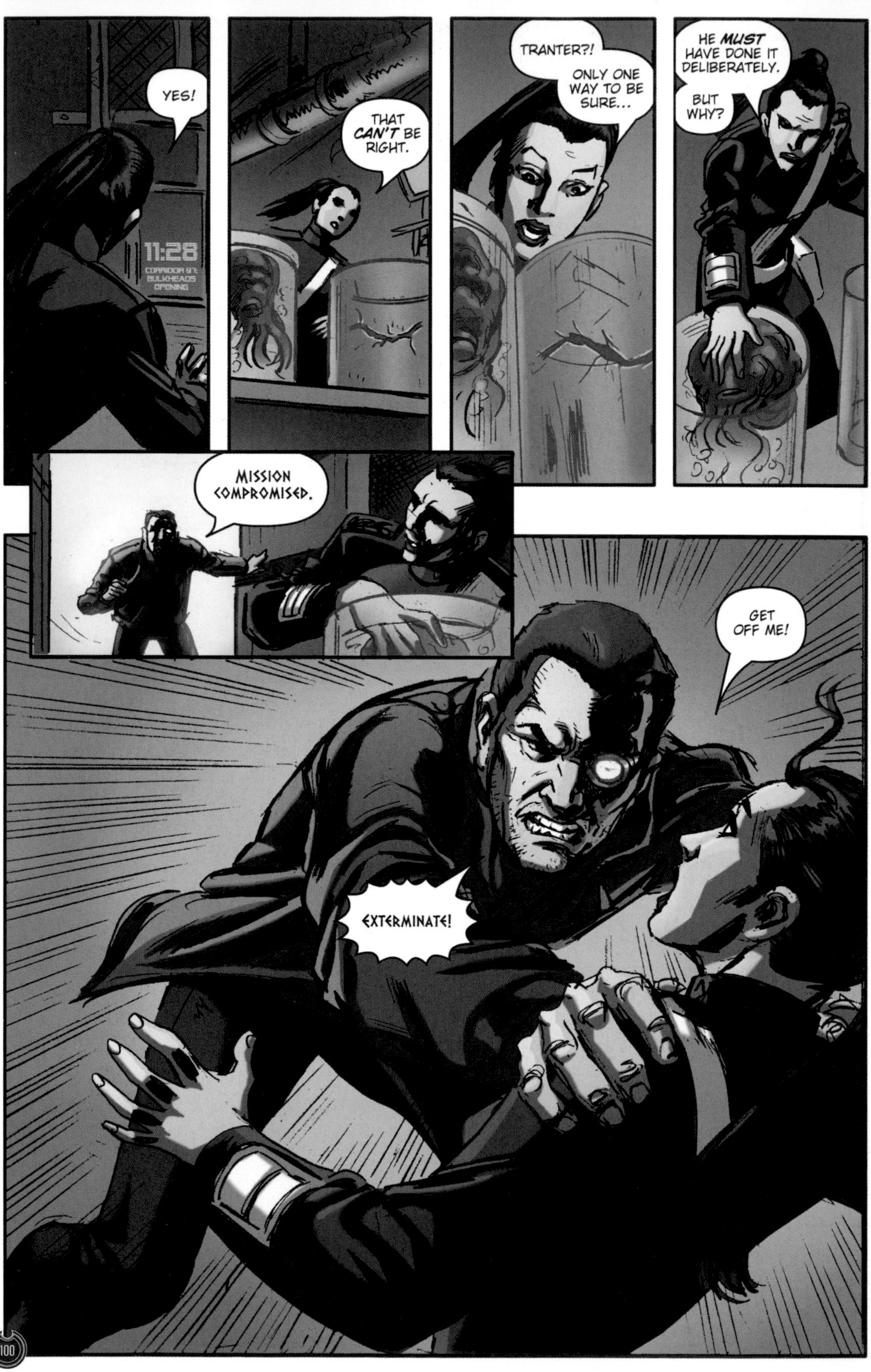
YES!
11:28
CORRIDOR 97: BULKHEADS OPENING
THAT CAN'T BE RIGHT.
TRANTER?!
ONLY ONE WAY TO BE SURE...
HE MUST HAVE DONE IT DELIBERATELY.
BUT WHY?
MISSION COMPROMISED.
GET OFF ME!
EXTERMINATE!

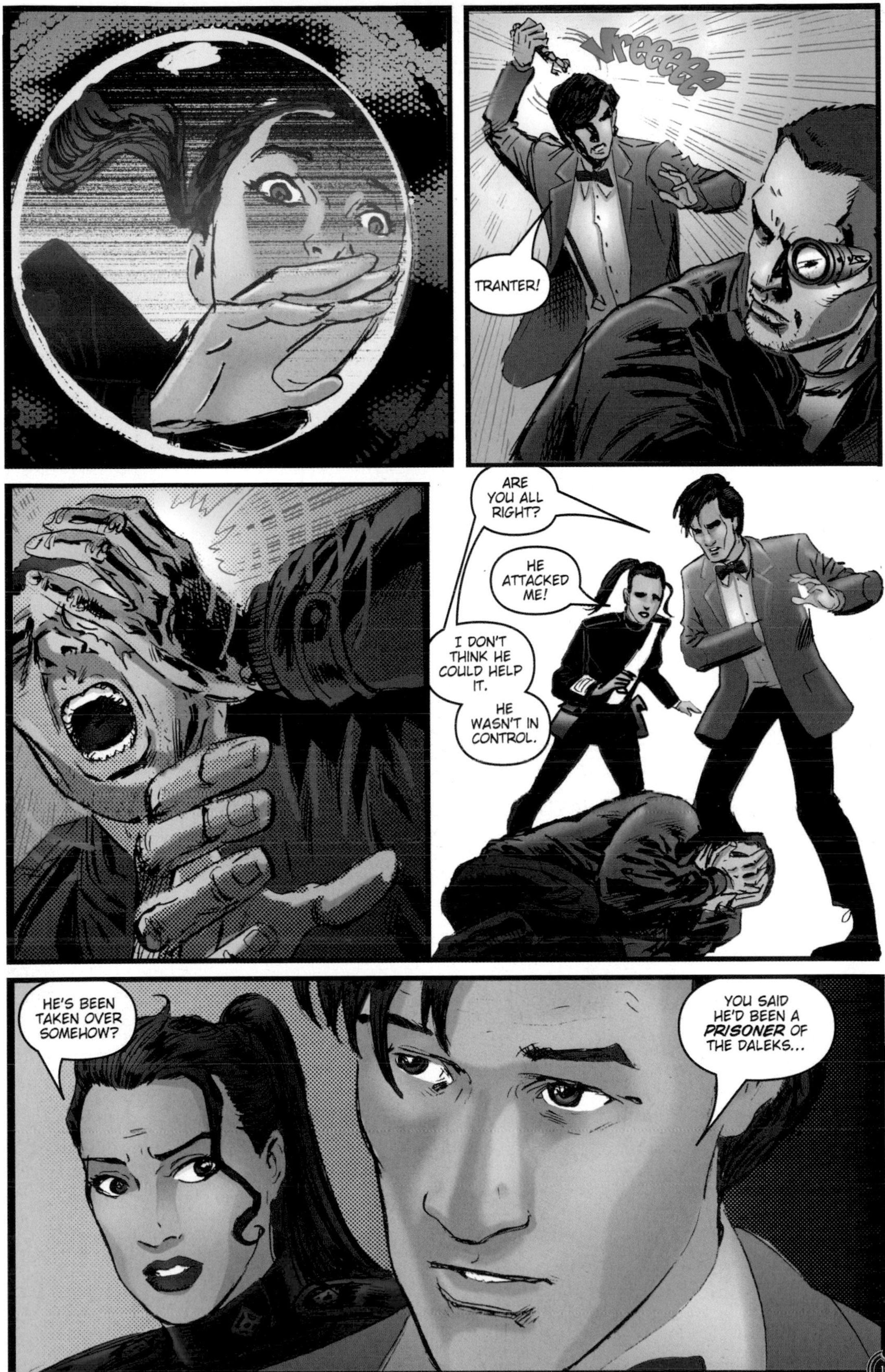
VREEEEEE
TRANTER!
ARE YOU ALL RIGHT?
HE ATTACKED ME!
I DON'T THINK HE COULD HELP IT.
HE WASN'T IN CONTROL.
HE'S BEEN TAKEN OVER SOMEHOW?
YOU SAID HE'D BEEN A *PRISONER* OF THE DALEKS...

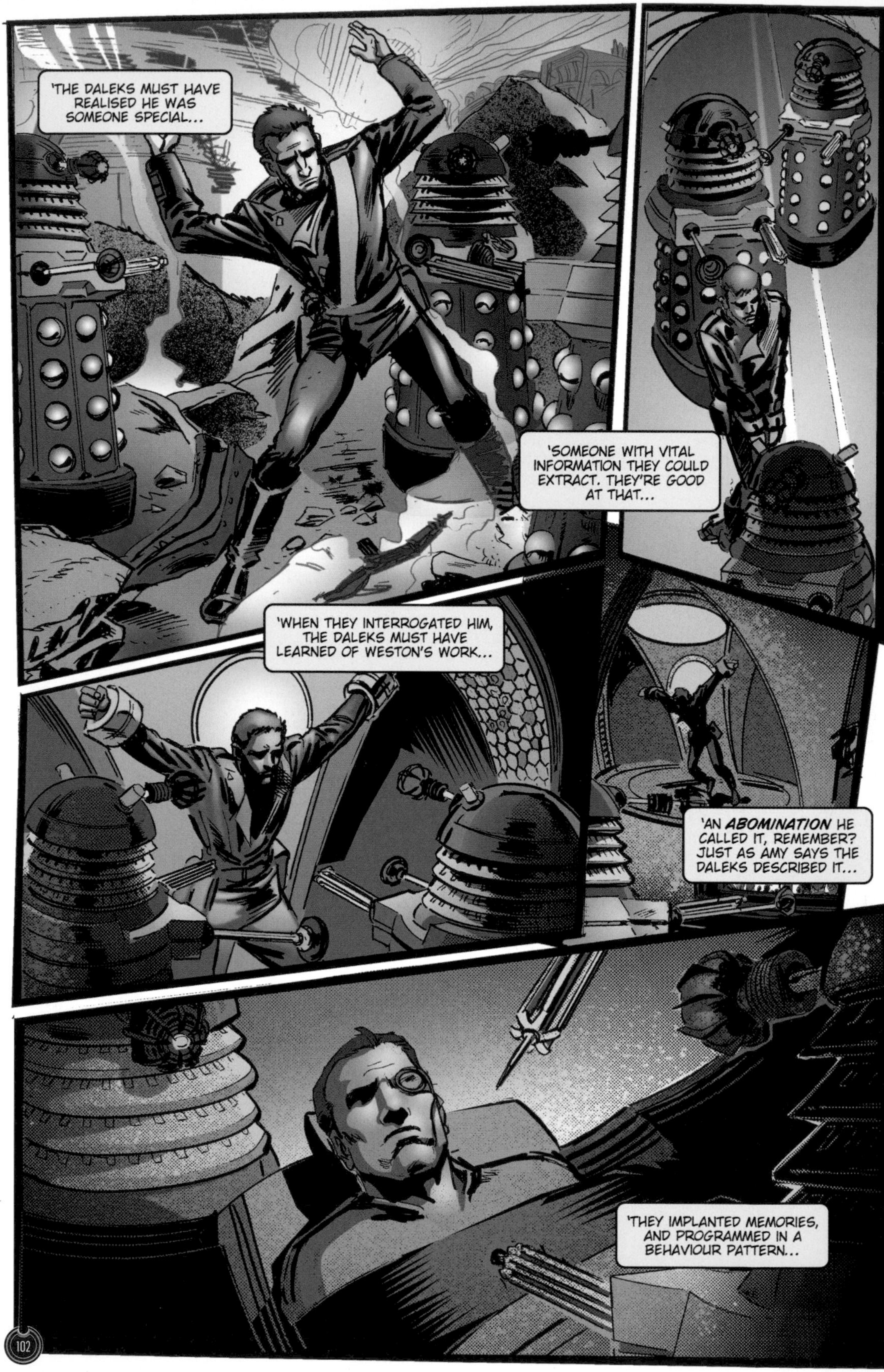
'THE DALEKS MUST HAVE REALISED HE WAS SOMEONE SPECIAL...
'SOMEONE WITH VITAL INFORMATION THEY COULD EXTRACT. THEY'RE GOOD AT THAT...
'WHEN THEY INTERROGATED HIM, THE DALEKS MUST HAVE LEARNED OF WESTON'S WORK...
'AN ***ABOMINATION*** HE CALLED IT, REMEMBER? JUST AS AMY SAYS THE DALEKS DESCRIBED IT...
'THEY IMPLANTED MEMORIES, AND PROGRAMMED IN A BEHAVIOUR PATTERN...

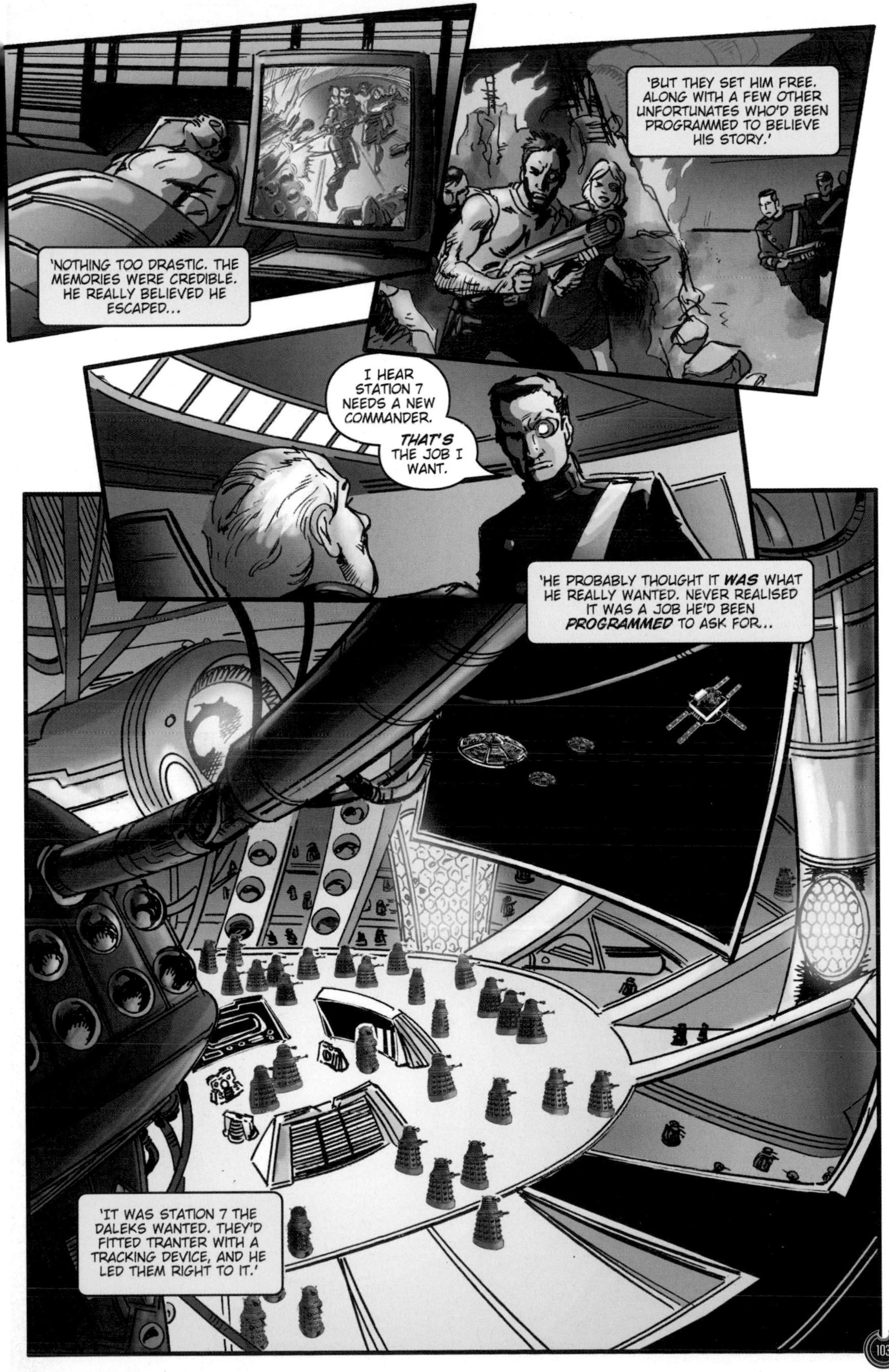
'NOTHING TOO DRASTIC. THE MEMORIES WERE CREDIBLE. HE REALLY BELIEVED HE ESCAPED...
'BUT THEY SET HIM FREE. ALONG WITH A FEW OTHER UNFORTUNATES WHO'D BEEN PROGRAMMED TO BELIEVE HIS STORY.'
I HEAR STATION 7 NEEDS A NEW COMMANDER. *THAT'S* THE JOB I WANT.
'HE PROBABLY THOUGHT IT *WAS* WHAT HE REALLY WANTED. NEVER REALISED IT WAS A JOB HE'D BEEN *PROGRAMMED* TO ASK FOR...
'IT WAS STATION 7 THE DALEKS WANTED. THEY'D FITTED TRANTER WITH A TRACKING DEVICE, AND HE LED THEM RIGHT TO IT.'

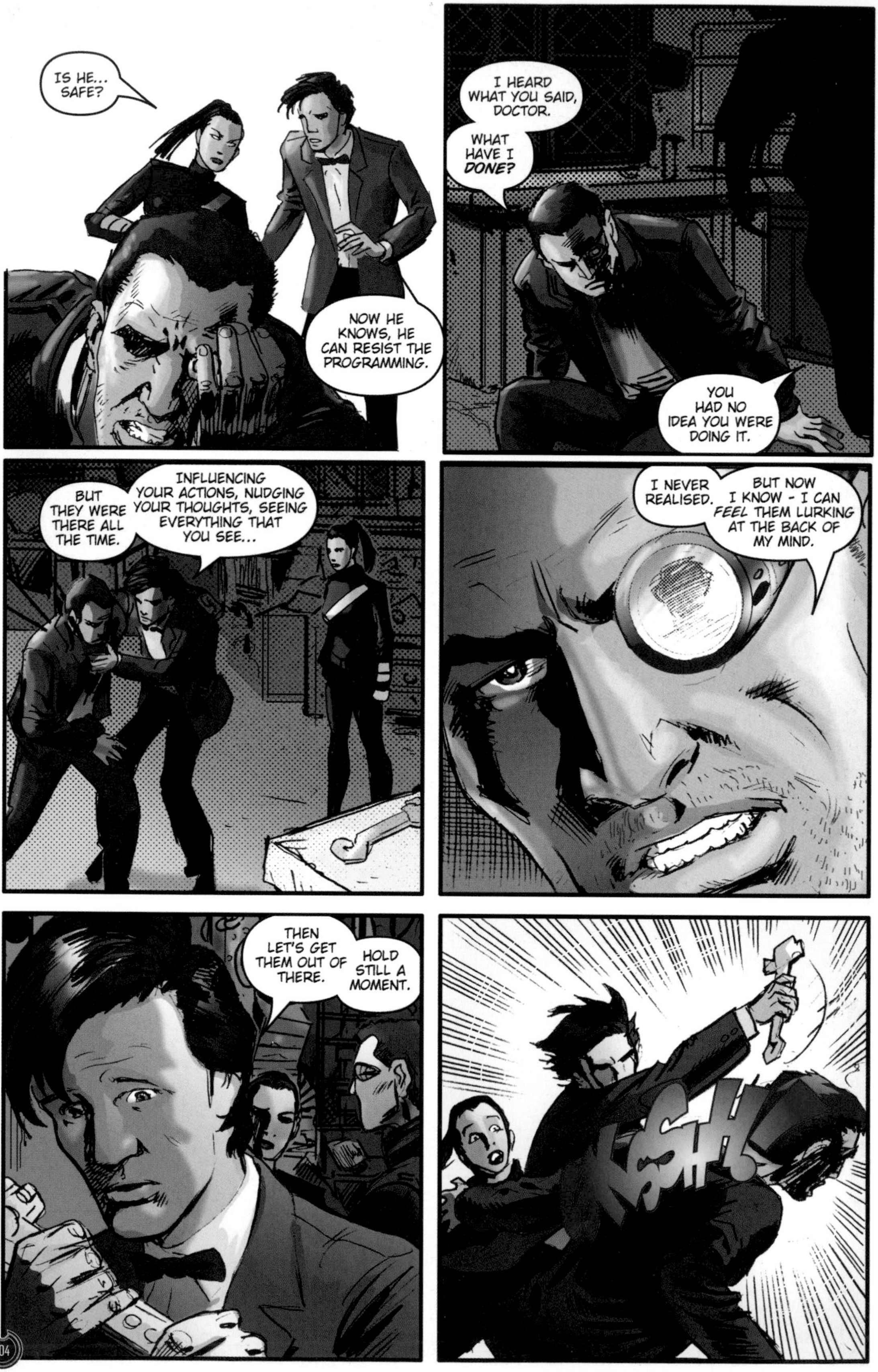
IS HE... SAFE?
NOW HE KNOWS, HE CAN RESIST THE PROGRAMMING.
I HEARD WHAT YOU SAID, DOCTOR.
WHAT HAVE I DONE?
YOU HAD NO IDEA YOU WERE DOING IT.
INFLUENCING YOUR ACTIONS, NUDGING YOUR THOUGHTS, SEEING EVERYTHING THAT YOU SEE...
BUT THEY WERE THERE ALL THE TIME.
I NEVER REALISED.
BUT NOW I KNOW - I CAN FEEL THEM LURKING AT THE BACK OF MY MIND.
THEN LET'S GET THEM OUT OF THERE.
HOLD STILL A MOMENT.
KSSH!

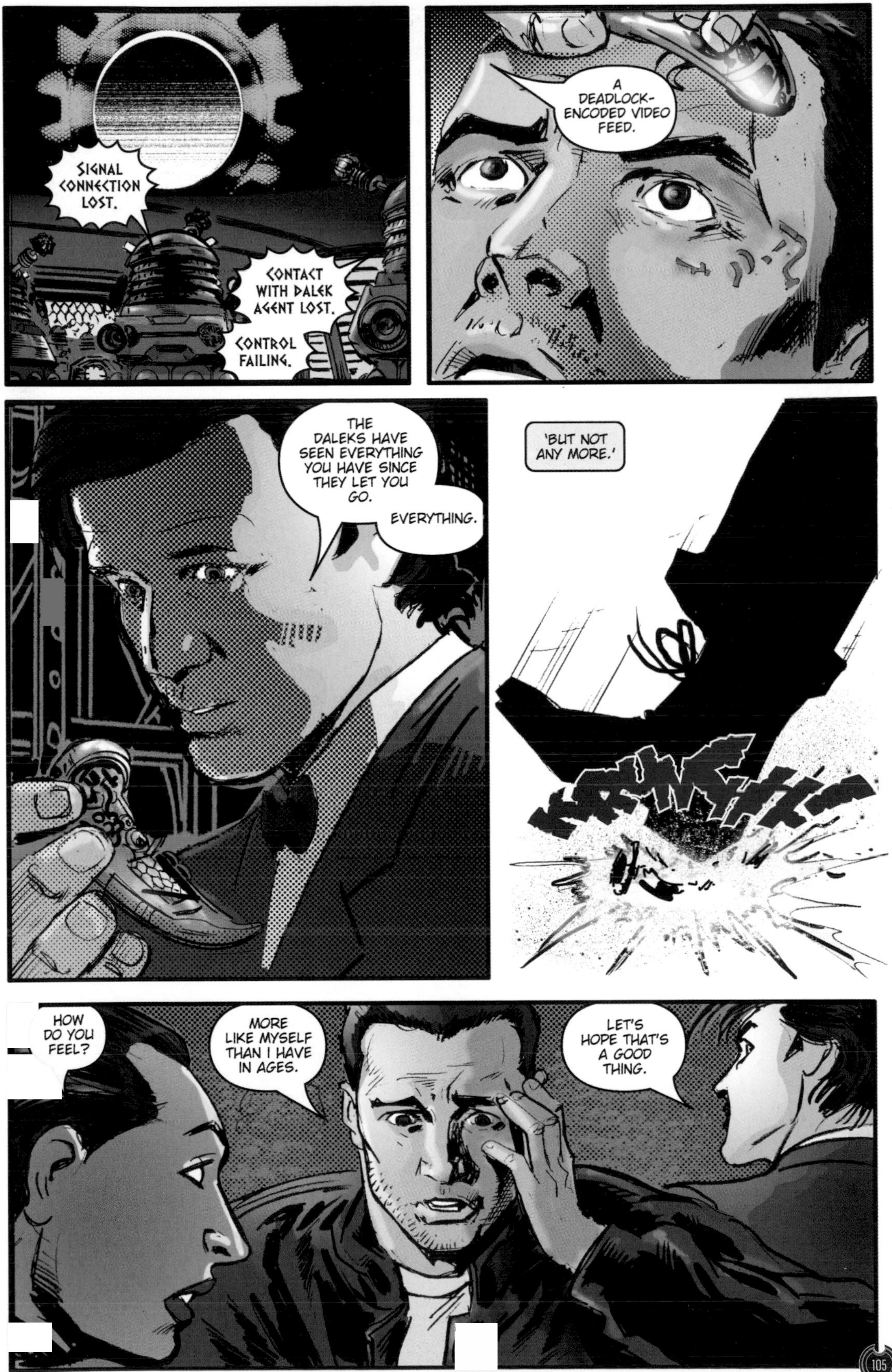
SIGNAL CONNECTION LOST.
CONTACT WITH DALEK AGENT LOST.
CONTROL FAILING.
A DEADLOCK-ENCODED VIDEO FEED.
THE DALEKS HAVE SEEN EVERYTHING YOU HAVE SINCE THEY LET YOU GO.
EVERYTHING.
'BUT NOT ANY MORE.'
HOW DO YOU FEEL?
MORE LIKE MYSELF THAN I HAVE IN AGES.
LET'S HOPE THAT'S A GOOD THING.

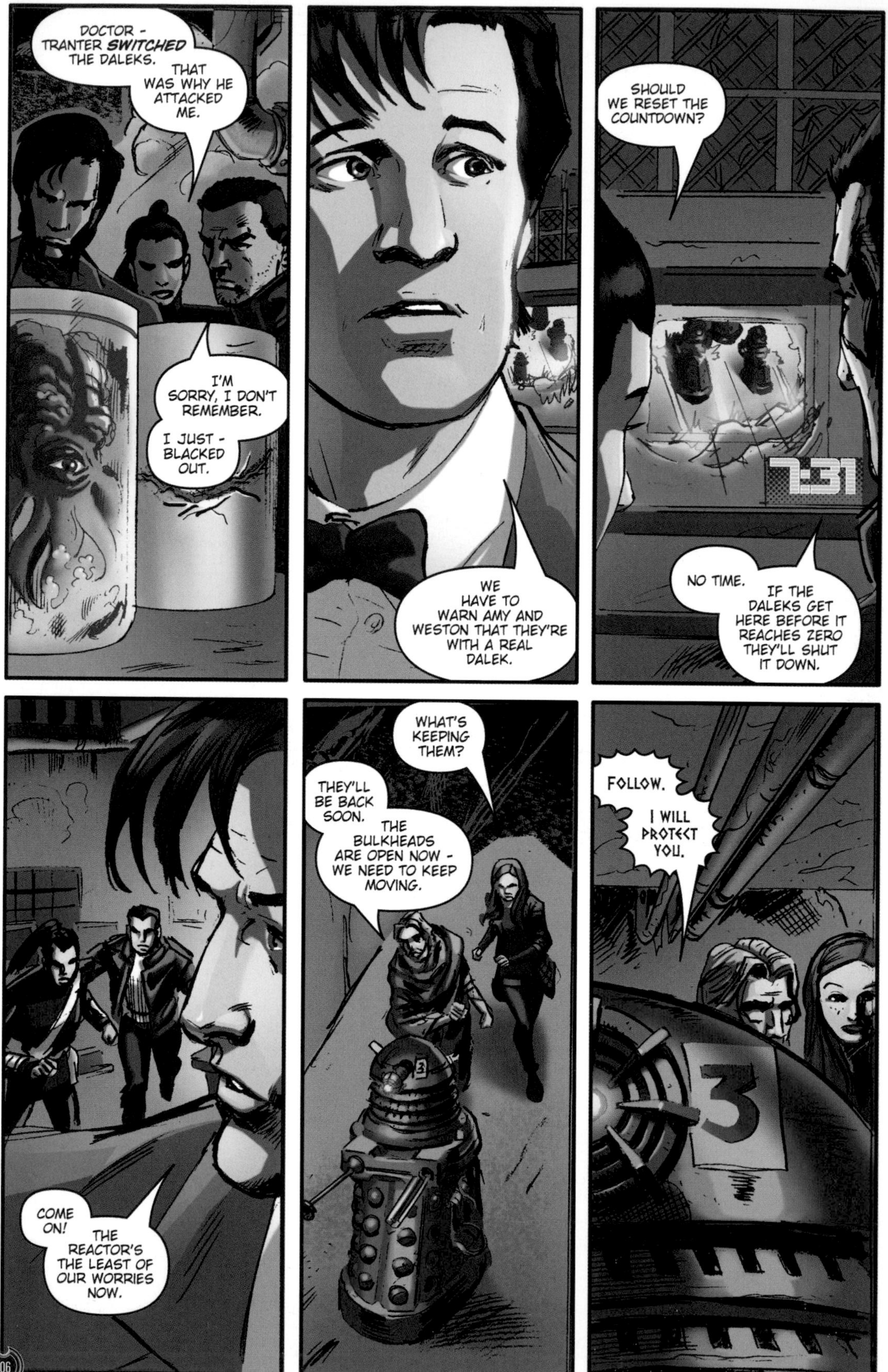
DOCTOR - TRANTER SWITCHED THE DALEKS.
THAT WAS WHY HE ATTACKED ME.
I'M SORRY, I DON'T REMEMBER.
I JUST - BLACKED OUT.
WE HAVE TO WARN AMY AND WESTON THAT THEY'RE WITH A REAL DALEK.
SHOULD WE RESET THE COUNTDOWN?
7:31
NO TIME.
IF THE DALEKS GET HERE BEFORE IT REACHES ZERO THEY'LL SHUT IT DOWN.
COME ON!
THE REACTOR'S THE LEAST OF OUR WORRIES NOW.
WHAT'S KEEPING THEM?
THEY'LL BE BACK SOON.
THE BULKHEADS ARE OPEN NOW - WE NEED TO KEEP MOVING.
FOLLOW.
I WILL PROTECT YOU.

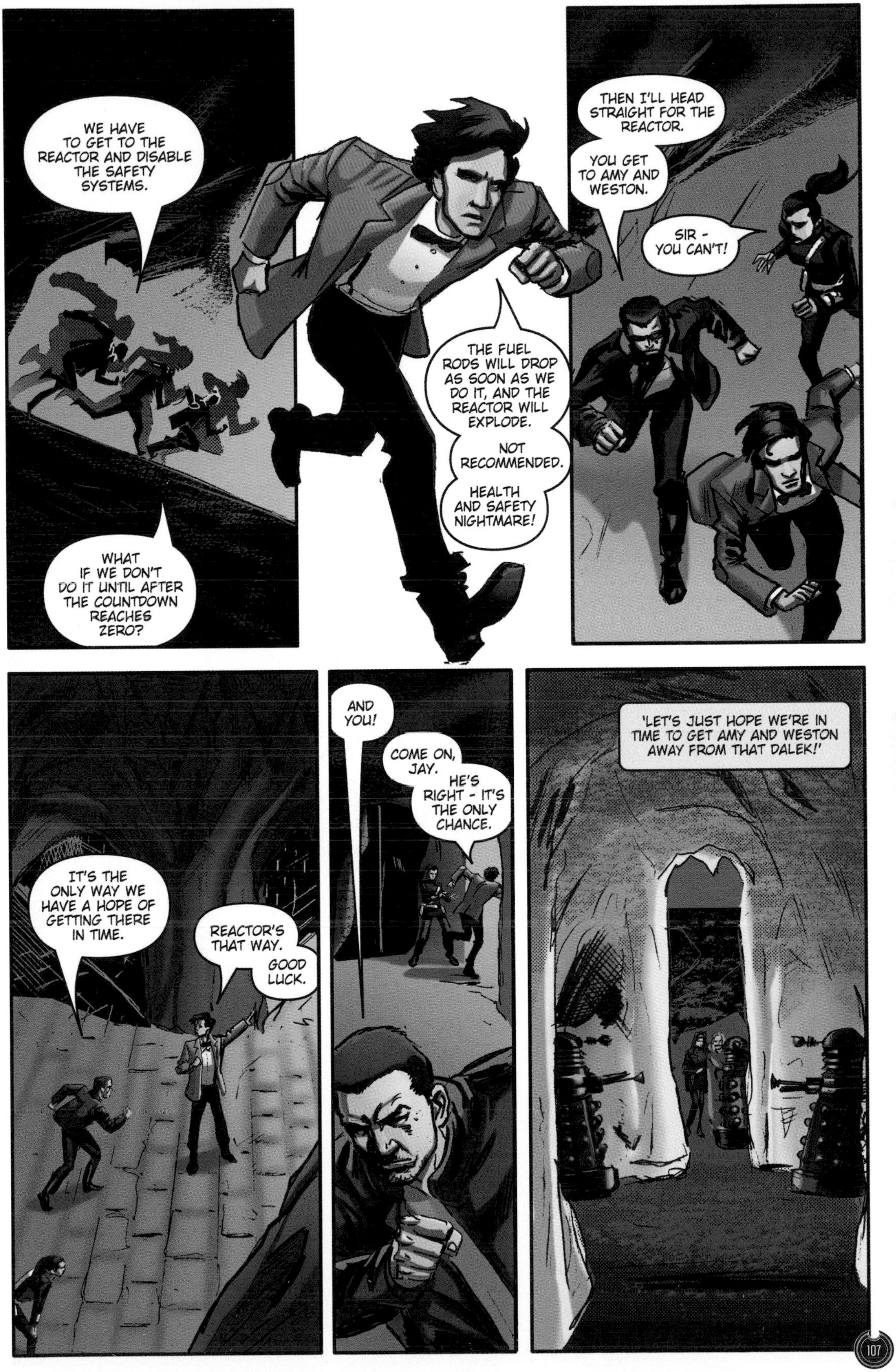

WE HAVE TO GET TO THE REACTOR AND DISABLE THE SAFETY SYSTEMS.
WHAT IF WE DON'T DO IT UNTIL AFTER THE COUNTDOWN REACHES ZERO?
THE FUEL RODS WILL DROP AS SOON AS WE DO IT, AND THE REACTOR WILL EXPLODE.
NOT RECOMMENDED.
HEALTH AND SAFETY NIGHTMARE!
THEN I'LL HEAD STRAIGHT FOR THE REACTOR.
YOU GET TO AMY AND WESTON.
SIR - YOU CAN'T!
IT'S THE ONLY WAY WE HAVE A HOPE OF GETTING THERE IN TIME.
REACTOR'S THAT WAY.
GOOD LUCK.
AND YOU!
COME ON, JAY.
HE'S RIGHT - IT'S THE ONLY CHANCE.
'LET'S JUST HOPE WE'RE IN TIME TO GET AMY AND WESTON AWAY FROM THAT DALEK!'

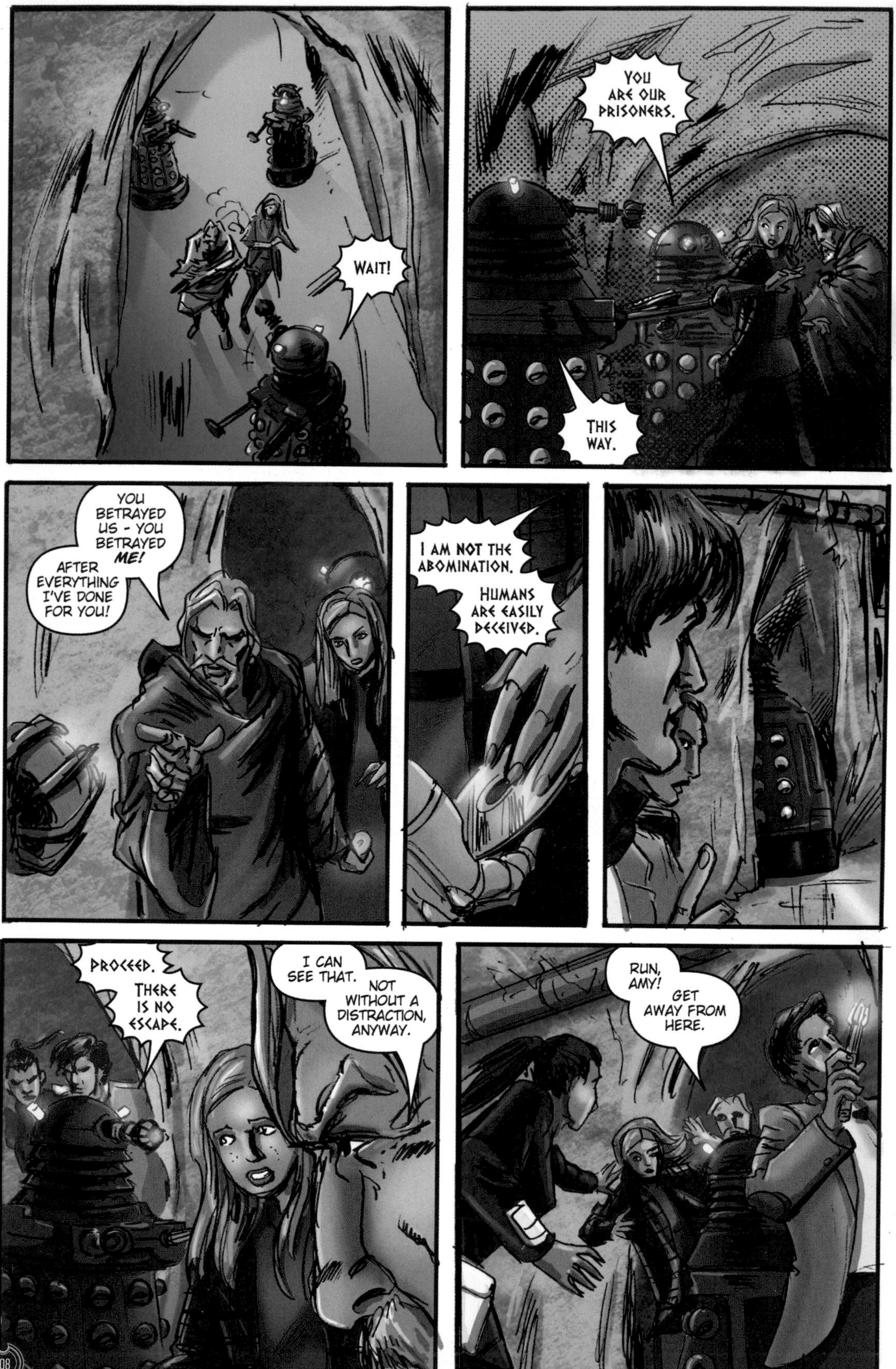
WAIT!
YOU ARE OUR PRISONERS.
THIS WAY.
YOU BETRAYED US - YOU BETRAYED ME!
AFTER EVERYTHING I'VE DONE FOR YOU!
I AM NOT THE ABOMINATION.
HUMANS ARE EASILY DECEIVED.
PROCEED.
THERE IS NO ESCAPE.
I CAN SEE THAT.
NOT WITHOUT A DISTRACTION, ANYWAY.
RUN, AMY!
GET AWAY FROM HERE.

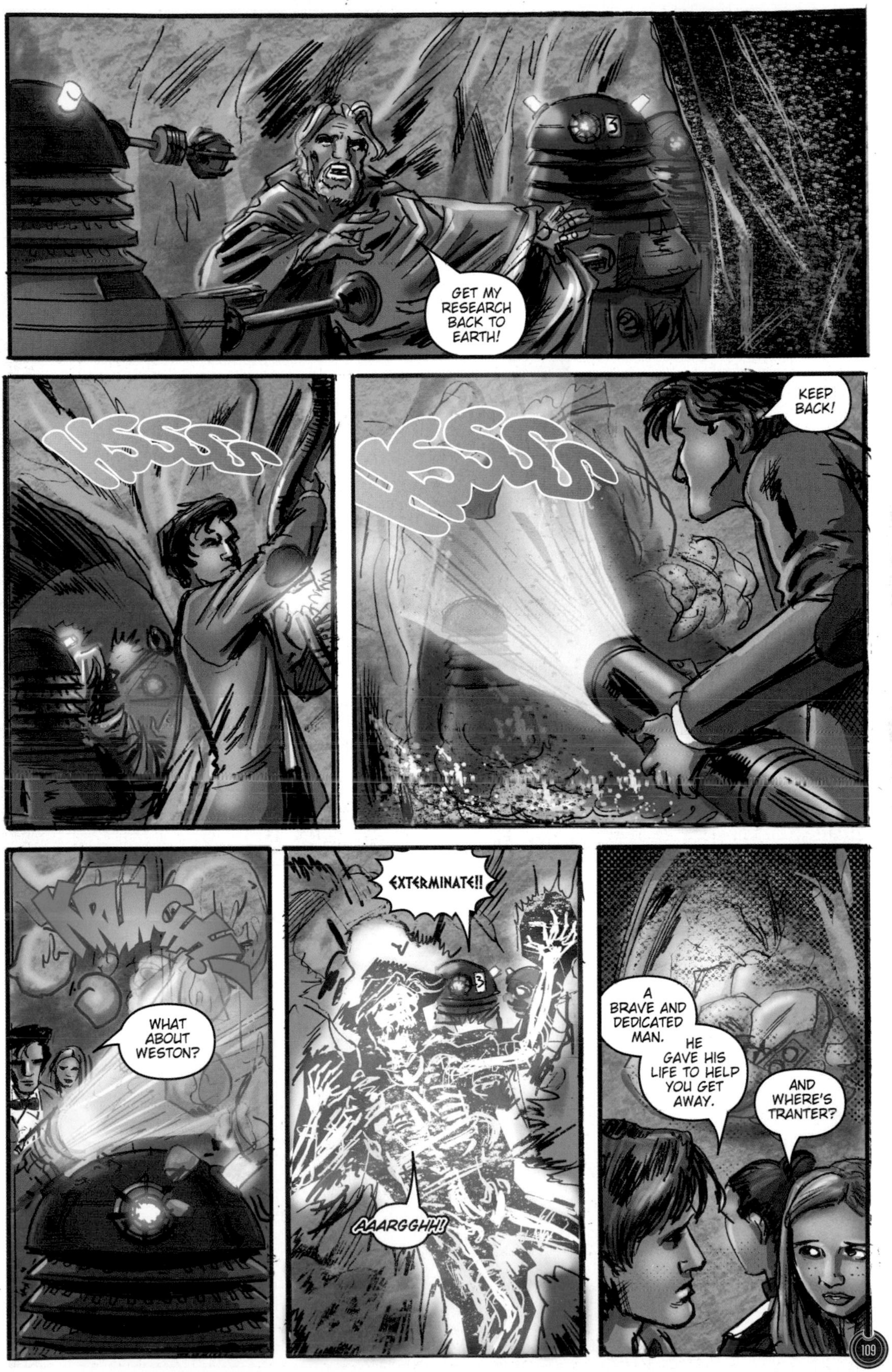
GET MY RESEARCH BACK TO EARTH!
KEEP BACK!
WHAT ABOUT WESTON?
EXTERMINATE!!
AAARGGHH!
A BRAVE AND DEDICATED MAN.
HE GAVE HIS LIFE TO HELP YOU GET AWAY.
AND WHERE'S TRANTER?

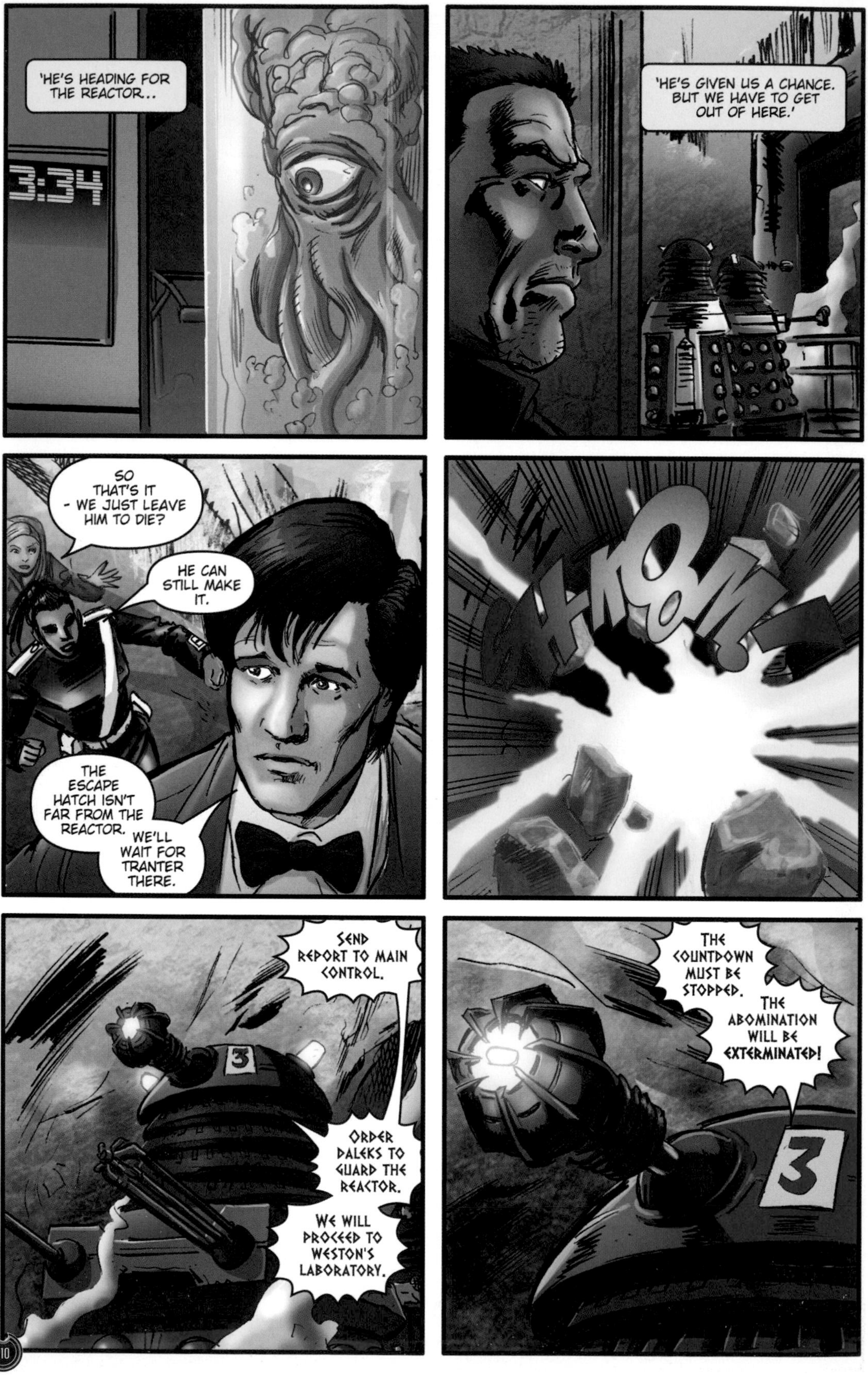
'HE'S HEADING FOR THE REACTOR..
3:34
'HE'S GIVEN US A CHANCE. BUT WE HAVE TO GET OUT OF HERE.'
SO THAT'S IT - WE JUST LEAVE HIM TO DIE?
HE CAN STILL MAKE IT.
THE ESCAPE HATCH ISN'T FAR FROM THE REACTOR.
WE'LL WAIT FOR TRANTER THERE.
KA-KOOM!
SEND REPORT TO MAIN CONTROL.
ORDER DALEKS TO GUARD THE REACTOR.
WE WILL PROCEED TO WESTON'S LABORATORY.
THE COUNTDOWN MUST BE STOPPED.
THE ABOMINATION WILL BE EXTERMINATED!

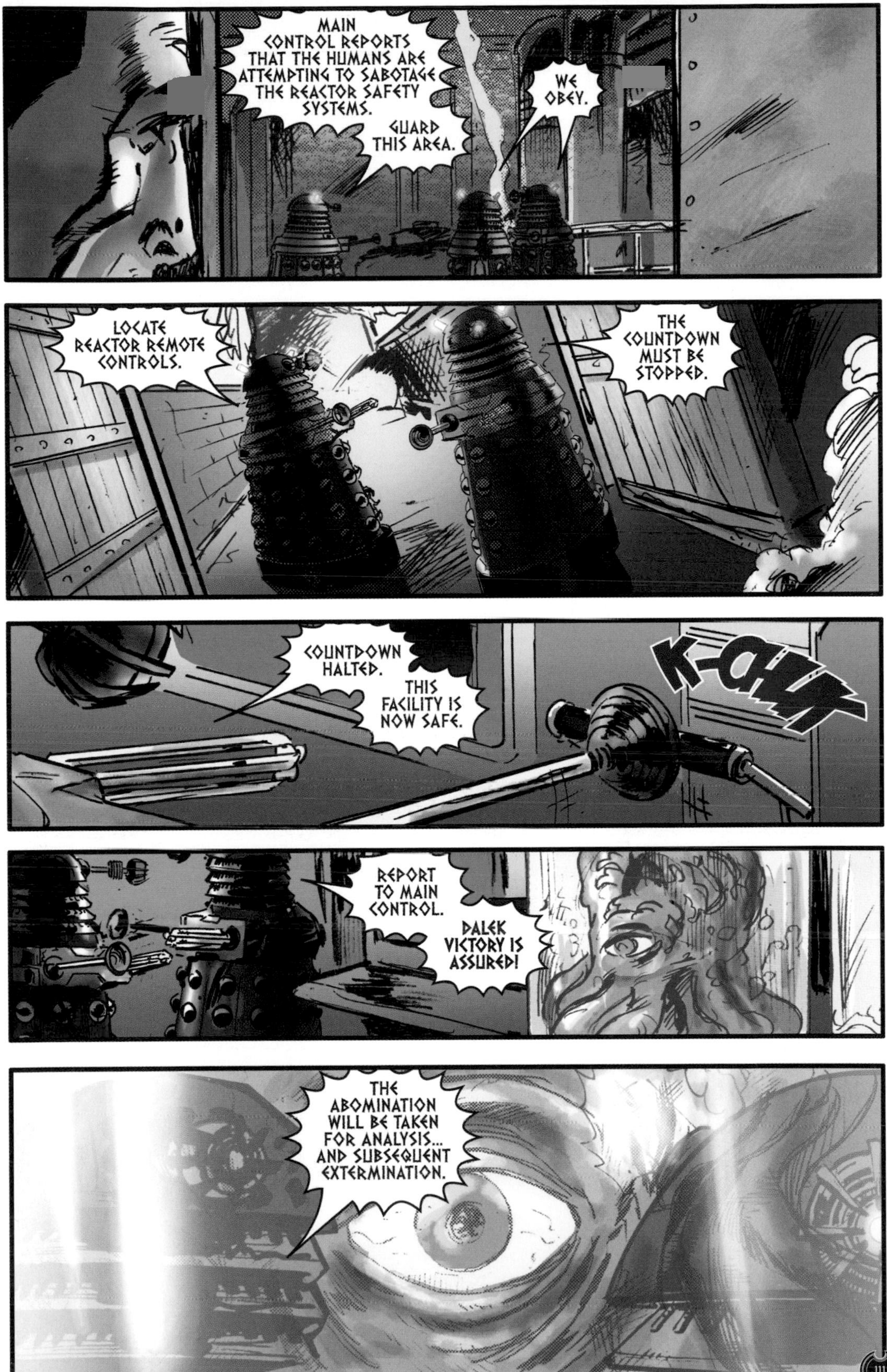
MAIN CONTROL REPORTS THAT THE HUMANS ARE ATTEMPTING TO SABOTAGE THE REACTOR SAFETY SYSTEMS.
GUARD THIS AREA.
WE OBEY.
LOCATE REACTOR REMOTE CONTROLS.
THE COUNTDOWN MUST BE STOPPED.
COUNTDOWN HALTED.
THIS FACILITY IS NOW SAFE.
K-CHUK
REPORT TO MAIN CONTROL.
DALEK VICTORY IS ASSURED!
THE ABOMINATION WILL BE TAKEN FOR ANALYSIS... AND SUBSEQUENT EXTERMINATION.

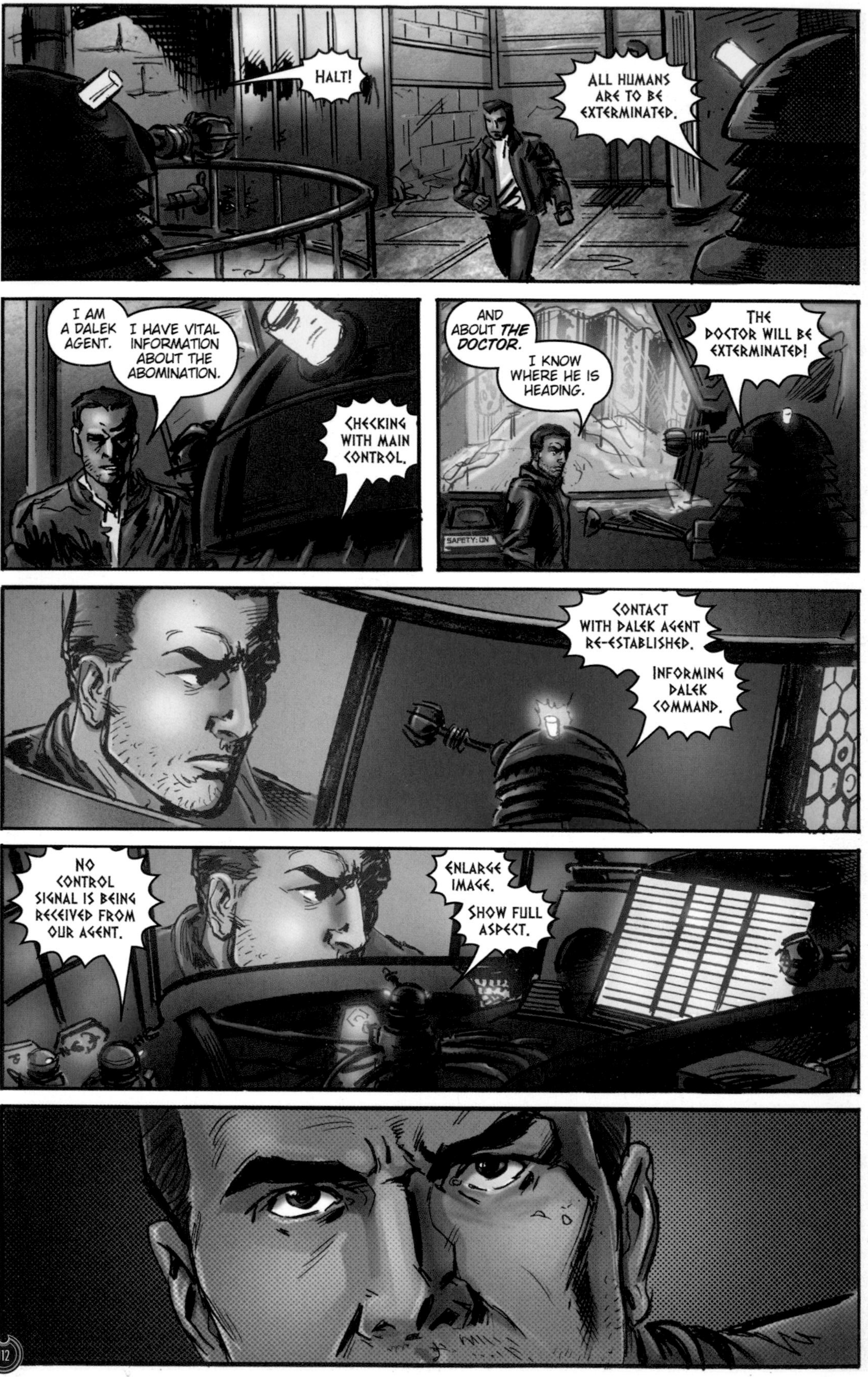

HALT!
ALL HUMANS ARE TO BE EXTERMINATED.
I AM A DALEK AGENT.
I HAVE VITAL INFORMATION ABOUT THE ABOMINATION.
CHECKING WITH MAIN CONTROL.
AND ABOUT *THE DOCTOR*.
I KNOW WHERE HE IS HEADING.
THE DOCTOR WILL BE EXTERMINATED!
SAFETY: ON
CONTACT WITH DALEK AGENT RE-ESTABLISHED.
INFORMING DALEK COMMAND.
NO CONTROL SIGNAL IS BEING RECEIVED FROM OUR AGENT.
ENLARGE IMAGE.
SHOW FULL ASPECT.

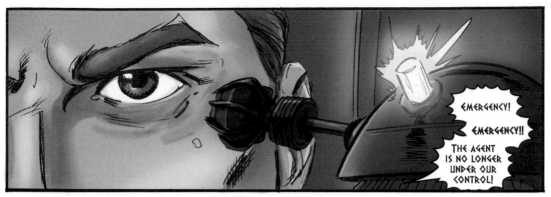

EMERGENCY!

EMERGENCY!!

THE AGENT IS NO LONGER UNDER OUR CONTROL!

WELL, IT WAS WORTH A TRY. DON'T WORRY — I'LL COME QUIETLY.

ALERT — SAFETY MEASURES DISENGAGED!

K-CLIK

RE-ENGAGE SAFETY MEASURES.

NOT POSSIBLE. CONTROLS DAMAGED.

STAND! YOUR ACTION WAS FUTILE.

THE COUNTDOWN HAS BEEN HALTED.

YOU'D BETTER HOPE IT DOESN'T START AGAIN BEFORE YOU REPAIR THOSE SAFETIES.

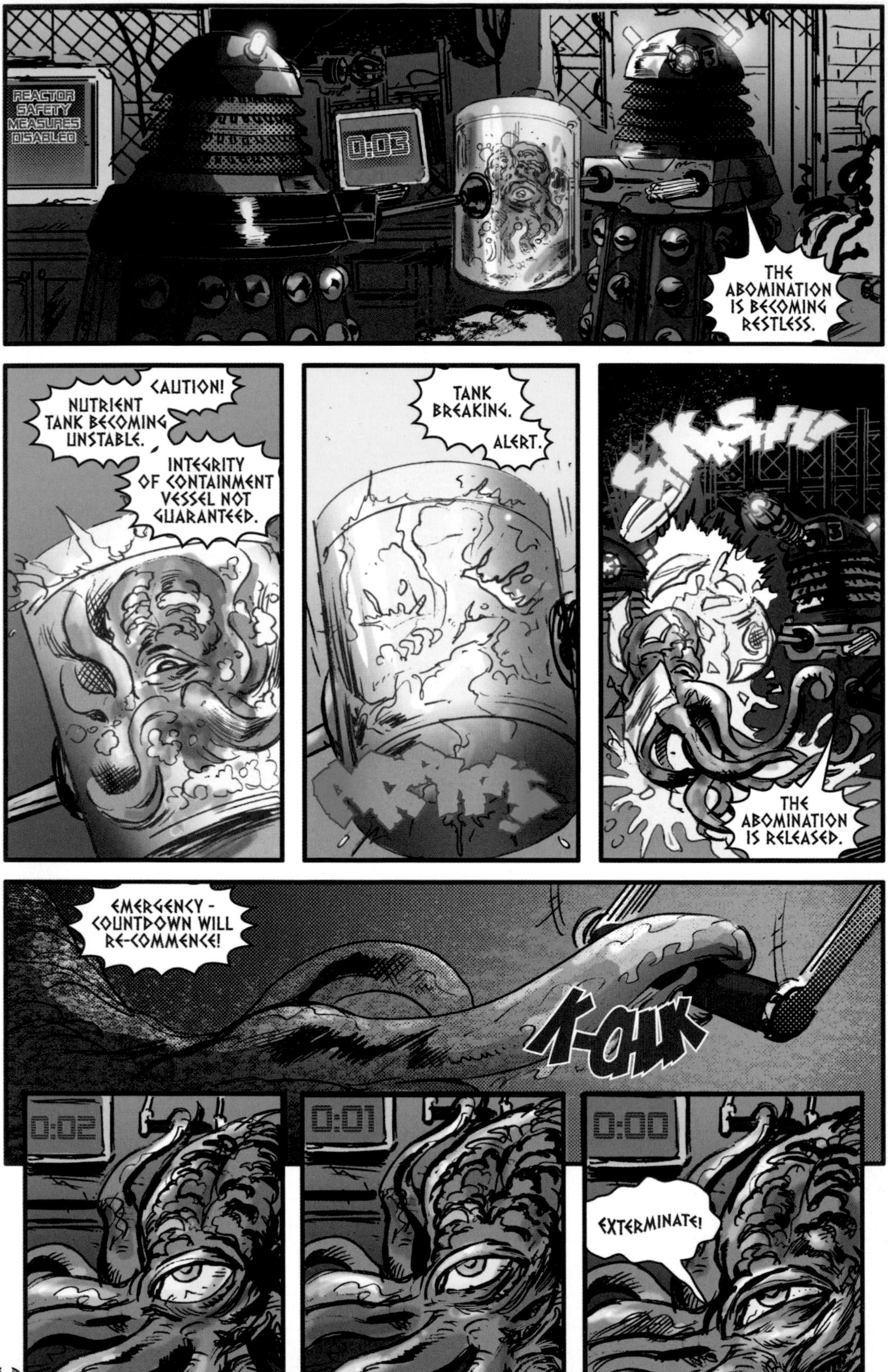
REACTOR SAFETY MEASURES DISABLED
0:03
THE ABOMINATION IS BECOMING RESTLESS.
CAUTION!
NUTRIENT TANK BECOMING UNSTABLE.
INTEGRITY OF CONTAINMENT VESSEL NOT GUARANTEED.
TANK BREAKING.
ALERT.
THE ABOMINATION IS RELEASED.
EMERGENCY - COUNTDOWN WILL RE-COMMENCE!
K-CHUK
0:02
0:01
0:00
EXTERMINATE!

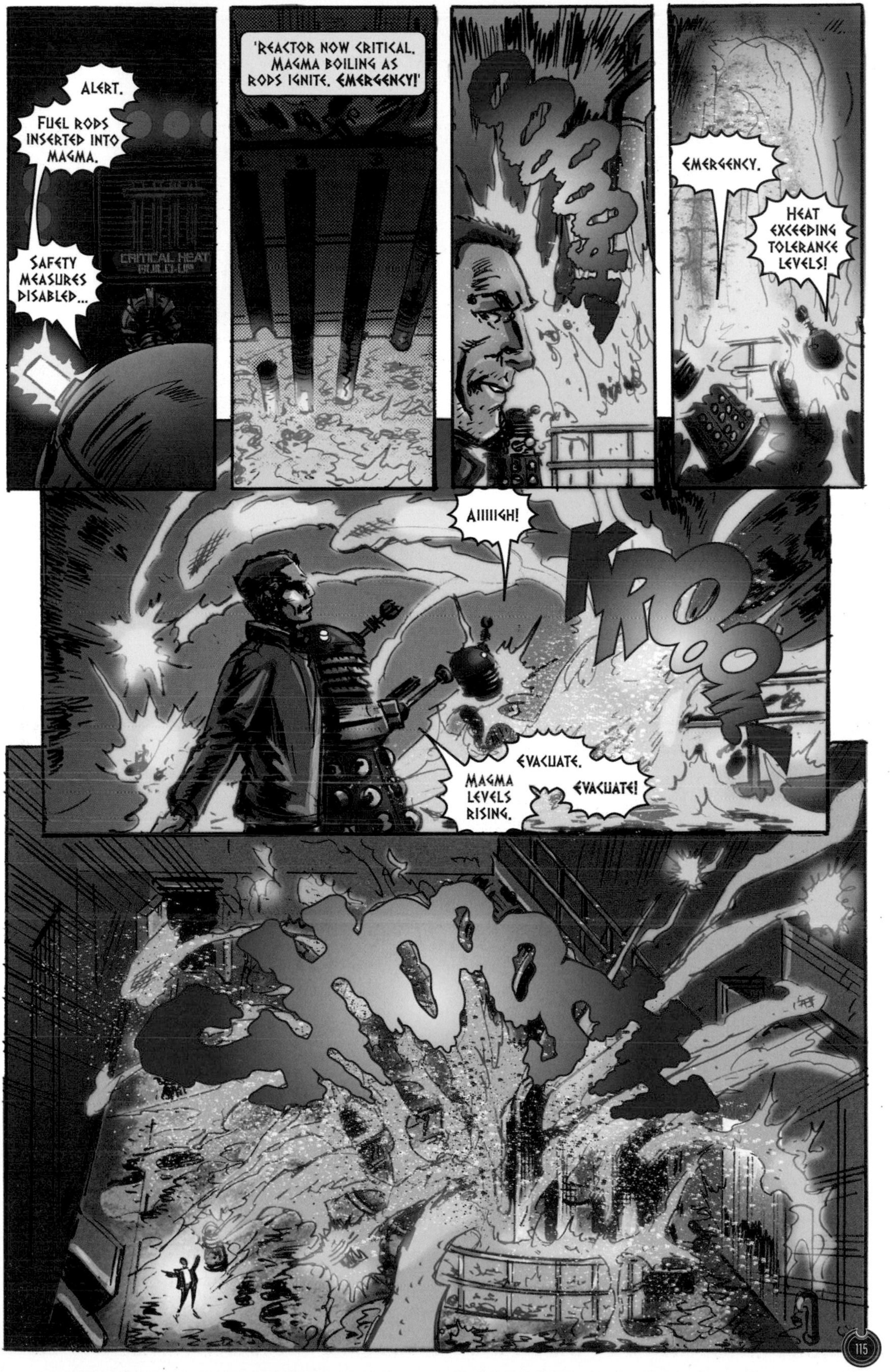

ALERT.
FUEL RODS INSERTED INTO MAGMA.
CRITICAL HEAT BUILD-UP
SAFETY MEASURES DISABLED...
'REACTOR NOW CRITICAL. MAGMA BOILING AS RODS IGNITE. EMERGENCY!'
EMERGENCY.
HEAT EXCEEDING TOLERANCE LEVELS!
AIIIIGH!
KROOOM
MAGMA LEVELS RISING.
EVACUATE.
EVACUATE!

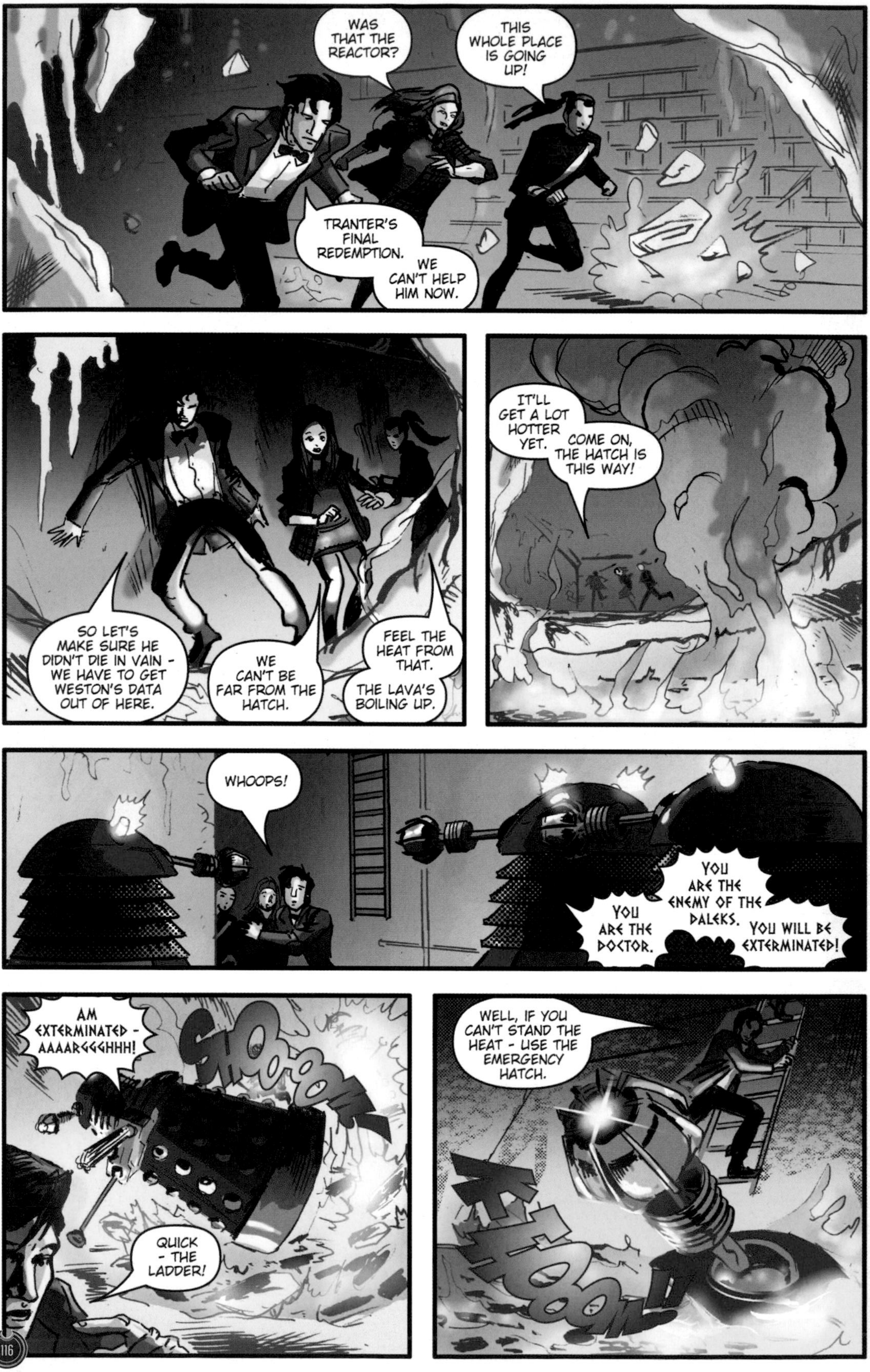

WAS THAT THE REACTOR?
THIS WHOLE PLACE IS GOING UP!
TRANTER'S FINAL REDEMPTION.
WE CAN'T HELP HIM NOW.
SO LET'S MAKE SURE HE DIDN'T DIE IN VAIN - WE HAVE TO GET WESTON'S DATA OUT OF HERE.
WE CAN'T BE FAR FROM THE HATCH.
FEEL THE HEAT FROM THAT.
THE LAVA'S BOILING UP.
IT'LL GET A LOT HOTTER YET.
COME ON, THE HATCH IS THIS WAY!
WHOOPS!
YOU ARE THE DOCTOR.
YOU ARE THE ENEMY OF THE DALEKS.
YOU WILL BE EXTERMINATED!
AM EXTERMINATED - AAAARGGGHHH!
QUICK - THE LADDER!
WELL, IF YOU CAN'T STAND THE HEAT - USE THE EMERGENCY HATCH.

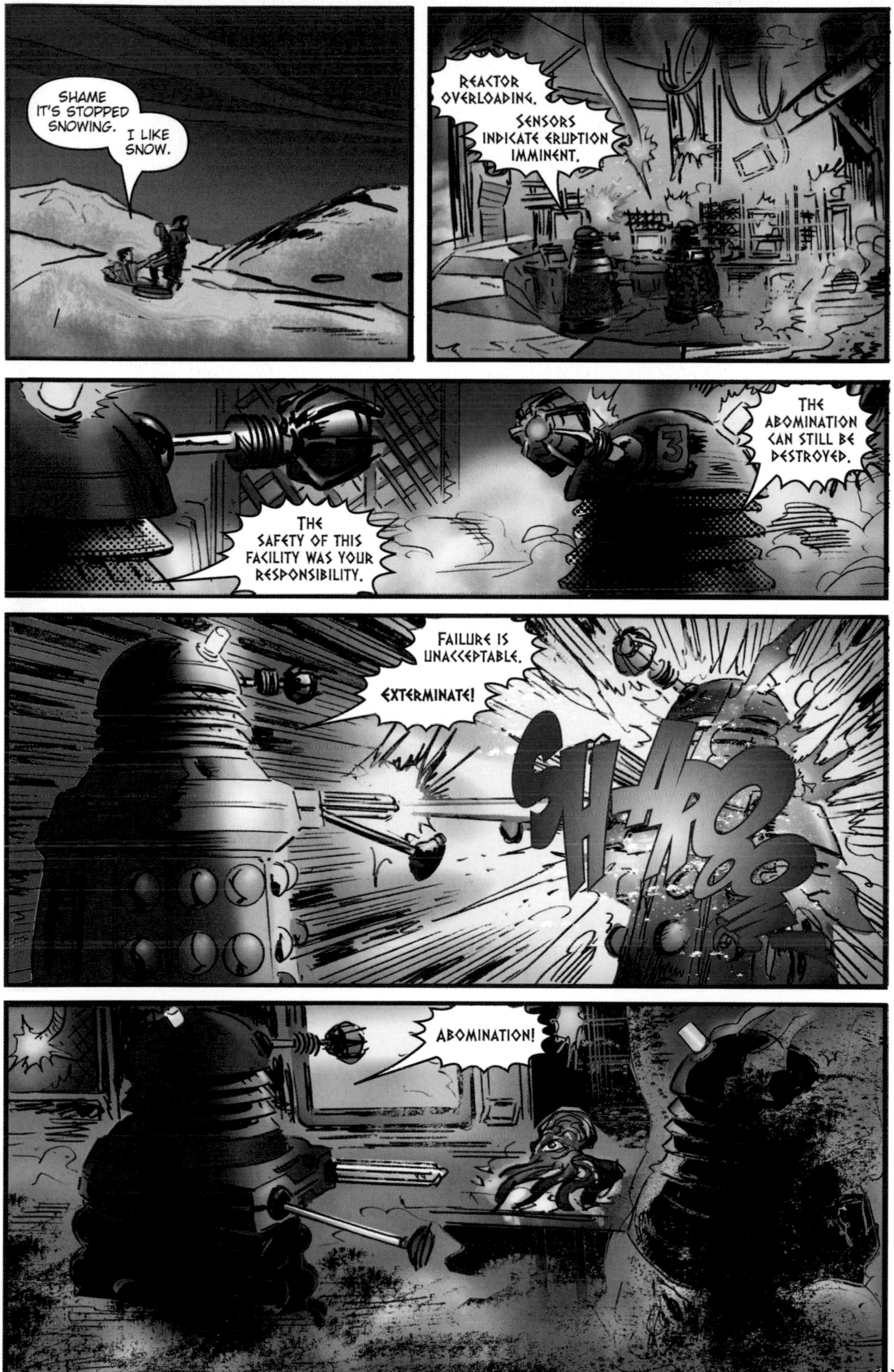
SHAME IT'S STOPPED SNOWING.
I LIKE SNOW.
REACTOR OVERLOADING.
SENSORS INDICATE ERUPTION IMMINENT.
THE SAFETY OF THIS FACILITY WAS YOUR RESPONSIBILITY.
THE ABOMINATION CAN STILL BE DESTROYED.
FAILURE IS UNACCEPTABLE.
EXTERMINATE!
SHHOO
ABOMINATION!

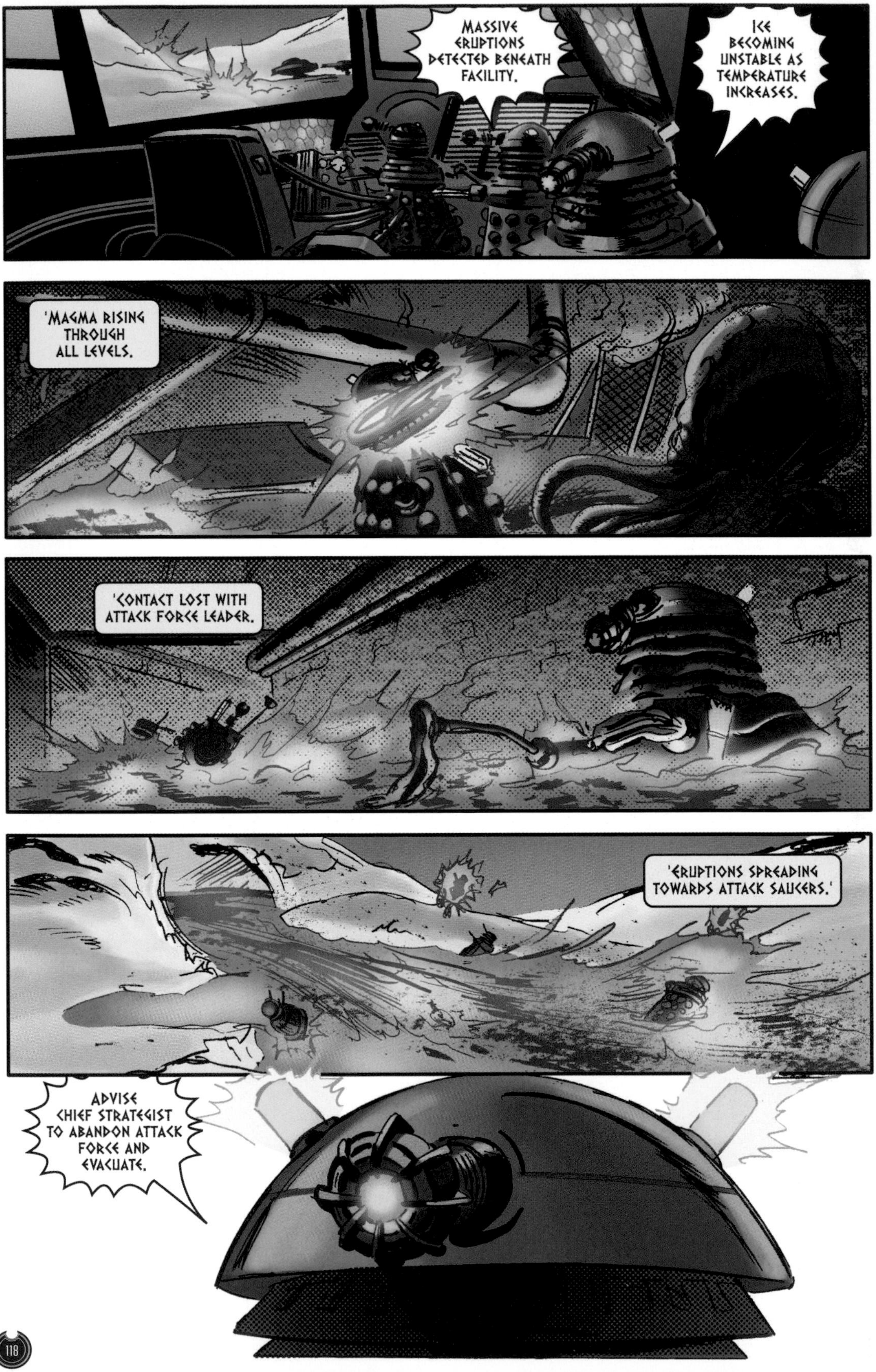
MASSIVE ERUPTIONS DETECTED BENEATH FACILITY.
ICE BECOMING UNSTABLE AS TEMPERATURE INCREASES.
'MAGMA RISING THROUGH ALL LEVELS.
'CONTACT LOST WITH ATTACK FORCE LEADER.
'ERUPTIONS SPREADING TOWARDS ATTACK SAUCERS.'
ADVISE CHIEF STRATEGIST TO ABANDON ATTACK FORCE AND EVACUATE.

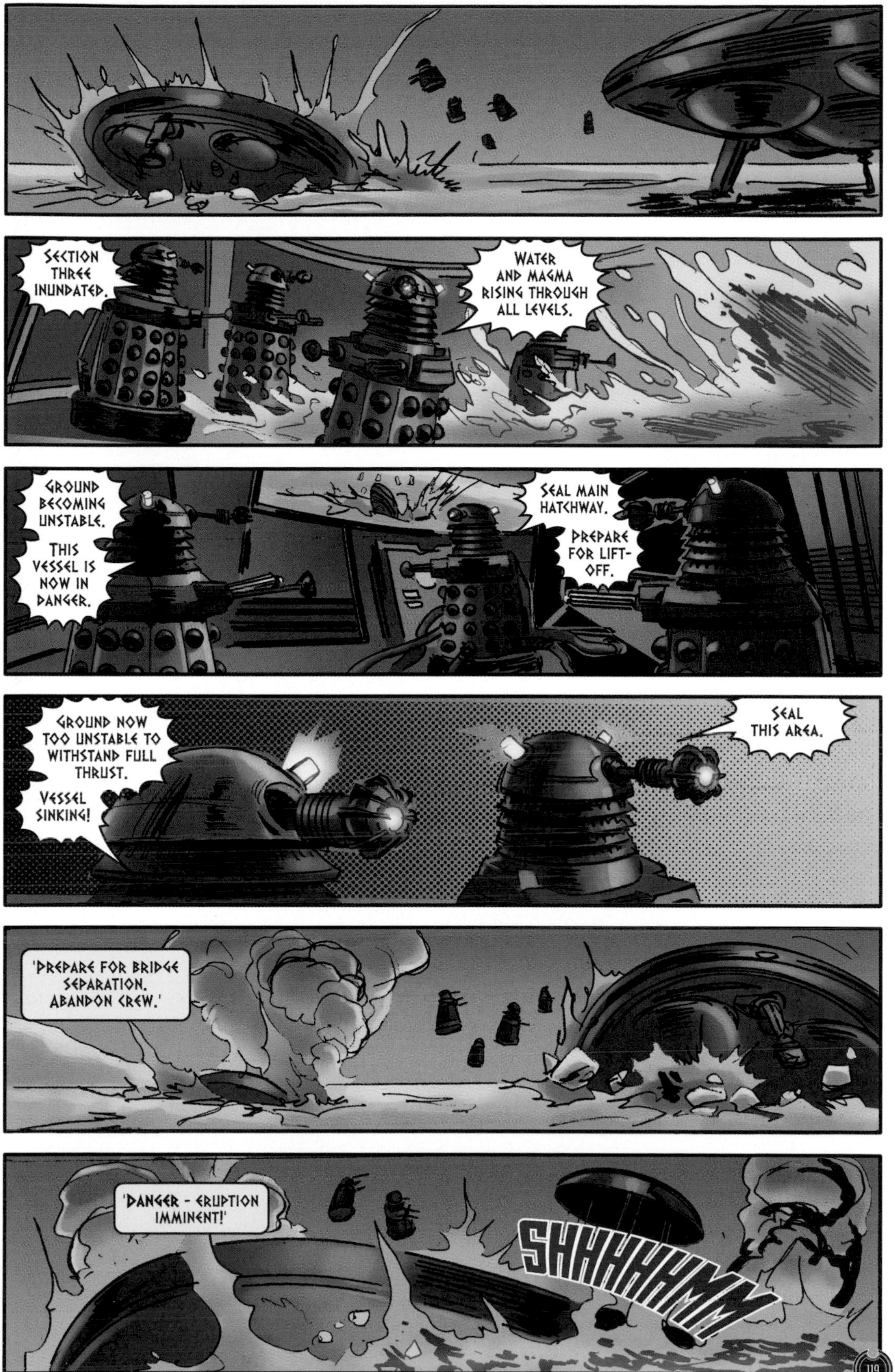
SECTION THREE INUNDATED.
WATER AND MAGMA RISING THROUGH ALL LEVELS.
GROUND BECOMING UNSTABLE.
THIS VESSEL IS NOW IN DANGER.
SEAL MAIN HATCHWAY.
PREPARE FOR LIFT-OFF.
GROUND NOW TOO UNSTABLE TO WITHSTAND FULL THRUST.
VESSEL SINKING!
SEAL THIS AREA.
'PREPARE FOR BRIDGE SEPARATION. ABANDON CREW.'
'DANGER - ERUPTION IMMINENT!'
SHHHHHMM

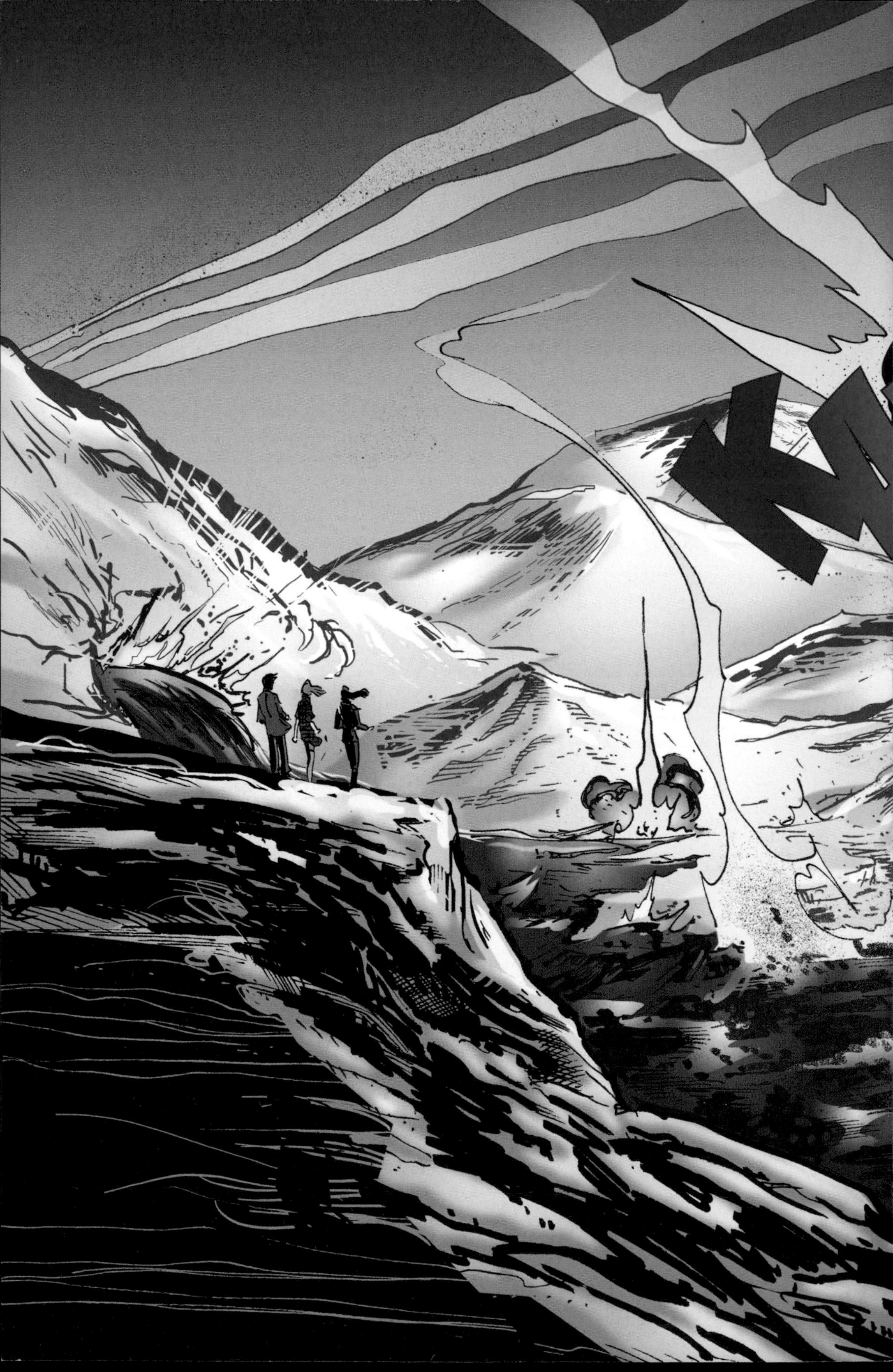

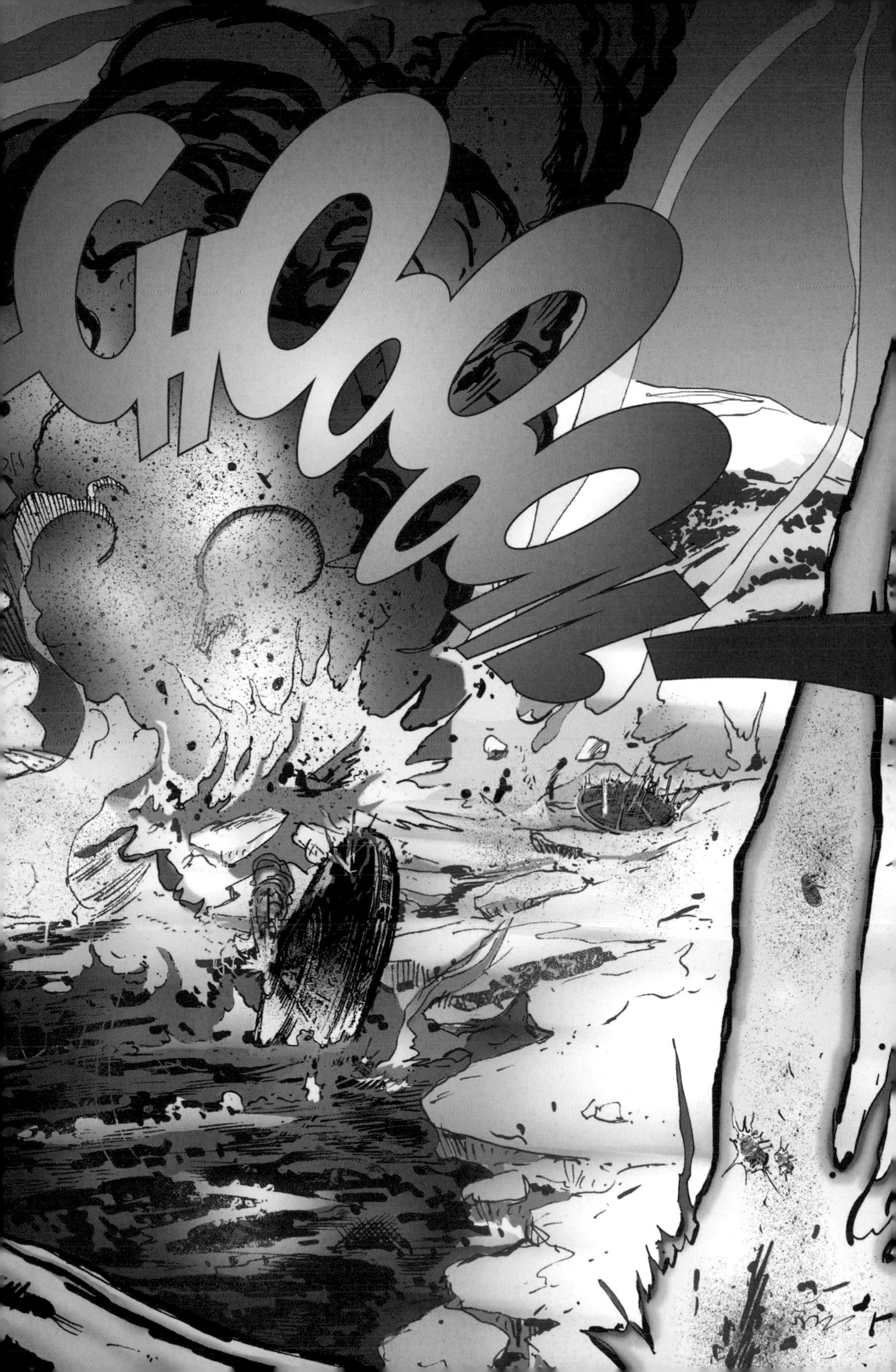

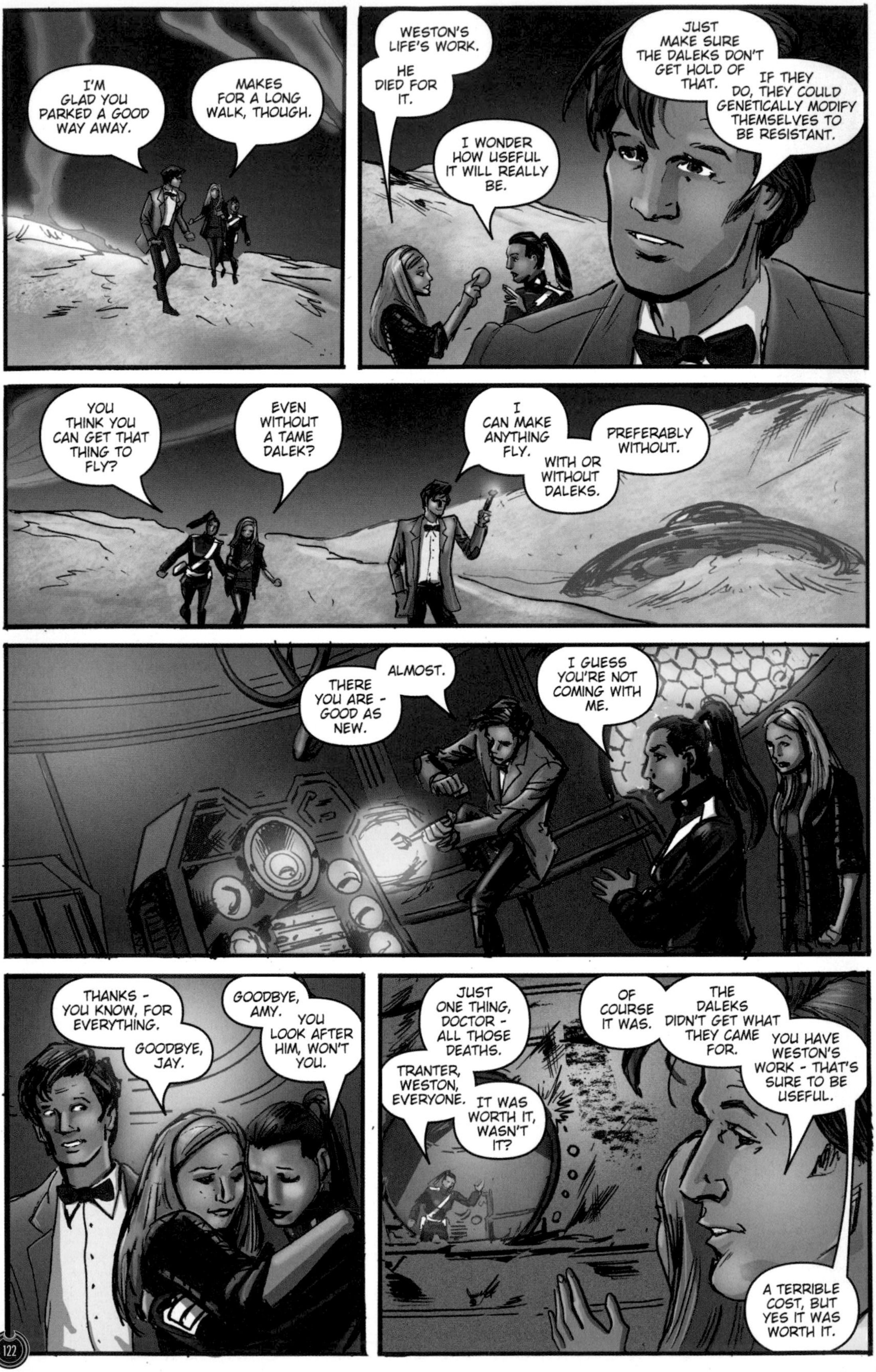
I'M GLAD YOU PARKED A GOOD WAY AWAY.
MAKES FOR A LONG WALK, THOUGH.
WESTON'S LIFE'S WORK.
HE DIED FOR IT.
I WONDER HOW USEFUL IT WILL REALLY BE.
JUST MAKE SURE THE DALEKS DON'T GET HOLD OF THAT.
IF THEY DO, THEY COULD GENETICALLY MODIFY THEMSELVES TO BE RESISTANT.
YOU THINK YOU CAN GET THAT THING TO FLY?
EVEN WITHOUT A TAME DALEK?
I CAN MAKE ANYTHING FLY.
WITH OR WITHOUT DALEKS.
PREFERABLY WITHOUT.
THERE YOU ARE - GOOD AS NEW.
ALMOST.
I GUESS YOU'RE NOT COMING WITH ME.
THANKS - YOU KNOW, FOR EVERYTHING.
GOODBYE, JAY.
GOODBYE, AMY.
YOU LOOK AFTER HIM, WON'T YOU.
JUST ONE THING, DOCTOR - ALL THOSE DEATHS.
TRANTER, WESTON, EVERYONE.
IT WAS WORTH IT, WASN'T IT?
OF COURSE IT WAS.
THE DALEKS DIDN'T GET WHAT THEY CAME FOR.
YOU HAVE WESTON'S WORK - THAT'S SURE TO BE USEFUL.
A TERRIBLE COST, BUT YES IT WAS WORTH IT.

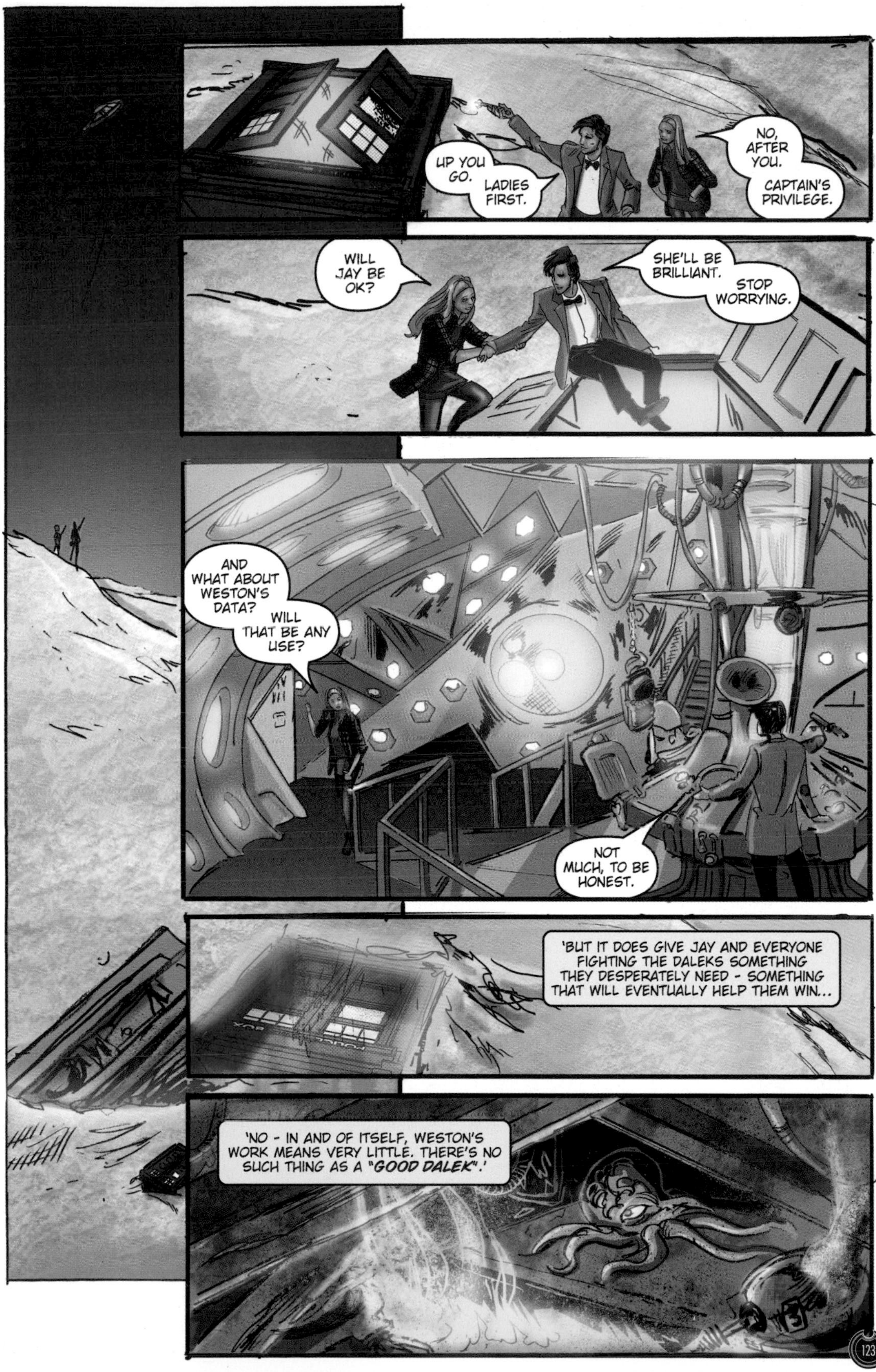
UP YOU GO. LADIES FIRST.
NO, AFTER YOU. CAPTAIN'S PRIVILEGE.
WILL JAY BE OK?
SHE'LL BE BRILLIANT. STOP WORRYING.
AND WHAT ABOUT WESTON'S DATA? WILL THAT BE ANY USE?
NOT MUCH, TO BE HONEST.
'BUT IT DOES GIVE JAY AND EVERYONE FIGHTING THE DALEKS SOMETHING THEY DESPERATELY NEED - SOMETHING THAT WILL EVENTUALLY HELP THEM WIN...
'NO - IN AND OF ITSELF, WESTON'S WORK MEANS VERY LITTLE. THERE'S NO SUCH THING AS A "GOOD DALEK".'

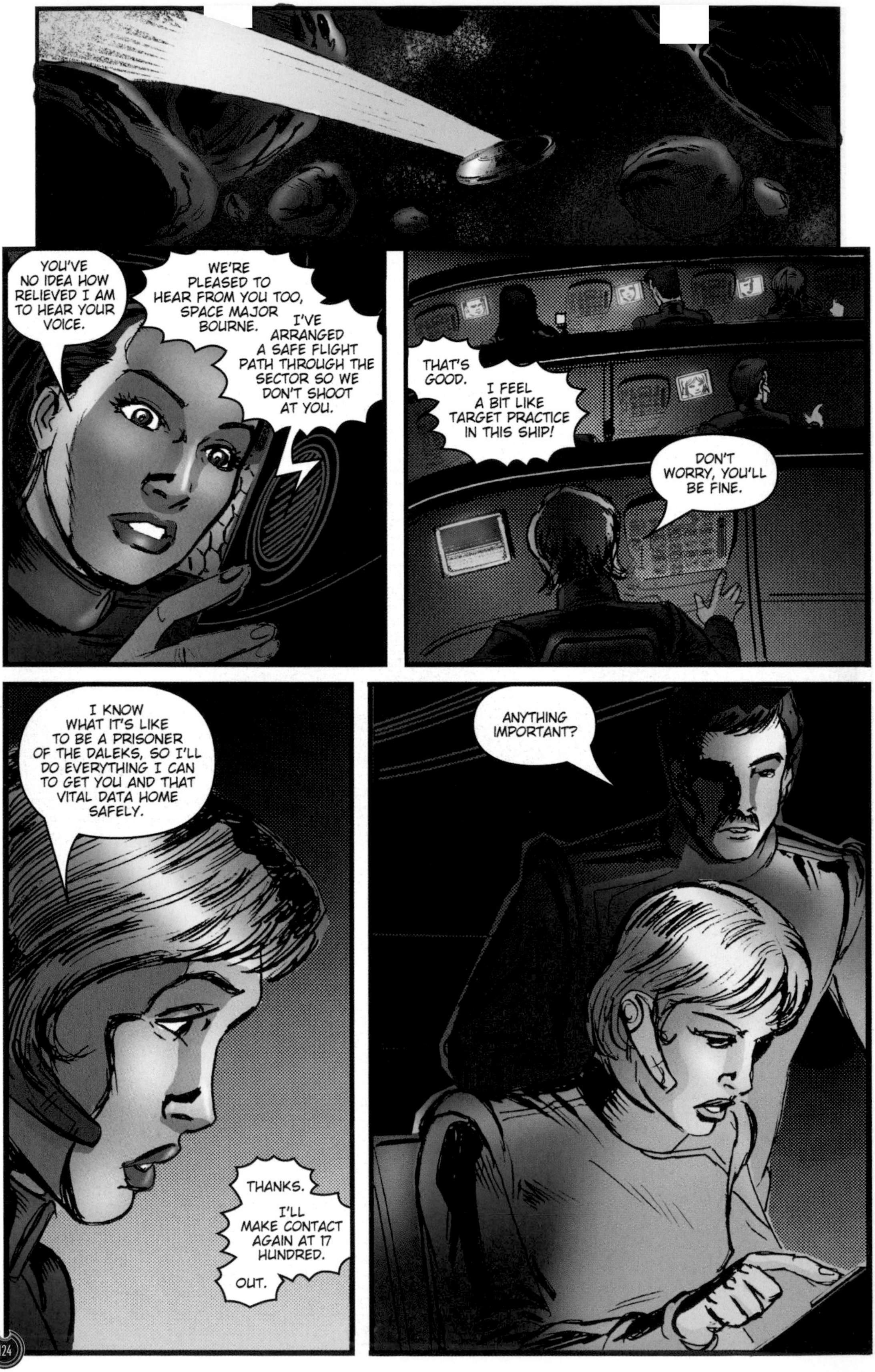
YOU'VE NO IDEA HOW RELIEVED I AM TO HEAR YOUR VOICE.
WE'RE PLEASED TO HEAR FROM YOU TOO, SPACE MAJOR BOURNE.
I'VE ARRANGED A SAFE FLIGHT PATH THROUGH THE SECTOR SO WE DON'T SHOOT AT YOU.
THAT'S GOOD.
I FEEL A BIT LIKE TARGET PRACTICE IN THIS SHIP!
DON'T WORRY, YOU'LL BE FINE.
I KNOW WHAT IT'S LIKE TO BE A PRISONER OF THE DALEKS, SO I'LL DO EVERYTHING I CAN TO GET YOU AND THAT VITAL DATA HOME SAFELY.
THANKS.
I'LL MAKE CONTACT AGAIN AT 17 HUNDRED.
OUT.
ANYTHING IMPORTANT?

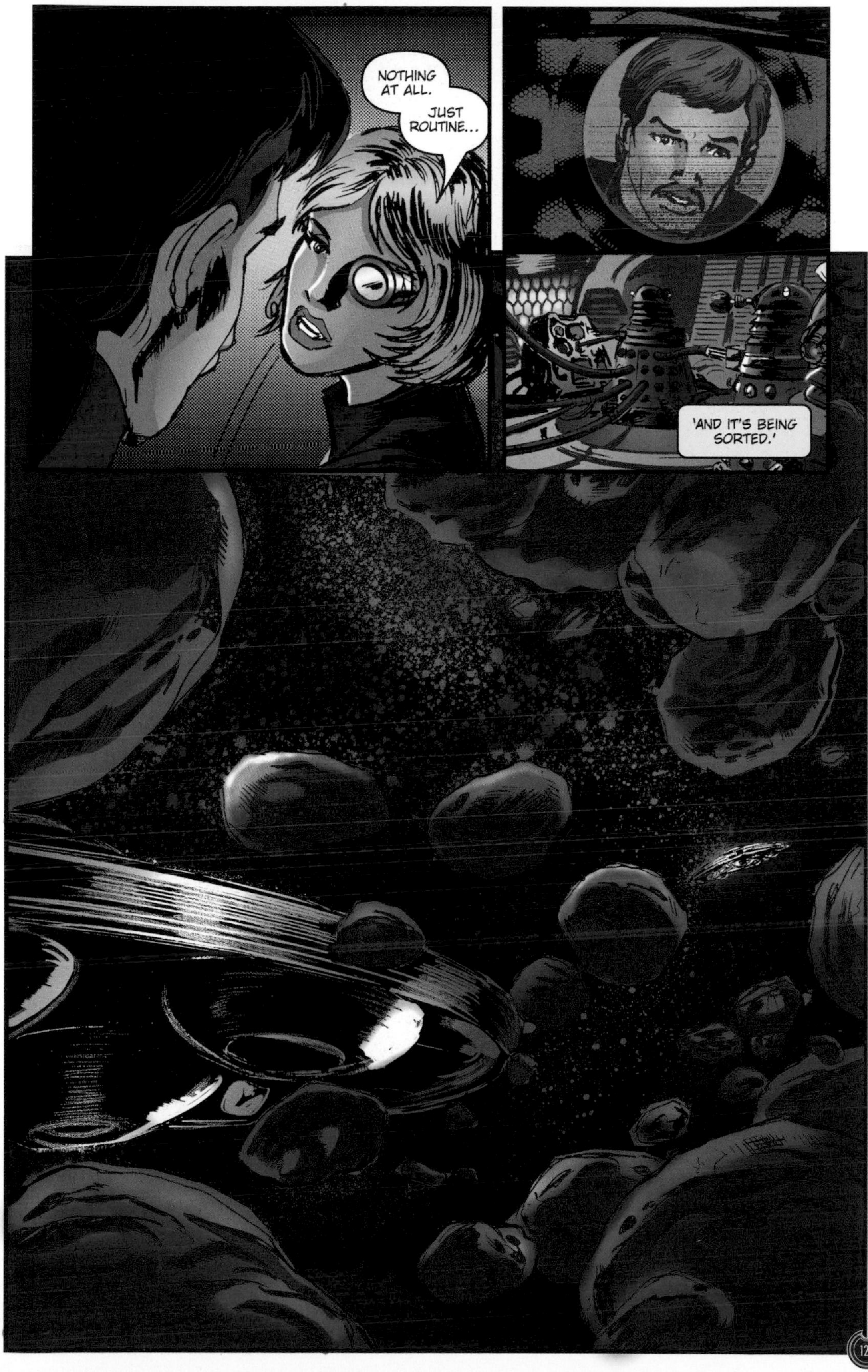
NOTHING AT ALL.
JUST ROUTINE...
'AND IT'S BEING SORTED.'

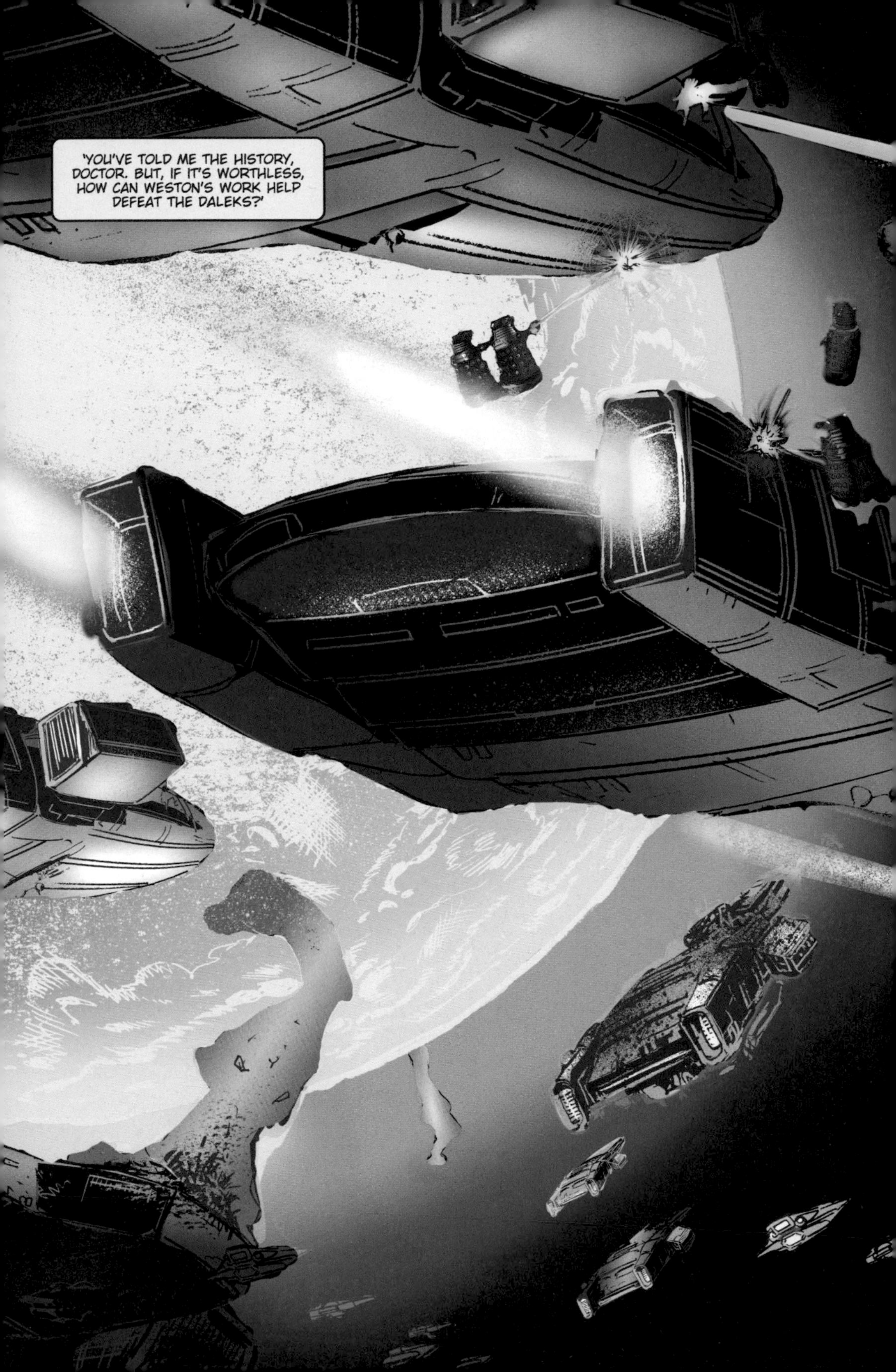
'YOU'VE TOLD ME THE HISTORY, DOCTOR. BUT, IF IT'S WORTHLESS, HOW CAN WESTON'S WORK HELP DEFEAT THE DALEKS?'

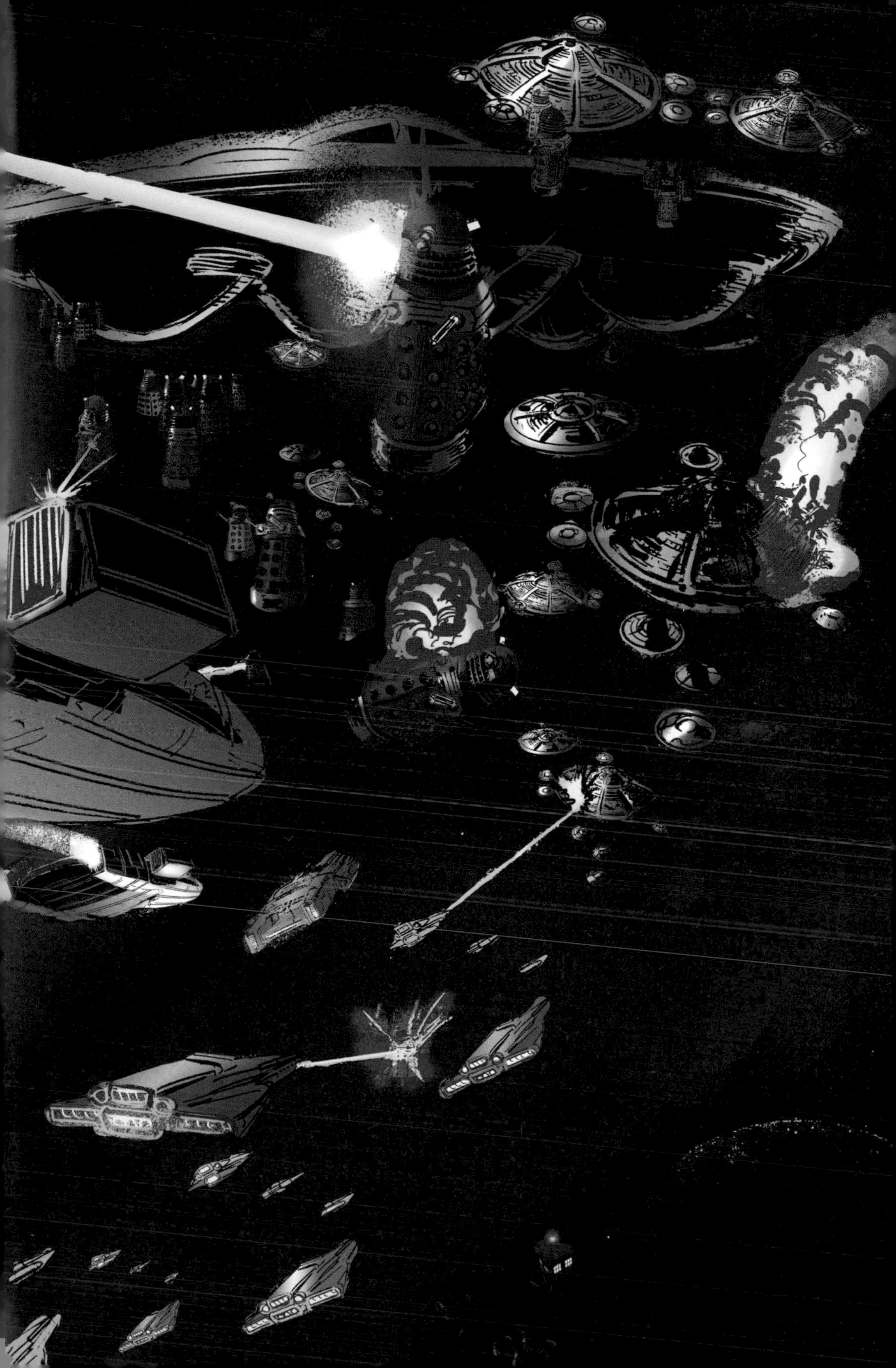

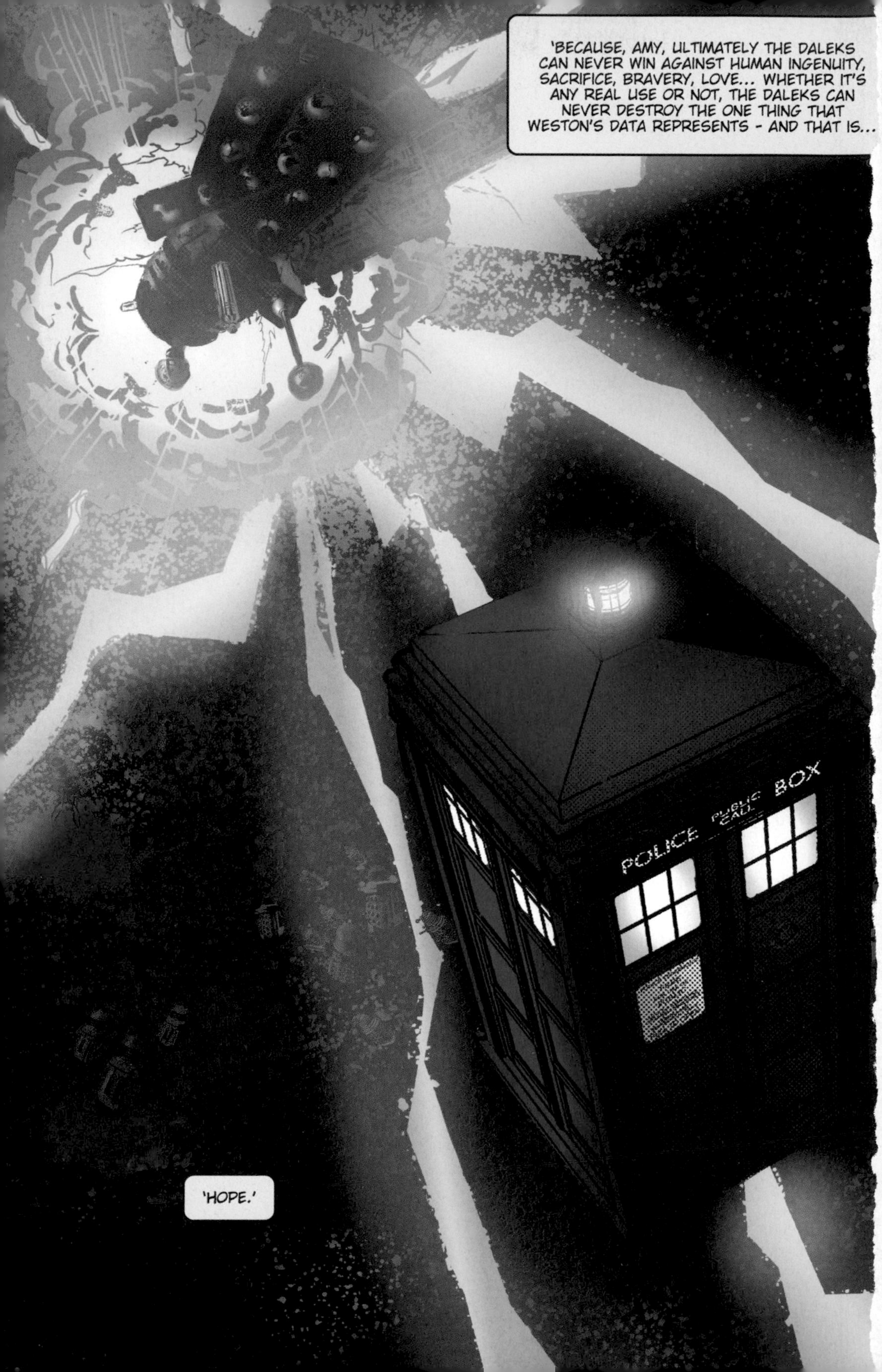
'BECAUSE, AMY, ULTIMATELY THE DALEKS CAN NEVER WIN AGAINST HUMAN INGENUITY, SACRIFICE, BRAVERY, LOVE... WHETHER IT'S ANY REAL USE OR NOT, THE DALEKS CAN NEVER DESTROY THE ONE THING THAT WESTON'S DATA REPRESENTS - AND THAT IS...
POLICE PUBLIC CALL BOX
'HOPE.'